Paula Lennon is the author of a murder mystery series set in the Caribbean and published by Joffe Books. Paula was born in the West Midlands to Jamaican parents. She worked as a commercial lawyer in London before relocating to Jamaica and turning to fiction writing. *Watch Her Run* is the first book in the Olivia Knightley thriller series.

ALSO BY PAULA LENNON

Detectives Preddy and Harris Series:
MURDER IN MONTEGO BAY
MURDER UNDER THE PALMS
MURDER AT SUGAR RUSH BEACH

WATCH HER RUN

PAULA LENNON

WILDFIRE

First published in paperback in 2023 by
WILDFIRE
an imprint of HEADLINE PUBLISHING GROUP

2

Cataloguing in Publication Data is available from the British Library

ISBN 978 1 0354 0177 2

Typeset in 10.75/13.75pt Carre Noir Std by Jouve (UK), Milton Keynes

Printed and bound in Great Britain by Clays Ltd, Elcograf S.p.A.

MIX
Paper | Supporting
responsible forestry
FSC® C104740

Headline's policy is to use papers that are natural, renewable and recyclable
products and made from wood grown in well-managed forests and other
controlled sources. The logging and manufacturing processes are expected
to conform to the environmental regulations of the country of origin.

HEADLINE PUBLISHING GROUP
an Hachette UK Company
Carmelite House
50 Victoria Embankment
London
EC4Y 0DZ

www.headline.co.uk
www.hachette.co.uk

For those who are not keen on flying,
but love arriving at new destinations.

PROLOGUE

THE WILDERNESS WAS beautiful and he adored the feel of clean air filling his lungs, revitalising him for the day ahead. He rather liked this campground. Then again, he liked them all. Parks, forest reserves, lush grasslands. Never-ending landscapes of towering trees, unique plants, fragrant flowers and delightful animals. Green was such a lovely, inoffensive colour; green and red, a particularly nice match, especially in the mid-summer sunshine. Claret and verdant. Magenta and emerald. Blood and grass.

Through binoculars, he watched more newcomers arrive. They did not disturb his tranquillity; the more, the merrier. The place was full of people. They were unlikely to notice someone like him in a sea of faces just like his. Summer was so much nicer than winter – and far more conducive to his activities. He didn't have to wait for people to come outside; they were often outside anyway. No one was all buttoned up – and even if they were, they wore thin clothes, making it easier for him to see who was well-built and who was spindly. Best of all, he didn't have to think too hard about the best placement for the knife. Exposed skin everywhere. Piercing a winter jacket with a thick collar could result in a snag; piercing an unprotected neck was child's play.

One of these men would be a headline in tomorrow's papers. A man who people would sympathise with for a fraction of a second, before studying celebrity news for an hour. A couple of potential targets were in sight, and he twisted the thumbwheel for a sharper view of each face. One man's features seemed more fitting than the other. He smiled to himself. What was this innocent man thinking of? His next meal, his next smoke, maybe his favourite sport? What would this man have chosen to do, had he known his life blood would be oozing from his body in less than twenty-four hours?

He had not yet made up his mind how to do the kill. Slit his throat, puncture his eye, stick his ear. Whichever way, the pain would be instant, death mercifully quick. Experience had taught him that. He inhaled another lungful of clean, fresh air. After decades of earnest endeavours, the universe had finally aligned in his favour. Now he had all the time in the world to do what he was born to do. This was his time to kill. What a time to be alive.

1

OLIVIA KNIGHTLEY CLUTCHED the steering wheel, pressed her back against the seat and willed her stomach to stay still. Why had she agreed to this? She should have stayed in London for the summer, which was predicted to be a long, hot one.

'Mom, you're driving like you've got a flat tyre.'

'No, I'm driving like a person should drive who's never driven in America before and wants to stay alive.'

Olivia was relieved to be on the ground after the long non-stop flight from London Heathrow to Denver. She had sought distraction through the in-flight magazine, comedy shows, an adventure novel and occasional small talk with Amy. Luckily, the temporary nausea she experienced as the landing gear was released and the ground rushed up to meet them passed quickly once they were on solid ground.

She kept her eyes straight ahead. Driving on the wrong side of the road was something she would never get used to, and ahead lay a daunting twelve-hour drive to their destination. Even worse, the SUV, the colour of which the car hire company described as 'tangerine tango', was hauling a large caravan, and she was fully conscious of the extra weight. When visiting the

East Coast as a carefree solo traveller many years ago, she had taken cabs and buses everywhere. Now she was heading west, accompanied by her sixteen-year-old daughter Amy, and for the Colorado-to-Iowa road experience, your own wheels were a must-have. Olivia had let Amy programme the sat-nav, and she took some comfort from the calm, robotic voice directing her along the unfamiliar route.

A knee brushed against hers.

'Mom, you can press the pedal, you know,' said Amy. 'We might just reach the campsite some time this decade. You drive like a maniac all over England, following people to God knows where. No need to crawl around in this country.'

'I've never gone above thirty miles an hour in England with you in the car.'

'You're in denial.'

For the past four years, Olivia had worked as a private investigator and was always on the way to somewhere. Some days, she was on her feet, bumping shoulders with passengers on the busy London Underground, or shivering in the wind and rain on railway platforms open to the elements. Most days, she was behind the wheel of her trusty Ford Focus, trying to avoid accidents while keeping sight of a target.

Olivia frowned. 'When have you ever seen me speeding anywhere?'

'You could wallpaper the entire IMAX cinema with the tickets you've collected, Mom. Your last one? Clocked doing thirty-five on Croydon Road, in a twenty zone.'

As she pulled up at a stoplight, Olivia squinted at her daughter, taking in her indignant face. She admired the tiny freckles on her brown skin, and the head full of thick, black hair that she liked to wear in cornrows all the way down her back. Amy could be quiet and moody sometimes, practically inevitable for a teenager. Olivia had learned to be grateful for any attempt at conversation led by her daughter, but this dig annoyed her, as all her tickets were hidden in one place. With great effort, she kept her tone even. Starting a three-week summer holiday with a fight would be a bad idea and could ruin everything.

'I asked you to keep out of my study, Amy. I try to protect you from seeing and reading things you really don't need to know about. I wish I didn't have to bring work home, but I can't do it all in the office with Bill around.'

The office, Dynamic Investigations Agency, occupied a prominent spot on the high street in Kennington, London, two miles from their family home in Camberwell. Bill Tweedy was Olivia's boss, a demanding type with whom she held face-to-face meetings once a week. She was grateful Bill had shown faith in her by inviting her to join him when he set up on his own, and had been delighted to leave her old job, which is where they'd first met: the accident claims department of a corporate mill in the Docklands, where she spent excruciating days inside a tiny grey cubicle.

Her private-eye work involved investigating civil, criminal and domestic cases, and sometimes placed her in hairy situations, but it was much more interesting. Tracking down a missing child in a bitter custody case was a highlight, particularly since the police had given up after two years and let the case go cold.

The stoplight turned green and Olivia pulled away at a quicker pace, hoping to avoid further criticism. 'My work is supposed to be strictly private and confidential. My clients wouldn't like it if they thought anybody else knew what I was investigating.'

'Can't blame a girl for being curious,' said Amy. She adjusted the air-con, which was on full blast, turning it down. 'You come home, walk through the front door and hide away in a small room, only coming out to check the microwave.'

Olivia winced. It was true she would never be a contender for Mother of the Year. She glanced at her ring finger, now minus the gold band that had been there for seventeen years. Placed there by Christopher Knightley, it had been discarded by Olivia three months ago. 'I've been doing much better, haven't I? Give me that, at least?'

'Dad doesn't lock any doors in his new apartment. It's big. Two huge bedrooms, two bathrooms. Plenty of living space, no separate study.'

'Sounds lovely.' Olivia forced a smile. 'Anyway, what would a games designer be doing with a private room? There's no need to protect your precious eyes from anything on his screen or in his workspace. My work isn't bright visuals and cool layouts, you know. Some of my cases are brutal, especially the domestic violence ones.'

'I'm sure I see far worse on TV shows.'

'You see corn syrup and food dye on television,' said Olivia. 'Anyway, who wants to talk about work? We're getting away from it all, remember?'

'Yeah, I know your idea of getting away from it all. That April weekend in Brighton was meant to be "getting away from it all". Ten minutes after getting there, you were following behind a man you swore had picked a woman's pocket.'

'It wasn't ten minutes; it was half an hour.'

'It was embarrassing. Fancy pouncing on a man putting his own wallet into his girlfriend's handbag.'

'Agreed, it wasn't my best moment.'

Olivia recalled that the couple had been nice about it and laughed it off. Amy was the one who had been outraged at the whole thing, sulking her way through the trip and declaring it the Worst Weekend Ever. Olivia wished she had made better use of those fleeting forty-eight hours, which covered the first weekend after the divorce had been finalised. Amy had shown her resentment of the family implosion by blasting music, slamming doors, refusing to wash dishes and dumping clothes everywhere.

The idea was that a mini-break to the seaside would help. It didn't – and Olivia blamed herself.

'I won't be following any suspected pickpockets in America, I promise. You're going to have the time of your life.'

Amy peered out the passenger side window. 'The size of some of these vehicles, Mom. I thought we had it bad in London with the Chelsea tractors, but look at all these monster trucks.'

'They do everything bigger over here. Not necessarily better, though.'

'We're the only ones driving a tangerine with four wheels, so I guess the joke's on us.'

'Hey, it's a new model and we got a good deal. Be grateful.'

'I am grateful. Extremely grateful that the caravan is just plain white.'

Olivia smiled. She was looking forward to these three weeks of freedom. Now Chris could not just stop by the house unannounced. She had been flooded with relief when he finally agreed that Amy could leave the country for America after weeks of putting all kinds of improbable obstacles in the way of her holiday plans. Multiple pile-ups and carnage on the highways was a thing, he said. Dangerous wild animals roamed around freely and could attack at will. Americans were always firing guns and were not particular about the targets.

Olivia rolled her eyes at the memory. Had she known for a second what horrors tomorrow would bring, she would have done a U-turn and headed right back to safety. Blissfully unaware of fate's plans, she smiled and kept driving.

'All I know is they better have good wi-fi at Hawkeye like they promised,' said Amy.

'You can go a couple of days without the internet, can't you?'

'No – are you crazy? I have to know what everybody is doing and where they're going. I'd die if I couldn't connect.'

'When I was your age, we didn't even have a telephone in the house — and no one had a mobile phone.'

'Yeah, the olden days must have been rough.'

They had picked up groceries and camping supplies at a supermarket. Two stops were made for bathroom breaks, and to grab oversized beef burgers and sodas to go. As they returned to the SUV, Amy settled into the passenger seat. Olivia climbed in and closed the door, her attention fixed on balancing the drinks in the cup holders between the front seats. A cardboard sign slammed against her windscreen, darkening the interior of the vehicle. Startled, Olivia jerked around and, with shaking hands, locked the doors. She stared at the holder of the sign, a man in tattered clothes. On the cardboard, in bold black letters, was a request for cash. A panhandler. She released a breath.

'Wow! He nearly scared the life out of me,' said Amy.

'Me too.'

The man removed the sign, rattled a tin can and shouted, 'Spare some coins, please?'

'Not today, sorry.' Olivia pulled away, watching as the man approached another vehicle.

'Could have given him a few coins, Mom.'

'No way. He's in dirty clothes, but I could smell cologne. His hands are clean, his nails are pristine. Those teeth belong to a regular at the dentist. I bet he's got nice wheels hidden away nearby. For some people, panhandling is their career and it pays the rent.'

'Trust you to see all that.'

Olivia drove on. As the hours ticked by, she pushed thoughts of the conman out of her mind. Plenty of other things were competing for attention in her brain, as much as she tried to push those aside too. It was hard not to think about work.

Amy held a cup of soda close to her mother and Olivia took a long sip through the straw. 'You know, you're frowning really hard, Mom. Relax. If you just pretended we were in England, you'd have an easier time around the wheel.'

'My love, if we were in England, what's going through my head right now wouldn't be any different.'

Olivia could not burden her daughter with her problems. The last in-person meeting she'd had with Bill had not been good. The life of a private investigator was not always exciting or fulfilling. There were not enough hours in the day, and those that were available could be tedious. Sometimes, things went badly wrong. Sometimes, the wronged sued. Clients could turn against you in the blink of an eye, and so could the targets of those clients. It would be a miracle if there was not at least one lawsuit waiting when they got back to London. She vowed to keep her troubles to herself and make the most of the mother-daughter time they had together.

Had the choice been Olivia's, she would have flown straight into Iowa rather than endure such a lengthy drive from Colorado. It was Amy who had planned this trip from scratch. Amy who had suggested a road trip around American campsites would be a great idea and selected their destinations. Amy who had decided it would be fun to mix with nomads and 'get in touch with nature', as she put it. Their first stop would be a campsite at Hawkeye Point, a flat, lush, green range offering panoramic views of the Iowa landscape. From the online advertisements, the campground looked vast and attractive, with twelve camping sites. The plan was to spend a few days at camp before taking to the road again. Their next destination would be Steer Creek Campground, near Nebraska National Forest, then they'd go onto the Yellowstone Loop, taking in Wyoming's famous Yellowstone National Park. The final week would be spent at Topanga State Park in Los Angeles.

Olivia had manufactured enthusiasm and gone along with Amy's infectious excitement, but it was not her idea of a good holiday. She would have preferred somewhere tropical, like

Jamaica, where her parents were born and laid to rest. Where she could sit on a sun-kissed beach in front of glorious blue seas and let the eager hairstylists braid her hair while she sipped coconut water and listened to reggae music. Jamaica had been the last family holiday for the three of them before things fell apart for good, a sort of last attempt at playing happily families. The holiday had been enjoyable, with plenty of distractions and fun activities that helped to disguise the problems temporarily. Olivia felt guilty that Amy, misled by all the cheerful civility, had obviously thought everything was going wonderfully well. Amy had happily taken selfies of the three of them smiling on sandy beaches and standing under spectacular waterfalls, and sent them to her friends. The girl was blindsided when, a few months later, her father moved out. For Olivia, the feeling was sheer relief that he was gone, as the pretence had been so exhausting. An angry Amy had raged, embarrassed when her friends teased her for not seeing it coming. Those had been some pretty tense days, and Olivia sensed that resentment was always simmering beneath the surface.

She shot a quick glance at her daughter. 'You alright, baby girl?'

'Oh Mom, come on. I keep telling you not to call me that.'

Olivia sighed. She had slipped up yet again. 'I forgot, sorry. Time really flies. It's like yesterday you were four.'

'Just think, soon I'll be old enough to have my own apartment.'

Olivia winced inside. 'Hold the soda up for me, please.'

She had three whole weeks to make things much better, and she intended to follow through.

*

The sign at their destination read 'HAWKEYE POINT CAMPGROUND – PUBLIC WELCOME'. Olivia had never driven such a long distance in her life and was thankful to have made it in one piece. Her arms were numb and her knees impatient to be flexed. Weary, she pulled into the campground as the sun faded on the horizon.

The site was as well-kept as the website had described. She followed the wide road leading to their reserved campsite, passing under imposing trees set in low-cut grass, and a sprinkling of picnic tables. The cars, motor homes and camper vans were evenly placed throughout the grounds. Olivia had expected to see a few tents among the vehicles, but there were none in sight. Pets were allowed; she observed a chocolate Labrador, which ignored their slow-moving vehicle and continued playing with a stick.

'Park Tango over there, Mom.' Amy pointed out a suitably large vacant area. 'There's lots of space for the caravan, too.'

'Looks good. We won't be too close to anybody.'

Olivia climbed out of the driver's seat and stretched towards the sky to ease her aching limbs. She then bent double and touched her toes. Amy followed suit and swung her body from side to side.

'You guys had one hell of a journey, huh?'

The approaching woman had thinning grey hair that hung in a limp ponytail. A broad smile covered her well-lined face.

'That obvious, eh?' said Olivia.

'Hi, I'm Darcy.' She stopped at a respectable distance, hands on hips. 'How're you doing?'

'Very well, thanks Darcy. I'm Olivia. This is my daughter, Amy.'

'Hi, Amy.' The woman waved a thin hand.

Amy stopped swaying and returned the gesture. 'Hi, Darcy. Nice to meet you.'

The Lab ambled over, tail wagging, desperately trying to get Darcy to admire his stick. She patted his head. 'Glad you made it before sundown. This place is much harder to find in the dark.'

'It was touch and go.' Olivia gazed around at the acres of green. 'This is a beautiful, quiet area.'

'Wow, I just love English accents. Don't hear any of that around here.'

Olivia could not identify the woman's drawl, and her sweats and slip-on shoes offered no clues. 'Oh dear, and I was hoping we wouldn't stand out too much.'

The woman took her time before giving a response. 'There was a family here that left last week, kinda looked like you guys.'

Olivia realised that Darcy's hesitation was born of a desire to avoid causing offence. She flashed the older woman a bright smile. 'Drop-dead gorgeous, you mean?'

'That too.' Darcy grinned.

'What's your dog's name?' asked Amy.

'That's Ben. He doesn't bark at strangers or bite. It's okay; you can pet him.'

Amy made a fuss over the friendly dog. As Olivia watched, she was overcome by a wave of optimism for the days ahead. Her daughter was happy; the woes of London family life were behind them; the world was at peace. Everything was going to be alright. Amy threw the stick and followed a few paces behind the delighted dog, who galloped after it.

A door slammed and Olivia glanced in the direction of the sound, a silver-coloured travel trailer. A miniature die-cast Harley Davidson motorbike dangled from the bumper on a short chain. Men of a certain age wanted a Harley, but if a real one was beyond their price range, a toy was not a bad idea. The man who'd slammed the door was tall and well-tanned, with a strong jaw that looked as if it hadn't seen a razor in weeks. He was dressed in black from head to toe. As their eyes met, he barely inclined his head. She nodded at him and stared at his broad back as he turned away.

'Security guard or cat burglar?' said Olivia with undisguised interest.

'Seen a coyote I'd trust sooner than that one,' replied Darcy with disdain. 'Good to look at don't mean good to taste.'

'Wasn't planning on biting him.' Olivia stared after him. 'Maybe I'll just say hello.'

'Trust me, he's hiding from something or someone.'

'Aren't we all?' murmured Olivia.

She decided against trying to get the stranger's attention for the time being. If he came over to talk to them, great. If not, well, there was always tomorrow.

The Hawkeye Point nomads turned out to be a welcoming bunch. Olivia and Amy met a wide array of Americans from East Coast to West Coast and everywhere in between. Darkness set in unnoticed as they mingled and talked. They ate ribs and steaks with peppers and tomatoes straight off the barbecue grill, the savoury, smoky odour filling the night air. Some were families who had been on the road for years and could not imagine being rooted in one place. A few were young couples, digital nomads enjoying a different lifestyle away from the rat race, earning a decent living while avoiding urban fumes. Others were in-state visitors, groups of friends on a short getaway from the grey concrete and shiny skyscrapers of Des Moines.

Too full for another bite, Olivia waved away the chef's offer of grilled s'mores. Amy made room for the dessert, her expression one of pleasure as the gooey, hot marshmallow-and-chocolate mix disappeared between her lips.

Olivia caught a flash of light and gazed at the dense trees, wondering if it was her imagination. She thought she saw a shadow of a person, but every object became the shadow of a person at night. Anyway, even if it was someone, this was a safe area, and wandering around at night was something the nomads probably felt quite comfortable doing. Maybe one of them had just grabbed a torch and gone exploring. She wondered if it was the mystery man; he had not joined in with the meal, and there was no light coming from his trailer. Soon, she fell back into easy conversation with the others, grateful that there were no rain clouds around to dampen the lively spirits.

By the time they turned in, Olivia had warmed to the idea of spending time in this amiable community and looked forward to a great holiday. Amy's choice was a good one after all.

2

OLIVIA OPENED THE caravan door and the cool morning air rushed in, bringing with it the fresh smell of dew on leaves. The sun was barely visible as a sliver of bold orange above the trees. She pulled on her trainers and vowed never to think of them as sneakers, despite being in America. She descended the three small steps to the ground. Amy jumped from the top step and followed behind her. They planned to take an energetic walk around the outskirts of the campsite to work up an appetite for breakfast.

Olivia caught a glimpse of a belly-button ring below Amy's tank top as the girl stretched. This addition to her daughter's anatomy was new, and had never been seen or mentioned. Olivia pasted a smile on to her face and resolved to bring up the subject later on.

She gestured with her chin. 'Let's follow the path down that way.'

'Nice and empty,' said Amy. 'We might spot some shy animals.'

Olivia thought it was just as well Amy did not know that the idea of encountering a shy animal had already crossed her mother's mind. The path in question would take them past the mysterious man's camping vehicle. Olivia had learned that his name was Rick Seagal, but none of the campers seemed to know much else about him.

She slowed her pace as they approached the trailer. The chassis was old, its many dents and scratches evidence of a rough life and poor care. The door was wide open, an invitation Olivia could not resist. Couldn't hurt to introduce herself, since she hadn't been able to last night.

She veered off the path and raised her voice. 'Hello!'

Other than birds singing in the elm trees, the silence was near complete.

'Come on, Mom, nobody's in there,' said Amy impatiently, continuing to walk. 'They've probably gone for an early walk too.'

Olivia could not imagine Mr Brooding taking a stroll through the campsite to enjoy the dawn chorus. By all accounts, he kept himself to himself. Maybe it took a persistent person to get him out of his shell, and Olivia felt up to the challenge.

She approached the door and tentatively placed a foot on the bottom step. 'Hello! Rick, is it?'

'Er, Mom?' shouted Amy. 'You might want to come around here!'

'Give me a minute, love. I want to say a quick hello to our new neighbour.'

Had she not been so focused on her goal, Olivia would have noticed that her daughter's previously breezy tone had become sober. Instead, she leaned into the trailer. Paper plates and food boxes littered the countertop, next to a couple of beer bottles, and a strong odour of stale savoury food filled the space. The pull-out bed was bare, the sheets piled up in a corner. The owner was clearly absent, but Olivia was determined to satisfy her curiosity about his humble home.

'Mom, say what you like to him. Quick or not, he's not gonna answer.'

This time, Olivia detected the change in her daughter's voice. 'What?'

She turned abruptly and walked around the outside of the trailer. She noted in passing that the emblem was missing from the bumper, the miniature Harley die-cast that had caught her eye last night.

That was the least of her discoveries. A breath caught in her throat as her brain fought to process the unwelcome sight. Rick lay on his back in the grass, his face ashen, blank green eyes staring unseeing at the skies. Surrounding his matted hair was a large pool of dark red blood. The broad handle of a knife protruded from his neck, the business end buried in his flesh. His lips were parted as if his speech had been cut short, and his arms and legs were wide apart as though frozen while making a snow angel. Mud-caked waterproof boots pointed to the heavens.

'Amy, get back!' ordered Olivia.

Amy rubbed her throat self-consciously, but made no move to retreat. Olivia's stomach churned. The last dead body she'd encountered had been that of a man who had been pushed off the roof at a building site. That crushed, bloodied body would never leave her memory, even though it had happened nearly a year ago. She'd hoped such grisly scenes were behind her for good, and had never imagined it would happen again, thousands of miles across the pond. Everything within her wanted to believe that this was a mannequin and not the person she had been so eager to meet.

'Amy, I need you to move away!'

'He's way past being able to hurt me, Mom.' Amy cleared her throat as she retrieved her mobile phone from her shorts pocket. 'So, it's nine-one-one, not nine-nine-nine, then?'

Olivia was surprised yet relieved that Amy was maintaining her cool. Not even a stifled scream. Regardless, she wanted her daughter away from the gruesome scene. She pointed. 'They must have a security post here. Check the notice board for a number. Go, quick!'

As Amy ran off in the direction indicated, Olivia quashed the revulsion that ran through her entire body and went into private-eye mode. She crouched beside Rick's still body. No point checking for a pulse, as the unmistakable smell of death was heavy in the air. Her finger barely brushed his forehead. Stone cold. He was clothed in the same black jeans and black long-sleeved polo shirt he'd been wearing last night. The previous day had been hot and the night warm. Why would anyone dress in thermal gear with the temperature in the mid-eighties?

After a quick glance around to ensure no one was watching, she rolled up one of his sleeves. She checked his bare arm and returned his clothing to its original position, then did the same with the other arm. Tattoos on both. She undid the two top buttons on his blood-soaked collar and stared at the strange mark a few inches below his neck. An indent rather than a tattoo, it bore more resemblance to what a branding iron would do. Sweat pooled in her underarms, soaking through her cotton vest.

She looked towards the notice board. Amy was talking to a man and woman while gesturing with her hands. More and more campers were leaving their motor homes to see what the commotion was about. Any minute now, Olivia would have company. Swiftly, she buttoned Rick's damp shirt and wiped the tips of her soiled fingers on the grass.

Struggling to keep from retching, she stood erect and briefly closed her eyes. Scenes like this could send her hurtling back to the bad old days of plucking her hair out by the roots, and trying to entice more rum out of an empty bottle. They should have gone to Jamaica.

*

A sheriff and his two deputies were on the scene, flashing blue lights drawing attention to the tragedy. Yellow caution tape was strewn from tree to tree around the motor home, extending the forbidden zone to around forty feet. Residents from the other campsites swelled the growing crowd of onlookers. A brunette with long, curly hair waved her microphone at various individuals, most of whom shied away. Unsure whether she was a citizen journalist or a reporter, Olivia decided it was best to avoid the woman. Appearing on screen sharing personal views with the public was the least sensible thing to do. Olivia made her way through the anxious crowd listening to bits of conversation, questioning the spectators.

A man stood on tiptoes, trying to see over the mass of heads. Olivia approached him. It was Eddie, who had been one of the first to introduce himself yesterday evening. A jovial sort, he was pale skinned with well-groomed salt-and-pepper hair. He was a barber, and claimed responsibility for keeping the nomads smooth-jawed and neatly coiffed. Hairdressers and barbers were always first to spill the tea — and what they didn't spill wasn't worth knowing anyway.

'Welcome to small-town drama, Olivia.' Eddie made no effort to hide his excitement. 'When I sit my clients on a log today, there'll be just one topic of conversation.'

'Don't get carried away and scalp anyone,' said Olivia. 'Did you see Rick last night?'

'No, didn't notice him. He's a stubborn one; he wouldn't surrender to the razor despite my twice trying to convince him. Said his momma taught him to cut his hair at five, and his daddy taught him to shave at fifteen. Said he could take care of himself, in that deep voice of his. And now look: somebody took care of him.'

'I didn't know he talked to anybody. You'd think from what Darcy said that he pretended to be mute.'

'Darcy always exaggerates.' Eddie flicked a dismissive hand. 'Rick was really quiet, though. You had to fire two or three questions to force even one sentence out of him. He liked his own company.'

'I can understand that,' said Olivia.

A sombre man ambled towards them, the fabric of his T-shirt and cargo shorts straining to contain his plump figure. Channing, the chef who had manned the barbecue with pride last night.

'Eddie, Olivia, how you guys doing?'

'Still taking it all in, Channing,' said Olivia. 'Do you know much about Rick?'

'I don't think anyone other than God himself knows anything about that man. Offered him my finest rib steaks from time to time, but he wouldn't take them. Couldn't tempt him with a burger, a hot dog or even a shrimp. Did his own grilling and ate alone.'

Olivia nodded knowingly. 'If you're used to spending time alone, the idea of group meals is probably a bit overwhelming.'

'Never even tried my prime steak and it's to die— Forget that.' Channing flushed. 'Not a nice welcome for you. Hope this doesn't get you thinking you need to move on?'

'Not sure what I'm going to do yet.' Olivia glanced across the crowds to where Amy stood chatting with a young couple. So far, her daughter showed no signs of fear or distress. 'I'll have to discuss it with Amy.'

'Seen some vehicles disappearing already. Running like rats abandoning a sinking ship,' said Channing.

'Beats drowning, I suppose?' mused Olivia.

'Don't let nobody frighten you away,' said Eddie. 'If needs be, we can run a neighbourhood watch around here. Take turns to walk through the campsites all night.'

'Good to know.' Although it was nice of him to say it, Olivia did not take much comfort from his words. Rick was a big chap, and he'd been murdered. Both Eddie and Channing were small in stature, though Eddie was considerably slimmer. A knifeman could immobilise either camper without much effort. 'Later, people,' she said.

As she moved on, Olivia passed an overtly religious couple she had encountered briefly last night. Having no wish to repeat the meeting, she averted her eyes. To her surprise, the woman reached out and touched her bare arm.

'I hope you have repented, my friend? The day of His coming is nigh!'

'I'll bear that in mind,' said Olivia in the friendliest voice she could muster.

Her male companion said, 'Now is the time to get right with God; tomorrow may be too late. I told Mr Seagal that, but he did not heed my warning.'

Olivia stared at him. 'Oh, when did you last see Mr Seagal?'

'Yesterday. Could not get him to accept a Bible, though I tried to press it into his hands.'

Olivia immediately thrust her hands deep into her jeans pockets. Trying to force religion on someone was such a bad take. She could not begin to understand why these sanctimonious types would even think of it.

'Did you see Rick talking with anyone?'

The woman shook her head. 'No, although there was a man quite near to the poor soul's trailer yesterday, taking photographs.'

'Do you know the man? Is he someone you've seen around here before?'

'Did he say his name?' she looked quizzically at her husband.

'Kent Hilson,' he replied. 'Very amiable person, retiree. Spends his time touring the country, snapping nature shots.'

'Nothing unusual in that. I see a lot of people taking photos around here, including me and my daughter.'

'He had one of those big, heavy-looking cameras though, like a professional.'

Olivia immediately recalled the flash of light she'd seen last night and wondered if the shadow in the trees had been the camera man lurking before selecting a victim.

'Maybe I'll run into Mr Hilson later.' Olivia waved goodbye. 'Have a good day.'

Eventually, Olivia made her way back to where Amy was standing chatting with her new acquaintances. It was all Olivia could do not to roll her eyes when the pair described themselves as social media influencers. Generation Z. Lifestyle influencers who advocated for a life of leisure over work, yet their entire lives were a workplace. Neither of them had met Rick Seagal. Hadn't even noticed him. Way too busy with podcasts, videos, filming and editing content, over-sharing everything through a filtered lens. If Amy ever opted for this career, Olivia would disown her.

She rested her hands on Amy's shoulders as the girl stood just in front of her. She observed that her daughter had grown over the past year; the two of them were nearly the same height now. She gazed past Amy at the female medical examiner, who was bent over Rick's body as she talked with the sheriff. Too far away to hear the conversation, Olivia narrowed her eyes and tried to follow the ME's inspection. She could not see whether the doctor had adjusted Rick's clothing. The knife remained embedded in his neck.

The microphone-wielding woman was being escorted from the area by a deputy, and the two seemed locked in a heated conversation. Olivia wondered how those three-inch heels were working out for the determined lady. She tried without success to make out the woman's name from the dangling lanyard around her neck, but the typeface was too small.

Olivia suspected she would suffer the same treatment at the hands of the deputy if she tried to get closer to the crime scene. Staying away from the action was not an option, though. She wanted in. While contemplating her next move, she noticed one of the lawmen looking straight at her. She guessed one of the nomads had pointed her out to him. About time, too, she thought. After all, she and Amy had been the ones to find the body, and should have been interviewed first.

The badge on the man's light-brown uniform identified him as the sheriff, and his gait identified him as a tired person. He was heavyset, with indulgence rather than muscle. Olivia guessed he must be approaching retirement age and looking forward to it. Even from a distance, his disposition seemed stony. As he approached, she steeled herself for the interrogation.

'Ma'am, I'm Sheriff Brancombe. Are you Olivia Knightley?'

'I am.' Olivia squeezed Amy's shoulders. 'And this is my daughter Amy. We found the body.'

'So I hear,' he drawled. 'What time was that?'

'Around six forty-five.'

As the sheriff scribbled on his notepad, she noticed tufts of hair growing from his knuckles. 'See anybody near the victim, ma'am?'

'No, no one at all. We were just out on a morning walk, and there he was. I'm told his name's Rick.'

'So it is,' he said in a flat tone. 'Hear anything strange in the night?'

'Not a thing,' said Olivia.

Amy shook her head. 'We went to bed around midnight. I slept like a log.'

'Not from around these parts, are you?' Sheriff Brancombe glanced at Amy, then scrutinised Olivia from head to toe. 'Understand you flew in from London yesterday?'

His facial expression and tone seemed a deliberate attempt to make her feel out of place, and Olivia took an instant disliking to the officer. 'Business class, sheriff.'

'Uh huh,' he mumbled and continued to stare her out. 'I hear you've been moving around asking a lotta questions — why would that be?'

'I'm a naturally inquisitive person.'

'She is that,' said Amy.

'What say you leave the questioning to me and my deputies, ma'am?'

'If you insist, Sheriff.'

'I insist. You want to be helpful? You tell witnesses to contact me or my deputies if they have any information about the crime.'

'I'll do that, sir.'

Olivia offered a strained smile. The man had a bad attitude, but she would not hold it against him. A murder on your home patch would put any officer in a bad mood, and having a lot of tourists milling around wasn't helpful either.

'You see anybody with the deceased at any time?' asked the sheriff.

'No,' said Olivia. 'Didn't notice anybody talking with him last night. This morning, I noticed his door wide open, but he wasn't inside. Dead behind the trailer.'

'Not just dead,' said Amy. 'Sprawled out, dead.'

Olivia made a mental note of the comment. Her daughter had paid way more attention to the corpse than she had realised.

One of the deputies sauntered over and engaged the sheriff in whispers, which Olivia could not hear. As none of the officers had even gone near the entrance to Rick's trailer, Olivia wondered if the sheriff was familiar with the dead man and not overly concerned about his death. Maybe Rick was a known nuisance and they were secretly grateful for his demise? The lacklustre processing of the crime scene suggested this was a murder case about which they didn't care too much.

Well, somebody cared about the murder. She did.

3

TWO HOURS LATER, a dark blue Jeep with heavily tinted windows rolled up to the crime scene. Three people emerged from the vehicle: two men and a woman. Although all three wore casual clothes, Olivia had no doubt they were something to do with law enforcement. A knapsack dangled from the woman's arm. Shielding her head was a flat sunhat, from under which protruded a long, black ponytail. So, a Girl Scout and a couple of Boy Scouts were the cavalry. Olivia watched as they spoke to the medical examiner, who raised a hand and pointed out the sheriff.

The Boy Scouts headed towards the sheriff. The taller man led with a purposeful stride, as if he was in charge. Olivia guessed he was the older of the pair. A cowboy hat sat above brown hair, heavily grey around the temples, and rimless glasses circled sharp eyes. He wore a plain cotton shirt with long sleeves, and loose-fitting trousers tucked into workman boots. She wouldn't call him handsome, but despite his low-key look, he carried a certain aura of authority that drew attention. What also drew attention was a holstered gun at his side.

'Sheriff Brancombe?' He held up a palm and displayed a gold badge. 'Special Agent Jack Tyler, National Park Service, Investigative Services Branch.'

'Special Agent Tyler,' grunted the sheriff. 'Have to admit I had to look you gentlemen up. Never heard of ISB.'

'We're working on our media presence,' said the second man, 'one Tweet at a time.'

'This is Special Agent Martin Morelli.'

Olivia glanced at Morelli, who flashed a similar badge and inclined his head. He looked a year or two under forty. Dark blond hair with barely any white specks was cropped close to his scalp, and part of a chewed toothpick projected from his lips. Wrap-around sunglasses hid his eyes and, like his leader, he had a weapon holstered to his side.

Tyler pointed into the distance. 'The officer with the medical examiner is Special Agent Francesca Perez.'

As the men shook hands, Olivia's mind went into overdrive. Not the Boy Scouts — and definitely not the Girl Scouts, either. Like the sheriff, she had never heard of the Investigative Services Branch, and had no idea the National Park Service employed special agents. Movies had taught her special agents were an FBI thing. American law enforcement must be a mystery to the very citizens of the country, let alone outsiders. She wondered why this team would be at Hawkeye Point Campground, which was nowhere close to being classed as a national park. A campsite murder in a small town should not have attracted a team of special agents.

'Get me all eye-witness reports,' said Special Agent Tyler. 'We'll talk to as many people as we can within the immediate vicinity, then take on the perimeter.'

Sheriff Brancombe drew himself up to his full height, which still failed to put him at eye level with the lead man. 'We've already made arrangements to do that, Special Agent Tyler.'

Those last three words oozed sarcasm, and Olivia glanced at Tyler, wondering if the less than subtle blow was felt on his hard jaw. The sheriff might well have expected the National Park team, yet he clearly was not used to being dictated to on his own territory.

'Of course. My apologies, Sheriff.' Jack Tyler lightened his tone, yet his hazel eyes remained steely. 'Not at my best when I've had to endure Marty's bad driving.'

'He means he's grumpy on account of I wouldn't play blues rock music,' said Morelli. 'Keeps his pressure down, makes my toes curl.'

'So, any signs of a struggle, footprints, Sheriff?' asked Tyler.

'Not that we've seen.' The sheriff's tone was defensive. 'Still looking. This is a lot of land to cover.'

'And we're here for you, Sheriff,' said Tyler in a polite manner. He removed a sealed envelope from his breast pocket and pressed it into the sheriff's hand. 'The director asked me to leave this with you; he strongly believes in formalities. Read it in your own time.'

The sheriff pushed the unopened envelope into his trouser pocket, while his narrowed eyes suggested he already knew the content. 'Mighty nice of you,' he said, through barely opened lips.

Olivia eyed the two agents. They were stepping on the sheriff's feet and grinding his toes while remaining personable. Something serious was afoot. Rick must be a major-league criminal after all, perhaps a wanted mobster in hiding, successfully evading those in pursuit. For a while, anyway. Law enforcement must have been hot on his heels, but his vengeful cronies tracked him down first and ended his life at Hawkeye.

'Any ID on the victim?' asked Tyler.

'Driver's licence. Name's Richard Seagal.' The sheriff offered the identity card, which Tyler swiped from his fingers with barely a nod of thanks.

Olivia got the impression that Jack Tyler was a man who readily gave orders with the expectation of being answered and obeyed. She wondered whether anyone ever dared say no or went up against him. Rather than wait to be barked at, she opted to jump right in.

'Special Agent Tyler? My name is Olivia Knightley and this is my daughter, Amy. We found the body.'

'I was just about to say that.' Sheriff Brancombe glared at her.

'Time is essential in a murder investigation, Sheriff,' said Olivia evenly. 'Thought I'd save you some.'

Prominent veins in the sheriff's forehead throbbed.

Agent Tyler's expression was one of great curiosity as he looked at her. His tone was neither sharp nor friendly, strictly probing. 'What can you tell me, ma'am?' he asked.

'We were out having an early walk,' said Olivia. 'The path took us past the dead man's trailer and he was just lying there on the ground. I gave a statement.'

'British.' Tyler stated.

'Feel free to add it,' said Olivia.

Tyler looked towards the sheriff. 'Let me see her statement.'

The sheriff handed over the leaf of paper and, as the special agent stretched his hand, Olivia caught a glimpse of wrist beneath the shirt cuff. He wore an ordinary Timex watch. She wondered if he dressed like this all the time, or if this was his one-of-the-people act for Hawkeye.

Agent Tyler read Olivia's statement. He glanced over at the victim's trailer and swiftly back to Olivia. 'So the trailer door was wide open?'

'Completely,' said Olivia. 'One hundred eighty degrees.'

'Wonder who opened it, victim or killer?' Tyler looked at Morelli. 'Might get prints from the outside of the door or handle.'

'Chesca's already on it.' Morelli shielded his eyes from the sun as he gazed across the greenery at his female colleague. 'Come with me, Sheriff Brancombe. I'll introduce you to Special Agent Perez. It's not good to leave the kid on her own for too long. She'll annoy the ME or your deputies, and we're all about harmony.'

Morelli placed a hand on the local lawman's shoulder and chatted in a jovial manner as they walked away.

Special Agent Tyler waved the page in front of Olivia. 'Your statement complete, Miss Knightley, or is there anything you can add?'

'*I'm* Miss Knightley,' said Amy. 'My mother is Mrs Knightley. Still.'

Jack Tyler appeared bemused. He gave Amy a brief nod of acknowledgement. 'I appreciate it,' he said.

'I've got nothing to add to what my mom said.'

'The statement's complete.' Olivia cringed inside. Amy was determined that they should keep the same surname, and Olivia had not argued the point. Reverting to her maiden name was not a big deal in the circumstances.

'My thanks to you both. If you'll excuse me?' Tyler delivered a short bow and headed towards the deceased's battered silver trailer.

As Olivia watched the investigators from a distance, an awful thought crossed her mind and jabbed at her temple. Of course, there was something she could – and should – add to her statement. She groaned inwardly. Fingerprints. She had placed a palm on at least one side of vehicle's entrance when she leaned inside. The sensible thing to do was to confess as soon as possible, face up to her blunder head-on rather than avoid the issue.

'Oh, Christ no,' she murmured as embarrassment pricked her skin.

'You alright, Mom?'

'Yes, sorry, ignore me. Didn't realise I spoke out loud.'

Stupid, careless mistakes like this had landed her in trouble before with her boss Bill. But how was she to know Rick would go and get himself killed? All she had wanted to do was break through a handsome stranger's rigid exterior, eke a smile out of him, get some friendly conversation going, maybe flirt a little. No harm in that.

'I'm starving,' announced Amy.

Olivia glanced at her watch. All thoughts of breakfast had vanished in the early morning excitement, and it was close to noon. A teenager's appetite showed up no matter what external distractions competed with their stomach juices. Olivia's own appetite for food had rather deserted her, replaced only by an appetite to find out more about the victim and evidence of his killer.

'Mom, did you hear me?'

Olivia looked at her daughter. 'There's something important I need to say to Special Agent Tyler. You can go put on some sausages and potatoes, can't you?'

'I think we're supposed to call them franks and hash browns,' said Amy. 'And yeah, I could go cook on my own – and I know I'll end up eating on my own.'

'I'll be five minutes.'

'No, you won't.' Amy adopted a mocking tone. 'What was that about "We'll cook and eat meals together on holiday"? Went out within twenty-four hours, didn't it? You're straight back in your zone, Mom. A stranger gets murdered and no time for breakfast. Dump daughter, time to investigate.'

Olivia silently recalled that Amy had abandoned cooked breakfasts for weeks on end and stormed out of the house early to punish her for the divorce. On the odd mornings that Amy had hung around, she'd poured herself cold cereal and walked through the house eating it before tossing the half-full bowl in the sink.

'Franks and hash browns it is, love.' Olivia took her daughter's arm. 'Come on.'

Olivia's phone rang as they set off walking towards the

caravan. Chris, her ex-husband and Amy's father. Olivia had promised she would ensure Amy called him when they arrived, but it had flown from her memory when she was busy meeting new people. The man had predicted bad things could happen in America, and lo and behold, something bad had gone down on day one. What a visionary.

'Answer the phone, Mom.'

'It's your father.'

'Yeah, I kind of guessed that from the expression on your face. So answer it!'

'No,' said Olivia. 'Why doesn't he call you?'

'Because he knows I do text only. Phoning people is so twentieth century, and he obviously wants to hear a voice.'

The phone continued to ring.

'Mom! If you don't answer it, he'll think something's wrong.'

'Something *is* wrong, Amy.' Olivia answered the phone with a polite, 'Hi, Chris, just a minute.' She covered the speaker and whispered, 'Talk to your father. If you tell him what's happened, this trip is over. He'll get on to the Foreign Office and demand they get you out of America.'

'I get it. I won't tell him.' Amy snatched the phone. 'Hi, Dad. Yeah, sorry, Mom's kneading dumplings and got her hands all covered in flour. Wait . . . right, you're on speaker now.'

'How was the flight?'

Olivia listened to the cool English voice that used to make her heart leap all those years ago. They had drifted so far apart that nowadays she could listen to it with complete detachment, and slight annoyance. Even though they were officially split, Chris continued to call with mundane questions. Sometimes, he called even when Amy was staying at his flat. It was as if he was determined to keep track of Olivia at every point and know the details of her life. She wished he would let go so they could both get on with their lives in peace.

'Fine,' said Amy. 'We had the longest drive ever, though that's cause Mom's scared of the road. The scenery was great, and we made it to Hawkeye camp before dark.'

'What do you think of it?'

'It's great so far. The people are really nice and there's the absolute sweetest dog.' Amy made a faux scary face at Olivia. 'The things you see around here, Dad! Would take your breath away.'

Olivia pinched her daughter's side, and Amy squirmed away.

Chris said, 'Take a few pictures for me.'

'I will. We're going sightseeing at Hawkeye Point across the road from the campsite after breakfast. I'll take one standing at the highest point in Iowa, even though it's only twenty feet above the flat land. There's a mosaic, a silo and a little museum over there.'

'Sounds lovely. Sox misses you, by the way. He wonders where the chief cuddler has gone.'

'Aww, give him lots of kisses for me, Dad. Tell him I miss him too.'

Olivia smiled despite herself. Sox was a ten-week-old kitten, a beautiful little thing, black and white with brown spots. Chris had never shown any particular interest in keeping pets during their marriage, and had downright rejected the idea of getting a cat. She wondered about his motives. She hoped the kitten had been bought because he truly loved the pet, and not merely to lure Amy over from time to time.

The tension eased from Olivia's body as her daughter chatted gaily with her father. She listened to her give a description of the location and the individual campers. Part of her cringed at the idea of Amy misleading her father, but at least she wasn't downright lying. Leaving out gory details was not lying. It was a truthful, if economical, round-up of their journey so far.

Olivia allowed herself a wry smile. Amy was indeed her

mother's daughter. She was not fazed by the turn of events, and obviously did not want her father to rescue her.

'Anyway, gotta go, Dad. You know I hate when fried dumplings go cold. Talk to you later.'

Amy clicked off the phone and handed it to Olivia. 'Remind me to text Dad every day, maybe first thing in the morning, will you? Or we'll be getting that all the time.'

'That was all so smooth. I thought I raised you to do better?'

Amy smiled sweetly. 'You raised me to do exactly what I did.'

Any thoughts she'd had of needing to leave Hawkeye immediately for Amy's sake began to fade away. Olivia wanted to know who murdered Rick Seagal and why. Darcy had suggested he was a bad one, but provided no evidence to back it up, despite prodding.

Such a death would not be reported on internationally, so she had no fear of Chris picking up the story on the BBC's morning news, the only news he ever paid attention to. He never watched nightly news, claiming he wanted to sleep in peace at night. It was one of the things they crossed swords about, as Olivia preferred to know all that was going on in the world before she went to bed. Whether it helped her sleep or not was beside the point. Burying your head in the sand never solved a thing.

'Right, let's go rustle up breakfast, young lady.'

'Am I ever ready.'

4

WHEN SPECIAL AGENT Jack Tyler had taken the disturbing phone call that morning, he was standing on a rocky ledge with an eighty-foot drop at Stone State Park in Sioux City, right there in Iowa. Surrounded by rich woodland, imperious trees and rippling waters, yet unable to spend any time appreciating that beauty, and forced instead to concentrate on the hunt for a busy killer that saw him working around the clock seven days a week.

He had hiked through the bluffs and past ravines adjacent to the Big Sioux River in search of evidence. The victim stabbed in the heart was found close to that scenic spot six days ago, and his taskforce's efforts were concentrated in that area. Then came the latest unwelcome news. A new dead body discovered at Hawkeye Point, just north of Sibley, a small town about eighty miles away. Time to hit the road again.

Most people assumed that working for the National Park Service was an easy gig, that he ambled through the national parks, and brushed dust from national monuments most days, that on other days he visited a range of natural, historical and recreational properties, quietly enjoying the sights. Other people thought that his working life was all strolling along man-made trails, warning visitors about wild animals, intervening in lovers' tiffs and ticketing litterbugs.

Only those who had once been close to him knew that his twenty years with the ISB included solving complex cases, including murders. He twirled the gold band on his ring finger. As long as he remained committed to this hazardous career, it was unlikely that Sophie would ever take him back.

He stared at the bloody knife sticking out of Richard Seagal's neck. Violent people were violent wherever they went, and were just as likely to commit murder in front of a stunning waterfall as they were on a busy road, outside a bodega, or in a dark alleyway. All that changed was the scenery on which the blood spilled.

This killer was very different to those Jack had pursued before, and in moments of low morale, he wondered whether he should have fought so hard for jurisdiction of this case. The FBI were the ones with all the fancy technology, the latest gadgets, high-tech vehicles, analysts, technicians and every facility needed for success. Budgets were low in the National Park Service, equipment and manpower limited. He was thankful that Tom Walsh had joined the team. Tom was an FBI special agent with particular expertise in criminology, psychology and conflict study. As well as being a fellow professional, he was also a friend, the two men having formed a bond at police academy decades ago.

Jack worked most of his cases solo, but he could have done with a dozen ISB Special Agents for Operation Dean, the code name given to this murder probe. Though frustrated by the lack of investigators to cover such vast regions of park lands, he was relieved when the directors gave the greenlight for Marty Morelli and Francesca Perez to get involved. Morelli had been with the ISB for twelve years, following an initial career as a traffic cop. 'Got tired of writing tickets and inhaling gas,' was his reason for jumping ship. Perez had joined the team six years ago after spending her first few years out of college teaching high-school students mathematics. Kids were fine, she said, it was the parents who drove her mad. Both agents had extensive training to bolster their sterling records as investigators, and were his first choice.

Jack pulled on latex gloves and crouched close to the body. 'Clean wound, no messing,' he murmured.

'Left carotid artery ended it for him,' said the medical examiner, a lanky woman with an air that suggested she'd seen it all before. 'No signs of blunt-force trauma anywhere. Even with the knife stemming the blood flow, he bled out mighty quickly. Didn't stand a chance.'

'The killer opts for a sharp kitchen knife,' said Jack. 'Out of all the knives he could have used to do the job, a kitchen knife.'

'A real solid knife, made right here in the good old US of A,' said Perez in a tone of admiration.

Perez was a slender, confident woman with an optimistic outlook that Jack admired. In her book, there was a solution to every problem, whether mathematical or logical.

'I bet he's not married,' said Morelli. 'My wife would go crazy if I removed her best knife from the kitchen.'

'That wouldn't bother me. Knives disappear from the kitchen all the while, and I'm the only one using them.' Perez shot Morelli a teasing look. 'Your wives are always strange, Marty.'

'Hey, the first two were fine. It's the third one. She's a little . . . off sometimes.' Morelli grinned at her. 'Don't be feeling sorry for me, Chesca. You're the one still swiping left and right every day.'

'Dean never left the murder weapon before,' murmured Jack. 'Maybe something startled him and he had to leave. Or maybe he just had difficulty pulling it out.'

'Wound's pretty deep, just like the others.' Perez raised her camera and flashed shots of the body from all angles.

'You've seen his handiwork before, then?' The ME stared down at the body dispassionately.

'Unfortunately, yes.' Jack took in the man's muddy soles and scanned the surrounding grass. 'Caked mud on his boots. The grass around here is dry, too dry for mud. He walked wet mud over from somewhere near here.'

'A witness says they're pretty sure they saw the victim late last night, after midnight, down by the standpipe.' Perez indicated towards distant trees. 'People don't tend to go there at night for fear of critters. I guess he wasn't the fearful type.'

'We'll check it out,' said Morelli. 'Maybe our vic had company on his midnight moseying.'

'He's been dead less than twelve hours, so the time is about right.' The ME looked at Jack. 'I'll give the victim a thorough examination at the lab, but I'm willing to state the cause of death won't change, and that'll be what you get in my report. Excessive blood loss from a major artery. If you're finished with him, Special Agent Tyler?'

'I'm done with the photos.' Perez made the sign of the cross on her chest.

'Can we get the knife out, doc?' asked Jack.

'Sure, I'll get it,' the ME said.

Jack noted it took some effort for the blade to emerge. The exposed stainless steel was at least eight inches long. He held open a plastic evidence bag and she placed it inside.

'All done now?' she asked.

'All done. Thanks, doc,' said Jack.

He watched as the medical examiner and her assistants zipped up the body in a black bag, placed him on a gurney and wheeled him off into the ambulance. The road ahead was daunting. The director had called in favours between the FBI and the leaders of the state parks and national parks to secure partnership between the different organisations in order to pursue this killer. There was always top-level kow-towing to be done and egos to soothe when it came to lengthy, complex cases crossing many internal borders. The cooperation of every entity was essential to get a grip on this case, and despite the mammoth task, failure was not an option.

Jack stared at the body shape pressed into the grass and the large puddle of congealed blood beside it. He jerked his head away as if the sight angered him. 'Other than the knife – which I really hope we get prints off – what else have we got to work with?'

'Georgia plates.' Morelli gestured towards the rear of the trailer.

'Run a background check,' said Jack. 'His ID doesn't look fake. If he's like the other bodies, then he's just some unlucky random victim.'

'Well, look what we have here.' Perez lifted a broad piece of fingerprint tape from the exterior wall of the trailer and held it up to her colleagues. 'Prints.'

'Good ones?' asked Jack.

'Clear babies.' Perez continued to scrutinise the exterior. 'Someone placed hands on either side of the door frame. I've got small hands and large hands, so more than one person. Guessing one pair belongs to the deceased. You think Tom can put priority status on them with the lab?'

'I'll let him know what's coming.'

With Tom Walsh's help, Jack had built an initial sparse profile of the person he sought to apprehend. Early indications suggested the killer was a white male and possibly a loner, which accounted for a good few million of the population.

'Dean posed all the bodies.' Jack placed his palms together as if in prayer and brought his fingers to his lips. 'This one is the most blatant. No one drops dead and falls in that position, with sprawled out legs and arms so far apart.'

'Except a drunk, maybe?' said Perez.

'That how you look when you make it to bed after a girl's night out?' asked Morelli.

'At least I make it to bed. No one's ever had to scrape me off the ground beside a trash can at some Delaware dive.'

'Remind me never to share secrets with you again.'

Jack walked up the few steps into the trailer. 'Messy sort, wasn't he? Uses paper plates and boxes, doesn't use the trash can. Would be hard to tell if anything was missing or out of place.'

He opened a few cupboards. Tins of food lay on their sides. Plenty of cutlery inside the drawers. All of the knives were ordinary kitchen knives, yet none matched the murder weapon. Under the small sink lay an empty bucket and cleaning rags, which were bone dry.

Morelli joined Jack inside, leaving not much room for either of them to move. 'Cosy in here. Couple of beer bottles. He certainly wasn't running a bar.'

'Mr Seagal, much like the unidentified victim in Illinois, doesn't seem to own much,' said Jack. 'His truck isn't in bad condition; trailer looks sound but old. No phone, tablet, computer. No notepads or pens anywhere.'

'He's got the right idea.' Morelli gazed around. 'The only way to truly be free living off the grid is to get rid of anything with an internet connection. Keep it, and you're tied to the world. To think otherwise is delusional.'

'I hear you,' said Jack. 'But if he hated people that much, he'd go live in a forest with creatures that can't speak.'

Morelli picked up a small transistor radio and turned it on. Country and western music filled the air. 'Good old country boy.'

'In the wrong place at the wrong time,' added Jack. 'Just like every other good old country boy.'

'I'll go check if anyone noticed visitors sniffing around this place,' said Morelli as the two men left the trailer van. 'Haven't spotted any CCTV cameras anywhere around.'

Jack had already noticed that, and knew it would make his job so much harder. Many a case had been solved with the use of crisp CCTV images. People lied or people were mistaken. The camera never lied.

'There's a whole lot of farmland every which way you look,' said Jack. 'Need to see if the farmers noticed anyone creeping through their property.'

'I'm on it,' said Morelli, crunching on a new toothpick.

'I'll go lock this away and get to canvassing.' Jack waved the evidence bag containing the bloody knife. 'The sheriff's done some work so we can coordinate reports.'

'Sheriff on board?' asked Perez.

'Thanks to my winning personality,' said Morelli. 'He's not so keen on Jack.'

'Don't write off that relationship.' A slight smile appeared on Jack's lips. 'I'll seduce him yet.'

5

AFTER BREAKFAST, OLIVIA left Amy in the company of the social media influencers and started off down the path towards the crime scene, reciting the words of apology she would say to the special agents. Darcy spotted her and threw a spanner in the works.

'Hey Olivia, can't believe this is the welcome you got.'

'Yeah, it was a bit rude.'

'We never have any trouble around here.' Darcy shook her head. 'I just knew from the first day I set eyes on Rick that he was trouble.'

'Why, though?' Olivia reluctantly stopped walking and frowned. 'Just because he kept himself apart and didn't like socialising? Some people are like that.'

'Yeah, well, now he's not "like that" anymore.'

Annoyed at Darcy's tone, Olivia barely managed to keep her own pleasant. 'Didn't he have even one friend around here?'

'Not that I'd seen,' said Darcy. 'He'd only been around a week, but some nights he'd sit outside by himself. Nearly bumped into him one night sat on a log, dressed all in black as usual, and still as a stone. Scared the living daylights outta me. Seemed he was just staring at the stars.'

'Did you talk to the investigators already?'

'Yep, told them what I'd seen. Which is pretty much nothing.'

Olivia could see the agents in the distance. All of them with gloved hands, holding notepads and scribbling away. She watched as Jack Tyler held a phone to his ear and moved away from a group of campers.

'I'm just going to have a word with them now.'

'I thought you done talked to them already? You thought of something else?'

'You could say that. See you later.'

Olivia tried to steady her nerves. Part of her wanted to walk away, but the other part — the one that sympathised with over-worked investigators — told her to get on with it. She had to stop them from wasting precious time. With shoulders back, she inhaled deeply and headed across the grassy field towards Jack Tyler. As soon as he lowered the phone, she cleared her throat behind him.

'Excuse me, Special Agent Tyler?'

'Yes, Miss . . . Mrs Knightley.'

'I'm fine with Olivia.' She delivered a bright smile, which was not returned.

'What can I do for you?'

'Er, I believe your Special Agent Perez was searching for fingerprints, around the dead man's campervan?'

To Olivia's alarm, Perez raised her head and almond-shaped eyes looked straight at her. 'She heard me, from all the way over there,' Olivia whispered incredulously.

'Like a cat hears you pop a can of food,' said Tyler. 'Prints are her domain; she can't help herself.'

Olivia's stomach fell another notch as Francesca Perez closed off her conversation with a nomad and strode towards her.

'This is Mrs Olivia Knightley,' said Tyler, once Perez was at his shoulder.

'Pleased to meet you, Mrs Knightley.' Perez nodded at her.

'Please, call me Olivia. I prefer it to Mrs Knightley.' Olivia gave a nervous laugh. 'Divorced, though. My daughter is at a touchy age; she'll get over it.' She hated herself for babbling on, and cursed Darcy for having interrupted her clear train of thought.

Perez glanced up at her unsmiling leader. 'I know I heard the word fingerprints.'

'You did,' said Tyler.

Perez wiped her dripping brow with the back of her wrist, then straightened up, hands on hips, her piercing eyes focused on Olivia. 'What about the fingerprints?'

The woman's tone had changed from pleasant to prickly with unsettling speed, and Olivia swallowed. 'I might have placed a palm on the trailer. Sorry.'

'You *might* have placed a palm?' repeated Perez.

'Possibly both hands. I'm sorry. I never dreamed this vehicle was about to form part of a murder site, or I wouldn't have touched it.'

This interaction attracted the attention of Agent Morelli, who wandered over, raised his sunglasses, and stood beside Perez like a sensitive big brother. Olivia got the impression that to mess with one was to mess with both. She expelled a breath. Three whole agents to witness her shame. Couldn't get any worse.

Tyler folded one arm across his stomach, while the other hand stroked his smooth chin. 'Did you arrange to rendezvous with the victim before you left England, or did you and he make friends last night?'

Rendezvous? Blood surged through Olivia's veins. She could see why her position looked bad, but did not appreciate the insinuation. 'I certainly did not rendezvous with Rick. Never been in contact with him. Never met him. And I didn't go any-where near him or his trailer last night.'

'Rick?' Tyler nodded slowly. 'That's a bit familiar. Richard Seagal said you could call him Rick?'

'That's what everybody here calls him, not just me.'

'Just checking.'

Olivia silently seethed and fought off the urge to retort.

'So, you weren't inside Rick's trailer last night,' stated Tyler. 'But you were inside this morning?'

'Well, not *inside* inside. I just sort of leaned inside from outside.'

'Just decided to go trespassing, sort of. In his trailer. A complete stranger?'

'As I said, I didn't trespass, Agent Tyler . . . not technically, anyway. I just glanced in for two seconds, then turned around when my daughter called out to me.'

'We live in tense times, ma'am. Ever heard of Stand Your Ground?'

'I would think the entire ten billion people who live on this planet have, sir,' said Olivia. 'Isn't that the law that allows you to shoot, stab, kill whoever you want once you declare you are afraid of them?'

Agent Tyler fixed her with an icy stare. 'It means a person who reasonably believes they're in imminent danger does not have to retreat, and can take the action they feel necessary to defend themselves.'

Olivia shrugged. 'Like I said.'

'You want to tell me what you were looking for inside the trailer, Mrs Knightley?' asked Tyler.

Olivia couldn't think of a credible response. She could hardly say she was searching for Rick when a split-second glance had already told her the vehicle was unoccupied. She could not admit that her natural curiosity would not allow her to leave the man's quarters without a good nose around.

'You work, ma'am?' asked Tyler.

'Oh, I see,' said an indignant Olivia. 'I'll have you know that I'm not some failed burglar or some stupid little tourist. I'm actually a private investigator, with a lot of experience and a whole lot of satisfied clients.'

The gentle summer breeze seemed to freeze; even the birds stopped chirping. Olivia's throat went dry as all eyes fell upon her. Morelli even removed his sunglasses to study her more closely. In that moment, Olivia wished she had not been so forthcoming. The need to set Jack Tyler straight had been too strong to resist, yet there was no way her misguided outburst could serve to improve the toxic situation.

'Well, what do we have here, a private eye?' said Morelli.

'Marty, you cannot give the answer when you've already heard the answer,' Perez chided him. 'That's cheating.'

'You were investigating Richard Seagal?' Tyler's tone was hard.

'No, nothing like that.' Olivia took a step back and held up both palms. 'I know nothing about him, honest. I was introduced to many of the campers last night, and I wanted to be introduced to Rick. He stayed holed up, so I couldn't. This morning, I decided to try again. The door was wide open. That's it.'

Tyler checked the content of her witness statement, then glared at her. 'We're going to try again, ma'am. And this time, you're going to tell the whole truth.'

'Of course. I just forgot, that's all.' Olivia stared at his rigid face and firmly set jaw as he made notes. If her excuse sounded lame to her, it must sound like a cover-up to him. She would never confess to having touched the body; that would really set him off.

His phone rang and he pressed the screen. 'Special Agent Tyler.'

Perez and Morelli ignored Olivia and spoke to each other in whispers while their boss took the call.

'We've got a runner,' Tyler said as he hung up. 'An RV just left here. Took off from a routine traffic stop a mile down the road, but they held him. Marty, go pick him up.'

'He'd better have a good story,' said Morelli.

Olivia watched as Morelli ran to the Jeep. Within seconds,

the vehicle sped off for the exit and blew past a police cruiser. She turned her attention back to Agent Tyler. 'No murderer runs away from a crime scene in front of a load of cops.'

'Had a kidnapper ask me for directions once,' said Agent Tyler.

'Oh dear, I keep forgetting we're talking about Americans.'

'Excuse me?' Agent Perez's narrowed eyes carried a distinct look of menace.

Tyler stared at Olivia and said nothing. Olivia felt like an ant waiting to be crushed underfoot. Why couldn't she shut up and mind her own business?

'Well, aren't you something?' said Perez in a less-than-appreciative voice. 'Screw up a crime scene and then tell us how to investigate it.'

Olivia bit her lip. Despite knowing she should be dedicating her time to bonding with her daughter, she wanted to gather evidence and interrogate eye witnesses. Not even the wrath of the agents changed that.

From the corner of her eye, she saw Darcy approaching. Despite her earlier uncharitable feelings towards the woman, she was relieved that someone had turned up to take the pressure off.

Darcy walked up to Agent Tyler and said, 'Do you know lots of people have left here since the murder, sir? How come you didn't cordon off all the campsites? There's twelve sites, you know? Why'd you not set up roadblocks on the streets, stop all the cars going in and out?'

'Oh great, another one,' mumbled Perez.

'Ma'am, I appreciate the concern,' said Tyler. 'We'd rather visitors stay and talk to us, but as much as we'd like to, we can't bring the state of Iowa to a complete stop. People are allowed to go about their legitimate business.'

'Even a killer?' asked Darcy.

'The killer's most likely still here, anyway,' said Olivia.

Darcy rubbed her throat and looked at her. 'You sound mighty sure of that. How come?'

'Please do answer, ma'am.' Tyler's hard eyes bore into Olivia.

'You want to save us heatstroke and give the confession right now?' asked Perez.

Olivia tried not to wither under the intensity of their glares. Taking on special agents was such a bad idea in the scheme of bad ideas — and she'd had plenty of bad ideas in her time. 'Mouse never moves with the cat around,' she said. 'The chance of being caught in a place like this must be low when you can trek through forestry. Wait out the tired cops. They'll soon give up and leave.'

'You really don't know when to quit, do you?' said Perez.

Even to Olivia's ears, her words sounded overly dismissive of the law enforcers. 'I'm sorry, Agent Perez. I'm not trying to say I know this place better than you do. As I said, I'm a private investigator. I can help if . . .'

Olivia was cut short by Jack Tyler. 'Thank you for warning us about your fingerprints, Mrs Knightley.' The sarcasm was heavy in his tone as he handed her a business card. 'If you think of anything else you might have done, please contact me. We're here all day. Or sleep on it. We'll be right back here in the morning.'

Olivia bristled. 'You're just going to dismiss me?'

'Could arrest you, if you prefer?' Tyler turned his back and wandered over to another prospective witness.

'Come on, Olivia,' said Darcy as she walked away. 'Let them get on with it.'

Olivia stormed away, angry at the agents, and even more angry at herself for making a mess of things. She hoped she was wrong. It would be the best result if Rick's killer had made a run for it and Morelli caught him on the road.

'Did you mean what you said, about being a private investigator?'

'Sort of.' Olivia mentally kicked herself. Her job was not

something she'd planned on sharing with any of the campers. 'I dabble in a little sleuthing any chance I get.'

'Like that one over there.' Darcy gestured with her chin.

The object of her attention was the pushy brunette, who still lingered on the grounds with microphone in hand.

'You know who she is?' asked Olivia.

'Said her name's Kimberly Grant from the *Quad City Tales* . . . some kinda true-crime blog. Not that I follow those things. Persistent little minx, that one.'

A true-crime blogger. In Olivia's experience, some of them were way more persistent than police and fellow private eyes.

'Cops told her to leave, but she's not going anywhere,' added Darcy. 'Firing off questions left, right, and centre like she's Nancy Grace. I'm sure she'd love to talk to you.'

The question Olivia asked herself was, did she want to talk to Kimberly Grant? She watched the keen woman focus on her next target.

'I'll think about it. See you later, Darcy.'

6

I T WAS NOON when Olivia and Amy set out on their second attempt at a leisurely walk around the grounds. This was supposed to be the start of a beautiful holiday, precious alone time with her daughter that, if wasted, could never be regained, and Olivia vowed not to get involved in any murder investigation. Making the vow was one thing; keeping it was easier said than done. Her instincts were such that if she came across people who seemed distinctly out of place, her brain shifted gear.

She recalled with a wince an incident at a large phone store in Oxford Circus, when she'd anticipated trouble from a number of loitering youths. Their form of dress was what first caught her attention. Twelve boys in identical blue stretch denim trousers and ballet slippers, although their tops were different. They circulated around the store without talking to each other, and she guessed a smash-and-grab was imminent. Police came in good time for once. Turned out the group had planned an innocent flash-mob dance, which was to be livestreamed. Olivia never set foot in that store again, and would rather sit naked in an ant nest than tell Amy about the episode.

This time, she would close her eyes to the diversions. The ISB agents were not interested and the sheriff sure as hell didn't want her input, either. She would curb her natural instinct to investigate and leave it to the all-American heroes.

As they walked past the playground area for small children, she noted it was largely abandoned. She could not recall seeing any young children, though there were a few teenagers. Some families were having lunch at picnic tables and seemed equally determined to enjoy their holiday, despite the murder in their midst.

Olivia and Amy discussed the landscape with fellow visitors and nomads. They learned that the land around Hawkeye Point was privately owned, but the landowners were happy to work with the county in making the site a tourist destination. That they'd succeeded was a triumph for the remote Midwestern farmland, which certainly was not on the cutting edge of tourist entertainment and could not compete with theme parks.

Watching her enthusiastic daughter, Olivia felt grateful that holiday mode had been restored. Amy in a good mood was a delight to be around. A lot about the girl reminded Olivia of herself at that age, except that her own parents, as wonderful as they were, could not afford family trips abroad. Still, Olivia had enjoyed those holidays spent with relatives in London, which to a young girl from the West Midlands seemed like an enormous, exciting place. Even then, it was inevitable she would end up living in London one day.

Amy turned her freckled face up to the warm sun. 'It's brilliant not to be in school, not to be doing homework or swotting for some test. Being free to do what you want is so underrated.'

'True talk.'

Olivia recalled her own school days, back when there was no internet to help with research, when studying meant taking books out at the library and copying whole paragraphs by hand. No one had a phone to check Google every minute, and everybody had at least one set of *Encyclopaedia Britannica* volumes in their homes. She was glad that despite the distractions of the modern world, Amy was doing quite well at school, and thankful that the divorce had not put her off her studies. Olivia smiled to herself at the latter thought, and remembered Chris had promised Amy £100 for every subject passed with a grade 8 or 9, which was incentive enough to keep the girl focused. Praise and encouragement were great, but sometimes a good bribe worked way better.

Amy chatted non-stop, discussing a mixture of informative subjects and inane things, but Olivia was happy to engage in all conversations. Amy would soon get used to this new normal of being with either her mother or her father, and not both together. Olivia hoped that this trip would break her rebellious nature, and so far all signs had been positive. Things were going to work out just fine.

Much to Olivia's annoyance, however, her mind strayed and refused to be diverted from Rick Seagal's murder for long. Despite promises made to herself that she would not entertain thoughts of motives and evidence, here she was, blocking out her daughter's voice and thinking instead of a dead stranger, wondering why he'd been killed and by whom. Guilt filled her, seeped through her veins and emerged as tiny pinpricks on her arms.

In the distance stood Rick's trailer with the yellow caution tape all around it. One of the sheriff's deputies guarded the vehicle. She could not see any of the special agents, and imagined they were engaged at one of the other campsites, interrogating people.

'Did you hear me, Mom?'

'Sorry, say that again, love.'

'I said, let's go cross the road. I'm ready to pose at the mosaic. Should have brought a British flag to stake my achievement.'

'You try that and I'm pretty sure they'd tell you where to stick the British flag.' Olivia smiled. 'Never forget: 1776 happened.'

Olivia and Amy walked down the long driveway to the exit and passed a patrol vehicle bearing the sheriff department's logo. The deputy barely glanced at them, although Olivia nodded at him. She wondered how long it would take them to find Rick's killer, and whether law enforcement officers manning the pictur-esque property would become a thing. Hawkeye was billed as a safe place. It would be a shame if that were to change.

A thought crossed Olivia's mind. She had not raised the issue of the belly-button piercing, and despite not wanting to rock the boat, she still wanted to know about it.

'So, when did you get the navel ring?' she asked in a light tone.

Amy bent forward and looked at her flat stomach, admiring the silver ring. 'Oh, that's been there ages, Mom. Have you just noticed it?'

'Yes, I have.'

'Cute, innit? Innit?'

The conversation was not going the way Olivia had planned, and she concluded that showing displeasure would just spoil what had been an enjoyable walk. Besides, there was no getting around it: time was passing and her daughter was growing older. The things teenagers did nowadays were more risky than in her day – and there was nothing she could do about the piercing, anyway.

'It suits you.'

'You don't like it, do you?'

'It'll grow on me.' Olivia noted the downturn in Amy's lips, and quickly added: 'Put it this way, I love your earrings. As soon as you turned four, I was straight off to the jeweller to get your ears pierced.'

Amy's smile returned. 'And Dad hated it, didn't he? Cos I kept crying when you had to twist them around every day for weeks until they healed.'

'I think you hated them too until they healed, although you'd been the one begging to have it done as you didn't want to wear the clip-on earrings.' Olivia laughed. 'I loved getting us matching earrings. Can't see myself getting a ring through my stomach to match, but then again, my stomach will never get as flat as yours.'

'Everybody wears them, though. Doesn't matter whether your stomach's flat or not.' Amy gave her mother a sly look. 'You know what? I think you should be a sport and get one.'

'I might just do that.' Olivia grinned at her daughter. 'And turn up at your school in a short tank top to meet your teacher.'

Amy squealed. 'Don't you dare. I'd just die!'

Olivia held up a hand. 'I promise faithfully not to embarrass you. I promise faithfully to always strive to make you proud.'

'Thanks, Mom. I'll hold you to that.'

They walked across the main road and into the Hawkeye Point elevated area, where most of the tourists converged. As expected, a large American flag mounted to a long pole was the only sovereignty marker. The raised mosaic marked the highest point of Iowa, which was 1,670 feet above sea level. Not exactly Mount Kilimanjaro as it was barely above the height of surrounding fields, but an interesting sight nonetheless. Directional signs surrounded the mosaic marking each of the other forty-nine states' highest points.

Amy turned out to be a good guide, providing commentary on what Iowa was famous for, and Olivia was pleased her daughter had made the effort to research the state in advance. They climbed the stairs of the old silo, which offered an observation deck and stunning views of the landscape, including acres of corn. Olivia enjoyed mingling with and chatting to other interstate tourists as they gazed at the scenery in appreciation. Back on solid ground, they ambled through the corn crib — a small walk-through museum — and admired a fine display of ancient farm machinery.

'Can you imagine ploughing the soil with this rusty thing?'

said a male voice. 'Now we have machinery that does it in a matter of minutes, saving hours of work.'

Olivia glanced at the corroded tool. 'Yes, and back then, it was probably state of the art.'

Another voice said, 'Ah, the good old days.'

Olivia smiled at the speaker. 'Some say the good old days were never that good.'

Olivia heard the sound of police sirens increasing in volume, but paid little attention. No doubt they were headed for the campsite. If they arrested a suspect, she would hear all about it later at Channing's barbecue. Or perhaps the murder was not the only crime in town, and there were other things going on that the cops were investigating. Still, it was hard to imagine any other major crime in such a laid-back area so far off the beaten track.

Olivia and Amy posed at a sign displaying the iconic Iowa painting *American Gothic* with cut-out holes to facilitate their heads. As far as the eye could see was lush green scenery that soothed Olivia's soul. Experiencing a non-stressful existence for a while felt so good.

Less than ten minutes after that zen-like thought crossed her mind, she heard the sirens again. To her surprise, two vehicles were heading up the driveway towards them. A black sedan and a patrol car from the sheriff's office rolled up and parked close to the mosaic. Jack Tyler emerged from the sedan with another man she did not recognise.

Olivia thought they must be there hoping to find other witnesses to interview. Strangely, the deputy did not alight from his car. Olivia locked eyes with Tyler, and her heart sank as he strode towards her with a hard expression on his face. Before she could interpret what his appearance could mean, he was towering over her. He gestured to the man at his side.

'This is Special Agent Tom Walsh. He's FBI.'

'Wondered if they'd turn up,' said Olivia.

'Mrs Knightley, good to meet you.'

The new agent had bright blond cropped hair. His tanned, unlined face hid his age. A fluorescent green bow tie topped a crisp white shirt and tailored trousers, the polar opposite in style to Tyler. Despite Walsh's chartered accountant-like appearance, Olivia had no doubt he was a professional criminologist.

'You can come quietly or under arrest. What's your pleasure?'

Olivia blinked a few times as Jack Tyler's improbable offer sank in. She had made it into her forty-fifth year of life on the planet without ever hearing such words, and quite reasonably expected to end her days never having heard them. Amy, who had been paying attention to the scenery, did an about turn and stood at her mother's side.

'Mom, what's going on?'

'I have no idea, love. What is going on, Agent Tyler?' Olivia glanced at Agent Walsh, who said nothing. She took this as an indication that he either condoned Tyler's actions or deferred to him.

'So arrest it is, then?' said Tyler.

'You don't have to make a scene in front of everyone.' Olivia's whole body prickled with sweat, aware that all eyes were on her. 'I haven't done anything. What could you possibly arrest me for?'

'We'll talk at the FBI field office in Sioux City. You can explain yourself there.'

Olivia's brain fought to make sense of the situation. 'What about my daughter? I can't just leave her.'

'She can stay right here or ride with the deputy. Your choice.'

Amy's face flushed with anger. 'You think I'm just gonna let my Mom ride off to God knows where with some crazy cops? You must be mad.'

'Special Agent Tyler and Special Agent Walsh, Miss Knightley.' Tyler's attention reverted to Olivia. 'You've heard the only offer I intend to make. What will it be?'

'Alright, I'm coming with you.'

Amy said, 'Well, I'm guessing you must be bad cop, Agent Tyler, so I'll follow with the deputy and pray he's good cop.'

'Let's go.' Agent Tyler gestured for Olivia and Amy to lead the way.

Olivia wiped damp palms on the front of her jeans as she walked. She watched as Amy entered the rear of the patrol car and the deputy closed her in. This was some bad dream, some mistake that could be sorted out quickly; of that, she was sure. It was just a case of over-excited American lawmen picking up the first easy suspect they could find, and as a foreigner, she could expect nothing less. So her fingerprints were near the victim's door? Big deal. They were certainly not on the knife, so what had got the agents so excited?

As Olivia settled into the back seat of the sedan, she said angrily, 'What's this about, Agent Tyler? I just know you cannot be arresting me for Rick Seagal's murder, so I want to know what it is.'

'It's best if you say nothing, ma'am,' said Walsh in an even tone. 'Wait until the tape is rolling.'

7

THE JOURNEY FROM Hawkeye to Sioux City was seventy-six miles. A little over an hour later, Olivia was sitting in a small, grey room inside the FBI field office. There were reflective window panels on one wall, and she had no doubt that someone was on the other side, watching and listening.

In the corner stood a relaxed woman in dark jeans and a white T-shirt, arms folded across her ample chest. In front of Olivia sat Jack Tyler and Tom Walsh. Walsh had a smooth, calm voice and she wondered if he really had been an accountant at some point in his career. Despite his easy warm-up questions, he searched her face with such intensity she was certain he counted every blink.

'No, there isn't anything else I want to tell you. I told him what I knew, and I told the sheriff the rest of it.' Olivia stretched across the table and tapped on her witness statement. 'Everything is right there.'

A padded manila envelope sat on the table in front of Agent Tyler. Turning it upside down, he shook out a transparent evidence bag and slid it towards her. He leaned back and said nothing. Recognition dawned on Olivia, and as the seconds ticked by, she lost her voice.

'Guess you know what that is?' said Walsh. 'A strand of hair the medical examiner brought over to us.'

'Kind of her,' said Tyler. 'She knows we're desperate for leads.'

Olivia was mesmerised by the single hair, and couldn't bring herself to look up at the face of either agent. A hair. About ten inches in length: a curly black hair that, if stretched, could reach twelve inches. Freshly washed, it shrank to eight inches. She ran a finger up and down the outside of the cool plastic in a nervous gesture.

'The ME told me this is African-American hair,' said Tyler. 'And I corrected her. I said African heritage, yes. But I'll bet my entire Aerosmith collection the owner of that hair is not American, she's British.'

'So what? I found the body. It wouldn't be unnatural if a hair fell on him.'

'It was removed from his face, right up close to his cheek. What was your head doing by his face?'

'I was checking to see if he was alive, Agent Tyler.'

'Most people who spot a body with a knife in it take two steps back or run in the opposite direction.'

'So I've got a stronger stomach than most. What is this?'

'We're not the morality police, Mrs Knightley.' Walsh's tone was sympathetic. 'If something happened between the two of you last night, we need to know.'

Olivia was silent only because she was incredulous at this one-track line of thinking.

'I know you'll be keen to give us a hair sample to test against,' said Tyler.

'You really think I just jumped off a plane and climbed into bed with a complete stranger at a campsite?'

'We don't judge,' said Jack.

'He says, in the most judge-y tone I've ever heard,' retorted Olivia.

'Lying to the FBI is a crime, Mrs Knightley,' said Walsh. 'You can go to jail.'

Olivia fought to keep her temper as she stared at Walsh. The man spoke as if he was advising her which savings account was best while talking about her liberty. 'Oh, so that's why I got dragged in to see you?' She jerked a thumb in Tyler's direction. 'Lie to the ISB and he can't do more than bristle. Lie to the FBI and go to jail.'

'Five years maximum,' said Walsh. 'It's never a good idea.'

'You need to tell us what you and Rick Seagal talked about,' said Tyler. 'Did he mention meeting anyone or having a confrontation with anyone?'

Olivia realised that this pair would never let up. Five years was a long time, followed by the shame of deportation.

'Alright, alright. It's not what you think. I did not know Rick. Never spoke to him at all. Not one word.' She looked from one man to the other. 'I told you, I'm a private investigator. Investigating is in my blood. What can I say? I touched his forehead: stone cold. Couldn't resist checking why he was so covered up. I rolled up his sleeves, checked his arms. Noticed a few tattoos. Unbuttoned his collar and checked his neck, noticed an odd scar on his chest. Buttoned him back up again and stepped away. That's it. That's all, I swear!'

'That's all?' said Tyler, his jaw taut. 'You contaminated a crime scene.'

'Look, go get your tweezers or whatever you use to collect your hair sample, and stop with the lecturing.' Olivia unwound one of her plaits so that a lock of hair hung down over her shoulder. She thought bitterly that once upon a time, she would have been able to give them handfuls, roots intact, to test for DNA.

Tom Walsh beckoned to the female agent, who moved forward.

'We'll do the prints first, Mrs Knightley,' she said.

Belatedly, Olivia realised that the woman held an ink pad and paper. She placed them on the table in front of her. Mortified, Olivia pressed her fingers into the ink and rolled wet digits on the paper.

'Okay, hold still.' The woman pulled out a strand of hair by the roots with a tweezer, placed the sample in a plastic envelope and sealed it. 'Thank you for your cooperation,' she said, and closed the door behind her as she left the room.

'You know the hair's mine, so I don't know what all the pantomime is for. I overstepped the mark. I get it, gentlemen.'

'You don't seem to get it,' said Tyler. 'You're a private investigator and you're all over a fresh crime scene without the presence of law enforcement? Exactly what kind of an investigator are you?'

As the question hung in the air, Olivia recalled leaving a top-secret folder on a train and paying a £200 ransom to get it back. Bill had chewed her out over it, and they didn't speak for two days after. So what if sometimes she screwed up? Cops screwed up all the time, and she was pretty sure the special agents did not have clean hands. Angered by the slight, she was not going to stand by and let him denigrate her.

'I spent about fifty seconds viewing Rick Seagal's body. He's about six foot two. Green eyes, slight cloudiness in the left eye, could be an injury or early glaucoma. I'd say he's probably late forties, early fifties. No earrings, but both ears were pierced. Pair of tan-coloured Timberland boots: one was laced to the top; on the other, he skipped the top eyelets. Could be his foot was swollen, or maybe one is naturally bigger than the other. Black polo shirt with one pocket. Black jeans, no brand name. Frayed at the rims and pockets – from wear and tear, not fashion. Oh, and that kitchen knife? Buried in his left carotid artery. Brand wasn't visible.'

As she rattled off her observations Olivia took great satisfaction in watching Jack Tyler's eyebrows rise further up his forehead.

Tom Walsh carried a look of amusement as if he found her comments entertaining. Neither man spoke.

'Now, let's see, inside the trailer — and my feet never went over the threshold.' Olivia tilted her head as if helping one side of her brain to remember. 'That view took maybe sixty seconds. He doesn't like using plates or hates washing-up. Had a whole lot of plain boxes, the ones you can buy in bulk. Couple of empty beer bottles, one regular Bud, one Heineken light. Grey cotton sheet rolled up by the bed. Blue-and-white striped duvet cover. No duvet, though. Had an old style transistor radio marked "JVC". A hunting jacket hanging by the door. I think that's what you call it . . . black with padded elbows? A plain sun-visor cap on the countertop, purple I think. Give me a minute, I'll see what else I can remember.'

Jack Tyler reached for another manila folder and took out photos. Tom Walsh sat forward, hunched over the photos as the two men scrutinised them. Olivia craned her neck. Even upside down, she could identify the interior and exterior of Rick's trailer. Close-ups of every square foot of the place. When Tyler finally looked up, she saw a flicker of something in his eyes. New-found appreciation for her skills, she hoped. At least it was not disdain — and his poked-bear expression had disappeared. He and Walsh exchanged subtle glances.

'Good going,' said Walsh.

Olivia felt relieved, both in a professional and a personal sense. She had long prided herself on her ability to see details, small and large. Not so much faces; she was never that great with faces. Objects and items were more her thing. Her memory had not deserted her, and she was not terrible at her job.

'So, right on every point, yes?' Olivia announced triumphantly. She waved at the reflective glass, aware her action would annoy whoever was watching the interview.

'Looks like it,' said Walsh with a smile.

'I'm not that big on Aerosmith, Special Agent Tyler, but if you've got Lauren Hill?'

'We have only your word for it how long you were looking around,' said Tyler.

Olivia held his gaze. 'Why don't I hold the photos face-down, and you tell me what's in them? You must have studied them for way longer than a hot minute?'

A fleeting look of discomfort crossed the ISB agent's face, giving her some satisfaction. He did not rise to the challenge, and merely shuffled his photos back together and pushed them into the envelope. She could tell he was buying time and felt certain he was impressed. Stubborn man would never admit it, though.

Walsh said, 'I should tell you straight, for the record, we do not think you're involved in Rick Seagal's murder.'

'Good to finally hear it,' said Olivia. She stared at the still-quiet Tyler, annoyed that he offered no apology. 'So what was that about, up at Hawkeye Point? In front of my daughter and all those strangers? Threatening to arrest me? Dragging me here?'

'You rode with your hands free in air-conditioned comfort,' said Tyler.

'Are you mocking me, Special Agent Tyler? You had my fingerprints and hair sample taken like I'm a criminal, and now you're mocking me?'

'You'd been less than straight with us,' said Tyler with no hint of regret. 'We wanted to know what you know. It's taken three conversations to get the truth out of you. Interview people in the right setting, they tend to remember things they didn't even know they knew.'

'Well, you succeeded, sir,' said Olivia bitterly. 'Thanks for upsetting Amy.'

'Your daughter can take care of herself. Gave the deputy a good earful of unladylike talk, I'm told.'

'Hope he understood her accent and got every word.'

Olivia made a mental note to check with Amy what the deputy said to her by way of conversation. If she cursed at him, he deserved it. Olivia wanted to curse at the two special agents, but bit her lip instead. Getting angry with these men was not going to help her get any information out of them, and they had to be hiding something.

'Look, are you going to tell me what's really going on here? What's so special about Rick Seagal that brought you good fellows to Sibley?'

Tyler said, 'He was murdered. We intend to catch the perpetrator.'

'Don't give me that. There must be a hundred similar murders all over America every day, and all they get is local police officers.' She looked at Walsh. 'I'm guessing I won't find your name on any door in this building? The sedan licence plate tells me you're not local either?'

Olivia was sure she caught something in the faces of the men. Their feathers were ruffled alright.

'There's nothing else we can tell you at this point in the investigation,' said Walsh in his cool, calm tone. 'Thank you for being open with us.'

'We appreciate it,' said Tyler. 'As always, if you think of anything we need to know, just pick up the phone.'

She stared at Tyler for a long while. So, interrogation over, he was dismissing her yet again. Although the dismissal angered her, she was more interested in finding Rick's killer than she was in misleading the agent.

'Rick's trailer is missing a little Harley toy bike. I noticed it last night, stuck to the rear bumper.'

'You sure about that?' asked Tyler.

'One hundred percent sure. Gone this morning.' Olivia tapped on her phone and brought up an image, which she held towards the agents. 'Looked just like this.'

As the men studied it, she added, 'It's not in the grass. You can go check for yourselves. Somebody must have stolen it during the night.'

'I guess the killer took a trophy,' said Tyler thoughtfully.

'What happened to the runner Special Agent Morelli went chasing after earlier?' asked Olivia.

'Wasn't murder on his mind. He was high on illegal drugs,' said Tyler.

'It would kill you to admit I was right, wouldn't it?' said Olivia as she got to her feet.

'Tom will find Amy for you.' Tyler leaned back in his chair and gave a short nod. 'We'll be in touch.'

Walsh stood and gestured towards the door. 'Follow me.'

'By the way, my daughter and I don't want to be accompanied by an agent or police this time,' Olivia said pointedly as she followed him. 'You drive flash cars; you can spring for a decent taxi.'

8

LATER THAT AFTERNOON, Olivia approached the Lantern, a small coffeehouse and roastery on a quiet street in Sibley. She glanced at her watch. Just on the wrong side of four o'clock. So much for wanting to make a good impression; she had taken a wrong turn and got lost on unfamiliar streets. The café had seemed relatively near to Hawkeye, so she had not bothered to programme Tango's sat-nav. Ninth Street. She would never get used to the fact that so many streets had numbers rather than names.

The interior of the café was cosy and carried the delightful smell of fresh roasted coffee. Chalkboards mounted at eye level listed the varied menu in different-coloured letters. A long glass cabinet displayed a wide array of appetising pastries. The wooden tables and chairs were sparkling clean and all were occupied. Kimberly Grant sat close to the back at a corner table, curly brunette mane hanging loose around her slim shoulders. Her legs were crossed at the knees, exposing plenty of flesh leading down to those three-inch heels. A lady who liked to be seen, thought Olivia. Carefully made-up smoky eyes locked onto Olivia as she walked over.

'Kim? I'm so sorry I'm late. Thanks so much for coming.'

'Time is money, lady, and I don't have much of either.'

'Forgive me. I'll pay for dinner. What will you have?'

Kim pointed at a plate on the table, which held a few diced green leaves. 'Already had all I'm having. Chicken, feta and almond salad.'

'I'll have piece of cake if you will?'

'If I look at anything with sugar, my hips swell.' Her face took on a pained expression. 'The camera adds ten pounds, and I can't afford to have any padding when I'm competing with all the glamorous reporters, educated journalists and skinny girl activists out there. Everybody has to look like they're on a movie set to get attention, and I'm just an ordinary citizen with a true-crime blog.'

Olivia thought Kim would look just fine with the extra pounds, as she appeared painfully thin, but decided it would not be a good idea to share her opinion. 'You look great to me. I've been reading some of the stories on your blog; you're brilliant at chronicling events.'

'Hah! You learn quick, Olivia, but you can cut the BS.'

A friendly waitress appeared and beamed at them both.

'Can I just have a lavender vanilla latte, please?' said Olivia. She had learned of the existence of such a concoction ten seconds ago. It sounded pretentious, but a woman at the table beside theirs had the label on her plastic cup and seemed to be enjoying the drink.

The waitress looked at Kim. 'You sure I can't get you something else, ma'am?'

'Bring me a mineral water,' said Kim. 'Can't talk on a dry throat.'

'Put everything on my bill,' said Olivia.

As soon as the waitress disappeared, Kim lowered her voice. 'So, Jack Tyler interrogated you good and proper, huh?'

Despite the blogger's attempt at nonchalance and her apparent lack of appetite for food, Olivia sensed an intense thirst for information. No way would this determined lady have abandoned the crime scene for a secret meeting in a café had she not thought there was plenty to gain. The stories on her blog, *Quad City Tales*, were quite well researched, though most were of interest only to people in the states covered.

'Look, Kim, I'll help you if you'll help me to understand what's going on.'

'Okay. Ask your questions, Olivia.'

'By all accounts, Rick Seagal was sullen, but not a bad guy,' said Olivia. 'Stereotyped because he didn't smile or talk about himself. Now I know a murder must be a big deal for a small place like this, but not a matter for special agents. So far I've seen three from the National Park Service and one from the FBI. Why are they on it? Seems like overkill to me.'

'Interesting. I knew about ISB; didn't know the FBI were on board, too.'

The waitress handed them their drinks. Kim Grant twirled her cold glass, drawing attention to her long, red fingernails. Although she seemed to be observing the faces of her fellow diners, Olivia suspected the woman's brain was working away.

Olivia turned the screen of her phone towards Kim, forcing her attention. 'I mean, I know you've only had a few hours to write your latest story, but it's so short. It's basically "man found dead, next story". Who does that? Not you. You've got some very detailed accounts on your pages.'

'You weren't joking. You really are a private eye, aren't ya?' Kim smiled, flashing over-white teeth. 'My blog covers real-life crime stories from Iowa, Illinois and the Quad Cities, that's . . .'

'I know what they are, Kim, I looked it up.'

'I bet you did.' Kim took a long drink of water. 'When two people know a secret, it's no longer a secret. In the media world, if a private investigator and a blogger know a secret, it stays secret only as long as it takes one of them to log on to the internet. People post every bit of information, and now they can do it on their TikTok, Twitter, Instagram, Facebook – or all of them at once. Don't have to wait on some editor to read it first. Still goes down as an exclusive under your name.'

'I'm not here to steal your thunder, Kim. I promise. Yes, I'm a private investigator, but I'm not working a case. You won't see a report from me anywhere. I'm just confused. It seems like something serious is going on. Was Rick Seagal a kidnapper or a murderer or something? There's a scar on his chest, and a few tattoos and marks on his arms, but I don't know if it means anything. He's not on any wanted lists — and trust me, I've been scanning them.'

'For someone not working a case, you've done a hell of a lot.' Kim spoke with a hint of suspicion. 'Jack Tyler promised me an exclusive if I keep this low key. I intend to be low key.'

'On my honour, I won't breathe a word. I swear.' Olivia waited, squeezing her cup as Kim took her time considering what to say.

'Well, from one gal to another, I'm going to tell you what I think is going on.' Kim took a sip of iced water. 'Rick was just an ex-con from Georgia. Spent some time in prison for multiple burglaries, got released five years ago. He's not Illuminati or anything exciting like that.'

'No? Then why are the ISB so interested in his murder that they've teamed up with the FBI?'

'I can't get over that the FBI are involved in this. Now I think about it, makes perfect sense. They'll need each other's help.'

'Kim, come on.'

'This isn't about Rick at all.'

Olivia fought to keep her voice light, although her lungs were about ready to burst. 'So what is it about?'

'Jack Tyler was at a state park in Illinois in June, investigating the murder of an unidentified man. Last month, he was at a murder scene at another park in Sioux City, right here in Iowa. I wondered about the significance of that at the time; seemed too much of a coincidence. No amount of digging led me anywhere. Now Tyler turns up at little old Hawkeye, and I got to thinking, that's really weird and definitely no coincidence.' Kim shook back her vast mane. 'Both of those murder victims had been brutally stabbed, just like Mr Seagal. Three stabbing victims, three park sites.'

'One killer?' murmured Olivia.

'One killer.' Kim cast a careful eye all over the café again before fixing her gaze on Olivia. 'That's Tyler's theory, anyway. But get this: there were other park murders before the ones I mentioned. They're tracking a serial killer.'

Olivia gulped her latte before a cough could explode, and her eyes watered from the effort.

'And Agent Tyler's not ready to tell America about it. Wasn't ready to tell me about it, either. Mind you, he didn't actually use the phrase "serial killer". Just said they were investigating "a disturbing pattern of murders".' Kim played with her long, curly tresses. 'I thought the silence might be to do with not wanting to scare the park community senseless, but now I think they don't want to alert the killer that they're coming for him.'

'I imagine it's probably a bit of both,' said Olivia. 'Jack Tyler told you about the other murders?'

'Nope.' Kim delivered a broad smile. 'I told him I was going to run a story suggesting that a serial killer was on the loose. That sure got his attention.' She laughed at the memory, and tiny dimples appeared in her cheeks. 'The last thing they want is me putting out a half-assed story before they're ready to go public. Agent Tyler gave me a basic rundown.'

Olivia wanted to laugh, too — a laugh of the maniacal sort. The whole situation was bizarre. Here she was, sitting in a cosy café in a foreign country, discussing murders in parklands. Murders committed by a serial killer, no less. 'How many victims are there?'

'Rick Seagal makes body number six. Six bodies in ten months.' Kim stared at her as if thrilled to be revealing such gory news. 'He wouldn't give me details about the other bodies or where they were found. Said they had no conclusive evidence it was the same killer, but that's a lie. They know it alright. I'm not one to give up when I sense a big story, and I sense a big story. I'll hound him to the grave until I get this one.'

Olivia placed moist fingers in her lap and twisted her hands beneath the table. She had to keep them occupied to avoid them inching towards her scalp. What had she led her only child into? From England to America, thousands of miles, they had come a long way to die.

Common sense told her that getting out of the country was the best thing to do. Getting away from Iowa, where a serial killer had already picked off two victims, would be a good start in the interim. Her initial fear when arriving in America was that Amy would hook up with the wrong people in her eagerness to get along with the locals. Now she had to fear a prolific serial killer. Six dead bodies.

'You good, hun? Vacation not going as you expected, huh?'

'You could say that.' Olivia gave a weak smile. 'I'm thinking the best thing I can do is take my daughter and get on the next plane back to London.'

'Hey, don't knock a whole country just because of one mad man. We've got great people here.'

'Oh, I know.' Olivia nodded and drained the last drop of latte.

Yes, there were great people here. She had met quite a few of them living at the campsite and sightseeing at Hawkeye Point. There were also serial killers here. She wondered if she had already met one of them, too. Would that person show up, all smiles, for a barbecue tonight? The very thought sent an involuntary shudder through her bones. She mustered up a smile and signalled to the waitress.

9

HE POLISHED HIS steel blade until it glowed in the moonlight. Keeping the tools of his job clean was a mark of professionalism. His expertise with the knife was unquestionable. That flow of endorphins when sharp steel met weak flesh was a feeling second to none. He sheathed his prized possession and tucked it into his knapsack, then reclined against a tree, staring at the dark skies.

The first murder at French Creek in Elverson, Pennsylvania, was both terrifying and exhilarating at the same time. He remembered the way his heart had palpitated so wildly he was afraid he would have a stroke and collapse before taking out the target. Literally falling at the first hurdle would have been awful when he had much more work to do. Paramedics would have wondered why a man of his age was wandering outside at that time of night in freezing cold November weather with a nine-inch blade in his pocket. The gloves he would have been able to explain away, but not the kitchen knife. He could hardly have said he carried a kitchen knife in case he ran into a birthday cake.

Earlier on that day, he had engaged his target in friendly conversation about the cost of living, only one of them knowing there were only a few hours of living left to do, and that costs no longer mattered. The blade pierced the man's inner ear, going straight into the brain, sending out a powerful gush of blood mingled with grey matter. A brief look of disbelief crossed vivid blue eyes before their eyelids closed forever.

The large body had crumpled in an ungainly fashion and twitched for a few seconds, those last few jerks before inevitable death. He had turned the heavy lump onto its back, straining his own in the process, and straightened out its arms and legs into positions he thought more fitting. He hoped that future bodies would fall backwards, so he did not need to exert so much effort.

The second murder was of a fine figure of a man, tall and broad shouldered. The kind both men and women admired. Every inch of his body was covered against the biting cold of the winter night. Without much pressure, the blade sank into his soft temple. The man sank to his knees, lips moving in horror as his brain lost all ability to assist his vocal cords. Warm blood cascaded down the sleeve of his winter coat and pooled in the light snow. The local paper had made a big deal about the deceased being a magazine writer, a nice family man who coached Little League. No comments about the killer's precision with the knife, which seemed much more noteworthy.

Leaving Pennsylvania was a bold move, and it had taken him quite some time to feel confident enough to do so, but he had always intended to get on the road and explore the beautiful United States of America. All the wonderful poetic words that had been written about his country of birth were true. Land of the free, home of the brave. Now he was free and brave enough to travel thousands of miles and meet hundreds of friendly people in the open air.

He smiled, amused by the memory of that jovial baker at Cuyahoga Valley National Park in Ohio, the third corpse. He encountered the baker walking the towpath trail by the canal on an icy February night. One minute the man was telling him how expensive it was to run industrial ovens, the next he was staggering back with a blade in his eye, clutching at the handle. Helpfully, the walking dead had pulled out the knife in a futile effort to save his own life, taking out part of his eyeball with it. That death was not pretty, and he hoped it hadn't been a child who had discovered the maimed body.

The first daytime murder he had ever attempted took place in Indiana in the spring. He'd stuck the guy straight through the jugular. Blood everywhere. Almost immediately, people turned up, screaming and shouting, and he'd had to run. The memory overwhelmed him. He lifted the whisky flask to his mouth and drained it, then wiped his lips. He didn't like to dwell too much on that one. Way too close for comfort. The useless local cops had slapped murder charges on some poor schmuck. As much as he wanted the credit, it didn't hurt that they were on the wrong track. He smiled. Wrong track. They weren't even near the railroad.

The body in Illinois was still unidentified by the cops, but he recalled the man said people called him Sonny. Strange thing was, the man had actually come up to him and started chatting, annoying him; he'd already picked out someone else for death. Well, he had a surprise for old Sonny Jim. The blade went straight into Sonny's forehead, deep. When he'd pulled it out, blood coursed down the body's nose like a waterfall off a cliff. The body wasn't easy to reposition, as Sonny had suffered a bowel movement upon death that delivered a revolting scent. It was the fastest he'd ever worked repositioning the arms and legs. Sonny had said he came from Maine. He frowned. If police didn't identify Sonny, he might have to call the helpline and drop hints to send them in the right direction.

Iowa was a nice state with a fine history. He liked Sioux City, all that history about the indigenous people. He would never go after an indigenous man; they'd suffered enough brutality without him adding to their misery. Not one had ever done a thing to hurt him or put him down. No matter how he looked at it, his own kind were always the ones causing trouble. He loved Stone State Park with its natural bluffs and ravines, and wonderful variety of prairie plants on the slopes and ridges. He'd wandered through yucca, blazing star, silky aster and pasque flowers. Seen red fox and white-tailed deer and turkey vultures. And when he had taken in most of the beautiful wilderness, he set his eyes on the next masculine body and slit its throat.

The Hawkeye man was a tricky one to kill. Tricky Ricky. At first, he had thought about leaving him alone. The man was gruff and looked strong as an ox. But just thinking about getting the better of him was exciting — too exciting to ignore. Rick had wandered into the fields behind the campsite during the day and startled him. Concerned the nomad might have noticed his little campfire and gear, he determined that this one had to go.

After spending much of the evening watching Rick's trailer through binoculars, he was finally rewarded shortly after midnight when the man came out to collect water from a standpipe. The target stood staring at the stars while his bucket slowly filled. Rick had barely grunted in response to his small talk. Rick's lack of friendliness was one of the reasons why he felt not an ounce of remorse. He followed him back towards his trailer, pointed out a shooting star. As Rick's firm chin tilted to the sky, he buried the blade in his thick neck. It was too dark to see the expression in the dying man's eyes, so he had to imagine it. He would have liked to see the fear and outrage, but it was not to be. So much time was wasted arranging and rearranging the heavy limbs that the blade got left behind. He frowned. Bad mistake. That knife was good for slicing beef. But no problem; he had two more just like it.

He would miss the Hawkeye campground. The playful

Labrador followed him all over the place, eager to be petted, and never barked. He wasn't sure who owned the dog, as it seemed to enjoy spending time with many of the campers. He could not imagine why cops thought killers did not like dogs. He was quite fond of them, particularly the family chihuahua back home. Dogs were trustworthy creatures. Didn't talk back, didn't judge. Just wagged and licked and showed affection. Loved it when you ruffled their ears. Much nicer beings than humans.

Watching the cops chase their tails was fun. He'd stayed a good distance away and spied through binoculars as they gathered evidence, examined the trailer and questioned the rubberneckers.

For a while, he had contemplated approaching the lawmen to be interviewed. Thought about making up a phantom suspect he'd seen casing the campsites. Ultimately, he decided against tempting fate that far. On true-crime shows, there were always fools who had gone to the cops and drawn suspicion to themselves by asking too many questions and being too helpful. He would not fall into that trap. He'd worn gloves, so there were no fingerprints to be found on the knife, and although he didn't think he had made any errors, other than leaving the knife, one never knew. Cops had all sorts of fancy technology to work with nowadays.

Anyway, he would speed things up a bit. Show them something to really give them sleepless nights. Soon, he would reach his goal of lives taken. Ten was a nice round number. A couple more picturesque states to pass through. When he got to his final destination, he would end his crusade in spectacular fashion. Maybe he would get a good name: something like 'The Cross-State Killer'. Nice. Then he would go back to his normal life.

Decades after his passing, the world would still speak about him in hallowed tones. The one that was too good to be caught. The one that got away.

10

JACK TYLER RUBBED the back of his sore neck as he strode down the corridor towards the forensics lab at the FBI office in Sioux City. As usual, he was functioning on little sleep. Yesterday had been a long day; after Olivia Knightley had left, he'd returned to Hawkeye and searched surrounding farmlands for clues way into the night, with only a flashlight and an outraged screech owl for company.

This morning he had spent poring over his own notes in addition to those taken by the sheriff's men. More paperwork to add to the mountain of photos and notes from Dean's other murder scenes. Keeping all the relevant information at the forefront of his mind was getting more difficult. There were a multitude of other cases on his roster, including cold cases, but Operation Dean had priority.

During his twenty-year career with the National Park Service, he had encountered a variety of criminals, including serial rapists, kidnappers, drug cultivators and traffickers. His last big case had involved chasing elusive animal poachers through brutal terrain over the course of a particularly rainy night. Sleeping in a tent was something he hoped not to repeat; not because of cold, but because his back had had enough of stones piercing lightweight sleeping bags. Propping up his neck with a rucksack didn't help, either. Hotel beds were necessary for the foreseeable future, until he was back to full health.

As he walked, he remembered the British private investigator's words. His team must have questioned a hundred possible witnesses at Hawkeye, and hers was the only report documenting a missing decorative item from Rick Seagal's trailer: a die-cast model Harley. At forty-five, she was four years his junior, and certainly had a better eye for detail. She was sharp and noticed things he wouldn't have seen without the benefit of photographs to study. A woman not afraid to speak her mind, she clearly shared a keen interest in the case.

Jack stopped at a hot beverage machine and grabbed a strong coffee, some of which managed to spill on his sleeve. He did not really feel at home in the FBI office; he'd never felt comfortable in any of their offices, and he had been inside many. His discomfort was self-inflicted, born of professional jealousy, as his surroundings reminded him of all the crime-fighting tools the ISB did not have — and could not afford. The use of the forensics lab was a blessing for which he was grateful, and he tried to curb his envy. He drained his coffee and tossed the empty cup into the bin before entering the lab.

Jack gave a brief nod to a technician in a corner, busy with a pipette and test tubes, and headed for a table where his special agents were studying evidence. 'What have we got?'

'One of the shoeprints from near the standpipe matched Rick Seagal's boot.' Perez turned the cast to face Jack. 'Timberland, size twelve. Same damage to the sole.'

'That's not all we got.' Morelli crunched a toothpick and pointed out a second cast. 'That print came from a shoe about six feet from where Rick was standing. He was shooting the breeze with someone; probably his killer.'

Jack took the mould and ran his fingers along the tread patterns. 'Unusual print.'

'It's called a Furlowe boot, size ten,' said Morelli. 'Their tagline says it's built for comfort and walking, with arch support. Not the height of fashion, but according to the blurb, their clientele is mainly people over fifty.'

'Good to know.' Jack nodded. 'I never thought we were looking at a young person.'

'Could be a younger person with a foot problem?' suggested Morelli. 'Fallen arches, painful heel, or maybe someone who spends all day on his feet?'

'Younger people tend to buy fashionable boots and stick orthopaedic inserts inside.' Perez wriggled her stylish riding boot in the air. 'Trust me, I'm not ready to give up fashion for comfort yet.'

Morelli winced. 'Now we only have to check the six murder sites for people over fifty and hope the killer registered for a camping space as opposed to being a walk-in visitor.'

'Should run into a few thousand people,' said Perez. 'Take us maybe a year.'

'I need to add another pair of eyes to our team,' said Jack.

'And the good Lord knows they'd be welcome,' said Perez.

Jack did not comment. The person he was thinking of had not left a great impression on these two agents yesterday, and now was not the right moment. Besides, he had not shared his thoughts with Tom, and was not even sure in what capacity Olivia Knightley could be brought in.

'Are Furlowe boots sold around here?' he asked.

'They can easily be bought online or at bricks-and-mortar stores,' said Morelli. 'I'll see if any stores local to any of the crime scenes stock them. It's a long shot.'

'We need a face to go with the feet.' Jack rapped his fingers on the countertop. 'We have to find a way to narrow down the list of prospective owners. The print is quite good, so the boot is probably new or not worn regularly. We don't know the colour. Maybe print off a picture in various colours and show it around? See if anyone remembers an older gentleman wearing them?'

Jack's phone rang and he frowned as he spoke to the caller. 'Goddamn,' he muttered. 'Where?'

'Please tell me that's not another body,' groaned Perez, her face creased in dismay.

Jack closed off the call. 'Wish I could. Palisades State Park, Minnehaha County.'

*

Jack sat in the passenger seat while Tom drove the sedan on the one-hour journey across the Iowa border into South Dakota. Agents Morelli and Perez followed behind in their Jeep. This time, the victim had been killed in broad daylight under sunny blue skies. Another scenic setting, once peaceful and quiet, now marred by a brutal death. All of the other murders had been night attacks, and this one was pretty brazen by anyone's stand-ards. Palisades State Park had opened at six am. It was not even noon, and Dean had already added another corpse to the tally.

Jack's whole body was tense. He desperately wanted to pop some pills, but the effect of Xanax was temporary. Taking them too often might get him addicted, and he vowed not to go down that slippery slope. He hoped the coffee he'd gulped earlier would give him the stamina he needed to get through the day.

The killer was getting the better of him. He was playing catch-up while Dean continued to raise havoc in the most tran-quil places in the country. The man was cocky. No one knew what he looked like or what vehicle he drove. The agents were struggling through mounds of leads, and it would take weeks to weed out the good leads from the frivolous ones.

Constantly on edge, wondering if he had bitten off more than he could chew, Jack had thought about asking the director to spare another special agent, but opted against it. What he needed was someone else with a clear head, someone mentally equipped to gather a lot of information in a short space of time, someone who could see details that even seasoned officers might miss. He looked across at Tom, who was concentrating on the busy highway.

'Tom, I'm going to ask that private investigator to come on board.'

'Private investigator? Who, the lady we interviewed yesterday?' Tom risked a quick glance at Jack, who nodded.

'I could use a fresh pair of eyes and ears. Olivia Knightley has both.'

'I know you're a man to think things through, Jack, but have you really thought about this one? She'd have to be told everything about the investigation.'

'She's an experienced private eye, though, so won't need handholding. She doesn't know our methods of operation, which is a good thing. She won't be led in the directions you or I might take. I really think her insight could be a great advantage.'

'Has she got a licence?' asked Tom.

'Doesn't need one in England. Anyone can hang a shingle if they decide that investigating is the career for them.' Jack waved a hand to silence Tom. 'She's not an American citizen, I know. These are desperate times.'

'How will you get that past your director? I'd never get it past mine.'

'She won't be deputised to the ISB, Tom. I'll get around it.'

'You don't know anything about her.'

'Dynamic Investigations is her place of business; website's secure. Operation is run by a guy named William Tweedy, and it is legit. No rap sheets for either of them. Plenty of experience in criminal investigations, including murders and missing persons. Whether the testimonials are true or not, we've seen what she can do.'

'I'm not knocking the idea, Jack, but if this goes south, you could go south with it.'

'The last stop south is Hell, but it is a stop.'

'I hear it's hot down there.' Tom grinned. 'Aren't you forgetting something? She was pretty pissed about being hauled to the office. Can't see her welcoming any request to buddy up with you.'

'One thing about that lady, she's very curious. I think this is right up her street.'

'We'll see.'

Palisades State Park was set in 157 acres of land, featuring breathtakingly dramatic cliffs and stunning rock formations with an unusual pink tint, surrounded by rushing water. For millions of years, Split Rock Creek had flowed through the park, cutting deep gorges lined with Sioux quartzite formations, which varied from shelves a few feet above water to fifty-foot vertical cliffs. The site was popular with sightseers, campers, photographers, rock climbers and hikers, all of whom were out in their masses. Compared to Hawkeye, this park was huge, with thirty-four campsites and thousands of day-trippers.

Park rangers in their iconic broad-brimmed tan hats prevented the sizeable crowd from approaching the crime scene. Some visitors still held their phones aloft, hoping for a glimpse of something interesting. Jack and his team were briefed by the park rangers who had phoned in the murder report. Internally, the word was out that a possible serial killer was at large, and ISB should be notified of any incidents and given full cooperation. Jack was relieved about that. The problem was, local police and sheriffs were also notified of murders, and they could cause headaches. Other entities, like the Drug Enforcement Agency and even the FBI, could get touchy too. As for the US Marshals, they were a whole other ball game; they needed more females in the ranks to dilute the testosterone.

Two young police officers approached as Jack chatted with a park ranger. From their expressions, he sensed they were about to activate his ulcers.

'You Special Agent Tyler? National Park Service?'

'Investigative Services Branch, huh?'

Jack sighed and reached into his breast pocket. 'Save it, guys. Here's your love letter from the ISB director.'

'Check it out, they even have a director.' The officer scanned the letter and handed it to his colleague, who crumpled it up and pushed it into his pocket.

'You here to interview the flowers or the trees?

'Can they, like, plead the fifth? Or is it one petal dropping off means yes and two petals is no?'

Jack's smile did not reach his eyes. 'You guys are really funny, you know that?'

'If you need any help, don't hesitate to send a pigeon.'

'Thanks, gentlemen.' Jack bowed and watched them lumber away. He really could do without the politics and ego. All he wanted to do was stop a busy serial killer.

Jack noted that the crime scene was partly shielded from view by a protruding rock formation, an explanation for why Dean was comfortable enough to kill in daylight. After circumventing the rock face, the team was greeted by the county medical examiner and her assistant. At their feet, a white sheet covered the corpse, the soles of blue sneakers visible.

Jack lifted the sheet. The victim lay on his back: a white man with pallid skin, dressed in jogging clothes. The knife wound in his temple created an impression similar to a fish gill. His eyes were rolled back in his head with the whites exposed. Blood had pooled on the rocks below him. A few feet closer to the edge, and the body would have plunged into the creek.

'I understand you know who did this?' said the doctor.

'We know his MO,' replied Jack. 'He repositions the arms and legs.'

Morelli removed a wallet from the pocket of the man's jogging bottoms. 'Name's Daniel Bailey. Colorado driver's licence. Business card says he's a realtor.'

'Whole lotta people out there would like to stab a realtor,' said Perez.

'Tell me about it,' mumbled Morelli.

'It's him alright.' Jack stood upright, his face ashen. 'His confidence is super high. There are a lot of visitors and staff walking around, yet he feels invincible.'

'I'll round up help from a couple of rangers to assist with canvassing the area,' said Morelli.

'You do that.' Jack glanced at his watch. 'Stay on it until I get back, guys. There's something I need to do. Tom, lend me your key.'

Jack snatched the car key from the air as Tom under-armed it in his direction.

'Remember what I said, Jack.'

'Yeah. Hell is hot.'

11

MIDDAY WAS APPROACHING when Olivia hitched the caravan to Tango. Her only plan was to get the holiday back on track by doing the things they'd planned to do, enjoying a road trip, taking in nature. Leaving Hawkeye would be a bittersweet experience, and Olivia had deliberately arranged to leave the campsite late to give Amy time for a last look around and to say goodbyes. The sudden change in their holiday plans had annoyed her daughter, who had wanted to stay put and enjoy life with the nomads. They had argued all night, with Olivia trying to convince Amy that it made sense to move on to a safer campsite.

'Where could be safer than here, Mom? Cops are all over the place.'

'They can't be everywhere, though, love.'

'This is just great. I get to plan the itinerary, you get to change everything?'

'I'm not changing everything. It makes sense to find somewhere more peaceful and just as beautiful.'

'It was too much to hope that I'd get to do things my way for once. Should have known you'd take over at some point.'

'I'm doing this for both of us. It'll work out just fine, you'll see.'

'Can't wait till I'm eighteen!' And with that fiery declaration, Amy had turned her back on her mother and pretended to go to sleep.

Olivia had no intention of discussing the potential presence of a serial killer with her offspring. The lawmen were experts at their jobs; they could get on with it. She would get on with her own job: maintaining family health and happiness. To do so, she needed to remove herself from any temptation to get involved in what she now knew to be a multiple-murder case.

In a few weeks, she might read all about it in a Kimberly Grant exposé. She had considered calling Kim to tell her that she was leaving Iowa, but ultimately decided against it, as she had no new information to share with the blogger, and Kim was probably busy chasing other leads for her big story.

As she buckled into the driver's seat, Olivia glanced across at Amy and was relieved that none of last night's rage was apparent in her face. Amy was consulting her itinerary, reading up on their next destination, Steer Creek Campground near Nebraska National Forest. The deep frown had disappeared and she was almost smiling.

'You okay?' asked Olivia.

'Sure.'

Olivia's heart shrank a bit. She remembered when Amy was very little, and the question 'You okay?' always brought out the chuckles.

Her daughter would respond, 'No, I'm A. K. Dad is C. K. and you're the only one who's O. K.' They would roll around on the floor, tickle each other and laugh. Amy would eventually concede and scream, 'I'm okay, Mom, stop!'

Olivia smiled at the recollection. Those were the days of young innocence, long before Amy rocketed into her teens, long before the family fractured.

Steer Creek was over three hundred miles away, travelling

west on the highway. It would take just under six hours. Shortly after they set off on the road, someone rang Olivia's phone from a local number she did not recognise. She concentrated on driving and placed the phone on the dashboard. No one should be calling her. Anyway, if it was important, they would call back later. Calls from England were the only ones she would expect: Chris Knightley, for starters.

'Remember to call your father, Amy.'

Amy lowered the phone from close to her face and switched to text. Olivia watched as Amy's lithe fingers tapped out a long message to her father, stubbornly adhering to her vow to text only.

'What are you saying to him?'

'Don't worry. I'm just telling him we'll be leaving Iowa heading to Nebraska, and giving him a rundown of what we expect to see.' Amy clicked the send button. 'Got to admit, Steer Creek looks stunning.'

'I'm sure we'll have a great time, love.'

'This has been some start to the holiday,' said Amy. 'If you'd have told me there would be a murder, I'd have said never in a million years. I mean, I get to say I rode in the back of a cop car too, and didn't even get a slap.'

'I should think not.' Olivia grinned. 'Maybe the visit to the FBI office is something we should keep between ourselves?'

'I know, I know . . . you don't want Dad to find out. Neither do I.'

Olivia's phone rang again on the dashboard.

Amy picked it up and waved the screen at her mother. 'It's Bossman Bill. Want me to answer it?'

Olivia frowned. 'No. Put it on mute and leave it there.'

Bill Tweedy would not have called her unless something was amiss. He was strictly an email kind of bloke. She would await the inevitable email or voicemail instead. If there was one thing she had learned in her job as a private investigator, it was not to be caught off guard. Being forewarned was forearmed. There would be plenty of time to think up an excuse or an explanation for anything she might have left unfinished or done wrong if she had written correspondence to look at or a voicemail to listen to. Her brain fought to figure out what the issue could be.

'I'll call him this evening when we've settled in at the park.'

'You know, you're worse than me sometimes, not wanting to talk on the phone. My excuse is I'm a teenager. What's yours?'

'I'm driving and I don't want to risk an accident. Good enough for you, madam?'

'Oh, please. Speakerphone? I've seen you drive and hold one-hour conversations with people you want to talk to.' Amy gave her a severe side-eye. 'Has Bill done something to annoy you, or the other way around?'

Olivia smiled. 'I'm on holiday. This is our time. Everybody and everything comes secondary to our time from now on. Deal?'

'Deal,' said Amy.

Before taking to the highway, they stopped at a convenience store. Olivia wanted a bottle of alcohol; rum or white wine would have done. The cashier told her regretfully they had no liquor licence. He was friendly and pointed out the liquor store nearby.

Inside the liquor store was a wealth of bottles with international labels, many of which Olivia had never heard of. No Jamaican rum; Cuba and Barbados represented their Caribbean selection. Nice, but not what she was after. She asked the clerk for white wine. As long as it was not too sweet and tasted good chilled, she would take two bottles of it. The cheerful clerk recommended a bottle of dry white and glanced at Amy as he placed them on the counter.

'Watch out for the cops. They're hot on alcohol for minors,' he said, while wrapping the bottles in brown paper. 'Twenty-one is the legal drinking age.'

'Oh, it's not for her, honest, but thanks for the tip anyway.' Olivia gave him the thumbs-up. The last thing she needed was another run-in with cops. Knowing her luck, they were sure to arrest her on the spot and charge her with supplying alcohol to Amy.

Olivia placed the bottles on top of a box of groceries on the back seat and threw a bath towel over it. She had barely pulled away from the shopping area when flashing blue lights became visible behind them. Surely the friendly clerk had not done this? Sold her alcohol and sent the cops after her for a laugh? She stared in the wing mirror in disbelief. A black sedan with tinted windows was drawing closer to them.

'You know, if I was having a bad dream, I'd swear that FBI man, Tom Walsh, was right behind us. I'm sure that's his car.'

'He can't be flashing you, Mom?' Amy arched her neck to stare at the approaching vehicle. 'Why doesn't he just pass us? Slow down a bit and he'll go around.'

'Oh boy, he's not going to pass,' said Olivia.

She could see no good place to stop, not with enough space that allowed the caravan a comfortable port. She continued slowly for a further quarter mile, and finally came across a lay-by. The sedan rolled right up on her tail and Special Agent Jack Tyler climbed out, sleeves rolled up to the elbows.

'It's not him, it's the other one,' whispered Olivia. 'The ISB man, Tyler.'

'ISB, FBI; a cop is a cop,' said Amy.

Olivia rolled down the window and decided not to utter a word. She glanced at her purchases in the box on the back seat and was glad he couldn't see the wine bottles.

'Hello again, Olivia.' Tyler leaned forwards and looked at her daughter. 'Hello, Amy.'

Amy did not respond. Olivia could not respond. Shocked into silence from hearing him address her by her first name, she hoped her expression did not reflect her complete surprise. No Mrs Knightley and no ma'am. He'd even managed to tilt the corners of his lips. Suspicion immediately enveloped her. She glared at him and was quietly satisfied to see his expression change to embarrassment as his cheeks flushed.

'I'm sorry about the stop, ladies.'

'Have you been demoted to traffic cop?' asked Amy.

'Not quite.' He offered a tight smile. 'Olivia, I think we got off to a bad start yesterday. Truce?'

'What can I do for you, Special Agent Tyler?' asked Olivia.

'You can call me Jack.'

Olivia could not hide her surprise this time, and gave up trying. 'You must really be worried about something. I know Americans are big on litigation for every little thing, but it's not like that where I'm from. I'm not going to sue anybody for that drama yesterday, if that's what's bothering you?'

'You have every right to be angry, Olivia. I apologise, I really do. I'm here because I have a proposition for you. Hear me out; I think you'll be interested.'

'Really? You could have phoned with your proposition. You've got my number.'

'I tried your number, you didn't pick up,' he said. 'Went back to Hawkeye and they told me you'd gone.'

Olivia glanced at the phone. So it was Jack Tyler who had called. She had never thought the special agent would call her for any reason once she'd confirmed her witness statement was complete.

'Phone's off. Can't be driving and chatting on the phone, can I? Wouldn't want to be hauled over by the cops and get arrested or anything.'

'I need your help with my case, Olivia.'

'Do you ever say please or make any attempt at humility?' she asked.

'I'm sorry. I'm wired this way.' Jack Tyler stared up at the blue sky and twisted his neck as if trying to stretch the muscles. He lowered his eyes to meet her gaze. 'I'm not too proud to admit I'd like you to work with us on our murder case. Please.'

Olivia arched her eyebrows. 'Run that by me again?'

'There was another murder, this morning, in broad daylight. In South Dakota — that's the next state over. Place called Palisades State Park.'

'Another murder?' said Amy breathlessly.

Familiar pin pricks that Olivia recognised as both excitement and fear gripped her. She fought to curb both. 'My daughter and I . . . we're going to Nebraska.'

'You've got a good eye, Olivia. You'll see things we don't.'

'When I wanted to work with you, you didn't want to know.' Olivia's tone was accusatory.

'I was wrong,' said Jack. 'I'm wrong, once a year.'

'We're going to Nebraska,' repeated Amy in a sullen tone.

Curiosity was definitely winning this fight, and Olivia hoped her voice did not betray her thoughts. 'You think I'm going to hold up my hand, swear on some Bible and recite the American pledge so I can work for you?'

'I can't think which one of a million TV shows you've been watching.'

'Never mind. I don't remember, either.'

'Nebraska calling,' said Amy impatiently.

'Can I count on your help, Olivia?'

Olivia sensed from his voice that he was exhausted. Dark circles surrounded his still-sharp eyes. Sympathy rose within her, which she struggled to stave off.

'Look, it's not just me. As an adult, I can put myself in any situation I want to, but I've got responsibilities. I don't want my daughter around murders.'

'I understand. Right now, I'm just asking for a few hours of your time. We can put Amy nice and safe in a hotel or some-where while you're with the team?'

'Oh no, you don't,' said Amy forcefully. 'Where my mother goes, I go.'

'What she said.' Olivia could hear the plea in his impassioned voice, but she blocked it out. 'I'm really sorry, I can't go back with you.'

Jack Tyler seemed to be racking his brain. 'You would be paid, Olivia.'

'Too right she would be paid,' said Amy. 'My mom works, my mom gets paid.'

'Good of you to make that clear, Agent Tyler, but we're here to holiday, not to work,' said Olivia firmly. 'Now, if you'll excuse me. I've got a six-hour drive ahead.'

'Nice try, Agent Tyler.' Amy waved a hand at him. 'Bye!'

The special agent took a step away from the vehicle and nod-ded abruptly at them. 'Ride safe, enjoy your vacation,' he said, and headed back to his car.

Olivia pressed on the accelerator and took off again. She watched in the rear-view mirror as his vehicle gradually grew smaller until it was barely a speck, and then she could no longer see it.

'A murder in South Dakota,' said Amy. 'I never even thought about looking up the murder stats before we got here, but when you think of the size of North America, they must have multiple murders every single day.'

'You'd think so,' said Olivia absently.

As she drove, Olivia glanced in her mirror again. No sign of the sedan. She guessed by now he must have taken an exit off the highway heading to the latest murder scene. The man had not said a word about the ISB hunting a serial killer or, as Kim had said, following a pattern of murders. Either he thought she would speed away if he mentioned what he was up against, or he was sparing Amy's ears from the horror of it all. She hoped it was the latter.

Another murder victim. Past criticism from Chris about putting work before family, and from Bill about not concentrating on the job, had bruised her. Jack Tyler asking for her help made her confidence soar. There was no way the special agent would want her if he didn't think she was good at her job. If nothing else, working with the team would be good for her ego. All she had to do was head to South Dakota.

An insistent knee knocked against her own.

'Answer the question, Mom.'

'Hmm? What question?'

'Yeah, I know you don't know what question,' said Amy peevishly. 'I've asked you two questions, but you're alone in your headspace again.'

'I'm sorry, Amy. What was it?'

'Forget it. You want to go to South Dakota, don't you? You want to go to Palisades State Park? Admit it. You're sitting there wondering what the crime scene looks like, and who the victim is.'

'Of course not!' Olivia tried as best she could to sound truthful.

'I know you, Mom.' Amy sighed. 'Don't worry, I'm not mad. I wish you could see yourself when you go into PI mode. You're so focused you can't see or hear anybody else.'

'I don't know what to say.'

'Don't say anything, Mom. It's cool.' Amy pressed away at buttons on her phone and studied the images. 'Palisades looks really nice, too. Just spin around at the next exit.'

Olivia looked at her daughter with concern. 'Are you sure?'

'Absolutely.' Amy leaned over and began readjusting the satnav. 'We can cancel the reservation in Nebraska. They won't charge us.'

'I shouldn't even be thinking of doing this. Taking you to a murder site.'

'As well as being a murder site, Palisades has four hiking trails, a gorgeous creek, lots of campsites, and the registration is still open.' Amy winked at her mother. 'If you put your foot down, we'll be there in just over an hour.'

12

OLIVIA HAD WONDERED if Palisades State Park would be closed to visitors, and was surprised to find it open. With 167 acres to showcase to eager tourists, nothing was going to stop business as usual. A dead body could always be discreetly dealt with, leaving most visitors blissfully unaware that anything untoward had taken place.

All parks sought plenty of personal information prior to allowing motor homes entry, and this park was no different. Olivia handed over the required information and watched as the clerk checked that Tango's licence plate matched up to what she had written on the registration form. His baby face suggested this must be a holiday job straight from high school.

'Welcome to Palisades. I hope you both enjoy your stay.'

'Thank you.' Olivia smiled as she took back her driver's licence.

'Go straight ahead and take a left to your campsite; you'll see the signs directing you to the right spot.'

Olivia decided that a direct question about the whereabouts of the body was not a good idea. There was no sign of any police cars at the entrance. 'Is anywhere out of bounds today, or can we tour wherever we like?'

'You can pretty much go where you like. There's an area

blocked off about a mile past your campsite because of an earlier incident. Members of the public are not allowed to walk around there. The whole rest of the park is available for your pleasure.'

'Thank you,' said Olivia. 'We'll be sure to stay clear.'

'An incident?' whispered Amy as Olivia drove along. 'He calls a murder an *incident*?'

'Well, he could hardly say a murder, could he?' said Olivia. 'Management would have given him that line to deliver to all newcomers. They don't want people turning around and speeding away from here.'

'You mean arriving in droves to collect video footage to put online.'

'Yes, I forgot that tends to be the in-thing these days.' Olivia glanced at her daughter. 'Either way, it's not a good look for me, you know?'

'Yeah, but you're here to the rescue.'

Up close, Palisades State Park was one of the most stunning vistas Olivia had ever seen. With its magical trees, lush vegetation, scenic rocky overlooks and endless blue-green water, the reason for its popularity was clear. She soon located the campground, which contained numerous campsites identifiable by numbers. A few sites were for tents only, others for smaller campervans and motor homes. Olivia checked the number on her ticket and pulled into the area dedicated to larger motor homes and trailers. In close proximity to their campsite was a row of attractive log cabins for guests who preferred immovable lodging.

Olivia shielded her eyes from the piercing sun as she got out of the SUV. In the distance was a single white car with flashing blue lights. Although she could not read what was written on it, she guessed it belonged to the county sheriff or local police. No sign of Jack Tyler's Jeep or any of the agents, but the clerk had suggested the murder scene was further away. It crossed her mind that the ISB man could have gone to interview a witness elsewhere and might not be on site at all.

'This is just perfect, Mom.' Amy stood beside her mother and stretched. 'You never see places like this advertised anywhere. It's always Disneyland and the Big Apple.'

'The best places are always kept quiet for some reason,' said Olivia. 'The hidden gems are usually so well hidden you have to know somebody in the know to find them. Looks like a great place to camp, bar the occasional body popping up.'

'Now, straight to find the crazy cop, right?'

'I should phone him and tell him we're here.' Olivia softened as she stared at Amy. Yet again, guilt infused her thoughts. 'Tell you what, let's just walk till we find him. We can have a good look around.'

'Much better idea.'

They linked arms and walked around the park, taking in the glorious creek, with dark waters rushing though the rocks. They admired rock climbers showing off their scaling and rappelling techniques. Downstream, at the quieter area of the water, they found visitors silently fishing. A few tourists rode past on bicycles, following the cycling routes.

To any observers, they were carefree mother and daughter. Appearances were deceptive; although Olivia basked in the beautiful environment, she was anything but at ease. A lioness, a good mother, would lead her cub towards safety, not towards a wild dog. Maybe they should just spend a few days camped right here and not get involved in any murder investigation? They could lie low, avoid contact with any law enforcement officers. After all, she had not committed herself to any investigative work.

Before her brain could settle the many arguments for and against, she saw Jack Tyler up ahead, close to a mound of jagged rocks. From his side profile, he appeared to be scrutinising the terrain around his feet. He circled the rocks and was hidden for a few seconds before returning to his original position. A watch-ful police officer hovered close by and barred anyone who made an attempt to get close.

'I see Agent Tyler over there, Amy,' said Olivia.

'I don't need to see him.' Amy threw a small pebble into the gently flowing water. 'Remember, he wants to shut me away somewhere while you teach him his job.'

'I wouldn't put it quite like that.' Olivia winced and squeezed her daughter's arm.

'Did you know there's only thirty-three of them? ISB Special Agents, I mean. Thirty-three in the whole country, to police eighty-five million acres of land. Got hundreds of thousands of proper cops, though.'

'There must be some logic to it. All I know is his hands are full.'

'You go do your PI talk.' Amy promptly sat down in the low grass, crossed her legs and closed her eyes, tilting her face to the sun. 'Right here is just fine for me.'

Olivia ducked under the yellow caution tape and walked slowly towards the agent, whose back was towards her.

'Couldn't get here any earlier, Jack. The caravan's heavy and I'm not used to the roads.'

As he turned around, Olivia caught an expression of both surprise and relief on Jack Tyler's face. He reverted to profes-sional mode with speed. This man either did not like to show emotion or was careful about who witnessed it.

'Olivia, glad you made it.'

The police officer who had started walking towards her stopped when he realised they were acquainted.

'Where else would I be if the National Park Service called?' she said lightly. It annoyed her that she liked the way he said her name. She glanced at the uneven rocky area around them. 'Where's the victim?'

'ME's taken him. Follow me. Careful as you go; there's a lot of blood on the rocks.'

Olivia manoeuvred around a protruding slab of the monolith and Jack pointed out the exact spot.

'Nice secluded area to sit,' she said. 'Not too close to the cliff face. Hard for passing people to see you, which is good and bad. A dead body is evidence of the bad.' She caught him staring at her. 'What?'

'I was just thinking how refreshing it is that you get straight down to business.'

His comment warmed her, and she was glad he could not see that blood had rushed to her face. 'I tend to go into PI mode when I see something that really piques my interest,' she said.

Jack arched an eyebrow. 'And Rick Seagal really piqued your interest?'

'Not in the way you mean.' She could tell he expected to hear more. 'Just something Darcy said about not trusting him. I mean, you see a person, you've never talked to them, never seen them do anything wrong, yet you decide they're bad. It's not on.'

'Darcy Jemson. That would be the talkative lady with a lot of opinions? Not that helpful to my case.'

'What exactly is your case?' Olivia had no intention of telling him anything about her meeting with Kimberly Grant, and preferred to pretend to know nothing of the other killings. 'I turned around with my daughter. We haven't even eaten anything since breakfast, but we rushed back for your case.'

'I'll get lunch, anything you want.'

'That's not the most important part of what I said.' Olivia stared at him in frustration. 'Stop holding all the cards against your chest. If you won't tell me everything . . . well, I'll have a look at whatever you need me to look at today, but I'll head off to Nebraska tomorrow.'

'You're right, Olivia. I promise you're going to learn everything about Operation Dean.'

'Operation Dean?'

'It's just a codename for this investigation. We use random codenames for some cases, mainly for secrecy and ease of communication between the agents.' Jack waved away any questions. 'Right now, I need you to trust me. I'll walk you through what we know about today's murder, then I need you to come back with me to the FBI office. Got a taskforce meeting planned, and it would be great to have you there.'

'Do you chaps not have your own office?'

'That's not the most important part of what I said.'

'Touché.' The man was allergic to please and thank you, yet at least his tone was way less demanding and his words were encouraging. 'Your team, is that the four of you?' she asked.

'That's right, you've met them all.' He added, with a hopeful look, 'A fifth person would be great.'

'Alright, tell me about the dead man.'

'Daniel Bailey.' Jack stood at her shoulder and scrolled through his phone's image gallery. 'That's how he was found.'

Olivia swallowed bile and an involuntary shudder of revulsion. 'All that blood around his head. A knife did that, like with Rick?'

Jack nodded. 'Straight through the temple, traumatic to the brain. ME said he had no chance of survival with that wound.'

Olivia pressed the screen and scrolled through more photos, commenting from time to time. After a while, her motherly instincts kicked in and her thoughts went to her daughter.

'Can we go back on the other side of this rock, where the officer is?'

'Sure. Watch where I step.'

Olivia followed behind him and gazed over at where Amy was still relaxing. She narrowed her eyes. Two people were now sitting on either side of her daughter. Young males that looked around Amy's own age. Any older, and Olivia would have been over there in a flash to set them straight. The three were talking, and from the expressions on their faces, all seemed to be laughing. Amy had never been boy crazy. She liked someone this week and hated him the next. Making new friends was a good thing, most of the time, and the girl had been happy making friends at Hawkeye before being forced to continue the road trip.

'Olivia?'

'Oh, sorry. Got to keep an eye out for Amy, she's sitting over there.'

Jack looked in the direction she was pointing. 'That's fine, I doubt if we'll be too long. Do you see anything going on in the photos that I don't see?'

Olivia continued to study each of the images. 'Daniel was tall, probably similar build to Rick. His clothes are ordinary; nothing suspicious there. The only thing that looks odd to me is how his arms and legs are laid out. Looks deliberately arranged like that?'

'Correct, just like Rick. The same person has done multiple killings.'

Olivia nodded slowly. 'Did you get any useful information from the other campers at Hawkeye?'

'We're sifting through it. A couple of local law enforcers are still doing interviews back there. We've got a long and growing list of names of people from parks in four states.' With the back of his hand, Jack wiped the sweat from his brow. 'South Dakota is state number five, and we're adding even more names of people to talk to.'

'Getting out of hand?' said Olivia in sympathy.

'He's moving quickly. We have to focus in on the right people.'

'I only met a small portion of the Hawkeye community,' said Olivia. 'There's a real mixed bag of nomads around that area.

Talk to a couple in a red trailer with Jesus stickers all over it. I'm quite wary of overtly religious people; they've usually got ulterior motives.'

Jack pursed his lips and shot her a warning look. 'You might want to temper your words. The religious right in this country is a force to be reckoned with.'

'So I hear. I don't know their names, but they said they saw a suspicious man taking photographs with a long-lens camera. Kent Hilson. Someone was definitely walking in the woods that night, but I don't know if it was him.'

'I'll check if anyone has interviewed them or Mr Hilson.' Jack scribbled in his notebook. 'While we're walking around, Olivia, I want you to have a good look for any people or vehicles you may have seen around Hawkeye. Our killer blends in easily in this type of setting. He's a respectable, pleasant type, fifties to sixties. This man is walking around with a long, sharp knife, concealed and ready to do serious damage.'

'A lot of tourists fit that bill. Even the knives bit. There's so much untamed land around – and wild animals. I know you Americans like to hunt.'

'Not all of us. Some of us like to fish.'

Olivia shrugged. 'Something dies, at the end of the day.'

'Fair point.'

She patiently cooperated with his interrogation and tried to think of anything odd or useful. Her mind drifted back to her own London cases. She had investigated a few murders, deaths from strangulations and beatings. Thankfully, such cases were rare, and in each case the perpetrator was known to the victim and quickly apprehended. She did not want Rick's murder to go unsolved; if that wrapped up all the other murders too, it would be a blessing.

A distinct savoury odour drew her attention, and she noticed a quaint café off the path. She rubbed her stomach. 'I have to get something to eat, or the body count will go up.'

'I forgot my manners. We could grab a sandwich and drink to go? No time to sit down for me, I'm afraid.'

'I'll call Amy and get something for her.' Olivia looked towards her daughter. She seemed happy, talking and laughing with her new friends. In the girl's hand was a napkin, shielding what looked like a hot dog. The two boys with her were also eating. She watched as one youth turned a soda bottle to his lips. 'On second thoughts, she's already sorted herself out.'

As they walked the short distance towards the café, Olivia was surprised that she felt comfortable in the special agent's presence. He wasn't such an ogre after all. Professional and friendly enough, though she guessed he would be cordial with anyone who could point him to the killer.

As they approached the counter in the café, he asked, 'What will you have?'

'A pulled-pork sandwich please, and orange juice with plenty of ice. Thanks.'

'I'll take a bologna sandwich. Give me a cranberry juice, large.' Jack handed the woman some cash. 'Make mine to go.'

'You know, you can't walk around the crime scene eating,' said Olivia, as the waitress handed them the food across the counter. 'Sit down for ten minutes. Let's take the table over there.'

'You're right.'

Carrying their food, he escorted Olivia to a table close to the entrance. She was glad it afforded her a good view of the park. She could still see her daughter. He sank into the seat in front of her.

'Most days I eat in my car,' he said.

'I know all about that. In my car, in a cab, on a train – anywhere I can snatch food during work.'

'Can't even remember if I ate yesterday. Last time I remember sitting at a dining table was two weeks ago.'

'Last time you got home?' Olivia thought his face took on a cagey look, and he took a while to answer the question.

'Had dinner at Tom's house.' He took a long drink of juice from the paper cup. 'His wife's not a good cook, but she's great company.'

'Where do you call home?'

'I'm from Cincinnati, Ohio.'

Olivia noticed that as soon as he put down the cup, he absently twisted his wedding ring. No mention of his own wife. The look on his face suggested it was a touchy subject.

'Guess you guys go wherever the cases take you?'

'That's right. My taskforce was assembled at the end of February, weeks after the discovery of a stabbing victim at Cuyahoga Valley National Park. That's in Ohio, by the way.'

Olivia nodded. 'I've got you.'

'This sandwich is everything,' he said. 'I can feel my muscles waking up.'

She took a mouthful of sandwich and savoured the taste. 'I agree, this is good stuff. The chef certainly knows how to season pork.'

She glanced out at Amy again. Amy liked to behave as if she had it all together, but Olivia knew even thirty-something women who *did* have it all together could be attacked by men on a mission in what should be the safest of places. Strolling in a park, taking a shortcut, sitting by a lake. It could all end in a violent second, someone else deciding your fate. It had happened recently in south London, and it could happen in South Dakota.

'Is Amy your only child?'

Olivia was alarmed to find he had been staring straight at her while she had been looking past his shoulder. She gave an embarrassed grin. 'Does it show?'

'First kid, you're checking every five minutes to make sure they're fine. Second one, as they're born, you're ready for them to go work in the mall.'

'Ouch! I'm not one of those fussy mothers, honestly. Not in

England, anyway. She's free to go all over the place when we're in London.'

'Looks like you've done a great job so far. She sticks up for herself and for you.' He half turned in his seat and glanced at Amy. 'I can remember what my kids were like at that age. Time passes quickly, and before you know it they've grown up and gone.'

'How many do you have?'

'Boy and girl – or, I should say, man and woman. My son works in technology in New York; my daughter is part of a dance troupe currently on Broadway.'

Olivia was taken aback. 'If you'd have asked me to guess, I'd have said both worked in law enforcement. Detectives, maybe.'

'I'm relieved nobody followed in my footsteps. They get to be normal people.'

'So how long have you been "not normal"?'

'I did five years in homicide and have done another twenty in ISB. I think the day you join law enforcement in any guise, you lose normal.'

'I like to think of myself as pretty normal, though others would disagree.'

'Me, for one,' Jack said. 'Normal people do not investigate dead bodies like you do, Olivia.'

He laughed, a deep, throaty sound, and Olivia found herself laughing too. She was glad to see he could find amusement in their shared predicament. As much as she loathed to admit it, he was kind of cute. Maybe working with him would not be so bad after all.

'Seen some glowing testimonials on your website,' he said at length.

'And you're wondering if they're real or fake?'

'Mind-reading one of your talents too?'

'I assure you, the testimonials are one hundred percent real.

Now, I'm not going to lie and say I get everything right all the time, but I do have happy clients.' She stared at him closely. 'Wait, did you call Bill Tweedy before you called me?'

'Your boss? No. Should I?'

'Not necessary.' Olivia hid her discomfort behind a straw-full of orange juice.

She was sure Bill would have plenty of good things to say about her if Jack did contact him; he was a shrewd man. Their disagreements were kept strictly in-house. But Bill was bound to be angry that she was supposedly on holiday and working with American law enforcement while there was unfinished business in London. She would check her work emails later and respond to whatever was bothering him.

'Tell me, Olivia, that thing you do. The ability to recall the most unlikely of things in a short space of time? I must have interviewed thousands of witnesses in my time, including law enforcement officers. Most would not spot such minute details – and believe me, they get trained to look for them.'

'It's practised behaviour really. Takes a while.' Olivia was secretly pleased, yet unwilling to appear too much of a show-off. 'Walk into a room, scan the walls, walk out and see if you can remember at least thirty things.'

'Thirty things. I'll have to try it.'

'So, this taskforce of yours. Don't I need a work permit or something?'

'Don't worry about it.'

'That response worries me. I've got a tourist visa. I don't want to get thrown out of the country if I run into police who want to know what I'm doing.'

'I've got it all in hand, I promise.'

'Have you told your team about me? I mean, did you discuss it and all agree to approach me?'

'I discussed it with Tom.' He stared down into his cup of

melting ice. 'Marty Morelli and Francesca Perez will be happy to have the extra eyes and hands.'

'So you didn't discuss it with Morelli and Perez?' Olivia was sure that his failure to look at her told its own tale. Her first encounter with that close pair had left a lot to be desired, and if neither was enthusiastic about her presence, she could hardly blame them.

'Let's say I informed them of my decision and they accepted it with good grace.' Jack finished his sandwich and gave an encouraging smile. 'It's all fine, Olivia.'

'So you don't have an office, then?'

'You got a desire to see an office to check if ISB is real?' He smiled. 'Our headquarters are in Washington. We've only got four field offices across the country, none near here.'

'I know you're real; I checked up on your outfit.' She glanced out front again. At first, her gaze was easy. Then fear flowed through her.

'I can't see Amy.' She jumped up, leaving her meal half-finished and headed towards the open door. 'She's not there!'

'Don't panic; she won't have gone far.'

'Amy!' shouted Olivia, running towards where she had last seen her daughter. 'Amy!'

Jack caught up with her. 'Remind me, what does she have on?'

'A yellow short-sleeved top and white shorts.' Olivia spun around wildly as she spoke peering into the surrounding mass of people, trees and trails. 'Those boys with her . . . one's got dark hair and a light-blue polo shirt. The other has blond hair and a bright floral top, like a Hawaiian shirt.'

Jack was much taller than Olivia. First he stood on tiptoes and peered around. Next, he ran to a nearby rock about a metre off the ground, and leapt up on to it. He pointed towards a foot-trail winding its way through the leafy trees. 'This way, come on!'

Olivia ran behind him as he raced up the trail, pushing past startled people. 'Can you see them?'

'I think so,' said Jack panting. 'They've just taken a turn off the path, heading behind an alcove over there.'

Olivia's heart pounded in her chest as she ran and caught up with Jack. Her mind conjured up images of Amy, sprawled broken and bloody over jagged rocks, and it was all she could do not to scream. She had dragged her daughter into this, knowingly brought her into danger. She begged whichever god was real not to let her child become a statistic.

'Jack, can you see Amy?'

'No, but I'm pretty sure I spotted blondie in the Hawaiian shirt.'

Olivia's mind went into overdrive. The boy could have pushed her off a cliff by now. Her daughter could be lying limp and crumpled beneath the cliffs, unable to call for help. In her eagerness to help catch a serial killer, she had sacrificed her own flesh and blood. She rounded the alcove just behind Jack, petrified of what she might see. One boy was pulling on Amy's arm to follow him, while the other stood a few feet back, as if to block her path if she managed to get away.

'Let her go!' said Jack.

'Oh, come on, dude. We're just having a little fun,' said one of the boys.

'What's it got to do with you, anyway? You her old man?' asked the other.

'Special Agent Jack Tyler, ISB.' He whipped out his badge and waved it at them.

'I've never heard of ISB.'

'Ever heard of handcuffs? Listen, you little punks, you've got five minutes to get out here. If not, I'll make sure you do ten to life for kidnapping. How's that sound?'

'Whoa, we're gone, G-man!'

'Just having a little joke. No harm done.'

'Four minutes, thirty seconds,' said Jack. 'Ten to life.'

The boys backed away, hands in the air. Blondie smirked at Olivia, then both of them turned and sprinted away, leaving behind a distinct smell of marijuana.

Olivia hugged her daughter. 'Oh, God. You gave me the fright of my life.'

'Yeah, sorry. I'm alright, Mom, really.' Amy squirmed away and seemed embarrassed. 'Stop over-reacting. I would have screamed good and loud if I thought they were going to hurt me.'

'It's best not to wait that long, Amy,' said Jack, his tone sober. 'What seems to start out as friendly joshing can turn into something much worse pretty quickly.'

'I hear you.' Amy stubbed the soil with her toe. 'But it's all a fuss about nothing really.'

'Thank you, Jack,' said Olivia. 'I really appreciate it.'

'I really like how you did that, you know.' Amy gave Jack a warm smile. 'Showed them who's boss.'

'It's my best skill.' Jack smiled back and glanced at Olivia. 'Look, we're only about an hour and a half away from the FBI office, but I'll understand if you don't feel up to coming back with me.'

'Of course we're coming with you,' said Amy. 'Sort of like a civic duty and all that. Right, Mom?'

'Right, love.'

'We can find an agent to give you a guided tour of the office while your mom is with me. Is that okay with you, Amy?'

'Sure. And even though I said that stuff about civic duty, my mom better still get paid.'

13

As she entered the FBI boardroom, Olivia's attention was immediately drawn to a huge map of America covered with red pins and yellow arrows. Graphs, charts and diagrams cluttered the surrounding walls. Thumbtacks held newspaper clippings to an over-laden corkboard. A whiteboard headed 'Operation Dean' was covered in black writing: names of victims, places, dates and possible times of murder.

In the centre of the room was a long table with enough space for a dozen chairs. There were only six, spread out for the agents' comfort, she assumed. A few piles of papers and reports were stacked on it. Jack cleared these to the end of the table with one swoop of his arm.

Olivia made for the death wall. Photographs of victims, all identified except for one, which was labelled 'John Doe'. Dead bodies at multiple crime scenes, as well as images blown up from their driver's licences or passports, and close-ups of naked corpses in the morgue. The stark finality of death on an ice-cold slab for all to see.

'You okay with all this?' asked Jack as he came up beside her.

'Sure, nothing I haven't seen before.'

Olivia hoped he did not detect her unease. Only someone

with a rigid heart and no feelings would not be touched by the images. Real people with real lives brought to a vicious end. Seven men. As her eyes were drawn back to Rick's mortuary shot, a sickly feeling ran through her. All the marks and tattoos he had gone to such lengths to hide while he tried to make a new life were exposed in death.

'The team is on the way. Have a seat anywhere you like.'

Olivia chose a chair at the far end of the table. The door behind them opened, and Special Agents Walsh, Perez and Morelli entered.

Agents Perez and Morelli acknowledged her with a brief hello, then went to the opposite end of the table. The dark eyes of Perez focused on her for too long, and in that moment Olivia suspected the woman would not so much hold a grudge, as cuddle and feed it. No sisterhood there. Morelli's face was a blank. He stared straight ahead at the whiteboard and twirled a toothpick between his fingers, as if her presence was neither here nor there.

Agent Walsh paused briefly at the doorway to improve the lighting with the quick flick of a switch. He gave Olivia a broad smile and shook her hand.

'Good to see you again, Olivia.'

Tom placed his laptop on the table as he sat next to her, and then straightened his bold orange bow tie. Either he was naturally a more forgiving person, Olivia thought, or it was his role to put her at ease. So far, it was not working; self-doubt overwhelmed her. She knew nothing about serial killers and was surrounded by people who did. She placed her hands in her lap beneath the table and tried to concentrate on the task ahead.

'As you know, Olivia has very good experience as an investigator,' said Jack. 'We're extremely lucky to have her work with us, and I know you'll all appreciate her help. Please give her your full assistance to settle in.'

Olivia nodded as more civil grunts of welcome were made, ostensibly for the team leader's benefit.

'Thank you, everyone,' she said. 'I promise you'll get my best work.'

'I'm going to run through what we've got, make sure we're all on the same page.' Jack pushed his already rolled-up sleeves further up his arms and clapped together his palms once. 'Feel free to interrupt me at any time, Olivia, or anybody else for that matter.'

'Pennsylvania is where we believe the murders started. Two bodies in November. French Creek State Park first, then Bald Eagle State Forest.' Jack pointed out both locations on the map. 'Both bodies were found early morning, and the ME put the times of death around ten to twelve hours before. Sunset is at six pm in November, and the parks closed at nine pm. Plenty of time to commit the murders under cover of darkness.'

'Were the victims camping?' asked Olivia.

'No, both were day-trippers,' said Jack. 'We don't know if the killer was a day-tripper, a camper, or someone holed up in the woods.

'Based on our knowledge of how serial killers operate, we believe he either lives in Pennsylvania or once lived there, or has relatives there.' Jack looked straight at Olivia. 'Serial killers tend to start in their comfort zone and stay there committing murders, but some, like Dean, do cross states as their confidence grows. Right, Tom?'

'Or if it's where the job takes them,' added Tom, with a nod.

Jack continued. 'We have no movement from the killer in December or January. No idea what he was doing. Enjoying the thrill of his kills? Waiting to see if anyone would come after him, or if he had got away with it? Could have been ill. Or perhaps the weather was so cold, he wasn't tempted out.' Jack tapped on the map, moving his finger through adjoining states. 'By late February, he's moving west. Victim three: Ohio. That's when he first came to my attention. After comparing sites, wounds and the positioning of the earlier bodies, we concluded it was likely the same perpetrator.

'Nothing from him in March or April. He struck again in June in Illinois, our unidentified victim four. By late July, he's in Iowa, where he took out victim five at Stone State Park. August barely starts, and he turns up at Hawkeye for victim six. Next day, he's at Palisades and we've got seven bodies.'

'So he's headed west. He did Pennsylvania, Ohio, skipped Indiana, straight on to Illinois, Iowa and now South Dakota?' Olivia frowned. 'He just ignored Indiana?'

'That's how it looks,' said Jack. 'We've got nothing in Indiana. Each of the victims died from one stab wound: head, neck or chest,' he continued. 'That suggests the killer knows what he's doing. Takes them out in one motion. No defence wounds to indicate any of the victims fought back. As for clues, this guy has done a clean job at each scene. The only evidence we have is from Hawkeye. An ordinary kitchen knife you can get anywhere, with no fingerprints, and a Furlowe boot impression with no boot.'

'We know one set of prints on the trailer belong to Rick Seagal,' said Perez. She kept her gaze on Jack and gestured towards Olivia with a wave of her hand. 'The other set belong to the lady in our presence.'

'Sorry about that,' Olivia whispered, noting that the female agent was left-handed with short, neat nails.

Jack ignored the strained interaction. 'All we've got so far is a basic profile. The killer, we believe, is late fifties or early sixties, white male, possibly retired or with a mobile job that leaves him free to criss-cross the country unnoticed.

'Two witnesses from different parts of the Hawkeye camp-ground did see an older male talking to Rick Seagal.' Jack unpinned a composite sketch from the wall and pushed it towards Olivia. 'Neither witness got a good look at him, because of the distance, and we can't put all our faith in the composite. His height is around five-six to five-eight; much shorter than Rick and the other victims. Makes sense, because the angle of the knife each time suggests the perpetrator struck upwards.' He imitated an upward jabbing motion with his hand.

'You think it's significant that the killer is smaller than the victims?' asked Olivia.

'I do,' said Jack. 'He's got something to prove.'

'Not many small guys set out attacking much bigger men, unless they're mentally impaired, drunk or just plain foolish,' said Tom. 'He could be all of the above.'

'Or he could just have something against jock types?' suggested Perez.

'Who hasn't?' said Morelli.

'His confidence is growing,' said Jack. 'He's getting bold and careless. But we can't wait and hope that his carelessness will lead us to him. We have to find him.'

Olivia studied the composite sketch. A slim, white face; thin eyes; a narrow, pointed nose; closely cropped hair; thin lips below a neat moustache and short beard. The sort of face visible everywhere, every day, yet not a face she remembered coming across at Hawkeye.

'Are you going to put this image on the news and hold a press conference?' asked Olivia.

'At this point in the investigation, no,' said Jack. 'It will be circulated only to the affected parks in the five states and their local law enforcement.'

Olivia noticed that a look passed between Jack and Tom. She glanced at Tom, expecting him to speak. He said nothing, merely fiddled with his cufflinks. It made sense for them to present a united front in the circumstances, yet she wondered about the dynamic between the two men. She sensed a disagreement.

'So, there's no known link between any of the dead men?' asked Olivia. 'They're all random?'

'There's certainly nothing to suggest a connection,' said Jack. 'We've talked to families and friends. We've got a mix of victims with different lifestyles. None of them are regular nomads or die-hard campers.' He ran his marker pen down the board, pointing to each name as he spoke. 'The Penn victims . . . we've got a tailor and a magazine writer. Ohio is a baker. Illinois is the John Doe. No one has reported him missing; it's likely he drifted in from another state. In Iowa, the first guy is an advertising exec. Rick is an ex-con who did time in Georgia for burglary. Came out and worked as a mechanic for two years. The latest vic is the realtor.'

'Going back to Rick, because he's the only one I met, do you know what that mark is just below his neck?' asked Olivia.

Jack gestured towards Perez with his chin.

'He got that working as a mechanic,' explained Perez, looking straight at Olivia with dark, unwavering eyes. 'Hoisted up a car and the jack slipped when he was under it. The oil plate burned his skin like a branding iron. That's one unique scar.'

'He got good compensation for the accident,' said Jack. 'Used the money to buy the truck and trailer.'

Olivia felt gratified that her initial thoughts about Rick had been correct. The man was just trying to live in peace in a remote area, and evil had caught up with him.

'We've had all sort of crazies phoning in about Rick,' said Perez. 'This morning, a woman called saying she shot and killed him. Said she's got the murder weapon, and I can pick her up.'

'Kind of her,' murmured Morelli. 'Desperate for jail much?'

'She asked if we could drive to the jail past a waffle take-out,' continued Perez. 'Desperate for honey-coated waffles at my expense is my guess.'

'She doesn't know there's no chance of you ever picking up a breakfast tab,' said Morelli.

The four special agents laughed and Olivia managed a smile,

grateful that the tension was gradually easing away. She imagined that this lot could be fun, if they ever let her into their clique.

'Okay, guys.' Jack clapped twice. 'We have no reason to believe Dean will change trajectory. He'll keep going west.'

Olivia stared at the map and rubbed her throat. The next state west was the one she and Amy had been headed for before Jack's intervention. 'So you think he could go to Nebraska next?'

'Possibly,' said Jack. 'Or he could go to Montana or Wyoming. Each of them border South Dakota.'

'Or he could stay right here,' said Perez. 'He took out two in Penn, two in Iowa. Could do two here.'

The agents started a discussion about the various states, each giving ideas about Dean's possible movements. Their overlapping voices reminded Olivia of Bill shouting across the office while she was trying to concentrate on her own work. White noise. Years of practice allowed her to blot out the voices. She concentrated on the whiteboard. Investigating a serial killer across many states was a huge task. Vast acres of land to search through for evidence to identify one man. She glanced at the notebooks in front of the agents, and wondered how many full notebooks they had stored elsewhere.

'Is all of this information in a database?' she asked.

'We've managed to get some semblance of order,' said Jack. 'As you can imagine, it's impossible to put every piece of information in the database, but every day we try to add the most relevant points.'

Olivia's first thought was that what was considered relevant depended on an individual's thought processes. A different person who gathered the same information could consider something else more relevant. There was always a good chance that handwritten information that should be there did not make it into the database. She decided against saying so. No point alienating the people she would be working with.

'I get to see everything in the database?' she asked.

'Everything to do with Operation Dean, yes,' said Tom. 'I can get you logged in here. We do have other databases that you won't get access to. Strictly forensics business, like CODIS for DNA testing, and AFIS for fingerprints — not things that you'll need.'

'Not things that we need either, unfortunately,' said Jack in frustration. 'At least, not yet. We've got seven bodies and no useful fingerprints or DNA. No fingernail scrapings, no blood other than the victims'.'

'It does seem strange that none of the victims fought back,' said Olivia. 'Did the medical examiners check to see if he stuck them with a needle first — to paralyse them, I mean?'

'They've checked.' Jack shook his head. 'No dice. They weren't injected or poisoned or tased. No blunt-force trauma. Every one of them was fully conscious when they were murdered.'

'Brutal,' murmured Olivia.

'We believe he gets close to the victims by being friendly, and then catches them off guard. Before they know what's happening, he's done his job.' Jack paced back and forth in front of the whiteboard. 'This killer is all about stealth and precision. I'm beginning to think he could have a military connection — army or navy — past or present.'

'The last medical examiner thinks there's a possibility he's a trained medic — nurse, paramedic, EMT, doctor,' said Tom.

'Could just be a regular Joe,' said Perez. 'Someone with a fixation on knives and a fascination with killing. Taught himself about the human body and knows exactly where to strike for best effect.'

'Got a lot of knife fanatics posting their violent hobbies online,' said Morelli. 'They tend to be young males though. I've not come across any middle-aged weirdos.'

'So, you're definitely sure it's not a female?' asked Olivia.

Jack nodded. 'I'd say we're very confident it's a male.'

'A male prostitute?' suggested Olivia.

'No sign of anything sexual with any of the victims,' said Morelli. 'All of them were fully clothed. The body positioning didn't indicate a sexual motive.'

'Yes, I should have mentioned that. In my time, I've seen murder victims lying in grass, balanced on ledges, in ravines, at the bottom of cliffs, even in shallow rivers – and none were situated like these.' Jack pointed at each of the bodies as he explained. 'Imagine these victims as if they were standing on their feet. This one's right arm is folded to his brow, like a salute. This guy, his left hand is touching his brow, again like a salute. These two, their arms are straight down, parallel to their thighs, legs ramrod straight . . . almost as if standing to attention, military style. Rick looks like he was caught in the position most people call a jumping jack or star jump. The army call it a side-straddle hop.'

'That's interesting. The only thing I thought when I saw Rick was "snow angel",' said Olivia. 'With the benefit of the whole picture, I get what you mean.'

'While I remember,' said Jack, turning the pages of his notepad, 'did any of you interview a Kent Hilson? Seems he's a keen photographer. A religious pair spotted him near the crime scene and got suspicious.'

'Name doesn't ring a bell,' said Morelli.

Perez flicked through her notes. 'Nope. Not on my list, either.'

Tom pressed the keyboard of his laptop. Olivia craned her neck as he tapped away, fascinated by the speed with which the special agent could investigate a name. No doubt her own details had been run through countless databases.

'Nobody of that name has a record,' said Tom.

'I'll check through the sheriff's statements,' said Jack. 'If none of his men talked to this guy, I'll go find him myself. Pretending to be a photographer is a good ruse to get up close to a person without causing suspicion.'

Tom played with his bowtie as if it was helping him to think. Olivia imagined he was a big fan, with a whole drawer full of them.

'A photographer might arrange your clothes, your hair, even adjust your pose, and you wouldn't think them a threat,' he mused. 'What about the people you met at Hawkeye, Olivia? Anyone make you suspicious?'

'Not really,' said Olivia with a frown. 'But if you're looking for people who keep sharp tools, there's a chap, Eddie, seemed really nice. A barber. He did say he'd tried to get Rick to have a trim.'

'Eddie Ingram,' said Perez. 'I interviewed him. He's got alibis for the times and dates of the murders that were easy to check. I'm not looking at him. Mid-forties. Besides, he's wide about the middle; no one would describe him as slim.'

'Channing the chef,' said Olivia. 'Another nice guy. Bet he has plenty of knives.'

'I talked to him,' said Morelli, with a shake of his head. 'Quite happy for me to look around in his trailer. And yes, he's got a whole lot of knives.'

Jack began pacing again. 'Remind me to hunt down that religious couple, too. Sometimes the people who send you in one direction are the very people trying to mislead you and protect themselves.'

Olivia narrowed her eyes and strained her memory. 'I can picture their faces clearly, but the names are still blank. In my head, I named them Judas and Jezebel.'

'Well, that's not nice.' Perez raised an eyebrow. 'You need to say a few Hail Marys and hope for forgiveness for such thoughts.'

Olivia shrugged and said nothing. She was not one for hailing Mary, or Selassie, or any other deity for that matter. It was just her luck that Perez was religiously inclined. Getting on the woman's good side was going to take a lot of hard work, and

Olivia's only comfort was that she could hardly sink any lower in Perez's estimation.

Jack looked around the table. 'Right. Everybody ready to get back to it?'

Morelli said, 'Me and Chesca are heading back to Stone State Park to follow up a couple of leads — unless you want us back at Hawkeye?'

'No, that's fine, Marty.'

'I'll be here working on the database.' Tom closed his laptop and stood. 'Shout if you need me for anything.'

'Will do,' said Jack. He looked at Olivia. 'I need to go find out why Kent Hilson didn't make himself available for questioning. Got time for a trip to Hawkeye, or do you need a ride to Palisades?'

Olivia slid her tote bag over her shoulder and glanced at her watch. Nearly six o'clock, so a good few hours of daylight were still left. 'Sure. I can do Hawkeye. Amy liked the people there a lot. She can come too, right?'

'Of course. We'll pick up some food on the way.'

14

AMY PLIED JACK and Olivia with questions as the special agent drove to Hawkeye campsite. Annoyed at the lack of detail to satisfy her curiosity, Amy eventually put on headphones, ate her hot buttered popcorn and ignored them. Olivia, sitting beside her daughter, nudged her from time to time, but was unable to raise a smile.

She gave up trying and stared out of the passenger window. All Amy knew was that they were going to interview some campers, and that was all she needed to know for now. Visions of the death wall were forefront in Olivia's mind, images that were sure to remain ingrained there all night.

Occasionally, Olivia noticed Jack watching the two of them in the rear-view mirror. He had tried to engage Amy in conversation about London, to which she had responded with monosyllabic answers that were only a sliver away from being rude. The man had earlier saved Amy from who knew what abuse, and it annoyed Olivia that her offspring seemed to have forgotten that episode so quickly.

Jack drove deep into the Hawkeye campground, which was still bathed in late evening sunlight, and Olivia pointed out Darcy's motor home. Ben the Labrador raced towards the Jeep, placed his paws on the passenger window and tried to lick Amy. Darcy immediately appeared from behind her trailer and greeted them as they exited the vehicle.

Amy fed the dog tepid popcorn, which he gulped down, sniffing expectantly for more. 'Can I take Ben for a run, Darcy?'

'Sure, go ahead.' As her dog galloped away behind Amy, the nomad placed her hands on her hips and stared at Jack. 'Not caught the killer yet, Agent Tyler?'

'Not quite,' he said.

Olivia observed Channing approaching. As he offered an exuberant greeting, all Olivia could do was stare at the two kitchen knives in his hands. The steel blades glinted in the sun as he slashed them together, sharpening them. The very idea that the jovial chef could have anything to do with Rick's murder was ridiculous. Morelli had already discounted him, anyway.

'What's that about the killer?' he asked. 'Has he been found?'

'You'll be the first to know when he is,' said Jack sourly.

Olivia felt some sympathy for the special agent. The general public expected crimes to be solved in a day, or at least before the weekend. She looked around the site. 'I don't see the red trailer. What happened to our saviours, Judas and Jezebel?'

'Took their hallelujahs and left,' said Channing. 'Headed back to Missouri.'

'Said we should pop into their church anytime we're passing through.' Darcy cackled. 'Hell would freeze over first.'

'I can trace them if I need to,' said Jack. 'Either of you know where I can find a Kent Hilson? Retired, from what I don't know. Wanders around with a large camera?'

Darcy cocked her head to one side. 'No, can't say I do.'

'Don't know him, either.' Channing pointed into the distance. 'Look, there's Eddie. If anyone will know who that is, he will. What's this Hilson done? You think he's a killer?'

'Hopefully he'll be able to help us with our inquiries,' said Jack.

'Been thinking I shoulda brought my pistol with me,' said Darcy.

'I'm glad you didn't.' Olivia grimaced. 'I like the sound of birds, rustling leaves and Ben barking. I don't want to hear guns barking.'

'Speaking of barking . . .' Darcy shielded her eyes. 'Oh, I can see them. That dog has love for everybody. Wouldn't put it past him to go snuggling up to a killer.'

'We'll go talk to Eddie,' said Jack.

Eddie was on his knees, washing a floor mat he'd spread on the ground. He dipped a brush into soapy water and scrubbed at the fabric. His haggard expression changed to one of delight when he saw Olivia.

'You brought Mr Special Agent back for a shave, Olivia? Kind of you to bring me business.'

'I'm afraid not.'

Olivia had noticed that stubble was growing on Jack's chin, but the idea of suggesting that he shave was way beyond her pay grade. She made a mental note to clarify exactly what *was* her pay grade; he had merely thrown some figures in the air. The fact he had not given her any paperwork to sign made her think her taskforce position was not above board. He'd probably stuck her fees under 'miscellaneous' or 'petty cash'. Still, she had no reason to believe he would ever try to stiff her.

'You know of a Kent Hilson?' asked Jack.

Eddie screwed up his eyes, deep in thought. 'I wonder if that's the one with the good-sized Winnebago? I think he said his name was Kent.'

'Retiree, photographer?' encouraged Jack.

'That's him. Good-looking silver fox; said he used to be a chartered surveyor. Don't know about the surname, though.'

Eddie sat back on his haunches and put down the dripping brush. 'He's got the best goatee beard; I know, because I shaped it for him. And I trimmed that moustache. Made him look like the Marlboro Man came out of retirement.'

Olivia chuckled. Eddie was a sweetheart, never a murderer. In any other circumstances, she would have happily remained at Hawkeye and really got to know this disparate bunch, but duty called.

'Nice,' said Jack. 'Where can I find the Winnebago?'

'Way at the other end. About two campsites along. Tan-coloured vehicle. It's the only Winnebago in that area — you can't miss it.'

Amy came up to them, breathing heavily, and waved a hand of greeting at Eddie. She looked at Jack. 'You don't think Eddie's a murderer, do you?'

'Amy,' said Olivia in frustration.

'I sure hope not,' said Eddie. 'Last thing I murdered was a mosquito that bit me on the wrist. Clapped that thing to kingdom come.'

'You're not a suspect, Mr Ingram,' Jack assured him.

'So you think this Kent Hilson's got something to do with Rick's murder?' asked Eddie.

Amy's eyes widened. 'Kent Hilson . . . is that the suspect's name?'

'Dear God, I swear I'm going to send you to work in the mall,' said Olivia.

'What? Have you lost your mind, Mom?'

'Peace,' said Jack. 'No one is a murder suspect. Every person I speak to is a witness, unless they give me cause to believe they're a suspect.' He tucked his notepad under his arm. 'Thanks, Mr Ingram. We'll go find him.'

Jack drove the short distance, passing through two other campsites, until the Winnebago came into view. The spotless vehicle boasted polished rims and tinted windows. The door and windows were closed.

A neighbour spotted them as they alighted and waved. 'Hello! If you're looking for Kent, he's gone into town for drinks. Not sure when he'll be back.'

'Thank you.' Jack waved back.

'Guess he took a cab rather than drive this hulk of a thing,' said Olivia.

'We should have got one of these instead of Tango, Mom. Looks fun. And we wouldn't have to be hooking and unhooking the caravan.'

'Looks a bit cumbersome to me, like driving a coach.' Olivia ran dubious eyes over the vehicle, then peered underneath it. 'If Kent Hilson is the killer, he must have another vehicle he drove to Palisades. The grass under there is dark green, quite different from the parched area around.'

'You're right.' Jack knelt and ran his fingers over the grass beneath the Winnebago. 'It hasn't moved for at least three or four days. A killer in a hurry would not return and park the tyres in exactly the same spot, unless it was a super-skilled driver used to parking in precise spaces, like a valet or a tow-truck driver.'

'We can check whether he was seen in another vehicle,' said Olivia.

'Plate is Illinois,' Jack muttered as he circled the vehicle in slow steps.

When he was temporarily out of view, Olivia climbed up on the wheel, pressed her palms against the hot chassis and peered through the window.

'There's no probable cause to do that, Olivia.' Jack's curt tone came from behind her. 'You remember what I said about Stand Your Ground? If he was hiding in there . . .'

'Am I really that scary?' Olivia jumped down.

'Don't need to be scary; just give them a reason.'

'You folks really need to sort out your laws,' said Olivia.

'You still haven't caught on that it's a bad idea to be leaving your prints everywhere, have you?'

Olivia dusted off her hands and averted her gaze.

'So, see anything?' he asked.

Olivia crossed her arms and stared at him.

'Look, it was an uncalled-for action, but since you did it already . . . if you have something useful, I may as well know about it.'

'Can't see much through the tint, but it's neat and tidy. On the countertop there's a dark baseball cap with a large yellow capital "P" on it. Does that mean anything?'

To her surprise, Jack moved past her and climbed up onto the wheel.

'Hypocrite,' murmured Amy, and winced when Olivia pinched her side.

'What is it, Jack?' demanded Olivia.

'Pittsburgh Pirates. Professional baseball team in Pennsylvania.' Jack was deep in thought. 'All this started in Pennsylvania, at French Creek State Park. I really want to talk to this Hilson guy. Like, now.'

He strode away from them and Olivia watched him knock on the neighbour's caravan. She could not hear the conversation.

'Mom, this is great. We might catch a killer tonight!'

'Yes, love,' murmured Olivia absently, and continued her attempt to eavesdrop.

Jack returned after a few minutes. 'Okay, he's at a bar in Sibley called Alley 7. Married, but he travelled here alone. I'm going to call him.'

As he held the phone to his ear, Olivia tried to follow the one-sided conversation. Jack informed Kent Hilson he was outside the Winnebago and wanted to discuss a homicide. She watched his face for signs of how well the conversation was going, but the special agent showed little emotion. The last thing he did was ask the suspect for an hour of his time.

'We'll be right there.' Jack clicked off and announced, 'He's not leaving the bar until midnight, but he says we're free to come see him.'

'We're going to see Kent Hilson,' said Amy in wonder. 'Note, I did not say "the murderer" or even "the suspect". I promise I will not say a single word. You won't even know I'm there.'

*

Alley 7 was a small, cheerful bar where loud voices competed to be heard over relentless pop music, a lively atmosphere amidst a light odour of wine and beer. The clientele was a mixture of youth and seniors, all casually dressed and relaxed. Olivia got the distinct impression the customers all knew each other. That, or they were social butterflies who relished interaction with strangers.

Olivia recognised Kent based purely on Eddie's description. There was no missing him. He would stand out in any crowd. A handsome man with a perfectly groomed goatee beard and moustache, and sparkly grey-blue eyes shown off to full effect on a lined, deeply tanned face. He was bent double shooting pool as they entered the bar, and she observed the edge of a leather wallet in his jeans pocket.

Jack approached him discreetly once the man had potted a ball. 'Mr Hilson? I'm Tyler. We spoke.'

Kent Hilson tucked his pool cue under his arm and continued to follow the game. He made no attempt to shake hands. 'You found me. How can I help you?'

'Can someone take over your game so we can go talk?'

'Not long to go, sir. I'm winning anyway.' Hilson smiled at his competitor, whose ball missed a pocket and ricocheted off the woodwork. Calmly, Hilson took up position and potted another ball. Looking up, he seemed to notice Olivia and Amy for the first time, and nodded at them. 'These lovely ladies with you?'

'They are. Olivia is a PI. Amy's her daughter.'

'Ah, I saw you at Hawkeye, Olivia. How do you do?'

'Fine, thank you, Mr Hilson.'

Olivia noted his good looks and smooth voice. This one was a real charmer, alright. She vowed not to be taken in by the assured gaze and easy tone.

'Amy, how do you do?'

'Okay, thank you, Mr Hilson.'

Olivia looked at Amy, who hopped up onto a high stool, closed her lips firmly and made a zipping motion across her mouth.

'What lovely voices,' he said. 'Haven't been back to England since you guys laid on a great Olympics. Awesome place. I'm well overdue a visit.'

'Glad to hear you enjoyed it,' said Olivia, with a smile.

Kent rubbed chalk on the tip of his cue stick. Olivia's eyes were on his hands. No rings, no watch, no bracelet. Around his neck was a thin gold chain that held a solid gold ring instead of a pendant.

Jack asked, 'Where are you from, Mr Hilson?'

'Cedar Rapids, right here in Iowa.'

'Ever lived anywhere else?'

'Springfield, Illinois, for few years, before I realised the error of my ways and came right back.'

'So, if I said you've lived in Pennsylvania, Pittsburgh maybe, I'd be wrong?'

Kent missed his shot and murmured an expletive under his breath. His competitor pumped a fist in delight. Olivia was taken aback by the speed at which Kent's veil of charm fell.

'What's my birthplace got to do with anything?' he snapped.

'I don't know,' said Jack. 'Funny how you didn't think to mention it.'

'Look, I've lived in Iowa most of my life, for the last thirty-five years, in fact. I rarely go anywhere near Penn state. Most times, I don't even think about the place.'

'Travel by yourself?'

'There a better way to travel?'

Olivia looked from one man to the other. Both were stony faced. Hilson was of medium height and did not look much like the photofit, but she was mindful that they could not place too much faith in an image cobbled together based on the views of two Hawkeye nomads.

'You playing pool, Kent, or twenty questions with your new friend?' asked his companion across the table.

'Dave is taking over for me.' Kent handed the cue stick to a keen spectator. 'Don't you dare lose, or I'll never live it down.'

Kent indicated a corner table and led the way, followed by Jack, Olivia and Amy. Before they had even sat down, he said, 'I have no idea what led you to me, Agent Tyler, but I know nothing about any homicide.'

'When were you last in your home state? That's Pennsylvania, in case you forgot.' Jack gave him a hard stare.

'Sometime last fall, I think.'

'Last fall. So maybe November?'

Kent angled his head and seemed to contemplate. 'Yes, could have been in November. Yes, it was Thanksgiving, or just before Thanksgiving.'

Olivia noted that he seemed flustered, as if he had misspoken. Surely he would remember whether he was home for what was a big day for the majority of Americans?

'You go to French Creek State Park?' asked Jack.

'In November? No, I mean, I like to go to parks all the time, but I don't recall going to any park in November.'

'No? Sure you didn't make a trip to Bald Eagle State Forest either?'

'I'm sure,' said Kent. 'Listen, I need a drink. I'm thirsty. Ladies, what can I get you?'

'We'll save the drinks until after the questions,' snapped Jack.

'Well, actually . . .' started Amy.

Olivia's foot poked her under the table. She took out her purse and handed Amy some money. 'Get a juice or something. And don't even try it – they won't serve you alcohol without ID.'

Amy made a face at her mother and disappeared.

'Mr Hilson, I'm investigating a series of murders that started in Pennsylvania last year,' said Jack. 'We had one yesterday at Hawkeye, as you know, and one today at Palisades, just an hour's drive away.'

'How did I get to be a suspect?'

'You're not,' said Jack. 'You're assisting us with our inquiries. Did you know Rick Seagal?'

'No, never noticed him before. First time I heard about him was when the sheriff and the police turned up yesterday morning. I'm an amateur photographer. One day, I hope to go pro. I'm at Hawkeye because I love the scenery and the peace.' He sent a long, studious look Olivia's way. 'I didn't even go over and look at the man's body, like some others did. As for whoever got murdered at Palisades, I know nothing about it. Haven't been anywhere near that place in months.'

Kent's phone rang inside his front jeans pocket. Olivia watched as he stared at the screen, clicked it off and returned it to his pocket. It unnerved her to think this man had seen her beside Rick's body, and she had not seen him.

'I woke up this morning, and spent most of the day taking photos in the farmlands – got some great shots, too. Never left the campground until this afternoon, around four, when I took a cab into Sibley. And before you ask, I don't know whether anyone saw me. I was looking at the birds and the trees, not the humans.'

'Ever been to Cuyahoga Valley National Park?' asked Jack. 'Ohio?'

'I sure have, beautiful place. Must have been around March I passed through there.'

'March? Could it have been February?'

'You trying to trick me? Wait a minute, Agent Tyler, I did not kill anyone. If anything happened around the time I was there, I can assure you it's pure coincidence. Nothing to do with me. I'm into nature and nurture, not murder. Wildlife and wilderness are my things. Animals and plants. Forestry lands are great for taking photographs, whether in sun or snow.'

'And it's a coincidence a body is found at Hawkeye and you just happen to be staying there?'

Hilson shrugged his wide shoulders. 'So, I'm a bad-luck kind of guy.'

'Why were you taking photographs by Rick Seagal's trailer?'

'Why not? He parked in as scenic a place as anyone else, didn't he? Flowers and trees are right there. Even caught a glimpse of what looked like a fox. I didn't know he was going to get murdered. As I said, I'm an amateur, and my aim is to be a professional. All I look for is an opportunity to take a good shot.'

Olivia pretended to adjust her sandal strap, and took the opportunity to study his footwear. No Furlowes. He wore canvas loafers without socks, revealing hairy ankles. Large feet. They could possibly be a twelve. Surprisingly, he had another wallet in one of his front pockets. Strange that anyone would carry two wallets. She wondered if he was juggling identities. Or juggling girlfriends.

'Visited any parks or campgrounds in Cook County, Illinois, recently? Say around June.'

'Not that I recall.'

'That a yes or a no?'

'I said I don't recall. I travel extensively by myself, Special Agent Tyler. It's not easy to remember where I was week to week.'

Olivia wondered why he was doing all this travelling, seemingly without his spouse. She watched his face as he spoke, trying to detect any inflection in his tone. After his initial alarm, he had reverted to a normal voice. His speech pattern remained regular, his exterior calm. She wondered if, internally, his nerves were running amok.

'Give it some thought,' insisted Jack.

'I passed through Illinois sometime in late spring.'

'What were you passing through for?' asked Jack.

'I was at a photography exhibition, showing some of my best work. After that, I went home to Cedar Rapids.'

'You always drive the Winnebago?'

'Yes, had it seven years.'

'Would you mind me taking a look inside it? It would go some way to showing you had nothing to hide.'

'You won't get me falling for that one.' Kent smirked. 'I certainly would mind special agents rummaging through my place, no matter what bureau you belong to. Whatever intel led you to me is way off base.'

The questions continued, with Kent Hilson growing increasing flustered as he sought to offer alibis for the murder dates. None of them sounded like strong alibis to Olivia.

'Agent Tyler, I'm done with your questions. This is my social time. You messed up my game, and I'm thirsty. I've been nice, because that's the sort of person I am. If you want to ask me anything else, you can talk to my lawyer first.'

The amateur photographer glanced at Olivia as he rose. 'You shouldn't hang out with him. This is a friendly town.'

As soon as he was gone, Olivia said, 'You were quite demanding you know, considering he wasn't under arrest. You'd have got more out of him with a smile or two.'

'Not my style.'

Amy came back, sipping juice from a bucket-sized cup. 'Mr

Hilson's not in handcuffs, so I guess he's not confessed to being a killer?'

'We don't know what he is,' said Olivia. 'His alibis need to be checked, right Jack?'

'Right. There's a whole lot of work ahead to do.' He stood up. 'No bed for me. I need to start the ball rolling on this guy.'

'Amy and I will hang around here awhile,' said Olivia. 'It's a nice place.'

'You sure you want to stay?' asked Jack.

'Absolutely. We'll be fine. We'll get a cab back to Palisades.'

Olivia wanted wine, but she ordered a glass of orange juice and snacked on a family-sized bag of potato crisps, which the label described as 'potato chips'. She fought to follow the flow of Amy's conversation while carrying out her surveillance of Kent Hilson, hoping to detect something odd in his mannerisms.

After he'd made a series of poor shots and been beaten in a second pool game, she noticed a swift change in tone. His voice hardened and he slammed down a fist on the table, causing the balls to jump. Although his anger was clearly directed at himself, Olivia determined that he had a hidden temper, like most people.

At one point, Kent wandered over and offered to buy them drinks, which Olivia politely declined. She watched him remove a phone from a knapsack and place it to his ear. Unable to read lips, she frowned. The man had two phones and two wallets. Wore a distinctive wedding ring around his neck. No wife in sight. Something was off with this picture. Had he been there in the woods at Hawkeye, watching them socialise? As she studied him, she tried to imagine those strong hands wielding a knife in anger, slaughtering victims in a precise, efficient manner, then rearranging their limbs.

He seemed nice — but by all accounts, Ted Bundy seemed *nice*. Sparkly-eyed, suave killers were not unique.

15

THEY LEFT ALLEY 7 just before it closed at midnight. Outside, the skies were dark, the road illuminated only by a thin
sliver of moonlight and dim streetlights. Olivia flagged down a
white car with 'Best Taxis' emblazoned on the side above a local
phone number.

'I hope these cabbies aren't like the ones in London,' she said.
'Refusing to drive south of the river after dark.'

Amy's forehead wrinkled. 'We crossed a river? I must not
have been paying attention.'

'Crossing state lines, I mean. It's only an hour to Palisades. Not
much different than going from central London to Croydon.'

The driver rolled down the window. 'Where to, ma'am?'

'Palisades State Park, South Dakota.'

'Hop right in.'

Olivia breathed a sigh of relief as she climbed in. Had she
been more alert, she would have noticed the vehicle that set off
from the bar right behind their taxi. As it was, she carried on a
conversation with Amy, comparing England and America,
unaware of the storm ahead.

Eventually, the driver, who was listening in on the conversation, decided to chime in. 'All the way from London, huh? How

you enjoying America?' He was a stout man whose stomach brushed the steering wheel. Heavy eyebrows shielded dark eyes.

'So far, so great,' Olivia said.

'I've been to England once before. To Birmingham, you know it?'

'I certainly do. I've got family not too far from that area. I live in London now, though.'

'Oh, you like the big cities, then?'

'Well, you go where the work is, I guess. Once you've got settled and put down roots, you tend to stay put.'

'I know what you mean. I settled in this town and can't see myself uprooting anytime. All my memories are here.' The driver made eye contact with Amy. 'You liking it here too?'

'Yeah, the place is beautiful. Seems like you've got a lot of murderers here, though. Serial killers.'

'Say what?'

'Amy, really?' Olivia nudged her daughter's knee with her own.

'Well, it's true. I looked it up. At any one point in time, there are twenty-five to fifty serial killers on the loose in America.'

'Keep thinking that way, little lady, you won't go out, let alone sleep at night,' warned the man. 'This is a quiet, friendly place. Ain't no serial killers around here.'

'Quite so,' said Olivia firmly.

She could imagine the tales the driver would spread if he heard how she had spent her day. People were as fascinated by murderers as they were afraid of them, and this man was unlikely to be any different. Up to fifty serial killers on the loose? If Kent Hilson was one of them, she hoped it could be proved quickly and the number reduced.

Olivia was shaken out of her musing by the change in the taxi man's voice.

'You know something, I'd swear somebody is following us.'

He stared into his wing mirror. 'Can't see who that is, but he's turned every time I've turned.'

'I really hope you're mistaken,' said Olivia.

Amy spun around in the back seat and looked out. 'You mean the red car?'

'Can't tell if it's red from here.' He switched his gaze to the rear-view mirror and locked eyes with Olivia. 'Watch this.'

At the next stoplight, he turned right. The mystery car followed. He performed a U-turn, and the two vehicles passed each other.

'Okay, it's red alright,' he said. 'Toyota Land Cruiser. Can't see who's behind the wheel.'

Olivia did not recognise the vehicle. She tried to sound confident for her daughter's sake. 'Well, looks like he's gone.'

For a few untroubled minutes, Olivia breathed easily, until the driver's urgent tone returned.

'He dropped back, but he's coming again,' he said. 'Third car behind us.'

This time, Olivia sensed that the danger was real. She was in no mood to put herself or her child at risk. 'Get us out of here, quickly. Find the nearest police station.'

'You got it. Sheriff's office is the nearest place to here.' The driver gripped the steering wheel and pressed down on the gas. 'You guys in some kinda trouble?'

'We are now,' said Amy. 'You think it's Kent Hilson, Mom?'

'I don't think so. He took a cab down here, too.'

'That your ex?' asked the driver in alarm. 'Lord knows they bring the worst kinda trouble.'

At the next red stoplight, the taxi driver slowed down and looked both ways before he raced through. Olivia held her breath, half expecting their pursuer to speed around them and pepper the taxi with bullets.

The taxi stayed ahead and eventually came to a screeching

halt outside the county sheriff's office, a red-brick building set back from the well-lit road. Only one official vehicle was in the open car park. No one came out, but Olivia noticed plenty of CCTV cameras on the premises. An attacker would have to be beyond crazy to assault someone there.

Olivia grabbed Amy's arm as they exited the vehicle. The taxi driver grabbed a small container in his palm and jumped out too.

'I'll Mace this sonofabitch if he tries anything.'

He stood behind his vehicle, arm extended, as the Land Cruiser came to a stop almost at his feet. The door opened. One high heel emerged, followed by the other.

'Olivia Knightley, we meet again.'

Olivia stared at the woman's flushed face. 'Oh my God,' she breathed. 'Kim.'

'They do say God is a woman. Wouldn't claim to be her.'

The taxi driver's voice was tinged with apprehension as he lowered his Mace and looked from one woman to the other. 'Guess you two ladies are well acquainted?'

'Yes, we are.' Olivia clutched her chest and exhaled. 'You gave me the fright of my life. I thought we were about to get shot or something.'

'Who is she, Mom?' asked Amy.

'Kim is a true-crime blogger,' replied Olivia.

'Actually, I'm going with investigative reporter for this scoop,' said Kim abruptly. 'Worldwide news business.'

'You mean you chasing down a news story driving like that, lady?' The driver fumed. 'Something going on around here I'm gonna read about tomorrow?'

'Stick to worrying about gas prices, mister. Never mind my driving.'

'It's alright, driver.' Olivia was apologetic. 'I really appreciate you looking out for us. Can you just give us five minutes, please?'

'Okay, ma'am. Meter's still ticking, though.'

The man had barely closed his door before Kim snapped. 'So, got anything you want to tell me, Olivia?'

The hostility was acute. Her hair sat messily on her shoulders, as if she hadn't brushed it recently. Olivia imagined the woman must have been dozing in her car.

'What on earth is wrong, Kim?'

'Don't try that sweet little British accent with me. I saw you today. You've been inside the FBI office for hours, and I thought that was odd enough. You and Jack Tyler took a trip to Hawkeye, and then you're both off to the bar for a fun night out.'

Olivia was indignant. 'You've been following me?'

'You bet your ass, I have. The idea was to follow Agent Tyler, try and get more information out of him. Then I realise you beat me to it. You've been shadowing this guy all along. Not a word to me – and I know you haven't lost my number.'

'Now, wait a minute . . .' started Olivia.

'After all you said, you're just like every other sleaze, trying to get one over on me.'

'Wow, don't talk to my mother like that! Who do you think you are?'

Kim's long eyelashes barely flickered Amy's way. 'Cute girl,' she said.

'Look, Kim, you're wrong. It's not like that.'

'What is it like then? Charmed your way into the feds' good graces, God knows how. Ready to file your story now? Got an exclusive for your cab driver to read first thing in the morning?'

'There won't be an exclusive, I swear. I have no story to file.'

'Who are the suspects?' demanded Kim, her eyes flared. 'Tell me.'

'Stop shouting at her,' said Amy, her voice raised in anger. 'Mom knows as much about Dean as you do!'

'Oh, Dean, is it? And what's his surname.'

Olivia could barely speak. She could not remember mentioning the words 'Operation Dean' in front of Amy, but she must have. 'Look, that's not a real person's name, Kim. It's just a random code name for the operation.'

'I get it.' Kim tossed back her mane. 'My story was already half-written, waiting to add details. But you know what? Light on details it may be, but I'm posting before you do.'

Olivia felt the blood leaving her face. 'Kim, please, I'm begging you not to do that. You know Jack is not ready to go public.'

'Whoa! Jack, is it?' Her tone was mocking. '*Jack?*'

'Special Agent Tyler said he's not ready for the news to be in the public domain until he has more facts. You told me yourself he made you a promise that you'd get the scoop. He hasn't broken his promise.'

'I trust him about as much as I trust you.' Kim Grant delivered a dangerous smile. 'Watch out for my blog, Olivia Knightley. If this doesn't get attention, nothing will.'

She climbed inside her cruiser and slammed the door shut. A stunned Olivia followed her and grabbed the door handle. 'Kim, wait!'

The fiery woman wound down her window. 'You might want to back away if you want to avoid going under. This baby weighs a ton.'

Olivia did as instructed. With a shriek of tyres, Kim pulled away. Olivia stood, shaken, staring after the accelerating vehicle.

'Scary lady,' said Amy. 'You alright, Mom?'

'Yes, love.'

Olivia was anything but alright. She thought about calling Jack to warn him, but decided that Kim must be bluffing. The woman had created all this drama because she wanted Olivia to call Jack. Kim would now be keeping her phone to her ear, expecting Jack to call and offer more information to appease her. That must be the plan. Well, it wouldn't work.

Olivia took Amy's arm and headed to the waiting cab. She pictured the bottle of white wine nestled in a mound of crushed ice in the cooler, and vowed to drain the entire bottle that very night.

16

THE MORNING WAS still dark, although it was nearly 5.30 am. The hotel shower sent a burst of cold water onto Jack's back. Turning his face up to the powerful stream, he allowed it to engulf his entire head. Having moved to a new hotel in Iowa, he was just getting used to the facilities. He wondered why hotels had such tiny bars of soap, each one no bigger than a cookie and wrapped in glossy white paper. Too fiddly to get a grip on. He needed to remember to buy a couple of decent palm-sized blocks for travelling, soaps like those he'd used at home. Home: a stylish detached house in Cincinnati, Ohio, which Sophie had asked him to leave five weeks, three days and six hours ago.

Jack flinched at the sudden sharp nick of pain. Sophie was not a morning person. Often, she would express frustration at hearing the shower running at all hours of the morning when she was still trying to sleep. Nowadays, she was probably getting all the sleep she wanted before heading out to her accountancy job. They had not spoken in weeks. None of his messages had been returned, and he thought a fourth attempt might be down-right annoying.

How had he not seen this coming? The signs were there, and

he had ignored them. Sophie loved cooking, and used to love showing off the fancy meals she could prepare, going as far as decking out the table like a fancy restaurant, with all the trimmings and sterling silver. The past year had seen a gradual decline in the elaborate nature of the meals, and the table settings had disappeared altogether. His cancelling of date nights for work was par for the course. She accused him of lodging there, not living there. In the weeks before he was kicked out, he'd made it home only twice, both times to a plate in the oven. The day before he was kicked out, there was no plate; just a message on the fridge, announcing the locks would be changed.

Now that he thought about it, their conversations had been strained for a while. At the time, he'd considered the growing silence to be something that happened to all couples after the kids had flown the nest. He had not listened when she tried to tell him about her day, whether the day was good or bad, yet he had not hesitated to dump his troubles on her. If he could have his time over again, he would strike a much better balance between his personal and professional lives. Right now, he could not go home, knock on the door and offer her any real change to their relationship. He would be crossing states chasing a violent criminal for the foreseeable future, so could make no promises of a settled life for them both.

As he was savouring the cool spray of the shower, which helped to relax his nerves, the phone gave its distinctive ring. Grabbing a large towel from the rail, he padded a trail of wet footprints to the bedside table. His hands were still wet as he snatched up the phone, hoping for good news.

'Tom, what is it?'

Tom's voice sounded groggy, and Jack guessed he too had managed little sleep. 'Go online and check the breaking news.'

'My heart can't stand the suspense. Fill me in.'

'Kimberly Grant has posted an exclusive on her blog. The

headline is "ISB pursues serial killer from Pennsylvania to Iowa". Guess she hasn't picked up on South Dakota yet.'

'Oh, great. So this is what good citizens will be reading while trying to swallow their Cheerios.' Jack sank onto the bed. 'Might as well get my eyeful of what she's written before I call the director and tell him what's going down.'

'You know how I feel about it, Jack. I don't think it's a bad thing. Our killer is moving at speed, and we need people to be on the lookout for danger. Yes, some are going to be scared. They will cancel their vacations and the campsites will get less traffic, but that's not on us. It'll be worse if someone dies and they say we should have warned them.'

'I hear you, Tom. Thanks for the heads-up. Catch you later.'

Jack laid on his back. Tom could be right. He hoped he wasn't. The last thing the National Park Service needed was for the FBI to be right. Playing second fiddle to them was bad enough already. Second fiddle? Who was he kidding? To the general public – and many law enforcers – ISB wasn't even in the same orchestra. The sharp light from the phone took some getting used to, and he blinked a few times as he scrolled. Kimberly Grant had reported all the basics he had given her, along with a vague profile of the suspected killer.

He frowned suddenly. The woman mentioned the word 'Dean' as the killer's codename. No one in the taskforce would ever have mentioned it outside of the group. Kim had been warned not to question any other special agents, and to direct all enquiries to him. As far as he knew, she had followed those instructions. His anger surged. She was forever sneaking around with an open mic, and must have overheard it. He thought they had an understanding. He had fed her enough to keep her belly lined, and yet she had still done this. Well, from now on, she would starve. From now on, all media would get the same story to run.

First, Jack spoke to the director and filled him in on progress to date. His boss kept the faith, and Jack was relieved he was trusted to do his job. They concluded their discussion by agreeing to have the media spokesperson hold a hastily arranged press conference.

Once dressed, he put on the TV news in the background and kept the volume at a non-intrusive level, wanting to hear it yet not be distracted by it. Kent Hilson was foremost on his mind. Ideally, he would have liked to seize Hilson's camera and examine the memory cards used since November, when the first murders occurred. Before Hilson had shut him down last night, he had planned on asking him for the camera. The amateur photographer was no idiot, and knew he was a suspect despite being told otherwise. Jack worried that the man might have been spooked enough to delete some of his photos. Still, many keen photographers, both amateurs and professionals, liked to upload photos online.

He found Hilson's Instagram page without difficulty. At least the man used his real name. Social media could be both a blessing and a nightmare. So many hours were lost online, searching for people who used different screen names for various sites.

Although Hilson modestly claimed to be an amateur, his nature photographs were sharp and interesting. He knew how to blur the background of an image while bringing the target of the shot into full focus, something Jack always had difficulty with.

Hundreds of images filled the man's pages. Most photographers proudly displayed the locations of their images as if it was a badge of honour, showing their followers they led busy, interesting lives and managed to fit in worldwide travel. Not Hilson. Jack scrolled through and frowned. Many of the images were taken in parks, yet few were identified by name, as if the photographer wished to avoid anyone knowing his location. Instead, he named the beautiful flowers, trees and rocks, demonstrating good knowledge of flora and fauna.

Hilson was married, but not one single photo of his better half appeared anywhere online. Jack considered himself a private person, but even so, a few family photos were online, placed there by Sophie and the kids over the years, showing family gatherings, some including the grandparents. Women were keener when it came to posting family photos. He would have to track down Mrs Hilson. Her husband had no rap sheet, and Jack wondered if somewhere along the line, the man had changed his surname.

Multitasking, he grabbed his phone and checked the main national news sites to see which of the different media houses had picked up Kim Grant's story. In the background, the perfectly groomed TV anchors chatted away, concerned only with traffic and weather. By 7am, though, the hosts had picked up the serial-killer story, and were excitedly promising that viewers would hear from distinguished guests in later broadcasts. It never ceased to surprise him how fast the media could wheel out people to tell law enforcement how to do their jobs. Anchors and their rented law professors and psychologists forcefully gave their thoughts on who the killer could be, and why he killed.

Jack smiled wryly as the TV hosts took commercial breaks to sell viewers RVs, camping tents and hiking gear. He hopped channels and caught an ex-cop mid-interview. The chevron floating at the bottom of the screen said the man had done vice and narcotics. No mention of homicide. Everybody with an opinion had been summoned, and Jack had no doubt this would continue throughout the day.

He squinted at one of Hilson's tree images and checked it against a crime scene photo of Cuyahoga Valley National Park in his home state. There were some similarities, but he could not be sure. The Cuyahoga park rangers, who worked the land every day, were more likely to identify their own landscapes from a single tree with ease. He would run it past them.

He turned off the computer and picked up his knapsack, which was made heavy by the larger tools he kept with him day and night. A flashlight and binoculars were the main culprits. He looked over at the TV as he fastened the strap on his knapsack. The male anchor accused the ISB of putting people at risk with their silence, as Tom had predicted they would. Worse still, the anchor accused the ISB of being amateur pinecone hunters, and demanded to know why the FBI was not in charge.

Jack's knuckles turned white as his grip on the strap intensified. He wanted to punch the TV. He managed to calm himself enough to turn it off instead. This accusation could well become a mantra, if the bodies continued to pile up. He would rather lose an arm than concede jurisdiction to the FBI, as good as they were, and he knew the director would now come under added pressure. This part of the job always had him torn, balancing the need to alert the public to potential danger with the need to progress the investigation without distractions.

While driving, he made a series of phone calls to check that the media team had the right phone numbers to issue to the public. His was one of four authorised numbers given out, and he knew all lines would soon be inundated with calls. Might as well get ready for the barrage of nonsense that would soon flow his way. Damn Kimberly Grant. Now the investigators would be tied up chasing countless false leads, wasting important time.

He popped a single Xanax pill and rubbed his temples. Today would be another long day. Like yesterday, and the day before that, and the day before that.

17

OLIVIA AND AMY sat on deckchairs outside their caravan in Palisades State Park, eating bacon and sausages for breakfast. Olivia's phone rang and she frowned as she answered it, annoyed that the caller had not rung Amy instead. She gestured towards her daughter and put the phone on speaker.

'Morning, Chris. Or should I say afternoon?'

'Where's Amy?' His voice was taut and clear.

'Right here beside me. What's the matter?'

'Hi, Dad!' shouted Amy.

'Have you seen the news, Olivia? You must have been at Hawkeye when that murder happened. Are you still staying there now? It's all over the news.'

'Oh . . . is it?' stuttered Olivia. 'Just a minute.'

She had not checked any news this morning. She'd rolled out of bed with an alcohol-induced headache and gone straight outdoors to grill sausages and toast slabs of bread.

Amy clicked feverishly on her phone and grimaced. She held up the screen to her mother and whispered, 'The ISB gave a press conference about the murders.'

'Olivia? Are you there?'

Olivia had no intention of discussing anything with her

ex-husband until she knew what was going on. 'Chris, Chris? Hello? Sorry, you're breaking up. If you can hear me, we already left Iowa. Amy will call you back.'

Olivia cut him off and brought her chair closer to her daughter. The two sat shoulder to shoulder, watching the recorded video.

'Play it again from the beginning,' said Olivia.

Olivia had expected to see Jack Tyler or one of the special agents she knew. The person on screen was unknown to her, and carried the title 'Media Relations Correspondent'.

'Turn it up a bit, Amy.'

The media correspondent confirmed that most of the report in Kimberly Grant's blog was accurate. Olivia's stomach tightened. So Kim had written her piece as threatened, and no doubt forced the lawmen's hands. The spokesman insisted the name Dean was purely an operational name, and not that of a suspect. Olivia now wished she had warned Jack Tyler, rather than have him wake up to this.

The spokesman provided limited and basic information. The composite sketch of the suspected killer appeared on a split screen while the spokesman encouraged people who may have seen someone resembling the suspect to contact law enforcement. Next, he listed the murder sites by name and Olivia grimaced. Hawkeye Point near Sibley, Iowa. Words that had undoubtedly drawn Chris Knightley's attention to the press conference. They also mentioned that yesterday's killing occurred in Palisades State Park, South Dakota.

Olivia's stomach contents did a jig. Amy had provided her father with details of the itinerary, and Palisades was not on it. If Amy told him they were at Palisades, he would be irate. Despite knowing his daughter was alive and well, he would demand they leave. He had accused Olivia before of being turned on by gruesome murders, and would know it was no coincidence she'd moved from one murder site to the other. Lies would have to be told to placate him. She would let Amy ring him back after they'd finished watching the news.

Specific telephone phone numbers appeared on screen. Olivia recognised Jack's number as one of them. She noted that the spokesman did not take any questions, merely delivered his spiel and disappeared, leaving the screen to fade to black, with only the phone numbers displayed as the recording stopped.

'I wouldn't exactly call that a press conference.' Olivia stood up and stretched in an effort to release the tension from her limbs. 'They didn't answer any of the reporters' questions. I guess it's just a press statement to stop people speculating.'

'That blogger woman posted the story with a big mugshot of herself. It's well photoshopped, though. She looks way prettier here than she did last night.'

'She was mad last night, and had been following us for miles. You'd have looked haggard too.'

Olivia had some sympathy for Kim. Finding interesting true-crime stories was a cut-throat business, and as the lady herself had said, there was always someone desperate to get the story out there first. She wondered if Jack shared her sympathy for Kim, or if he was mad about Kim's betrayal of trust. A thought crossed her mind.

'Amy, you've not been going through my notepad or my phone, have you?'

'What notepad?'

'If you'd said "no", I'd have felt better. You know what notepad.' Olivia sighed deeply. 'I never mentioned the name Dean to you, did I?'

'No.' Amy had the grace to look sheepish. 'Sorry about that, Mom. It just came out.'

Olivia saw no point in being angry with her, knowing the girl must be feeling left out. Back in London, she tried to share the more pleasant aspects of her cases with her daughter. They'd had a good laugh when it turned out that a husband was not taking off to Hastings every weekend to cheat, but was busy refurbishing a seaside holiday home he'd bought as a surprise twenty-fifth anniversary present.

Now Amy had reverted to doing exactly what she did at home. She'd searched her mother's private space for information, despite knowing it was wrong. Olivia had to find a balance: feeding her daughter enough information to make her feel included, while not over-sharing. If she disclosed too little information, the girl would feel ignored, and this holiday was meant to be the complete opposite of ignoring Amy.

Olivia stared at her daughter, looking for signs of distress or discomfort. This could all be too much for a teenager, even one as smart as Amy. Suddenly, Olivia felt weary of it all. She was doing motherhood all wrong.

'Amy, we came here for a holiday. This is not what you signed up for. We don't owe the ISB anything. If you want us to leave, we'll go. No questions asked. We'll just get out of here.'

'I'm not afraid, Mom. It's exciting . . . in a gory way. Trust me, I've seen a dead body close up now, I can handle anything.'

'Never mind what you think you can handle. It's my job to keep you safe.'

'I'm safe. They said the victims were all white males.' Amy held up her bare arms and twisted them. 'Brown female here. Not white, not male.'

Olivia could think of nothing to counter that statement. She bit her lip.

'Relax, Mom. Do what you have to do; you're good at it. You'd never forgive yourself if you just turned your back and didn't even try to help them catch him. Actually, I wouldn't forgive you either.'

Olivia and Amy shared a long hug. Olivia discreetly dabbed at a small tear that had crept into her eye.

'I'd better phone Dad,' said Amy.

'Text him.'

'Huh? You've changed your tune.'

'I know.' Olivia grimaced. 'Be careful what you tell him. Say we left Hawkeye and are on the road. Tell him the signal is bad and you'll phone tomorrow.'

As Amy texted her father, Olivia cleared up their breakfast things, her mind on the press statement. She tried to think positive. The public had a photofit image and a physical description of the suspected killer. They knew the parks where he had struck between November and August, and the names of all identified victims.

The media spokesman had withheld some things. No mention had been made of where on the bodies the victims were stabbed, nor of the Furlowe boot prints. It made sense that no member of the taskforce appeared on screen. Dean could be watching, and no one knew whether he had spotted any of the agents at the crime scenes. Even if he had, there was no point giving him a close-up so that he could easily identify them while they worked to gather evidence.

Should she call Jack Tyler or wait for him to call her? A conversation was needed, for sure. Having given plenty of thought to the seven dead men, instinct told her that other than body type, something else had drawn Dean's attention to them. So far, that something eluded her.

And then there was Kent Hilson. She wanted to share her thoughts on him. Her initial feeling was that his two phones and two wallets suggested he was juggling life between a wife and a secret mistress living in different states. It would go some way to explaining why he was so unsure which states he was in at different times. And perhaps he had to keep removing his wedding ring, and thought it safer to just hang it around his neck.

Another thought did linger and refuse to budge. Hilson could indeed be a killer. It could be that his absent wife was missing and no one had realised it yet. The invisible Mrs Hilson could already be a dead woman.

18

OLIVIA WAS SITTING on the grass at the Palisades camp-site, reading through her case notes, when a sound to which she had become accustomed caught her ear. Distant at first, the sirens gradually increased in tempo, until a police cruiser with flashing lights pulled up close by. Two uniformed officers jumped out and, with their arms spread wide, ordered the visitors to leave the immediate area.

'What's this now?' said Amy.

'No idea.' Olivia frowned. 'Come on, we have to move back with the others.'

They followed the crowd away from the campervans and trailers, towards the trees, abandoning deckchairs and half-finished plates of food to the birds and insects.

Olivia caught sight of two young men who were being forced out of their campervan by an officer who was trying to clear the area. One of the youth's swore at the officer, while the other made a rude gesture with his finger. Surprise turned to anger as she recognised them as the pair Jack had chased away from Amy. The blond boy stared straight at Amy, winked and puckered his lips. Amy smiled and, with her hand lowered to waist level, gave a short wave of acknowledgement. Olivia caught the covert move and glared at her daughter.

'You knew those two were staying here, didn't you?'

'So? They have a right to stay, haven't they? Paid for a trailer space like everybody else.'

The sullen tone annoyed Olivia, and she mentally counted to five. 'Just stay away from them. I mean it, Amy. They're not your crowd.'

'They're not your crowd, you mean,' said Amy evenly. 'Some of us prefer to hang out with live people rather than spend time with dead ones.'

'There must be better company around here?'

'Maybe, but not as cute.' Amy rolled her eyes. 'Chill, Mom, I haven't given them my phone number. Yet.'

Olivia silently cursed herself. She had removed her daughter from the company of innocent social media influencers at one campsite and placed her in the arms of lewd potheads at another.

Just then, two more vehicles raced into the space. As the first Jeep passed, Olivia caught a glimpse of Special Agents Perez and Morelli. The dark sedan behind contained Jack Tyler and Tom Walsh. Their vehicles screeched to a halt and the agents climbed out.

'Festive around here, innit?' said Amy.

'Quite,' murmured Olivia.

The four agents all wore bulletproof vests. They headed to the back of the campsite, where a single log cabin was located in isolation on a low ridge, partially camouflaged beyond the trees. Until now Olivia had not noticed the cabin. The building was a sturdy looking single-storey structure. On one side of the solid door was a large casement window, closed.

Tom approached the front door while Jack, armed with a battering ram, followed immediately behind him.

Morelli took up position at the side of the building. Gun drawn, Perez dipped low and crept around to the rear of the cabin.

Tom shouted, 'Ralph Simmons. This is the FBI. Come out quietly.'

Amy squeezed Olivia's hand and whispered, 'That's not the man from last night.'

'No, never heard of this one.'

Olivia was bewildered by this turn of events. Having not heard from Jack, she had assumed he was being inundated with phone calls, not preparing to raid a log cabin right there in Palisades State Park. Around her, her fellow visitors muttered to each other, but no one knew what was going on. Olivia had not yet made friends with anyone, as there was a greater distance between each vehicle here, and these campers seemed to be more introverted types. They smiled and nodded to one another, but no one had seemed interested in conversation – until now. It took the arrival of the police to get them gathered in clusters, excitedly talking to strangers.

A female voice shouted, 'What's he done, officer?'

'Don't come any closer, ma'am.' Raising his voice, the officer addressed the entire crowd. 'Stay behind the trees. For your own safety, keep back and stay low.'

'I guess they think they've identified the killer.' Olivia pulled Amy further behind the broad trunk of a tree. 'Stay down. Just because he has a taste for knives, doesn't mean he hasn't got a gun.'

'Wow! This is like a siege,' said Amy.

'Ralph, let's talk,' shouted Tom. 'Come out quietly with your hands in the air.'

'I'm not coming out! Get away from me!'

'Well, at least they know he's definitely in there,' whispered Olivia.

'Come on out, Ralph!' shouted Jack. 'This won't do you any good.'

'Leave me alone, dirty pigs!'

Tom signalled to Jack. Using the battering ram, Jack hit the door with full force. It held strong. A loud shot echoed. A flash of light came from inside the cabin, simultaneous to the sound of glass shattering from a rear window. The agents instantly crouched and backed away from the door, firearms raised. Morelli, weapon in hand, ran in the direction Perez had taken.

Some individuals in the crowd screamed and abandoned their positions, preferring to flee further into the park. Olivia and Amy stayed put behind the tree. The police officers drew their weapons and took shelter behind their vehicle, watching the cabin.

Another shot came from the rear of the cabin and indistinct raised voices filled the air. Olivia couldn't hear the words. Jack retrieved the battering ram and attacked the door again. It splintered and flew back off the hinges.

More raised voices as Jack and Tom entered. For a moment, the place was eerily silent. Olivia's heart beat a rapid tattoo in her chest. After what seemed like an hour, but could have been no more than five minutes, Perez and Morelli emerged past the dangling front door, with a handcuffed man sandwiched between them. A white-haired man, who struggled, screamed and cursed as blood seeped from a shoulder wound.

'You shot me! You dirty pigs! You shot me!'

'You shot at my partner.' Morelli pushed him into the back of the Jeep and climbed in beside him. 'Lucky she didn't blast your head off.'

'I need a doctor. Get me a doctor, now!'

'Quit whining.' Perez rubbed her upper arm. 'I'm the one who took a fall. My shoulder's in worse condition than yours.'

The car doors slammed and they drove off with their combative suspect.

'Amy, stay here and don't move.' Olivia broke cover and ran towards the cabin, despite angry protests from the police officers, who had now holstered their weapons.

She entered to find that the back door was also swinging off its hinges, and she assumed Morelli had kicked it in. The cabin was a decent size, with a sofa bed, a table and two chairs, a fridge, a sink and a tiny countertop with a microwave. The rear window was shattered and glass lined the wooden floor. No bullet had done that. Simmons must have smashed it out to shoot at Perez.

'Jack, what's going on?' she asked breathlessly.

A police officer was close on Olivia's heels. 'Ma'am, did you not hear . . .'

Jack waved him off with a gloved hand. 'It's alright, officer, stand down. She's with us.'

'Who is Ralph Simmons?' asked Olivia.

'That's what we want to know,' said Jack.

Tom picked up a gun from the floor, emptied the clip and bagged it. 'A man not afraid to shoot, it appears.'

'We had a tip-off from a witness who took down the plate of a strange man he talked to earlier at the creek.' Jack gazed around the spacious interior. 'Said the man told him he'd drunk beer with Rick at Hawkeye same night he died, and said he might have killed him.'

'Simmons said he *might* have killed Rick?'

'You'd think he'd know whether he did or not. The only prints we got off the beer bottles were Rick's, but we figured whoever killed him wore gloves.' Jack gave the sink area a quick once-over. There was no cutlery. 'Ralph Simmons' vehicle is registered in Harrisburg.' At the blank look on her face he added, 'Harrisburg, Pennsylvania.'

'Where the first murders occurred.' Olivia gazed around the cabin.

'Did you recognise Simmons?' asked Tom.

Olivia shook her head. 'No, never seen him before.'

She pushed her hands deep into her shorts pockets to avoid touching anything. Clothes were piled on a chair: T-shirts, vests, shorts, jeans. On the table was a photo of Simmons and two young teenagers who resembled him.

'Got his ID.' Tom waved the card at Jack. 'Wallet has a couple hundred bucks in it, credit cards.'

Jack picked up a pair of training shoes and looked at the bottom. 'Size ten, and not Furlowe. We'll take a look in his car, see what he's got in there.'

Tom examined the label on a bottle of pills. 'Prescription medication. Haloperidol.'

'I really want to hear what our man has to say,' said Jack. 'A confession would be great.'

'I guess you won't get to talk to him for a while, since he'll be in hospital?' said Olivia.

'Shoulder graze.' Jack spoke firmly. 'Medics will stick tape on him. Whether he lawyers up or not, we're talking to him today.'

'Can I sit in on the interview?' asked Olivia.

'Tom and I will take this one,' said Jack. 'You can watch from behind the glass. The speakers will be on. He won't know anyone's there.'

As they were about to leave the lodge, a nervous young man, one of the campsite clerks, approached the doorway and surveyed the damage in awe. 'Holy Moly!'

'Do not go inside, sir,' said Jack.

'Who's gonna pay for those busted windows and doors?' asked the clerk.

'Geico? Allstate?' Jack shrugged and patted his arm. 'The doors can still be closed. Close them. Do not let anyone in until I say so. No cleaning lady, no visitors.'

'I get it.'

'Good man. Let's go see what he's got in his car.'

*

At the FBI field office, Olivia was seated behind the glass wall of a room adjoining the interview room. Perez sat perched on a table, leaving a considerable distance between them, which Olivia believed to be calculated. The lady agent was definitely not the forgiving sort. Morelli stood near Perez with one elbow resting on top of a filing cabinet and chewed his toothpick while staring at the interviewee.

In the interview room, in front of Jack and Tom, sat a wounded and miserable-looking Ralph Simmons. His solemn face represented a marked change in disposition from an hour ago, when Olivia had witnessed him screaming and cursing. A quick check told Olivia that the bottle of Haloperidol in front of him was a drug to treat schizophrenia.

'What can you tell us about the murder of Daniel Bailey?' asked Jack.

'Who, the poor man who got stabbed to death yesterday?'

'That's him.'

'I didn't do it.' Simmons tentatively massaged his bandaged shoulder. 'You got some painkillers?'

'You've already had painkillers,' said Jack. 'Four hours between doses. You've got a way to go.'

'Ralph, the quicker you tell us what we need to know, the quicker you'll get to go relax and nurse your wounds,' said Tom.

'I told you, I don't know nothing about the dead man.'

'What about Rick Seagal at Hawkeye?' said Jack. 'Did he make you angry? That why you killed him?'

The man flushed. 'That's why you don't joke with strangers.'

'What part of Rick's death was funny?' asked Jack.

'I didn't mean that. I mean what I said to the guy this morning. I was just shooting my mouth off. I didn't drink no beer with no one at Hawkeye.'

'What beers do you like, Ralph?' asked Tom.

The suspect shrugged. 'Bud mainly, or Coors.'

Olivia caught a breath. One of the empty bottles on Rick's countertop had been a Bud. She noted Jack and Tom exchanging glances.

'You told someone you killed Rick,' said Tom, patiently. 'Why would you do that?'

'I just said I might have killed him. But I didn't do it. I spent the day looking around the sights at Hawkeye and left around eight in the evening.'

'And returned later in the night?' asked Jack.

'Oh, man!' The suspect shook his head from side to side and slapped his own face hard. 'Shut up, shut up, shut up.'

'Don't do that, Ralph,' said Tom. 'You'll hurt yourself, and we don't want that to happen.'

'This is so wrong. My woman always tells me to stop lying. I should've listened to her. It's either her voice I hear or the voices.' Simmons stared earnestly at Tom. 'I was just showing off, pretending I'd seen Rick Seagal. I didn't go nowhere near the area where the RVs are parked. I swear. I was on the opposite side, by the mosaic.'

'I hope you've got a good alibi for that night,' said Jack. 'Your woman won't cut it.'

'But she is my alibi. Look, I live in Cloverdale, about seven miles from Sibley. I'm sure I was at home, drinking beers with her. We were both drunk by midnight and passed out. When I woke up it was around ten in the morning.'

'So your passed-out woman won't know if you left the house or not, will she?' said Jack. 'Not much of an alibi, is it?'

Behind Olivia, Perez said quietly, 'So which of us gets the pleasure of interviewing his old lady? She sounds a peach.'

'I volunteer you,' said Morelli.

'Why not tell us the truth, Ralph?' said Tom. 'It must be a burden on you. Let it all out.'

The man fell silent for a moment. Then he said, 'I didn't kill none of those men you mentioned.'

As Olivia stared at him, she wondered if this was all an act, and she was actually looking at a clever killer. The agents had not found any bloody clothes, knife or boots in his vehicle, although he could have buried them deep anywhere in the vast parklands. They had no evidence other than his confession to a stranger, which was of little use if he insisted he was muddled and it was all a mistake.

'What about the other dead men?' asked Jack.

'You really want to pin all them murders on me?' Simmons's worried eyes flicked between Jack and Tom. 'I've seen the news. You think I been travelling all over the country since November, killing people? What reason I got to hurt nobody?'

'You fired a shot that could have hurt one of my agents,' said Jack.

'I got scared,' said Simmons. 'Wasn't trying to kill nobody. When I get scared, voices start telling me that people are coming to get me. Don't even get to see my grandchildren anymore because of the voices. When you bawled out my name like that, I thought, that's it. They're coming for me. I got to fight back.'

Behind the glass, Perez said, 'He's lucky *my* voices told me to aim away from the head.'

Tom tapped his pen on the desk. 'Ralph, did the voices send you to Hawkeye?'

'No. It's the last place I took my grandkids, last summer.' Simmons's voice cracked and he sobbed. 'We had great fun there. They liked the little playground, and we had a picnic. Can't believe summer's here again already. The sun's shining, and I can't even see them, let alone take them nowhere for the day.'

'Do you do bad things when you don't take your meds?' Tom tapped the bottle of pills. 'The Haloperidol is for the voices, isn't it?'

'Yes, I take my meds every day, like I'm supposed to. Well, most days. The voices tell me all kinds of things, but they've never told me to kill nobody.' He stared at Tom. 'My daughter thinks the voices told me to slap her young'un, but it wasn't no voices. He was acting up, and I set him straight like she should a done if she was a good mama.'

Olivia remembered the photograph in the cabin, of Simmons and what she now knew were his estranged family members, the grandchildren he missed. Was he being clever? The voices and the broken family issues could all be a good cover.

'What do you do for a living?' asked Jack.

'Retired last year. I've had enough of working for the man,' said Simmons. 'Always planned to retire by fifty-five, and I did.'

'Retired from what?' asked Jack. 'Adviser to the president? NASA scientist?

'No need to get like that, Mr Special Agent. I used to drive for Greyhound. Drove those buses from one end of the country to the other in my day. Must have covered a million miles.' His gaze drifted, caught up in nostalgia. 'Say what you like about them, but they got a good pension.'

Tom looked down at Simmons's feet. 'Where are the boots you usually wear?'

'Boots? What boots? I'm always in my sneakers.'

'So, if we wanted to search your home in Cloverdale, you'd have no objection?' asked Tom.

'Well, I wouldn't like it, but no, I wouldn't object. Hell, I'll even give you the keys.' Simmons sat back and his voice became more forceful. 'You searched my cabin, found nothing. Searched my truck, found nothing. You know what you're gonna find in Cloverdale? Nothing.'

'Got a car from Harrisburg, I see. Got a house in Harrisburg?' asked Jack.

'My son lives in Harrisburg. He got a good deal for me at the car dealership. I got no house there.' Simmons pushed back his chair in frustration. 'Haven't even left Iowa since I retired last year. Can't believe I come to South Dakota and somebody gets murdered.'

Olivia watched as they plied Simmons with questions and he continued to deny involvement in any murders. After about two hours, Jack and Tom walked out. Simmons remained seated, his head bowed as if exhausted.

A minute later, the door opened. Immediately, Olivia stood up to face the special agents and waited for their report.

'You buying anything he's selling?' asked Morelli.

'Hard to be sure,' said Jack, his face a picture of frustration.

Tom sat on the edge of the desk beside Perez. 'I've had many a suspect claim to hear voices, say their judgement was impaired through no fault of their own. I'm not feeling him for murder, though.'

'Are you letting him go?' asked Olivia.

'We're not setting him loose. He can be a guest of the sheriff.' Jack stared at the suspect through the window. 'He probably knows he messed up badly, shooting at us, and he's going to rely on the medication to get him off that charge.'

'I feel sympathy for the wife already married to that sad sack,' said Perez. 'By the way, did you locate Kent Hilson's wife?'

'Still looking.' Jack scowled as he watched the schizophrenic. 'If Simmons is our man, I don't want to get tunnel vision going after Hilson.'

'We've got Hilson under surveillance,' said Morelli. 'If he runs, we'll have a tail on him.'

Olivia gazed at Simmons, who now sat back in the chair, staring at the wall. 'Both Simmons and Hilson have some features that resemble the photofit — sorry, the composite — but neither man really looks like the other.'

'Yes, it's always an issue,' said Tom. 'Sometimes you can find a dozen suspects who match elements of the composite image in one way or another. And in the end, you catch a killer who bears little resemblance to the image you put together.'

The agents began an urgent conversation about the two main suspects, each talking over the other. Olivia took a step back and watched them. They were a pretty united team with a whole lot of hard work to do, running from state to state trying to identify a serial killer before he claimed another victim. Her thoughts were interrupted by Jack's next words.

'Do not speak to Kimberly Grant. If you see her lurking anywhere with that damn microphone, direct her to the media team.'

'I'm really sorry about Kim and her exclusive,' said Olivia. 'I tried to stop her.'

'Wait a minute. You know her?' asked Jack.

'Well, sort of. I met her once. Actually, twice, if you include last night.'

Olivia felt all four pairs of eyes on her, and none were kind. Even Tom had a deep frown on his tanned brow. She wished she had stayed quiet and kept her apologies to herself.

'So, that's where she got the name Dean from.' The frostiness in Jack's tone was apparent. 'You talked to her.'

Olivia was not about to throw Amy under any bus, neither Greyhound nor Arriva London. In any event, she was the one at fault for not protecting the confidential information. She knew her daughter was prone to digging in places where she had no business to be.

At that very moment, Amy was with Liz, the female agent. She had wanted to stay behind at Palisades, and Olivia had a pretty good idea why. Desperate to keep her daughter away from her new male admirers, Olivia had demanded that Amy accompany her to the FBI office. She would never let these agents give the girl a ticking-off or make any disparaging comments in her presence.

'Sorry. It sort of slipped out. I know it shouldn't have.'

'And there I was thinking no one on the team would have mentioned it,' said Jack tersely.

Olivia was crushed at this terrible start to her new role. 'It won't happen again, I swear.'

'Glad to hear it.' Jack's sarcastic tone burned her ears.

Olivia thought about the things she had wanted to discuss with Jack when she got up that morning. Her ideas on Kent Hilson, her thoughts on the killer's state-hopping and skipping of Indiana. She had planned to scrutinise the death walls again in an effort to identify similarities between the victims. Now was not a good time.

'Time for me to get out of the way,' she said.

Without waiting for Jack's response, she headed down the corridor, her skin singed from embarrassment. No doubt they would discuss her, a stranger from a strange land who had let them down. Maybe they'd vote for her to be booted off the taskforce.

In the corridor ahead were Amy and Liz. Olivia inhaled deeply and fixed a broad smile, hoping her astute daughter would not see the pain in her eyes.

19

THAT AFTERNOON, AS they walked through Palisades State Park, Olivia tried to admire the beauty of the natural environment. The colourful trees and fragrant flowers swaying in the gentle summer breeze did little to soothe her tortured nerves. Everybody she knew was annoyed with her: the taskforce, the blogger, her boss, her ex-husband.

'You're miles away, Mom.' Amy prodded her arm as they walked along a wide trail. 'And you're picking at your hair.'

Olivia lowered her right hand from behind her ear. It had taken long enough to regrow that thinned spot, caused by her nervous actions over the years. At least Amy was not still annoyed with her, which was a blessing under the circumstances.

'Sorry, what did you say, love?'

'I said we should go down where the rock climbers are. I wouldn't mind having a go at it.'

Although Olivia had taken out travel insurance, she did not fancy the idea of spending any time in the accident and emergency ward of a hospital. Besides, she knew from experience in her previous job that insurers would find any ridiculous excuse to decline a claim, and American hospital bills were notoriously exorbitant.

'You sure you don't want to do something more relaxing?' she asked hopefully.

'I'll be relaxed,' Amy replied with confidence. 'Anyhow, they have harnesses, special boots and other gear. You did say no matter what happened, we were going to have a good holiday. Rock climbing sounds good to me.'

Olivia inhaled fresh, clean air. If only the exhaled air could take with it her clouded thoughts. She fashioned a big smile. 'You're right.'

Anything to keep Amy away from those predatory young men. Confronting them was out of the question. If they were ignorant enough to taunt cops, they would not hesitate to curse her, and she had no intention of engaging in a slanging match with kids. She had thought about seeking Jack's help in getting them evicted from the park, but decided such a move might antagonise her daughter and cause a major rift.

'We'll go do whatever you wish, madam.'

They linked arms and walked through the canopy of broadleafed trees, down a well-trodden path full of tourists and locals. Despite trying to concentrate on the remarkable scenery, Olivia found herself studying the face of every man that passed by who looked like he could be over fifty.

'Mom, do you think either Simmons or Hilson could have done the murders?'

Olivia chewed her bottom lip. So much for trying to put the serial killer out of her mind. 'For the sake of a successful end to the case, I sincerely hope so.'

'But did you get a vibe from either of them?'

'I try to ignore "vibes", as you put it. It's a bad idea to label people before you've checked their alibis. If someone is standing over a body with a dripping knife, then it's a bit more suspect.'

'Hmm, and even then, they could have just stumbled across the body and pulled the knife out?'

'Correct. That's exactly the way you should be thinking.'

Olivia did not disclose that she always took a view on whether or not an interviewee was lying at every interview. Searching for signs of deception was the most natural thing to do, even though getting it badly wrong was a possibility, as the most devious people could adopt an innocent persona.

Something was definitely off with Kent Hilson, whose mask of smooth politeness was covering a dark secret, possibly hiding a violent streak. Instinct told her that Ralph Simmons was more likely to be a disturbed man who'd bragged about something he didn't do than a murderer.

'You know, I think I could be an interviewer, and investigate just like you. Liz said she's been with the FBI three years, and they always need more people in law enforcement.'

'I'm sure they do.'

'I've got a good idea of the basics of your case. You should fill me in on the details.'

Olivia raised her eyebrows. 'Nice try. The answer's still no.'

'I used to think I'd freak out around dead bodies, but I didn't feel any real shock when I saw Rick. I dunno, I think I could actually work crime scenes, be a forensic analyst or a coroner.'

'There's a big leap between being an investigator and being a coroner. The coroner can't just look at the dead from afar and comment. They have to cut open the bodies and study the insides. Every day, they're wrist-deep in blood and entrails. You think that's you?'

Amy grimaced. 'Maybe not, but I can look for clues if you let me know everything you've got so far. I've been doing research on that Kent Hilson. He's got a load of nature photos online from exhibitions. Tell me more about Ralph Simmons. I'll look him up, too.'

Olivia sighed. She had exposed her daughter to this. If she had stayed in her tiny cubicle in the Docklands working accident cases, Amy would never have been around crime scenes and murder victims. Watching her mother being courted by the agents had encouraged thoughts that this could be an exciting occupation. Allowing her to survey the FBI field office with a female agent was also bound to have driven her thoughts towards law enforcement as a career.

Still, giving Amy something interesting to focus on would make her less inclined to go mixing with undesirables. She stared at her daughter's earnest face, cute freckles standing out prominently in the blazing sun, and hoped that in the weeks ahead she did not come to regret the choice she was about to make.

'I think they're missing something in Indiana. They reckon the killer skipped that one state while heading west, but I can't see why. Pennsylvania, Ohio, ignored Indiana, Illinois, Iowa and now South Dakota. What do you think?'

'Maybe it was too cold and he didn't fancy going to parks?'

'November and February are pretty cold months in Pennsylvania and Ohio, and that didn't stop him.'

'Or he could have been sick? Maybe he was following a particular timetable and when he eventually recovered, he'd run out of time and moved on to Illinois?'

'That's a possibility, I suppose,' said Olivia.

'Maybe he checked out a park in Indiana and just didn't see anyone he fancied knocking off there?'

'He'd have had a wide choice, I'm sure. We know he goes after well-built men, and there must be plenty of those in Indiana.' Olivia frowned. 'I'm thinking something could have scared him off, like the chosen victim spotted the knife and the killer ran? Or they had a fight and he broke free and escaped?'

Amy nodded. 'I could see that.'

'Park rangers must keep records of any altercations that happen on their patch. Like an accident book? The ISB agents must have enough clout to get their hands on those records.'

'Sounds like a good idea. You going to call them?'

Olivia's heart sank. 'I think I'll give them a wide berth for now. They're busy chasing leads, and I know they're not keen on any distractions at the moment.'

Amy scrutinised her mother's face. 'Have they been horrible to you, Mom?'

'No, of course not, love. Everybody is a bit on edge at the moment.' Olivia squeezed her daughter's arm. 'I'll try them later on.'

They approached the rock-climbing area and joined a short queue of people waiting outside the hire shop.

Olivia gazed up in awe. 'Look at that sheer rock face. That girl is nearly at the top.'

'I can't wait,' said Amy, with excitement.

They rented climbing equipment and discussed safety matters with the instructor. Olivia had not planned on climbing the rock face, but Amy insisted that she live a little. Now she found herself scaling a cliff in a hard hat and boots, attached to a rope and harness. She chose one of the less-imposing cliffs, rather than the tall one on which Amy was focused. As Olivia had pointed out to her daughter, she was out of her comfort zone, not out of her mind.

Olivia enjoyed the challenging session. Dangling many metres off the ground and relying only on a piece of rope was nerve-racking yet exhilarating. Observing the extensive parklands from on high was a beautiful moment to remember. She began her descent while Amy was still ascending, determined to touch the jutting ridge at the top. Close to the ground, Olivia broke a fingernail, deep in the nail bed. The pain was off-putting. As she stood nursing her forefinger, a man approached unnoticed.

'You okay there?'

'Yes, thanks,' said Olivia. 'Bound to get scratches and scrapes around here.'

'Wish I could climb myself,' he said. 'Bad knees. Make sure you get in all the fun physical activities before you get to my age.'

From a quick glance, Olivia determined he was not so ancient. Dark brown hair, possibly dyed. A few flecks of grey; clean shaven.

'I will,' she said, her attention on her throbbing finger. 'My daughter will make sure of it.'

'Welcome to America.'

'Thank you.'

He nodded at her and sauntered away.

'Wow, Mom, that was great!' said Amy, as soon as she got down to earth. 'I want to do it again.'

'You go on up. I need to get my breath.'

'Okay, you majestic cliff. Here I come, quicker this time.'

As Amy started her ascent once more, Olivia's phone rang. She stared at it long and hard, wondering whether she could ignore the caller. She had put off this conversation for too long. The man deserved an explanation, and there was no point in delaying the inevitable. She cleared her throat and walked a few paces away from the crowd of rock climbers, all the time watching Amy scale the cliff.

'Hello, Bill. How are you?' Her voice was as cheerful as she could make it.

'Hello, Olivia.'

'Sorry I couldn't get back to you,' she lied. 'Really bad reception where I am, and the internet's acting up too.'

'Hope you're enjoying the holiday. You read my email?'

Olivia could tell from his tone that he had little interest in her holiday and was focused strictly on work.

'I did. I typed a response, but the connection was coming and going so it didn't send.' She recited her practised words. 'I'll sort out the notes for those two files you mentioned as soon as I get back.'

'Olivia, the stalking case and the forgery case can wait. I can bluff my way around those.' Exasperation echoed through the ear piece. 'There's another matter I have a big problem with.'

Olivia let the silence take over. She had obviously slipped up with something else that he hadn't put in writing. Robbed of an opportunity to prepare a calming answer in advance, she pursed her lips and waited.

'Mrs Dupree said you failed to send the file on her husband's hidden assets to her lawyer on time. Big mistake. Now there's going to be a preliminary hearing to decide whether to allow the evidence in.'

Olivia swallowed. She had sent the file by courier when she realised the deadline was upon them. Copies of the file were sent to both sets of lawyers, and one to the court. One day late.

'It's not like the extra day prejudiced the husband at all, Bill.' Olivia did her best to sound upbeat. 'Courts tend to be more lenient about that sort of thing when the rich husband is avoiding paying the non-working spouse. We'll keep our fingers crossed it gets in.'

'Keep our fingers crossed? This extra hearing costs money, and she's insisting that we pay it, regardless of the outcome. There is no winning for us in this situation, Olivia. It's a question of how bad it can get.'

'I'm really sorry, Bill.'

'We'll know in the next day or so what the position is. A couple thousand for the hearing is painful, but we'll survive it. If the court excludes the new evidence, Mrs Dupree will sue us. And you know her lawyer is very good, because you recommended him. Our insurance will never cover all of what they'll be after.'

'I thought I'd sent it off weeks ago, to be honest.' Olivia's stomach churned. 'Even had a reminder in my diary. I did have a lot going on, but I don't know how I overlooked it.'

'I don't know how either.'

She could picture him, pink-faced with anger, rubbing a vein in his throbbing temple while his right eye twitched.

'You used to be so on the ball, Olivia. You've dropped it more times this year than you have in the past four years. I know the divorce was a bit messy, but it's over now.'

'How dare you bring that up?'

'I hate to say this to you, but you've got to shape up. I really hope you rest and clear your head on this holiday, because you need to decide whether to be a private investigator or find another position you can be comfortable in.'

'After all I've done for you, Bill? You want to get personal? I've been there for you from day one. I've covered for you on numerous occasions. I lied to your wife when I knew you weren't where you said you were . . .'

'Olivia, I—'

'You've made mistakes, too, and we've got past it. So I make a few mistakes and you're ready to push me out, just like that? I really hope you find your conscience. You need to go search for it.'

Olivia pressed the red key, dismissing Bill Tweedy. Her chest heaved and fell. She realised belatedly that curious eyes were on her; her voice had been raised.

She tucked away her phone, and fixed a rictus smile to her face in case Amy looked down at her. Thoughts of having to leave Dynamic Investigations occupied her mind. She could start her own business; she had plenty of experience. It would be fine on her own, maybe better with no boss around to manage her. Regardless of what Bill thought, she would make a great success of it, too. Hell, if she was not good at her job, Special Agent Jack Tyler would not have sought her help tracking a serial killer.

Olivia winced at the thought of Jack's grim face. She had failed him too. Nothing was going right, but crawling away in shame, abandoning the taskforce, was not an option. She would have to find the strength to get through this niggling sense of worthlessness, and put her all into getting a result in this murder case.

Amy, shiny-faced and grinning, came to her side. 'Whew! I'm going to need a strong shower after all that, Mom.'

Olivia hugged her daughter's shoulders and buried her chin in her soft hair.

'Me too, love.'

20

JACK TYLER HAD driven away from the FBI field office shortly after Olivia left. He preferred not to spend too much time at the borrowed facilities, where brash agents joked about ISB hunting lost pets, overstayers and pickpockets. Besides, he worked more effectively in his own space, which in winter was normally inside the Jeep, and in summer any remote outdoor spot where he would not be disturbed.

He found a quiet place along the banks of the Big Sioux River, planted himself on a smooth log under the cool shade of a low-hanging tree, and propped up his back with his knapsack. Amidst the calming sound of rushing water, he made phone call after phone call. So many tips from people eager to identify one man, as well as from those who just wanted attention. Inquisitive ants marched up his arm, along his pen and onto his notepad as he wrote. As long as they didn't sneak a bite, he was cool with them.

A handful of callers confessed to being the murderer, but had no details to offer and could not describe the murder weapon. Sifting through them had taken up a good portion of his afternoon, and before he knew it the sun was rapidly heading west.

He had wanted to go and see Mrs Simmons personally, to

drive to Cloverdale and scope out the house, but he was not ready for another face-to-face and badly needed some time to himself. Instead, the task was added to Morelli's already significant workload, which the stoic team player took with good grace.

Jack flicked through Ralph Simmons's interview notes and circled the name of his doctor. The address of the doctor's clinic was easy to find. Another man to add to the list of people to visit tomorrow. Jack knew little about schizophrenia, or the effects of the prescribed medication, and needed input from an expert.

As he drank cold water from a flask, he wondered if Simmons had indeed been banned from seeing his grandchildren. Jack's mind drifted to his own family then. Maybe if one of the kids had produced a grandchild, Sophie would not have ended things. They would still be together, bouncing the baby on their knees and indulgently comparing the infant's behaviour to the parent's behaviour at that age. Still, it was far from too late. Ryan and Holly were still young and had plenty of time to have kids if they chose to.

He hadn't spoken to either of them in a while. His son was working in tech in San Francisco. He was a quiet man who could be counted on to remember Father's Day and birthdays. Ryan had not been raised to be the hugging sort. If Ryan had called him, it would have been odd. They mainly talked about sports, as Jack understood little about the intricacies of software, and Ryan was not interested in what he termed 'murder business'.

Holly was off dancing on Broadway, and summer was a big time for her. She would post things on her social media pages, and sometimes he would leave a two-word comment below. She would always hit the like button.

The children visited as infrequently as tornadoes, even before the separation. Occasional short phone calls had taken place, but no one had come to see how he was doing, and he could spare no time to go and see either of them.

Thanksgiving was three months away. It was unlikely they would all meet up in Cincinnati for Thanksgiving this year. This would be the first time ever that the four had not spent the special evening together at home. He remembered last year, when they were sitting around the table and he had taken a work call. The disappointed faces that had stared back at him as he'd grabbed his coat, made his excuses and left was something that still haunted him. The lead had come to nothing. It was an evening he could never get back. What should have been a treasured memory of a great family day brought only regret.

Guilt coursed through his veins. His whole life consisted of making time for every family except his own. He placed a small stone on his notepad to stop the light breeze from lifting the pages.

On a whim, he phoned Holly, and could not hide the delight from his voice when she picked up. He knew his daughter was not keen on murder business either, and so he kept the conversation on her dance work, lauding her for getting great reviews.

He agreed with her when she told him he must eat proper meals, and decided not to confess that he'd lasted the whole day so far on a couple of energy bars. Yes, he would get room service this evening, he promised, knowing he would be too tired to order anything, never mind eat it.

Holly said her mother had called and was doing well, and would be starting a new job next month. That was news to him. He asked her to pass on his good wishes, and left it at that. He was sure the mother and daughter discussed him and the relationship, but they were women and probably had a different take on things. It was easier for him to talk about it with the happily married Tom, who had somehow got a grip on work–life balance.

Glad that he'd made the call, Jack hung up, his spirits lifted somewhat. Straight away, though, his thoughts returned to the murder case. Kent Hilson was another person in the headlights.

A deep frown set in his brow. Olivia Knightley had not yet shared her thoughts on Hilson, and he wanted to know what she'd gleaned after spending hours in close proximity to him in the Alley 7 bar. Olivia was supposed to be an asset, a bright lady with a keen mind. He still had confidence that she could show them her worth, but now he had a problem. There were rumblings within the team about her. The rumblings had always been there, but Perez and Morelli in particular were growing more vocal. Tom still had his back, as usual, but even Tom reminded him of his original fear that information could get leaked from a private investigator about whom they knew little.

Jack skimmed a stone across the dark green waters and watched the ripple effect. While it was true Operation Dean was being hamstrung by excessive phone calls, the mission itself had not been thrown off course. Olivia's mistake was one they could get over, and there was no cause to get heavy with her. No point canning the woman when he needed more people on the ground, not fewer. He regretted having been so abrupt with her, and knew the best thing to do was pick up the phone and talk it through. Failure to hash out small problems always led to bigger problems: a harsh lesson he'd learned at his own cost.

Despite this, he stubbornly ignored the phone and pulled out his notes on Kent Hilson. Maybe it was better to maintain silence, give Olivia time to calm down, allow her some space for the evening. He had no idea whether she was the emotional type, prone to crying and histrionics, although she seemed strong-willed and confident. Strangely, he found himself wanting to hear her voice, and it wasn't just because he liked her accent. Something about her interested him beyond her unconventional observations and insights. Maybe she would call him before morning.

21

WHEN OLIVIA WOKE up, it was late morning. Drinking that second bottle of ice-cold white wine had seemed like a great idea last night. Now she was slightly hungover and her eyes resented the bright sunlight.

Amy had opened the blinds and lay on the bunk, reading something on her phone.

'You know your eyes are going to give you hell someday, young lady,' Olivia mumbled. Her silk bonnet had slid off in the night, and her hair was tousled. She recovered the bonnet from the floor and grimaced as her brain matter reacted badly to the sudden movement. 'You've always got that thing pressed too close to your face.'

'Morning, grumpy,' said Amy brightly. 'No more wine for you. Fancy a cup of tea?'

'Two sugars.'

'Ooh, two not one? Living dangerously.' Amy filled the kettle with water and placed it on the portable stovetop. 'This thing is so annoying. We should have brought our electric kettle. I can't understand how Americans don't use them.'

'Thought you wanted to be adventurous? Real nomad living?

You should go outside, rub a few sticks together, start a wood fire and set a tin can on it.'

'Yeah, no, thank you.'

Olivia checked through her emails. A new message from Bill stared back at her. Relief flowed through her as she read the contents. Mrs Dupree was not going to sue them. Her new evidence had been allowed in by the court with a reprimand from the judge. The lawyer's fee for the extra court date was £1,500.

Olivia smiled to herself. £1,500. The lawyer might be happy diluting the Duprees' considerable fortune, but Dynamic Investigations was not there to be milked. The number of clients she'd sent that lawyer's way was worth tens of thousands of pounds, including Mrs Dupree herself. She vowed to keep an eye out for the lawyer's invoice and convince him to shred it.

At the bottom of Bill's email was an apology for his behaviour, and then he wished her a good holiday. Poor Bill. Despite their arguments, he was still one of her favourite people. They would get past this fight, just like they had got past fights before, and would continue to work together. She carefully crafted an apology, admitting to her own mistakes, and clicked send.

'I want to show you what Kent Hilson's got online.' Amy placed a cup of tea beside her mother. 'I did a search for the first murder site in Pennsylvania and "amateur photography exhibition". It came up with a place just ten miles away that shows amateur photography, a temporary venue.'

Olivia combed out her hair and set about making neat plaits. 'It was Illinois where he said he'd stopped at an exhibition, not Penn.'

'Yes, I did a search on Ohio and then Illinois, and they have these temporary venues too, within twenty miles of the murder sites. They're called pop-up galleries. They cater to amateurs trying to break through, and each gallery features photos taken locally.'

'Now, that really is interesting.' Olivia lowered her comb and stared at her daughter.

Amy held up her phone. 'Look at the last two searches I've done in Iowa. The pop-up gallery was open for two days in Sibley town, not far from Alley 7. It closed yesterday, unfortunately, but there's also a pop-up gallery right here in South Dakota — and it's open.'

'Close to here?'

'Twenty miles away. I'll bet Kent Hilson was at every single gallery, displaying his photos. Either before or after he does the murders, I don't know. What I do know is, he's a killer.'

Olivia was taken aback as she tried to process Amy's conclusions. She wondered how far Jack had got with breaking the man's alibis.

'What do you think, Mom?' Excitement made Amy's tone high-pitched. 'Am I right or am I right?'

'I certainly see your line of thinking.' Olivia stirred her tea slowly as she tried to imagine Kent's methods and motives. 'Where did you say the nearest gallery is?'

'Sioux Falls. It'll be there for the rest of the week. Sioux Falls is not a waterfall, by the way. Says here it's the largest city in South Dakota, with over one hundred and ninety-two thousand people.'

Olivia's initial plan had been to start the day with investigations into any possible fights or stabbings in Indiana parks, but this lead might prove even more helpful. She would track down Morelli or Perez later, not Jack Tyler.

She smiled at Amy. 'Get dressed. We'll take a run to Sioux Falls.'

*

As they entered the city of Sioux Falls, Olivia admired the historic sites and visitor-friendly environment. The bustling metropolis had a unique appearance. No sign of the usual chain stores. Slowly, she drove past dozens of historical markers, and wished they could take the time to stop and check out each site. The area was blessed with a good share of indoor museums and outdoor parks. She crawled past the magnificent Cathedral of St Joseph, a Romanesque and French Renaissance structure, its double spires contributing much grandeur and charm to the majestic building.

Olivia parked and they walked through Sculpture Walk, an area located on the sidewalks of the downtown region. They passed under the Arc of Dreams, which spanned 285 feet across the Big Sioux River between Sixth and Eighth Streets. The sign said the Arc was dedicated to the dreamers of the past and the present and served as an inspiration to the dreamers of the future. All along the route were fascinating sculptures with original designs.

The words 'Portray Your Wild Side' fluttered from a red-and-white banner atop a large white fully-enclosed marquee, home to the pop-up gallery. Inside, hundreds of photographs were pinned to the heavy-duty canopy. A young couple stood together, trying to attach another photo to the already busy walls. The man had a hippy look: colourful patterned shirt, bright trousers, and lots of facial hair. The woman had a broad face, reddened with heat rather than rouge, surrounded by thick auburn hair. Tiny sandaled feet protruded beneath her floral maxi dress as she approached.

'Hey, ladies, welcome!'

Olivia and Amy both smiled and greeted her, and nodded at the man.

'Do feel free to look around at the exhibits.' Her voice was warm and cheery. 'We're showcasing the beauty of the local area, nature and wildlife. All shots were taken by amateur photographers, some of whom will eventually go on to make a name for themselves.'

'Sounds exciting,' said Olivia.

'It is. It happens every year. One gal was hired to do travel shoots for a national hotel chain just through displaying at one of our galleries. We don't sell the photos, but if you want to contact the photographers direct, their social media handles are all right there.'

'Thank you very much,' said Olivia.

As they browsed through the gallery, Amy stopped abruptly and pointed. 'Mom, look at these. Kent Hilson.'

Olivia stared at the photographs. A stunning dawn image of Palisades State Park revealed a softly blended meeting of cliffs with the rising red sun. The other, also a dawn image of the creek, depicted low-hanging trees touching the shimmering waters. The photos were undated, yet the surrounding flora in full bloom suggested summer. She recalled Kent said he hadn't been to Palisades in months.

Olivia raised a hand and caught the attention of the attendant, who ambled over to them.

'How can I help?'

'These are lovely ones of Palisades,' said Olivia.

'It's a truly gorgeous place. Have you been there?'

'Yes, we're actually staying there right now.' Olivia beamed at her. 'This Kent Hilson is no amateur, surely?'

'He is.' The lady smiled. 'Kent has come with some really good stuff this year. Started out slowly, with blurry shots. Last year, we couldn't use any of his. Then again, he said Lucy was a distraction last year. That's his wife by the way, not a pet.' Her smile broadened.

'Ah okay. We actually met him in a bar last night in Sibley,' said Olivia. So, Lucy was not with him this year? Lucy could be sitting at home with her feet up. Or Lucy could be dead and buried under the patio. 'Nice man. Lovely photos.'

The woman handed Olivia a business card. 'Portray Your

Wild Side is the brand name of these pop-up galleries. We have partners in all the states mentioned here. If you're a fan of his work, you can contact them too. I'm sure Kent had work displayed in the Iowa branch, and I think Illinois and Ohio?'

'That's great,' said Olivia. 'I'd really love to follow his work.'

'Let me know if you need anything else,' the attendant said.

'Do the exhibitors come in personally, or do they just send you the images?' asked Olivia.

'Oh, all exhibitors attend for the first day. Most spend two or three hours hovering around, talking to patrons about their images. Some exhibitors may walk in the next day, too — depends on what business they have on elsewhere. We're here for five days.'

'Is it the same for the other states, too? Exhibitors attending for at least one day?'

'Absolutely. It shows that although they're amateurs, they are also serious. No way would any site display images people sent in from afar without the photographer making an appearance at the exhibition.'

'I see, thanks for that.'

Once she had moved away, Amy whispered, 'He lied, Mom.'

'Yes, he did. Keep walking and looking at the other photos.'

They continued their slow walk around the exhibition, admiring the many other local images.

'If we can prove that he was near the parks around the time of the murders, we've got him.' said Amy. 'It would be too much of a coincidence for him to be innocent.'

'It would be a great start. Not sure if it would be enough for a warrant to bring him in or search his property though.'

As they strolled back up the Sculpture Walk, Amy took the business card from Olivia. 'They have a pop-up in Indiana, Mom,' she murmured. 'The state the cops think Kent breezed through without committing any murders.'

'Let's stick with Dean, madam,' said Olivia with a smile. 'Don't hang Kent yet. First things first: we don't even know if anything happened in Indiana.'

'I'm still betting on it being him. I'll check out these businesses and see if Kent ever showed his work with them, and when.'

'Good idea. If you can't see anything online, phone them. Don't be all obvious, though. Pretend to be a fan, desperate to locate local nature photos or something.'

'Got it. I'll think of something.'

'Right. Time to go seek out a couple of special agents. See if they know whether anything went down in Indiana.'

22

OLIVIA PULLED INTO the half-full FBI parking lot shortly after 1pm to learn that only Special Agent Tom Walsh was on the premises. He came downstairs to the lobby to meet them.

'Guess everybody is super busy at the moment?' said Olivia.

'Yes,' said Tom. 'Jack's in the field, checking alibis. Is he not picking up calls?'

'I didn't call him.' Olivia ignored Tom's raised eyebrow. 'I was actually hoping to find Special Agent Perez or Morelli?'

'They're out in the field, too. Tell me what it is and I'll see what I can do.'

'I need to get hold of any accident reports of violent incidents at parks, nature reserves, forests in Indiana. I'm looking for mainly stabbings or fights.'

'Indiana?'

'Yes, Indiana,' said Amy. 'Maybe an attempted stabbing went wrong.'

'Or maybe somebody saw an incident that got overlooked because there was no murder,' added Olivia.

Tom looked dubious. 'Have you talked to Jack about this?'

'He hasn't contacted me.'

'I haven't got any information like that in our database.' Tom looked thoughtful. 'Actually, you're right to be seeking out one of the ISB Special Agents.'

'Can you get hold of them?'

'Follow me to my office.' He gave a boyish grin. 'Well, as you so rightly guessed, it's not exactly *my* office; I borrowed it while I'm here.' He whipped out his phone as he walked. 'I'll see who I can get on the line.'

Tom put the phone on speaker as the three sat in his office. Olivia gazed around. The small room was devoid of personalisation except for a single photo of the special agent, his wife and two small children. All rosy-cheeked and happy, they could have been starring in a Disney commercial.

'Marty?'

'Hey, Tom. You got good news for me? Mega millions come up?'

'No dice. I've got Olivia and her daughter Amy here with me. Olivia's got a couple of quick questions for you. You okay to talk?'

'I've just finished with Mrs Ralph Simmons. That lady doesn't know what day of the week it is. Give her a sip of liquor and she'll tell you any day you want. I won't be okay for another week.'

Tom smiled at Olivia and Amy. 'He's okay,' he whispered.

'Fire away,' said Morelli.

When Olivia relayed her question and repeated the reason for it, there was silence on the line for a moment.

'Marty, you there?' asked Tom.

'I'm here. Just thinking. The incident reports are centralised for the National Park Service, and there's a news release page online. It doesn't cover smaller parks or campsites that aren't part of the service. They would probably have their own incident reports, most likely on paper.'

'I guess there are a lot of parks in Indiana?' Olivia was disappointed. 'And the killer has picked both small and large places to strike.'

'You're looking at between February and June.' Morelli's sombre voice crackled down the line. 'Could take a week or so to sift through all that information.'

'Alright, thanks, Agent Morelli,' said Olivia. 'I'll think of another way around it.'

'Catch you later, Marty.' Tom clicked off the phone and looked at her with some sympathy. 'It was a good idea, Olivia.'

'I've got another idea, one that might be less time consuming.' Olivia furrowed her brow. 'Do you have a computer we can use, one with a large screen? I want to read through some Indiana newspapers. Local papers are great for local news. They cover things that the nationals don't care about.'

'Follow me.' Tom stood and gestured for them to follow him down the corridor.

'Actually, if I could get two computers side by side, one for Amy, that would be great.'

*

Inside the brightly lit room, six large-screened computers were arranged on desks, and a bulky laser printer sat on a table in the corner. The room had a single glass wall. Olivia could see through it into the adjoining room, which appeared to be a library, full of shelves with rows of books. A few agents were inside at different sections with their heads bowed, deep in research.

Olivia filled two cups from the water cooler next to the printer, then she and Amy sat side by side. She had expected only a handful of newspapers in Indiana, and was surprised that more than twenty were listed online.

'We'll start with the top five newspapers,' she said.

'I'll take the first two, then,' replied Amy. 'You do the next three.'

'Concentrate on every incident between February and June; that's when the killer would have passed between Ohio and

Illinois,' said Olivia. 'It must be in a park, forest, nature area or campsite.'

'Sure thing. Hey, this is really exciting.'

'Two hours from now, with nothing discovered, you might not think so,' Olivia warned. 'Now concentrate, and take it slow. We don't want to miss anything.'

They scrolled through pages of local news for hours. Occasionally, Amy would point something out and Olivia would lean over and read it on her screen. Both made notes of anything they deemed relevant. Olivia learned more about the good and bad of Indiana than she had ever wanted to know.

She looked up as a shadow crossed the window. A male agent she did not recognise was watching them. He lingered only a minute and then wandered off. Shortly afterwards, Tom knocked on the door, leading Olivia to suspect the unknown agent had gone asking questions about them.

'Everything alright in here?'

'Yes, sure. Thanks Tom.'

'Let me know if you need help. I've told Jack you're here.'

'Alright.' Olivia said nothing else, hoping he would tell her what Jack Tyler had said in response. That she cared so much what he thought about her was a source of constant annoyance.

'I'll leave you to it.' Tom closed the door and was gone.

Olivia continued with her task, but as her mind went into overdrive, her shoulders slumped. Maybe Jack thought she was a nuisance, that adding her to the taskforce was a bad mistake. She bit her lip. Who did she think she was, anyway? She had overthought the whole murder case, let her mind run away with far-fetched scenarios and wasted everybody's time. Her fingers inched towards her scalp.

'What do you think of this story, Mom? Look!' Amy tapped her mother's arm. 'Dated April. A stabbing at Hidden Paradise

Campground, St Paul's, Indiana. It's reported as two roommates having a drunken quarrel and one stabbed the other. At first, Lamar Webster denied stabbing Nathaniel Jeynes, and said a stranger did it.'

Olivia scooted her chair closer to her daughter so the two were rubbing shoulders. She stared into the sombre face of a forty-year-old Black man. His unlined smooth complexion made him look much younger than his years.

'Lamar Webster,' Olivia murmured as she read. 'Later he changed his statement and admitted to the attack, then changed it yet again and insisted it was a stranger who fled the area.'

'Why on earth would he keep changing his statement?' asked Amy.

'People do strange things under stress,' said Olivia.

'Or he did the murder, I suppose, and couldn't keep up the lies? It says the first statement he gave police he confessed to the crime, and said he'd tossed the knife into a lake.'

'The park rangers would never have listed this as a possible serial killer case because a man admitted to the crime,' said Olivia, overcome with a wave of excitement. 'It wouldn't have been referred to the ISB.'

She turned on the printer and, once it had warmed up, printed two copies of the story. She searched through other newspapers for the name Lamar Webster and found a few less-detailed mentions of the incident. Most were a short paragraph or two. Just another crime amongst hundreds of crimes that weary citizens had learned to ignore.

Amy found the website for Hidden Paradise Campground, and her eyes widened. 'The lake is beautiful, and it's got a water slide and paddle boats. You can do canoeing and kayaking.'

Olivia knew that tone and the look in Amy's eye. 'Amy, do you know how far Indiana is from here?'

After a few clicks on the keyboard, Amy said, 'St Paul's, Indiana, to be exact. It's about eleven hours' drive from the Palisades campsite.'

Olivia was deep in thought. 'Lamar Webster is in Hamilton County Jail in Indiana. I'll give Agent Tyler the lead. If anyone can get an interview with him, he can. The way things are going, I'm not sure if he'll let me sit in, but I'd really like to talk to Lamar.'

'I can go too, right?'

'I don't think jail visits to Indiana are on that itinerary you prepared so diligently before we left London.'

'Neither was South Dakota, nor seeing dead bodies.' Amy shrugged. 'A road trip to Indiana would be great fun, Mom, regardless of the case. I wouldn't mind staying at Hidden Paradise for a couple of nights.'

'Amy Knightley, you really do surprise me,' said Olivia. 'Well, if you're not worried about moving on to another murder site, I guess I'd better worry for the both of us.'

'If Lamar Webster didn't do it, you might be able to help him, Mom,' said Amy earnestly. 'Talk to Agent Tyler and tell him you're going to Indiana whether he likes it or not. You know you'll never forgive yourself if you don't at least try to get into the jail.'

Olivia stared at her daughter's flushed cheeks and bright eyes, pleased that Amy wanted to be on the side of what was right. Even more pleasing was the idea of putting distance between her daughter and the two enthusiastic young men camped at Palisades, who according to Amy were between jobs.

'You're absolutely right, love. We do not need anyone's permission to do a road trip. Tomorrow, bright and early, we'll leave. Eleven hours. We'll arrive in the evening, too late for a jail visit. Check what it says about weekday visitation times.'

Amy pulled up the Hamilton County Jail website and searched the pages. Her lips drooped as she looked at Olivia. 'Visits are by appointment only, it says. No walk-ins. And they have to be scheduled at least twenty-four hours in advance.'

'Come on.' Olivia stood and pushed her chair under the desk. 'Let's get out of here.'

Amy shut down the webpages and followed behind her mother. 'What are you going to do, Mom? You're not giving up, are you?'

Olivia smiled at her daughter. 'Never.'

23

JACK TYLER WAS at the small practice of a general practitioner, physician to Ralph Simmons. The visit was not prearranged, as he did not want the doctor consulting lawyers or declining to be interviewed. Jack explained the reason for his visit only after the nurse who'd escorted him into the doctor's office had left the room. The men sat across the desk from each other, the doctor frowning as Jack briefly related his search for a killer who knew how to wield a knife.

The doctor, a pale man with a noticeable hunched frame, read through a typed waiver of doctor–patient privilege handed to him by the special agent. 'I suppose you drafted this, Agent Tyler?'

Jack, unimpressed by the challenge to his authority, gave him a cold, fixed smile. 'Mr Simmons dictated it to me.'

'And I bet he didn't have a lawyer, either?'

'Any chance I can do the questions? It's why I'm here.'

'I am not trying to be obstructive, Agent Tyler.' The doctor spun in his swivel chair and tucked the letter into a folder inside his filing cabinet. 'I consider it a privilege to help law enforcement whenever I can.'

'Glad to hear it, doc.' Jack relaxed into his chair, tapping lightly on the arm rest. 'Mr Simmons speaks very highly of you.

Says the Haloperidol you prescribed is great for him. I'm wondering if failure to take the meds could lead him to do bad things?'

'You think he's a murderer?' the doctor asked.

'Here we go again.'

The doctor had the grace to flush. 'I apologise.'

'Does he have the temperament for murder?'

'My personal opinion is that lack of medication would not make him pick up a knife and attack anyone,' said the doctor. 'Quite the opposite, in fact. Without medication, he hears voices and his hands tend to tremble. He'd have difficulty clasping a knife, although I wouldn't say it's impossible.' The doctor flicked through his private patient file. 'He was taking a different medication back in May, and I switched him onto Haloperidol when he started acting in a disruptive manner.'

'Explain disruptive to me.'

'Shouting at people in the street, pushing over trash cans. Never hit anyone, though. I think his body got too used to the original medication.' The doctor stared at Jack. 'During that period of disruptive behaviour, I referred him to a mental facility for a six-week stay, covering June and July.'

Jack frowned. 'He was an inpatient in a secure facility?'

'Whether or not it's secure, I couldn't vouch for hand on heart.' The doctor uncapped his pen. 'I'll give you the address, Agent Tyler. You may get your answers there.'

*

Jack answered the phone to Tom as he drove to the Osceola mental health facility. So, Olivia Knightley was at the FBI office. Her reason for being there surprised him. The lady sure knew how to look at cases from different angles. Whether successful or not, it made sense to investigate whether they had missed a crime scene in Indiana. He'd been wrong to cold-shoulder her and would have to make it right, just as soon as he'd finished checking out the psychiatric facility.

The psychiatrist was a tall, stern-faced man in a white overcoat that swamped his skinny frame. The walls of his spacious office were a neutral oatmeal colour with abstract paintings carefully arranged throughout. A plush chaise longue stood in front of two small single-seat sofas. Jack chose a sofa and rested his arms on the comfortable armrests. The light, earthy odour of algae was in the air, and he noticed a large aquarium in the corner.

'Agent Tyler, I know you understand why I cannot give you any information about a patient or their care. If you provide a warrant, I'll give you whatever you need.'

'Time is against me, doc,' said Jack. 'So far, seven men are dead and I have no suspects in custody. You don't have to tell me anything about his medication. Hell, if you administered shock treatment, I don't want to know.'

'We don't do that here.'

'I want to give you two specific dates. You can confirm or deny whether Mr Simmons was here. That's all.'

'You wouldn't be recording me would you, Special Agent Tyler?'

'I would not. You don't have to speak. I'll write them down. You can nod your head yes or shake your head no, if you're that worried about it. One man was murdered in Illinois in June and another in Iowa in July.' Jack tore a page from his notepad and wrote on it. He held the page towards the doctor, who leaned forwards.

The doctor tapped his pen on his lip as he stared at the special agent. Eventually, he pulled a black appointment book closer and held it to his chest, preventing Jack from seeing the contents.

At length, the doctor closed his book. 'He was here with us, Agent Tyler.'

'And he couldn't have got out unnoticed?' Jack gazed around

the facility. 'Doors open everywhere. This place doesn't seem that secure to me.'

'It is an open place, but he had an electronic ankle bracelet to monitor his movement. If he'd set foot outside, it would have gone off.' The doctor held up a palm. 'And before you ask, it would be extremely difficult to remove the bracelet.'

Jack held up the composite photo. 'Would you say this looks like him?'

'I can see why you would get that idea.' The psychiatrist shook his head. 'Agent Tyler, don't waste your time with Ralph Simmons.'

Jack searched the doctor's face for signs he was withholding information. 'Would you tell me if you thought he was a murderer, doc?'

The psychiatrist fashioned his hands into a steeple and pressed them against his nose. 'If he confessed to me that he'd murdered someone and I thought for one minute he had done it, I would not hesitate to call the police. He's never mentioned any such thing, despite intense question-and-answer sessions during his stay. He's not your man, sir.'

As Jack drove away from the facility, he gave a deep sigh. In reality, he was glad to rule out the schizophrenic as a suspect. He wanted to get the right man, not just any man. Kent Hilson was still in his sights, and there were a few more people to canvass before the sun went down. About eight more hours of daylight were left in what was going to be a long day. With a bit of luck, he might even get back to the hotel before nightfall.

As he drove to his next destination, an address given for the unseen Mrs Hilson, his mind wandered back to Olivia. She had literally put her holiday on hold to help track down a killer, and he had behaved like a jerk. His phone rang before he could call her, and her name appeared on the screen. *Great minds think alike.* As he answered, he braced himself to make that long over-due apology.

24

HAMILTON COUNTY JAIL, Noblesville, Indiana, was a sprawling red-brown brick structure with an imposing exterior and large American flags flying from the masts. Despite still being weary from yesterday's eleven-hour drive from South Dakota, Olivia made sure to arrive with time to spare for the 8.30am visit. Jack Tyler was already there, pacing the entrance with his phone at his ear, and she hated herself for being so pleased to see him.

She grimaced at the memory of their last phone call. She wished she had let him speak first, but she'd gone off on a rant as soon as he'd answered the phone, insisting she would go to Indiana alone if he would not join them, promising to cause a scene at the jail demanding to see Lamar Webster if she had to. Without any resistance, Jack had agreed to meet her at the jail, his tone contrite, and he was apologetic about not contacting her. Her feelings towards him warmed somewhat. The man certainly had a softer side, despite his reluctance to show it.

Amy's irritated voice interrupted her thoughts. 'Under-eighteens are allowed in if accompanied by a parent or guardian. Mothers bring children to see their fathers all the time.'

'I hate to state the obvious, but Lamar Webster is not your father.'

'So? They won't know that.'

'I think they'll take one look at you and figure he's not the guy,' said Olivia.

'Hello? There is such a thing as adoption. Or he could be my stepdad.'

'Nice try.'

Olivia kissed Amy on the cheek and got out of the SUV. Her daughter was suffering a double disappointment, and she felt great sympathy for her. She would not be allowed to see Lamar Webster, and, even worse, despite intense research into Kent Hilson's cross-state travel, no connection could be made between the photography exhibitions and the crime scenes. Olivia leaned on the open window.

'I can't imagine we'll be in there more than a couple of hours. Once we're done, we'll go sightseeing wherever you want to go, I promise.'

'Cool, go do your thing. Tango and me will be fine. Besides, I've still got people to call. I've not given up on Hilson yet.'

Olivia waved at Jack as she walked towards him. She caught him giving her the once-over, and was glad she looked smart in her light cotton culottes and tucked-in fitted shirt. As he ended his call, she noted that he looked drawn, like a man carrying a whole lot of weight on his shoulders.

'I didn't expect you to be here already,' she said.

'Didn't go to bed. I drove through the night.' He gave a half smile in which she detected genuine warmth. 'Thought I'd better make it quick before you got here and started a violent demonstration.'

Olivia smiled back. 'Kind of you to want to prevent me getting locked up.'

'Actually, I have a reputation to protect. Didn't want my name dragged through the mud.'

'Ah, I see.'

Jack rubbed the back of his neck, twisting it as if in search of relief. 'I do appreciate your diligence, Olivia.'

'I never give up on a job.' Olivia chose her next words carefully. 'A general chat might work better with Lamar Webster than an all-out interrogation. Think you can show him your lighter side?'

'I'll do my best to find it.'

'And if you could throw in a please or thank you, that would work wonders.'

'You don't ask for much.'

The ceilings were high, the interior light and clean. They walked through a metal detector and were patted down for weapons. To Olivia, it certainly looked as though money had been spent making the institution a decent place for officers to work. She assumed the cells were not in bad condition, either, but being an inmate must be hopelessly depressing. Deprived of liberty, allowed out of a cell for a few hours a day, forced to adopt a timetable of strict rules.

'Commander said to expect you,' said the warden. His facial features were all squashed together as if pushed there by a great weight on his head. Flat lips, hard expression. Although Olivia smiled at him, he made no effort to conjure up a pleasant disposition.

As he checked Jack's ID, he took on a mocking tone. 'National Park Service Investigative Services Branch? We've got a couple elms that need urgent work, rotten trunks.'

Jack stared him out. 'I'm sure nothing's rotten around here, warden.'

The warden scrutinised Olivia's private investigator ID for longer than necessary before returning it to her. 'Understand you're not here on a warrant. You want to talk with Lamar Webster?'

'That's right,' said Jack. 'Hoping he can help with our investigations in a murder case.'

'You might have come all this way for nothing, because Webster's refusing to see anybody,' said the warden with a smirk. 'I cannot have him dragged to an interview room against his wishes. Next thing he'll be bleating about civil rights. He's always complaining about something.'

'What can you do for us?' asked Jack.

'All I can do is put you in the visitors' section and tell him his visitors have arrived.'

'We'll take it,' said Jack.

The warden showed them into the visitors' hall, where a large glass partition separated visitors from the incarcerated on the other side.

'Visiting time's eight thirty to ten.' The warden's thin lips curled. 'If he doesn't show for this one, the next visiting slot is one-thirty.'

As the warden turned to walk away, Olivia said, 'Can you tell him I'm here, please?'

'He know you?' The official stared at her curiously. 'Thought you were both strangers to him?'

'Yes, we're strangers.' Olivia squirmed. 'But if you tell him the private eye is a Black woman, it might arouse his curiosity.'

The warden raised an eyebrow as he stared at her.

'Hey, no need to look at me like that! I'm not trying to suggest I'm Miss Jamaica or anything, but I'm not that bad.'

'It won't hurt, warden,' said Jack. 'I'm willing to try anything that will get him out here.'

'ISB indeed,' said the warden in a scathing tone. 'As you wish. I'll go tell him a *sister* is here to see him. That all right with you, ma'am?'

'A sister will do nicely.' Olivia offered a dazzling smile. 'Thank you very much for your help, sir.'

The warden stopped smiling and seemed annoyed at her cheerful response. He walked away slowly, taking his time, glancing at other visitors and inmates as he went.

'That clown is deliberately wasting time,' said Jack. 'At the rate he's going, it'll be fifteen minutes before Webster even hears we're out here.'

'I thought all you law enforcers were on the same side?' said Olivia. 'Has this bloke got something against all acronyms or just yours?'

'Some wardens are territorial. He's probably worried Webster will try to do some kind of deal and get released.'

'Is that even a possibility?' asked Olivia in surprise.

'Even things that are not a possibility can be made a possibility.' Jack rubbed his rough jaw. 'Bond's set at half a million, he needs to find ten percent to get out. In this game, it just depends on who needs what from whom.'

Ten minutes passed, then fifteen, then twenty. Jack paced around. Olivia stayed seated. Occasionally, her eyes strayed to Jack, but mainly she kept her focus on the archway from where the inmates emerged into the visiting area. Just when she was beginning to think they were out of luck and might need to try again in the afternoon, an athletic man in an orange jumpsuit emerged. She recognised him instantly from the online article. Lamar Webster kept his eyes on hers as he threw himself onto a plastic seat in front of her. A glass panel perforated with holes was all that separated them. He stared at her through the glass, his appreciation apparent.

'My, I thought old boy there was lying, but it *is* a sister. A fine sister . . . and you a cop too? How you doing?'

'Private investigator.' Olivia smiled graciously. 'I'm very well thanks, Lamar. How are you?'

'Hot damn! Straight outta England?'

'I am, yes. My name's Olivia Knightley, Lamar. This is Special Agent Tyler.'

Lamar Webster considered Tyler for the first time. As his eyes raked over the special agent, his smile faded. 'Not everything looks good around here.'

'Hello, Lamar,' said Jack. 'Thank you for coming out to see us.'

'What do you want?'

'To talk about what happened to Nathaniel Jeynes at Hidden Paradise in April.'

'You come all this way to ask me about Nathaniel's murder?' The inmate glared at Jack. 'I already told everybody who'd listen that I didn't do it. I even told those who wouldn't listen, like that two-bit public defender. Now I gotta tell the feds, too?'

'You changed your version of events a few times, Lamar,' said Jack. 'Give us the real truth.'

'What you gonna do for me? You gonna get me outta here?'

'That's not a promise I can make.'

'In that case, no point me hanging around here, even for a fine sister.' The inmate got to his feet. 'Nice to meet you, Olivia. Come back any time you want. Don't bring the G-man next time.'

Olivia reacted swiftly. 'Lamar, please don't go! Just sit down a minute. I don't think you murdered your friend. If you can help us fill in the details, I'm sure Agent Tyler will do what he can for you.' Turning her head, she locked eyes with Jack. 'Isn't that right, Agent Tyler?'

They stared at each other for a long moment, and Olivia almost forgot what she had asked until he answered.

'Sure, that's right.'

Lamar retook his seat. He stared at the wall above their heads, avoiding eye contact, as if contemplating his position.

'Nathaniel looked like a really nice man,' said Olivia.

'Thank you, he was. I'll answer the questions if I get some smokes.'

'You can have a box of smokes later if you'll talk first,' said Jack. 'And I want the truth, no BS. What happened that day at Hidden Paradise?'

'We were camping for a couple of nights. Nathaniel's been my good buddy since we started sharing a two-bed apartment on the rough side of Bloomington. He's actually the first real white guy friend I've had, and he was the same age as me.' Lamar's voice took on a wistful tone. 'Cool guy. Wouldn't let anyone call him Nate or Nat. Said it sounded like a bug's name. Said people better call him what his momma named him.'

'I wish more people would do the same thing,' said Jack. 'Chasing aliases is the bane of my life.'

'We'd had a stupid argument earlier over an eye meds bottle he accused me of breaking,' said Lamar. 'Always rubbing his itchy eyes, he was. We'd had a little scuffle back at the RV. We're rough-housing all the time, you know? Wrestling and pretending to box at each other, so it wasn't nothing new. Never drawn blood. We would never do that.'

'But he wasn't stabbed inside the RV?' said Olivia.

'No, the wrestling around was earlier in the day. He said I broke his eyedrops bottle, but he had a girl in there the night before who could have broke it.' Lamar shook his head. 'Later in the afternoon, we were outside sitting on a bench on the outskirts of the campsite. Nathaniel on one end of the bench, me at the other, not talking. That's where he got stabbed. I didn't have a knife on me, and I did not stab him.'

'Why did you say you did it?' asked Olivia.

'The cops tricked me. Told me I'd just get a fine and it would be over if I said I did it. Now they talking about a trial, about first-degree murder. I mean, man, first-degree murder? Stupid lawyer telling me I should take a plea to manslaughter. I'd still have to do plenty time.' Lamar slammed his palm against the glass. 'I just wanted to go home.'

'I can see how that would happen.' Olivia nodded in sympathy. 'Sometimes it's quicker to get on with your life by just taking the easier option, rather than risking decades in jail.'

'Ain't that the truth, sister,' said Lamar nodding eagerly. 'So-called witness said they saw me toss the knife into a lake. Bald-faced lie. I threw a bottle of moonshine in the lake. Knew the cops would be after me for anything illegal. Man, I ran. Then when they caught me, I got confused when they kept saying I'd stabbed him. At one point they even got me believing I did do it, but I swear I didn't.'

'Tell us about the man who you say did it,' said Jack.

'A grey dude was sitting by himself on a bench about ten feet from ours, right up where there's this giant chestnut tree with the biggest trunk you ever did see. I got up to go take a leak in the bushes. As I was walking away, I saw Grey Dude get up and sit beside Nathaniel. Didn't think much of it, just went ahead and did my business.' Webster rubbed his hands together. 'Decided to let them chat for a while, because I was thinking it would help Nathaniel cool off.'

'Did you hear the man say anything to Nathaniel?' asked Olivia.

'I caught a bit of something. Sounded like Grey Dude said, "Scratchy eyes in doofus corner."'

'Scratchy eyes in doofus corner?' repeated Olivia with a frown, and threw a questioning glance at Jack.

'I have no idea,' he said.

'That's what I remember.' Webster shrugged. 'I couldn't have been gone more than ten minutes. When I got back, Nathaniel was lying in the grass. I didn't even realise he was dead. Thought he was playing around. I sat down on the bench beside him, right where Grey Dude had been sitting. I said something to him about playing around, and he didn't respond.'

'You didn't see all that blood?' asked Jack.

'Only when I knelt beside him and grabbed him up. Saw blood pumping outta the other side of his neck.' Webster clenched his fists and closed his eyes. For a moment, he fell silent, and a single tear rolled down his face. Lowering his head, he wiped it on his shoulder. 'I'll never forget how it feels to have warm blood running all over your hands, watching someone take their last breath.'

Jack's tone grew urgent. 'Did you get a good look at the man?'

'Said so, didn't I?' Lamar replied irritably. 'Old white guy. Grey Dude coulda been sixty or eighty, I don't know. They all done look alike to me.'

'We're going to show you three images. Tell me if any of these look like the man.' Jack held up an enlarged photograph of Kent Hilson and one of Ralph Simmons. Olivia held up the composite image of Dean.

'Definitely not either of the two you're holding, G-man.' The inmate pressed his nose against the glass and stared at Olivia's poster. 'More like that one. But Grey Dude's face was wider than that, and had more space between his hairline and his eyebrows.'

Olivia glanced at Jack, who lowered the photographs. She sensed his frustration as he briefly closed his eyes and massaged his temples. She'd never expected Lamar to pick Ralph or Kent, but had hoped he'd get excited about the composite. His lacklustre response was not encouraging.

'Anything else, Lamar?' she asked. 'Think about it, take your time.'

'His ears stuck out more too. I remember that because when

I was looking at the back of him, I thought, hey, he's got sticky-out ears.'

'That's good,' said Jack as he put pen to notepad. 'Anything else?'

'I already described him to them cops at the time,' said a frustrated Webster. 'I don't know what they wrote down, but I told them everything I could remember at the time. I actually saw Grey Dude walking away pretty fast into a really busy area. He disappeared into the crowd. If I'd have known what he'd done . . .'

'Was Nathaniel's body out straight when you got to him, like with his arms and legs stretched out?' asked Jack.

'Huh? No, he was sort of crumpled up. Why'd you ask about his arms and legs?'

Jack was silent for a moment, as if considering what to share with the inmate. Eventually, he said, 'Because other possible victims of the same man have been found with their limbs all straightened out, almost as if they were standing to attention.'

'He didn't get no time to do that.' Lamar stared at Jack, his eyes widening behind the glass partition. 'You know what? I don't think Grey Dude even realised that me and Nathaniel was friends. Some people don't think Black dude white dude can be good friends. He probably thought I was just hanging around the bench by myself, because Nathaniel and me didn't say a word to each other.'

Olivia nodded. 'When he saw you move off, he got busy chatting to Nathaniel, then he attacked. You came back before he had time to rearrange Nathaniel's arms and legs.'

'Was the killer taller or shorter than I am?' asked Jack.

'Way shorter than you, G-man. Nathaniel's six foot, and he weren't no way even as tall as him. Dude was maybe five-seven, five-eight.'

'Do you know what happened to the clothes you were

wearing that day?' asked Jack. 'If you sat right where the killer sat, you might have picked up his DNA on your clothes.'

'The cops took my clothes. I guess they still have them.'

'I'll follow it up,' said Jack. 'Anything else you can remember?'

'Rangers tackled me before I even got out of the park.' Lamar's voice became heightened and tears flowed. 'I didn't do nothing. Four months I've been locked up in this damn place! I lost my job. Right now, my landlord must've dumped out all my stuff. Man, I did nothing wrong, and I could be stuck in here for twenty years or more!'

'I'm so sorry, Lamar,' said Olivia. 'I believe you. I really do.'

Lamar sniffed and wiped his nose with his sleeve. 'My family believes me. My mom and dad and brothers and sisters. They know me.' He smiled out of the blue. 'My dad said he wants to kick my butt for saying I did it in the first place.'

'I'm with your dad,' said Jack, though his look was kind.

A bell rang, startling Olivia, who glanced around the hall. A loud voice over the tannoy announced that visiting time would end in five minutes.

'Lamar, was anything missing from Nathaniel?' asked Olivia. 'Like a ring or a watch or anything?'

He stared at her in surprise. 'Yeah. A gold chain with a little mermaid dangling at the end. He always wore it. His mom was looking for it. The cops said I must've taken it, but they didn't find it on me. Couldn't explain that one, huh?'

'I've got people in the US Attorney's Office I can talk to,' said Jack, as he rose. 'See if they can give your lawyer some assistance, or get him to pay a little more attention to your case.'

'You think you'll find the no-good rat who killed Nathaniel? And get me outta here?'

Olivia stared at his pained face. The desperate hope for freedom was apparent in his eyes and choking voice. From her experience, the legal system could drag its feet when it came to releasing the innocent. The truth will set you free, but not necessarily in the same year the truth becomes apparent. The truth can leave you rotting in jail for years.

'We're going all out to catch him,' said Jack. 'I promised to do whatever I can for you, Lamar, and I will.'

Lamar stood up as a warden approached him. 'Do I get my box a smokes, G-man?'

'I'll see to it before the warden throws us out.'

Olivia glanced around, and noted that some of the inmates clung to their chairs, as if they did not want visiting time to end. A young girl wailed uncontrollably as her mother tried to lead her away. The girl screamed for her father. Behind the glass, the man looked over his shoulder at his daughter as he was led away. Olivia swallowed. 'Bye, Lamar. We won't give up till we find Nathaniel's killer.'

'Thank you, my sister. Take care of your fine self, now.'

*

As they exited the jail, Olivia inhaled the fresh, clean air, never more grateful for her freedom, never more determined to catch the elusive Dean.

'That was pretty good work finding Lamar, Olivia. I appreciate an investigator who doesn't cut corners and doesn't give up. No way he would ever have come on my radar.'

A warm glow of happiness spread over her body as he stared at her. There was no mistaking the admiration in his expression and tone. She still remembered the first day, when he'd questioned her skills as a private investigator. He'd changed his tune now. Her sense of personal satisfaction was tinged with something else, something she could not or would not allow herself to identify. The only thing she felt comfortable enough to admit was that she liked working alongside him.

'What happens next?' she asked coolly.

'I know which police department caught the case. I'll get hold of the file and check what description Lamar gave for Nathaniel's killer. Get another composite drawn up and get that distributed to the media and the public.'

'Mom!'

Olivia turned her head slightly. 'Coming!'

'I'll ask the lawyers to request a DNA test on Lamar's clothes. Might be the break we need if the killer's in the system.' He drew a long breath. 'I'll do what I can do up here today. Tomorrow, I'll head back to South Dakota. Still got some possible witnesses I need to see. Then we need to regroup and see where everybody's at.'

'Alright, we'll head back to South Dakota tomorrow, too.'

'I'd really appreciate it if you would, Olivia. We really need you.'

Olivia wished he'd said, 'I really need you,' but it was good enough. She smiled at him. 'I have no intention of missing out on anything.'

'I guess you don't.'

They shared a smile, and she thought he was about to say something else. Amy chose that moment to toot the horn, breaking the spell.

'I'd better go. She's eager to know what we found out. She was doing research on Kent Hilson, digging and getting nowhere.'

'Tell me about it.' He waved off her questioning look. 'Depending on what's in Lamar's case file, I may need to take a trip over to Hidden Paradise Campground, have a look around. You two spending the rest of the day there?'

'Not until this afternoon.' She checked her watch. 'We're going to tour Noblesville, see what delights it has to offer. I asked Amy to look up some places of interest, so I'm not exactly sure what's on her agenda.'

'You deserve a break. Enjoy your day.'

Olivia wondered if she should at least attempt to shake hands with the special agent. One hand was in his pocket, the other clutching his phone. Always business-like. No need for her to make things awkward.

She gave a light, 'Bye!' then turned and walked quickly towards her daughter. She sensed Jack's eyes following, watching her, and she hoped he was having only good thoughts.

25

IN HISTORIC NOBLESVILLE Square, Olivia and Amy admired the splendid court house before enjoying a late lunch in Matteo's, a genuine Italian upmarket restaurant. Afterwards, they browsed in local boutique shops and bought pastries to go at a family restaurant.

Amy sipped an ice-cold cherry milkshake as they walked. 'I texted Dad, by the way. Told him we'd heard of a great campsite in Indiana and had turned around. Said I'd send him some photos later.'

'Good, that should keep him happy.'

'Do you think you two will ever get back together?'

The question came out of the blue. Olivia hadn't heard it in months, and assumed Amy had long given up on the idea. She swirled the ice in her fruit punch.

'No, we won't, love. We had a good run, but it's over.'

'Lots of people get divorced and get back together. Some of them even remarry.'

'And I hope they live happily ever after, I really do.' Olivia sighed. 'I get why some people remarry — better the devil you know and all that. It wasn't a decision taken lightly. You believe that, don't you?'

'Tricia's parents argue all the time. She says they've been arguing since she was born, and they're still together. They don't hate each other.'

Olivia knew little about the parents of her daughter's best friend. The mother taught music studies at the local community college, and the father worked in construction. Maybe Tricia's parents were tied together by financial issues, a hefty mortgage or school fees. Or maybe they were the kind who actually loved each other and argued as foreplay.

'We don't hate each other, Amy. Chris has some great ways and some not so great ways . . . yeah, I know, just like me. We stopped seeing eye to eye years ago.' She nudged Amy's side. 'Hey, everything is going to be alright, for all of us. It takes a bit of getting used to, but we'll all soon be fine with the new normal.'

'I know.' Amy offered her a forgiving look. 'Sometimes I like to remember when we were happy, though.'

'You're happy right now, aren't you?' Olivia asked hesitantly.

'Yep.' Amy held up her new purchase, a patterned cotton scarf, and smiled. 'If Dad was here, we'd never even have set foot in that boutique. Too girly for him. You'd think after being a girl-dad for sixteen years, he'd get used to doing girly things and just go along with it.'

'Well, I'm sure when you two go on your first holiday together, he'll be happy to do the things you want to do.' Although she said it to be encouraging, Olivia recalled that one of the problems she'd had with Chris was his insistence on doing things his way; he'd make plans for the family and just expect her to go along with it.

'Oh wow, I'd never even thought of that. Dad and me on holiday together.'

'You'll be fine if you pick somewhere with activities he considers masculine. He'd get really excited about rock climbing.'

Olivia's mind drifted and a vision appeared. She and Amy climbing a rock face with a man climbing beside them, smiling and urging them on. The man was Jack Tyler. He put out a hand to help her up and offered encouraging words. Shocked at the vivid image, Olivia looked around for a distraction.

'Where do you want to go next?' she asked.

Amy laughed out loud, surprising Olivia. 'I love you, you know, Mom?'

'I love you too, but what's so funny?'

'You're itching to go to the murder site,' said Amy. 'I can see all the signs. You keep going off into your zone. I know you're going over and over what Lamar said. Admit it, you were in PI mode when you walked into that jail, and you've been in PI mode since you walked out.'

'Not when I was eating that delicious pizza, though.'

'Yeah, I'll give you that.'

They both laughed, Olivia from sheer relief that Amy had got it wrong this time. If her daughter ever guessed where her mind was really at, she would never live it down.

'No point pretending around you, madam.'

'Tell me what you're thinking, Mom.'

'We know Lamar didn't do it,' said Olivia. 'And I got the impression from Jack that he's come to the same conclusion that we have: that Kent Hilson isn't a murderer, either. Ralph Simmons is out, too.'

'Well, now Lamar's provided a good description of what the killer looks like, it should help the cops nail him.'

'I hope so. They'll be relying on an alert person spotting him and making the call.'

'Suppose they don't catch him and Lamar gets convicted? Imagine spending your whole life in jail for something you didn't do.'

Olivia tried to imagine it. Definitely the stuff of nightmares.

It was little wonder some people took their own lives in jail, knowing they were innocent, despairing of ever getting out. A lone voice screaming into the void, watching the world continue as if your absence from it was of no consequence. She would not wish that on anybody. Identifying Dean was an absolute priority.

'Come on. Let's go find that giant chestnut tree Lamar mentioned.'

*

It was late afternoon, with the sun still high in the cloudless sky, when they arrived back at Hidden Paradise. The campground was located on eighty acres, with nearly two hundred RV sites and log cabins. A water lover's paradise, it was situated along the glorious Flat Rock River, with kayaks available for those who wished to explore by floating serenely along. Surrounding the visitors were high limestone cliffs and a whole wilderness of lush, leafy trees. Dream Lake, a stunning expanse of dark water, ran through the middle. A separate swimming area was popular with younger people, offering a huge floating trampoline and an obstacle course.

Enjoying the beauty of Hidden Paradise with her daughter was one thing, but Olivia could not lose sight of the fact that a gory murder had taken place there. A park guide pointed out the route to the giant chestnut tree, and Olivia mulled over Lamar Webster's account of his brief encounter with the killer as she walked.

An older man of average height and build walked past them, carrying a long-lens camera. Olivia found herself straining to see if his ears protruded.

'Hi, how are you?' she said.

The man turned, startled and nodded at her. 'I'm good. How are you?'

'I'm fine, thanks. Enjoying the scenery.' She took in his facial features in a split second and said, 'You have a great day.'

'You too. Bless you.' He smiled and continued on his way.

'Mom, I really hope you're not gonna stop every grey-haired man you see. I've seen you staring at every one of them who strolls by. It's hardly likely the Parkside Killer is going to be walking right beside you if he's supposed to be heading west.'

'You're absolutely right. Besides, we're not his type.'

'Yay for brown-skinned girls!' said Amy.

Olivia gave her daughter with a wry look. 'So we're going with the media's name for him now, are we? The Parkside Killer.'

'Sounds more punchy to me.' Amy smiled. 'Last night I read all about the Green River Killer, this serial killer who killed forty-eight women before he was finally caught.'

'You used to spend your nights reading about film stars and pop singers. I'm not sure if celebrities make for healthier reading, but at least their activities won't keep you awake.'

'I slept fine, Mom. Besides, I did my regular gossip reading too. But there's only so much you can read about celebrities before your eyes glaze over.'

'That's my experience, too.'

As they walked through the stunning grounds, taking in the picturesque landscape, Amy spread her arms wide apart and stared up at the canopy of overhanging trees, through which glimpses of blue sky could be seen.

'I just love living on the road, Mom. It's great to just be able to pick up and move to different locations. Far better than being stuck in a boring house with a mortgage for years and years.'

'It's summer, lovely and warm. You'd be singing a different tune if it was January.'

Amy laughed. 'No, I wouldn't.'

'You're not much better with the cold than I am, madam. There's no way you'd want to be without your central heating for even a day during winter. As for when it rains? Trust me, grey skies and muddy fields are not things you'd enjoy.'

'Next year, I fancy going to Glastonbury,' said Amy lightly. 'Plenty of grey skies and mud. It'll be my first outdoor music festival. Tricia's been before, a few years ago, with her parents. She and I can go together next time. The music's good, and it looks like fun.'

Olivia raised an eyebrow. The idea of Amy and her friend alone at a three-day music festival with boys and booze was not an attractive one.

'Glastonbury? We'll see.'

'I heard how you said that. I'll be seventeen, and you don't have to go with parents when you're no longer classed as a child.'

Olivia detected the arrival of the confrontational tone she had managed to keep at bay for longer than usual. No point getting into an argument over an event that would not be held until next summer. She had a whole year to prepare for that one.

'It's a long way away, Amy. Lots of things can happen between now and then. You might be on summer holiday with your dad.'

'Hmm, why do I get the feeling that if he suggests we go away on holiday over the Glastonbury dates, you'll be quick to agree?'

'Your father likes live music. He'd be happy to join you,' Olivia teased her.

'Noooo!'

'Look – there.' Olivia pointed to a huge chestnut tree. 'That's got to be the place Lamar mentioned. And there are the two benches.'

'Must be about eighty feet tall.' Amy gazed up at the majestic chestnut in admiration. 'And that *is* the widest tree trunk, for real.'

In the distance, the motor homes and trailers of the nearest campsite were visible. Nothing about the area indicated that a man had been brutally slain there months ago, that blood had pooled in the soft, green grass. The benches were set back in the grass, off the trail, and probably less frequently used by visitors, but Dean had taken a big risk launching a daylight attack there.

'People are passing by all the time,' said Amy. 'How can no one have seen what happened?'

'Yes, but look at their faces. Everyone is minding their own business, enjoying the scenery. They wouldn't expect an attack in such a peaceful place. Only a scream would get attention and the victim never got a chance to scream.'

'Scary. You can kill people in broad daylight with no one noticing if you do it quietly in a pretty place.'

Olivia looked at her daughter with concern. 'You okay?'

Amy smiled and gave her a double thumbs-up. 'I'm A. K., a chip off the old block.'

'Not so much of the old, cheeky.' Olivia stared at the benches. 'I'm still trying to work out what "scratchy eyes in doofus corner" could possibly mean. Is it a line from a film or something?'

'Not that I know of.' Amy shook her head. 'Looked it up online and nothing came up.'

'Lamar was a good distance away, near the tree, so it's unlikely he heard clearly anyway.'

Olivia put one foot before the other and measured the distance between the two benches. About twelve feet. So Dean had sat down twelve feet from a well-built stranger and just decided on the spur of the moment to attack him? Something in particular must have drawn him to Nathaniel Jeynes.

'You getting any ideas, Mom? Cause I'm not seeing anything other than green grass, shady trees, and a comfortable spot to chill.'

Olivia placed her hands on hips and glanced from one bench to the other. 'Sit on the edge of that bench, and I'll sit on this one.'

Amy did as she was told and stared across at her mother.

'Take off your sunglasses a minute, love.'

'What is it, Mom? What are you thinking?'

'It's okay. Put them back on.'

Amy did as she was told, her expression curious.

Olivia closed her eyes and her brow furrowed. In her mind's eye, she studied the faces of each of the seven victims on the death walls. She repeated the phrase Lamar thought he had heard the killer say. Her heart began to palpitate. There was something similar about all these men. Well, about most of them. She would need to double check the others, but if she was right, their medical records would most likely confirm it.

'Hello? You're freaking me out over here.'

Olivia opened her eyes. 'Lamar said Nathaniel had itchy eyes.'

'Yes, and?'

'I've got a good idea what the killer said to Nathaniel.' Olivia stared at her daughter's frowning face. 'I know what he does for a living.'

'Mom, you're driving me crazy!'

'The killer specialises in eye care.'

26

BEFORE DAWN THE next morning, they were back on the road. Olivia drove with speed and intense concentration for the eleven-hour journey back to South Dakota. Determined to make the 7pm taskforce meeting, she arrived in Sioux City at the FBI office a few minutes past the hour.

She speed-walked inside and pushed open the door to the situation room. 'Hello, everybody. Sorry I'm late.'

The four agents were talking amongst themselves. Jack immediately stood up and gave her a warm smile. 'You made good time, considering you must have driven all day.'

She could not ignore the warmth of the greeting and returned the look. She greeted Perez and Morelli, who both made polite noises, then she waved at Tom.

'I should tell you I've managed to fit a tangerine SUV and a caravan in the car park. Don't tow either of them, will you?'

'Don't worry about it.' Tom grinned. 'We appreciate your dedication to the cause.'

Olivia smiled back. The other cause to which she was dedicated was her daughter's safety, and she would rather Amy potter around in the caravan outside than drop her off at Palisades campground with those boys she found so interesting.

Were she in London, Olivia would have donned a smart suit for this particular meeting. A suit was like armour against people who might think she was not their equal, but not even one suit had found its way into her suitcase, as she could never have imagined being in such a position. Instead, her green cargo trousers, which had never met an iron, paired with a white linen blouse, were as close to smart-casual as she could get.

'The floor's all yours, Olivia,' said Jack.

Olivia walked up to the death wall and studied each face. New photos had joined the old. Under a new section for Indiana, Nathaniel Jeynes's photos appeared. The numberings had changed, with Nathaniel now classed as victim four. Eight victims. Seeing the victims up close again and studying their features made her even more confident of her theory.

Olivia turned to face them. 'You did say one of the medical examiners thought Dean might have a medical background because of the clean, precise nature of the kills. I believe he does have a medical background, just not the one you might think.

'Something drew him to these men.' She tapped on Nathaniel Jeynes's image. 'Yesterday, while I was at Hidden Paradise, I went over what Lamar Webster thought he'd heard — "scratchy eyes in doofus corner" — which made little sense. What he actually heard was something like, "Scratching your eyes will do for your cornea." That leads me to believe the killer works with eyes. Optician, optometrist, ophthalmologist.'

Morelli mumbled something to Perez that Olivia could not hear. Her confidence did not wane. 'Do speak up, folks,' she said, and stared him out.

'Take us through it,' said Jack.

'Ordinary people don't use the word cornea,' explained Olivia. 'You or I would say, "You'll damage your eyes if you keep scratching them." Someone who specialises in eyes would be more likely to refer to the cornea.'

Tom nodded. 'I get that.'

Olivia pointed out Rick's driver's licence, beside which was a mugshot from his prison years. 'Did you have a look at Rick's face? I mean, a really close look?'

'Yes, both at the scene and his IDs,' said Jack. 'Nothing about his eyes struck me as odd, I must say.'

'You can't see it that well in these photos, but when I was crouching beside him, I looked right into those green eyes. If his eyes had been identical, I probably wouldn't have noticed it. Would have thought the cloudiness happened due to death and the length of time he was lying there. One eye was partly cloudy, like he had a cataract. Early stages, though.'

Jack walked over to where she was pointing. 'It's barely visible.'

'That's most likely because of the lighting.' Olivia pointed at the body of the first victim from Pennsylvania. 'This guy, his eyes are not staring straight ahead; one looks a bit off to the right. Slightly cross-eyed.'

Jack looked. 'I can certainly see the issue with him.'

'This second one has a bloodshot eye; see all the tiny red spots? It's not the petechiae of death, as it's visible in his ID, too.' She picked up a stack of medical reports and pointed out the man's medical record. 'Look, the ME noted as much.'

'This one, the John Doe, I'm not sure about. Can't see anything obvious in his eyes. The ME didn't record anything about them, either.'

'Hey, now you mention it, the John Doe did have a pair of glasses right by his face.' Perez flicked through her notes. 'Thick lenses. Short-sighted.'

'Well, I'll be,' mumbled Morelli.

Olivia caught a look shared between her two detractors, a look that suggested they were finally coming around. No need for a suit, just a clear voice and a plausible explanation of her findings. 'The Palisades victim . . . look, there's a small stye on his eyelid.'

By now, all four agents surrounded Olivia, looking closely at the eyes of the victims in the enlarged photos.

'Vic three has bloodshot eyes, even in the passport photo,' said Perez.

'I never would have seen that.' Morelli's nose almost touched the victim's face. 'How did the killer get that close, though? I can't imagine any stranger getting close enough to comment on the cornea of my baby blues.'

'Your eyes are brown,' Perez reminded him. 'I told you eating toothpicks would rot your brain.'

'Let me have my Sinatra moment,' said Morelli.

'Of course no one's going to get close to you, Special Agent Morelli,' said Olivia. 'The nature of your job makes you more suspicious than the ordinary man.'

'I'll give you that,' he agreed.

'The Indiana victim, Nathaniel Jeynes, had itchy eyes; maybe asthma or hay fever,' continued Olivia. 'He's a big man. He was rubbing his eyes in broad daylight, not knowing that such a basic action would attract a killer to him.'

'And you think the killer talks to them about their eyes?' asked Jack.

'Eyecare is expensive,' said Olivia. 'If a smiley older person came up to you and offered suggestions for free care, or a free consultation, you wouldn't chase him away, would you? You'd be interested.' She paused briefly, wondering if she had caused offence. 'Well, I mean, not you guys personally – you've probably got great medical insurance – but you know what I mean.'

'We don't do so badly,' said Jack. 'But you're right. People without healthcare benefits have a rough time paying for any treatments they need.'

'I don't know if Lamar broke Nathaniel's eyedrops bottle. He suggested a girl did it.' Olivia stared at Nathaniel's photo, which showed a cheerful man unaware he was less than a year from death. 'I just hope it wasn't Lamar, or he'll never forgive himself. He'll think his friend would not have been rubbing his eyes, would not have drawn attention, and would not have been murdered.'

'I spoke to Nathaniel's parents,' said Jack. 'Good people. They don't believe Lamar killed their son. Said cops have been trying to convince them he did, but they refuse to accept it. Said their son only ever had good things to say about Lamar. For Lamar's sake, I'm glad about that. If you go to trial with the victim's parents on your side, your defence is off to a good start.'

'That's really something.' A spark of hope ran through Olivia. 'I wish they would visit Lamar and tell him, though. I don't think he knows they're behind him.'

'They're barely coping,' said Jack. 'Way too traumatised to even think about it. They're offering twenty thousand dollars to whoever catches the real killer.' He closed his eyes briefly, his expression pained. 'We overlooked their son.'

'Don't be too hard on yourself, Jack,' said Tom. 'We can only look ahead from now on.'

'I know.' Jack waved a hand in reluctant acceptance. 'On a more positive note, we won't need to spend any more time on Ralph Simmons or Kent Hilson. Ralph's alibis — well, the ones that don't include the drunken wife — all check out. As for Kent Hilson, that man is really something, but he's not a murderer.'

'What is he?' asked Olivia. 'Don't tell me, as well as his wife, Lucy, he's got a lot of girlfriends?'

'Lucy?' Jack's face registered his surprise. 'I found Vivien, Sarah and Ruth. And they're not girlfriends; they're all still married to him. Got a few kids between them, too. Families spread out in Iowa, Ohio and Illinois.'

'Phew!' Perez whistled. 'At least Marty divorces his wives before he marries the next one.'

'Damn right I do. Four wives at the same time? There's not enough Excedrin.' Morelli stared at Jack. 'You spilling on him?'

'Not sure if I need to,' said Jack. 'At least one of the women smelled a rat from the questions. The cat's not yet out of the bag, but it's certainly clawed a few holes.'

Olivia joined in the agents' laughter. At least the women were alive and well, not decomposing under a freshly built concrete patio. That the handsome Kent was a polygamist was disappointing, though. Why put the women and children through all this? With such a complicated love life, it was no wonder the man could not recall his whereabouts at any given time.

When the revelry eased, Jack said, 'Okay, back to business. So we need to know whether Dean is an optician or way more progressed in his profession. Opticians are allowed to test eyes, but they're not doctors, are they?'

'That's right,' said Olivia. 'Optometrists are eye doctors. They do medical treatments and minor surgical procedures. Ophthalmologists are the big players. They're medical doctors who specialise in eye surgeries. They'd treat things like cataracts and glaucoma.'

Tom stared at the row of dead victims. 'He's a big player, alright.'

'Ophthalmologists need to be licensed, and different states have different rules for licensing.' With a smile, Olivia added, 'Or so my daughter tells me. He can't just roam around practising his profession, although the victims wouldn't know that.'

Jack nodded. 'He's definitely retired. Another boxed ticked.'

'Retires from a good, honest profession, creeps around in Furlowes stabbing big guys to death,' muttered Perez. 'What the hell got into him?'

'Beats me,' said Morelli. 'You get tired of being a good guy and just decide to be a bad guy?'

'He's been wanting to do this for a long, long time,' said Tom.

'Most of the victims were killed at night,' Jack recalled. 'No matter how good an eye doctor you are, you wouldn't spot these issues at night. How did he see their eye problems?'

'He first met them in the day,' explained Olivia. 'Whether the same day or the day before. He's sociable and meets lots of people. Finds it easy to approach them.'

'And says what to them?' asked Perez.

'Starts a conversation, like I do in my job. Ask to borrow a phone or a phone charger. Pretend to have found a pen or a five-pound – five-dollar – note and ask if it's theirs. See people trying to take selfies and ask them if they want you to take the picture. Whatever it takes.'

'I can see that.' Morelli nodded. 'Befriend a person one day, murder them the next.'

'Wouldn't have happened that way with Rick,' said Jack. 'He wasn't the conversational type.'

'Maybe not.' Olivia perched on the end of a desk with one foot on the floor, the other in mid-air. 'So Dean sees Rick in the day. Says something about noticing Rick has an eye issue, and says, "If you ever need a doctor, let me know." Rick walks away. In the night, Rick is at the standpipe, and Dean wanders over. Tries to strike up a conversation again. Rick isn't interested and heads for his trailer, unaware a killer is following him.'

'He felt confident and brave enough to do that after previous successful kills,' said Tom.

'Got a new thrill from knowing he was about to take down moody Rick,' said Jack.

'We have our fair share of psychopaths in England. We've had a couple of serial killers in the medical field – Doctor Harold Shipman, Nurse Beverly Allitt – but they murdered their own patients, not some random beefy guys. What's he got against fit male bodies?'

'Haven't given up my original thought that there could be a military connection,' said Jack.

'That's possible, though we can't rule out the jealousy thing,' said Tom. 'This whole killing spree started in Pennsylvania. I think that's where he established himself in his profession. Probably still lives there.'

'The "why" part is way over my head,' said Olivia. 'I was thinking he's a madman seizing every opportunity to kill.'

'Oh, he's not mad,' said Tom. 'Certainly not mad at all, though you have to have some mental failing to act as he does. Could be any one of many events that led him here, and he may have more than one motive.'

Jack frowned. 'One thing's for sure. He enjoys killing, and I don't think he's going to stop of his own free will.'

'The ones who get away with killing in the daytime are the worst,' said Tom. 'Gives them a sense of invincibility. You're strolling through the park in the sunshine, next thing it's lights out.'

'And he's claiming trophies from the victims,' said Morelli. 'He stole a keychain, a Harley toy emblem and a ring – that we know of.'

'And a chain with a mermaid from Nathaniel,' recalled Olivia.

Perez added, 'We believe he would have swiped a memento from the others, too, but the relatives haven't identified it. My guess is, when we find him, he'll have a personal treasure trove.' She directed a look of admiration at the private investigator. 'Good job, Olivia.'

'Yeah, great work, Olivia,' said Morelli.

As the team all mumbled their appreciation, Olivia felt giddy with pride. Perez and Morelli were finally engaging with her as if she was of them. For the first time, she felt like a real part of the taskforce, not an add-on.

'Tom's guys did a great job with the new composite,' said

Jack. 'We need to get copies to all the murder sites and see if any-body recognises him.'

'What about the media?' asked Perez. 'They need to see this.'

'I'll talk to the media team,' said Jack. 'Under no circum-stances should anyone mention Indiana or say anything about his possible career as an eye doctor. He'll be watching, and I don't want him thinking we're any closer to identifying him.'

Olivia stared at Jack as he took control. The meeting seemed to have lit a spark in him, and he was more buoyant and enthu-siastic. Another thing she noticed was that he wasn't absently playing with the ring on his finger anymore.

'The killer is no ordinary Joe. He's smart,' said Jack. 'He knows how to stay off grid. To nail him, we need to go back to the beginning, back to Penn state, and start from there.'

'Makes sense,' agreed Tom.

'Chesca and Marty, you need to canvass the parks with the new composite. Call in favours from every ranger you know. Me and Tom will catch a flight to Philadelphia tomorrow. We'll visit every school for eye doctors, and talk to every ophthalmology practice if we have to. Olivia, you're with us — unless you can't make it to Philly?'

'I'll notify my wing-woman,' said Olivia, excited at the pros-pect. 'You can get an extra pair of plane tickets.'

27

THE ISB CALLED him Dean? How basic. He had always thought the feds lacked imagination as well as sense, and now they'd proved it. The media had a much better idea. The Parkside Killer was a more fitting moniker, although he much preferred his own attempt: The Cross-State Killer.

He drove with one eye on the late-night traffic and the other on the TV attached to the dashboard. South Dakota was nice, and Palisades was a lovely park. Now he'd set his sights on another place in South Dakota: Larsson's Crooked Creek Resort, five hours away. He hoped the truck would make it there. Brand new off the manufacturers' forecourt two years ago, it shouldn't be complaining now, despite the thousands of miles covered. But the engine was making strange sounds. At least, he thought it was the engine; he was not the kind to ever try and understand what went on under the hood. The last thing he needed was a broken-down vehicle. The sort of ridiculous unexpected issue that would have some helpful cop pull over and offer to assist. God forbid.

His body tally had climbed nicely. The latest body, he'd learned, had been a realtor. Most people had strong opinions about them. Loved them or hated them. Having never purchased a house in his whole life, he had no feelings towards realtors one way or the other.

The man had caught his eye almost as soon as he arrived at Palisades State Park that morning. Dressed in a muscle top stretched over his torso, he was the right type. It was hard to get a good look at his face, though. He'd followed the man behind a rocky outcrop to find him standing on a ledge, close to the cliffs, pretending to be transfixed by the waters in order to avoid eye contact and the need to be civil.

He had sized up two other men, but there was nothing wrong with them that would allow him to show off his expertise. He enjoyed speaking about his profession. Some people were bored by it, others were very interested. It was the one thing in life he had excelled at, and so was worth talking about.

Once he'd decided that Mr Realtor did indeed fit the bill, he'd perched beside him and delivered his usual spiel. The knife sunk deep into his temple with ease, sending an unexpected spurt of warm red blood onto Dean's shirt. Sticky stuff, blood. Luckily, the vest beneath his shirt had remained untouched. He had rolled up the soiled item and stuffed it into the bottom of his knapsack. A good morning's work.

As he pulled up at a stoplight, he stared at the latest TV news with interest. The new composite image was a big surprise. It was a vast improvement on the first, and, more worryingly, a good likeness. Somehow, somewhere, he'd made a mistake, and someone had noticed him. There were no surveillance cameras in the Palisades area. In any event, a video recording would never have picked up these new details, as he wore a wide sun hat and sunglasses to disguise his features. Those were definitely his ears. He frowned darkly. It must have been the busybody clerk at the entrance to Palisades; he'd briefly removed his hat to fan himself when speaking to him. In future, he would need to be way more careful.

Some comfort could be taken from the fact that no one who knew him in person really knew him. Colleagues, acquaintances, old friends: none would ever suspect it was him. The thought would never cross their minds. Avid reader, yes. After-dinner trivia specialist, yes. Cryptic-crossword expert, yes. Serial killer, no.

As the stoplight turned green, he pulled away. He was still way ahead of law enforcement and planned to stay that way. They had not one shred of evidence against him, other than a knife that could belong to anyone. He had left no fingerprints, no evidence that could ever lead them to him.

The idiots still only knew about seven bodies and would never get any the wiser. Some killers were stupid enough to get caught after just one or two kills. They did not take the time to cover their tracks and watch how law enforcement reacted to the killings. Staying too long in one place was a bad idea, for starters. Why stay in one state when there was a big wide world out there to explore? Fifty states, to be exact. Fifty states, each with glorious wildernesses to discover. Why not cause a stir in a few of them?

It had taken nine months before his deeds finally made their way on to the news, which just went to show how good his strategy was. Even though the feds now knew it was a single killer, they would never pick him up.

It rather annoyed him that no name had been attached to his Illinois victim. His list would look incomplete with just a John Doe on it. He supposed he could make up a name, but that was like cheating. An accurate list of names was necessary for the sake of completeness.

The talking heads on TV were a joke. They thrived on guesswork and supposition. Not one thing the academics and so-called crime experts said about him was true. Well, other than that he enjoyed his work, but it didn't take Lieutenant Columbo to work that one out.

A lady lawyer with bouffant hair and full make-up declared in a shrill voice that he was a soulless personality with no family or friends. He laughed at that. Why would these people associate murder with friendship? It wasn't as if he needed a sideman to carry his bags or act as chauffeur. Murder was a one-man thing, unless you were lazy or stupid. The lady lawyer should appreciate he had provided work so she could pay for her Botox treatments. Wrinkled witches like her got eighty-sixed from TV jobs every day.

He pulled over about a quarter mile away from his destination park and hid the vehicle in a secluded area of the woods, away from the streetlights. Might as well get a good nap before the sun rose. He set his alarm for 4am, curled up on the back seat and closed his eyes. For one unfortunate man at Larsson's Crooked Creek, dawn would be the first and last part of the day they would ever see.

28

THE NEXT DAY, Olivia and Amy took a flight from South Dakota and arrived at a fashionable hotel in downtown Philadelphia in the early afternoon. Reception was all swirling grey-and-white marble, with chandeliers dangling from the ceiling. The desk was staffed by two beaming young women in crisp red suits. As soon as Olivia gave their names, the receptionist directed her to the main boardroom.

'A Mr Jack Tyler reserved it for a meeting, Mrs Knightley. He and Mr Walsh are waiting for you.'

Olivia frowned. The special agents had taken an earlier flight, and she was surprised that Jack would arrange a meeting with no notice.

'Thank you,' said Olivia. 'Can someone take the bags up to our room, please?'

'Of course, we can arrange that for you.'

'Can I sit in on the meeting?' asked Amy.

'Sorry, love.' Olivia pecked her on the cheek. 'This place has got a pool and spa. Go relax and enjoy yourself. You'll have a whale of a time.'

Olivia headed off down a corridor, which led to an area dedicated to commercial activities. She could see business meetings in progress. The door to the boardroom was ajar. Both Jack and Tom looked up when she pushed it open.

'Another body found this morning,' announced Jack, his voice tight with rage.

Olivia struggled to overcome an acute sense of despair. 'Oh, no.'

The room was a windowless space with heavy wallpaper and small vases of fresh flowers that delivered a pleasant scent. Olivia sank onto one of the padded chairs arranged around a plush walnut table, discreetly slipped off her sandals and planted her bare feet into the soft carpet.

Jack continued, 'Second one in South Dakota. Larsson's Crooked Creek; it's a campsite about three hundred miles from Palisades.'

On a sixty-inch screen anchored to the wall were Perez and Morelli, surrounded by the trees and woodland of Larsson's resort.

'Name's Zach Harrison,' said Perez, her voice crystal clear over the speakers. 'Medical examiner says he was killed in the early hours of this morning — and I mean early, like between three and six.'

The latest victim was a forty-two-year-old white male found behind dense bushes in the campground. Olivia stared at the image of the dead man, flat on his back in the grass. Broad-chested and once handsome. His blond hair was matted with blood, his blue eyes shocked, wide and staring. There was a deep, red, vicious-looking wound in the soft spot just below his Adam's apple. His arms and legs were stretched out, a phone was clutched in his hand, and a pair of broken glasses lay close to his face. Olivia's stomach churned. The last face this man saw before everything went dark was a friendly killer.

'Get anything from his phone?' asked Jack.

'No, it wasn't locked though.' Morelli held up the bright lilac phone. 'Still got plenty of juice. I've scrolled through his photos for the last couple of days. Hoped to find a selfie of him with his killer. No such luck.'

'Any witnesses?' asked Tom.

'We're talking to campers who were up early this morning, but so far no one saw a thing out of the ordinary,' said Perez. 'The person who found the vic came out of his RV for a smoke. Didn't see anyone near the body.'

'I've shown the updated composite around,' said Morelli. 'Haven't caught a break yet.'

'Got a call from a farmer near to Hawkeye though,' said Perez. 'Reported a disturbed area on his land. I went to take a look, found a matchbox. Looked like someone lit a fire and could've camped there.'

'Could be him,' said Jack. 'He's comfortable in the woods. Either someone trained him to live rough or he trained himself.'

'You know, the more I look at the new image, the more the face looks familiar,' said Olivia. 'I'm not sure if it's because I've seen him before or because I've stared at so many people with a close likeness to him.'

'Give it some more thought,' said Jack. 'He's out of control, and we've got to stop him picking off anyone else.'

'Can't get my head around why anyone would do this, let alone an eye doctor,' said Perez. 'Whatever happened to that oath they take?'

'Maybe his clients back in the day were big guys, boastful sorts, and he grew to hate the sight of them?' offered Olivia. 'Or maybe he just felt inadequate around them, and hated them because he didn't measure up?'

'Human beings have various triggers. It's hard to second guess,' said Tom. 'I've come across people who have playground fights as kids and carry that grudge into adulthood.'

'If he's watching TV, do you think he might change direction now he knows you're after him?' asked Olivia. 'Like head up to North Dakota, maybe?'

'He'll continue west,' said Jack with certainty. 'This man knows what he's doing and he's stubborn. He's on a mission; he won't change track. He's showing us what he can do and relishing the fact that we can't stop him.'

Tom said, 'We can't suggest a lockdown of every campsite and park in South Dakota, Montana and Wyoming, but they do need to be on alert.'

'I agree,' said Jack. 'Marty, can you get on it?'

'Sure thing.'

'I'll show the latest composite at a couple of gas stations and food stores,' said Perez. 'Even a killer's got to eat.'

'This has to be the last dead victim.' Jack ran a weary hand through his hair. 'Tom, can we get the lab guys to imagine him around twenty years younger? We need a second composite we can show around. Maybe somebody will remember him from his younger days.'

'We're in a line for services, but I'll put a rush on it,' said Tom. 'Press them to get us something by tonight.'

'Great. Tomorrow, we knock on doors. Kick them off if they won't open. As well as the medical sites, I intend to hit the military camps.'

After the meeting, Olivia left the two agents in the room together and went in search of Amy. Her head was buzzing with the news of another murder. The victim's fixed expression of disbelief stayed at the forefront of her mind. The pain and shock of sudden death must have been immense. An involuntary shudder ran through her body. She could but hope to get through the night without picking every single hair out of her head. That silk bonnet would have to be secured firmly with hairpins.

She still could not shake the feeling that she had seen Dean before. She had stared at so many men at various parks that it was no surprise her memory would suggest a physical encounter. Even Amy had warned her off her habit of doing so.

She walked through the pool area, inhaling the chlorine as she gazed at guests enjoying the enticing water. She found Amy in the adjoining spa, reclining on a lounger, hair wrapped up in a towel atop her head, eyes closed. The elegant steam room smelled of lavender, and candle flames flickered softly in the low light. It was certainly the place to rejuvenate your mind and soul. Her daughter looked so serene, Olivia hesitated to interrupt her. She undressed, slipped into a soft, white gown and took the lounger beside her.

'Enjoying yourself, madam?'

'Yes, I am,' murmured Amy. 'What's with the meeting? The cops found more evidence on Dean?'

Olivia could not bear to relate the latest horrific news. Her soul needed five minutes of peace. 'I'll tell you about it later, love. For now, relax.'

'Who knew such luxuries existed?' Amy closed her eyes and nestled down into the lounger. 'This is all on the ISB, right?'

'Right.'

'Good, because I've booked a deep massage, and they said it was extra. A lot extra.'

Olivia smiled. 'Jack said the ISB budget is nothing like the FBI budget. Let's not go overboard.'

Amy's eyes flew open and she sat up abruptly. 'Mom, these cops have you holed up in a room looking at dead bodies every day. They've got you out on the road before cockerels are awake. They've got you flying from state to state — and I bet they never thought to check how you feel about flying? We're entitled to go overboard. Nothing less than overboard will do. In fact, if we do not go overboard, I will never, ever forgive you!'

Olivia laughed at the sudden outburst. 'I hear you loud and clear. Overboard it is.'

Her daughter was right. What with Chris and Bill and threats of litigation, and now the hunt for a serial killer, she needed to spend more time on self-care. The whole idea of getting away from London had been to get away from work and the stresses of her personal and professional life, and bond with her daughter. Yet here she was, thousands of miles off the original itinerary, filling her already over-extended brain with thoughts of how to identify a killer and where to look for him. Bill would be taken aback by it all. If they caught Dean, she would tell him all about it. If not, he would never hear about her impromptu job.

She and Amy deserved every perk the hotel had to offer, but she would not stick Jack Tyler with the whole bill. The luxuries she would pay for herself. She had not thought to bring swimming costumes with them, having urgently packed just a few changes of clothes in the rush to leave Palisades. The hotel had a gift shop selling everything a guest could need, and was sure to have a few decent one-pieces to choose from.

'Do you want to go for a swim before that massage?' she asked.

'Love to! Hope they have swimming caps here. I really don't want to get my hair wet.'

'Let's pop into the shop.'

Amy gazed at her mother slyly. 'How much are they paying you, by the way?'

'Never you mind.'

Though not a strong swimmer, Olivia enjoyed the swim, and her limbs thanked her for stretching. She savoured the warm water against her skin. Amy showed her prowess, doing length after length with ease, and Olivia made no attempt to keep up with the younger limbs. When Amy eventually tired, she slowed down and the two swam side by side. This was how it should be: she and her daughter, in sync. She would not let the murder investigation interfere with their relationship. Tomorrow, they would also work side by side.

'Massage time, Mom.'

'Right behind you, love.'

29

B ACK IN HIS hotel room, Jack Tyler drained the glass of bourbon, pushed the half-empty bottle towards the end of his
desk and massaged his temples. He had already knocked back
two with Tom at the bar before calling it a night, and drinking on
his own was never a good thing. The loss of another innocent life
weighed heavily on his mind. One step forwards, two steps backwards. Nine bodies.

The latest victim was a manager of an independent grocery
business. A hardworking young man who'd taken a few days off
work to enjoy the countryside. Dead on his second night at the
park. Local police officers would inform the parents. That was
the worst part of the job, the part Jack was keen for others to take
on. He remembered all those years as a homicide detective when
he was that man who knocked on the door and delivered a
sledgehammer blow to the lives of a family. Some fainted. Some
crumbled and screamed uncontrollably. Others just stared at
him. Not everybody could get their heads around devastating
news in a split second. He would never forget the father who
insisted his teenage daughter was in bed. Jack accompanied him
to the girl's bedroom, and watched him collapse in misery on the
unslept-in bed as the truth hit him.

Jack drew the bourbon bottle forwards and poured another shot. He had tried getting some sleep, lying on top of the standard-sized bed without bothering to remove the duvet. The sheets were tucked in so tightly he wondered how the maids had the strength to manage it when they must be changing dozens a day.

The desk and floor were littered with gruesome photos of dead people and newspaper clippings he'd brought with him. The maid would get a terrible shock if she happened to walk into his room. When this crossed his mind, he got up and hung the 'Do Not Disturb' sign outside the door, in case he forgot in the morning. He did not want to be the cause of anyone else's trauma. The morning. It was already morning, nearly 2am.

He stared at Dean's composite photos, one showing him in around his mid-fifties, the other mid-thirties. Impressive what the lab tech guys could do with their software. For a long time, he studied the younger image and wondered what could have happened over the decades to make someone turn to violent, bloody crimes? Could he have committed murders many years ago, stopped, and now resumed? Although it was possible, it did not seem likely. According to Tom, few waited until they aged considerably to continue their rampage. The only ones the FBI knew of who temporarily stopped their murder rampages were forced to do so because of incarceration for other crimes. Once they got out, they went back to their homicidal ways. Jack was convinced Dean had no criminal record; it was more likely that he appeared to be a pillar of the community.

Jack popped a Xanax as a pang of guilt went through his stomach, mixing uncomfortably with the alcohol. If he had made the connection with Nathaniel Jeynes's death in Illinois, maybe he would have caught Dean by now. Four men died after Nathaniel. He tried to rid himself of the thought. The park rangers, sheriffs, police departments, all were overwhelmed with work, and the loss of life was down to one man. A ruthless knifeman.

Now he must concentrate on stopping the killer in his tracks. Jack turned on his laptop and added more institutions to the list they needed to hit at opening time. As the list grew, he became aware the mission could take a few days. Universities, colleges, eye doctors galore: every place connected with eye medicine that he could think of went on the list. Penn Medicine's Department of Ophthalmology was top of the list, followed by Wills Eye Hospital, which served as the Department of Ophthalmology for Thomas Jefferson University's medical school. He assigned most of the institutions to Tom and Olivia.

He would personally investigate the likely military connection. He looked up Pennsylvania military camps. Three looked promising: Valley Forge Military Academy, Philadelphia Military Academy and Carlisle Barracks. Someone here might know Dean's identity, whether because he had once been a military officer, or because he had provided optometric services to their men.

Olivia Knightley had proven essential to the case, and he was glad she had joined them in Philadelphia. Tom had welcomed her input quite early on, and he was relieved that Perez and Morelli were now all in favour. Olivia had a clear head for the case. Unlike himself and Tom, she had no behavioural science training to rely on, just clever thinking and a keen eye for detail. The lead that the killer could be an eye doctor was a good one and he hoped it panned out. If it did not, well, they would have lost a day or two, but as the team had not made much headway since their formation in February, he still considered it worth investigating.

Kent Hilson had wasted his valuable time. He could not imagine why the photographer would prefer to be a murder suspect and mislead them, rather than hold his hands up to a lesser crime. He was not a killer, but a man who had shattered lives in a different, painful way. How did the man find stamina for four marital relationships? Jack could not keep even one wife happy. No way would he have been able to maintain the lies and remember which wife he'd told what. At one point back in his single days, Jack had tried juggling two girlfriends, and that had proved one too many.

No doubt Hilson gave the women good reason why he could not wear a ring. Easily irritated skin was probably the excuse. Less problematic than wearing four rings and having to keep changing them. Those kids were going to be traumatised when they realised that they had previously unknown siblings all over the place. That the dad they thought they knew was a liar and a criminal. Filled with a sudden intense dislike for the man, he vowed to nudge the police in Hilson's direction rather than wait on the wives to do so.

His mind went back to Olivia and he frowned suddenly. Instead of bringing the meeting to a close earlier and bidding her goodnight, he should have at least asked her and Amy to join him and Tom for dinner. Too busy mentally formulating plans for the mammoth task ahead, it had not crossed his mind. He hoped Olivia was content spending time with her daughter and would not hold it against him.

He kicked off his shoes and laid on the bed fully clothed, hands looped behind his head. He stared at the ceiling and found himself wondering what really motivated this private investigator from Great Britain. Clearly she was a good person who cared about others. Spurred on by the death of Rick Seagal, she had dived in head first, and the incarceration of Lamar Webster had undoubtedly added fuel to her fire. A spark of a temper was always there, simmering beneath the surface, yet she was pretty good at keeping her composure. It was good when women had that confidence and would not cower when they were right.

He was lucky to have her on board; for how long, he did not know.

The daughter Amy was smart, a real handful, but Olivia seemed to have things under control. He thought of his own daughter, Holly, now twenty-one; he remembered her as a rebellious teenager, always challenging her mother. Perhaps it was a rite of passage with girls: test Mom to the limit, be friendlier with Dad. A frown lined his brow as he wondered what Olivia's ex-husband was like. Amy's complexion suggested her father was white, but that was all he knew about him. As soon as the thought hit him, he chided himself. Her family life was none of his business. Still, he could not help but wonder. Olivia Knightley intrigued him, and there was no point denying it. He gazed at his ring finger. If the circumstances were different, he probably would have invited her for a one-on-one dinner by now.

30

IN THE MORNING, Amy insisted they make use of the hotel pool as soon as they woke up. Although Olivia was keen to start on the list of businesses and institutions Jack had emailed to her, she had to accept that it was way too early to visit any of those places. Nowhere opened for business until nine o'clock. In any event, she did like the idea of a good swim.

After an hour doing laps in the pool, they helped themselves to breakfast from the buffet. Amy piled her plate high with sausages, bacon and eggs, while Olivia opted for a fluffy omelette and rich muesli. As they ate, Olivia glanced around at other diners, most of whom also had stacked plates. Something about hotel buffets seemed to make a pig of everyone. Either being away from home made people hungrier than usual, or the immediate availability of ready-cooked meals was too much to resist.

'Just as well you're stuffing yourself. Once we start working, I'm not sure if we'll get a break for lunch.'

'Oh come on, Mom. It's not like we're going down a coal mine, is it? Philly is a big city with restaurants and cafés everywhere.'

'Today you're going to be a dedicated private investigator, and you'll learn that it doesn't work like that,' said Olivia. 'Keeping up the momentum is important. When you start, it's best to stick at it, even when your throat is tired from asking questions. Even if that means you keep going until sunset.'

'I'd have to take at least one break.'

'I'm sure we'll fit one in. You can lose leads by taking a break, though. You'll be watching someone and think you've got them covered, pop into a shop for a bag of crisps, come out and they're gone. It's happened to me more than once.'

'I can just imagine your face.' Amy impersonated a hangdog look.

Olivia poked her under the table with her trainers. 'I put as much into the day as early as possible. If I get information that I can follow up in the afternoon, I'll do it. Keep the energy going for the entire day, and take it down a notch at night.'

'I'm not afraid to be out working at night.'

'I know you're not.' Olivia savoured her tasty omelette. 'Good thing I've got enough fear for both of us.'

Amy's phone rang and she quickly pressed the cancel button.

'It's Dad. I'll text him.'

Olivia watched as her daughter's fingers typed a message at speed.

'I told him the truth; we're going on the road and I'll call him later. He doesn't need to know which road.' Amy took a mouthful of sausage. 'And I'm not calling him.'

Olivia felt a sense of disquiet. 'This is so bad, you lying to your father. Alright, not outright lying, but keeping him in the dark. You'll have to call him later, or he won't stop. He'll probably guess something's up and start ringing my phone again.'

'What should I say?'

'Say we're in Philly. Tell him you found the original itinerary too restrictive and decided to go elsewhere.'

'I'll tell him I woke up yesterday with an overwhelming need to see the Liberty Bell, so we dumped Tango and took a plane.'

'I think he'll appreciate the reasoning.'

As she gazed around the tables, Olivia picked up various accents, mainly American with varying drawls, but she caught a hint of German from one couple, and a few words of Japanese from another. A sprinkling were casually dressed for a holiday; some were in crisp business suits with ties, despite the summer heat.

Reaching across to the nearest table, Olivia retrieved a discarded newspaper and flicked idly through the pages. Local news, business, politics, entertainment, sports. She had little interest in the types of sports most popular in America: basketball, baseball, football. Football – with helmets, shoulder pads and an oval ball you picked up. Overleaf was a story about athletes training for the sprint races. She was a big fan of sprinters from all over the world, particularly the Jamaican women who dominated at every major championship. She folded the paper and glanced over at her daughter's feet.

'Ready to go, madam? Are you not going to change out of those sandals? You need to be comfortable.'

'Relax, I'll be fine, Mom.'

*

Shortly after nine o'clock, Olivia and Amy, both carrying tote bags containing stacks of 'Wanted' posters, headed out of the hotel. The smiling concierge in a gold-studded uniform nodded a greeting and prevented the automatic doors from closing on them.

'We can hire a car, can't we?' suggested Amy. 'Something nice and luxurious with air-con and big rims. Remember, you can claim the fee as an expense.'

'No, there are cabs everywhere. My, you're determined to rack up a bill for the ISB, aren't you?'

'We deserve comfort.'

'We do, and we'll get it taking ordinary cabs.'

'Oh, well. It was worth a try.'

During the course of the day, they visited many ophthalmologist practices, sharing the posters and asking for information. Some of the businesses were mere blocks apart and did not warrant a taxi ride. The wide pavements were busy with pedestrians whose morning commute was accompanied by the tune of horns blared by irritated motorists struggling through traffic. A real bustling metropolis. The unusual sight of trolley cars caught the Londoners' attention; their old-fashioned, classic look differed from the more modern looking tramcars they were used to seeing in Croydon.

In Center City, they passed the impressive Philadelphia City Hall and headed on to Walnut Street. As they walked, Amy pointed out other interesting places. Olivia, in her private-eye zone, barely noticed anything; her only focus was the apprehension of a dangerous and seemingly unstoppable killer. No one they spoke to could identify either photofit image of Dean, the young or the older. Occasionally, Olivia glanced at her phone, which remained silent. If either of the special agents had caught anything, they would have contacted her by now. Tom was at a university and Jack was at a military barracks.

Olivia had her ID card at the ready, as she expected to be challenged on her role as private investigator, but seeing the 'Wanted' posters was enough for citizens to be willing to have a good look at the suspect's image without asking her detailed questions. Many had seen the original report on the news and were well aware the killer was still on the move.

'You think he's in Philadelphia?' asked one alarmed assistant at an eye clinic.

'No, not at all.' Olivia delivered a bright and, she hoped, reassuring smile. 'He may have lived in Pennsylvania at some time. Might still have a home here, but at the moment he's believed to be in South Dakota.'

'Shouldn't you all be there looking for him?'

'There are lots of police and special agents doing just that, I can assure you.'

'Well, good luck! I really hope you get him soon.'

As they left the clinic, Amy glanced at a poster critically. 'They should have printed his nickname, The Parkside Killer, on it. The page looks bland with just a photo and a statement that he's wanted for murders in the listed states.'

'Tom says they try to discourage the media from naming them. Some killers enjoy the Hollywood-style publicity. Take pride in their notoriety. It encourages them. Worse still, some otherwise normal citizens tend to hero-worship killers with catchy nicknames, and root for them.'

'Did you ever hear from that evil blogger woman again?'

'No, but I see she's still hot on this case. Kim Grant's her name – and she's not evil, Amy. Any information I'm free to share, I'll send her way.'

'You are joking, Mom? After how she spoke to you? She'd have plucked your eyes out if we weren't in front of a police station.'

'It's business with her, love, not personal.'

They tried a few opticians and optometrists as well as ophthalmologists. Although everyone was sympathetic and interested, no one could offer any leads.

'Can we not take a ten-minute break, Mom? That must be the twentieth shop we've been in. My feet are killing me.'

'I knew this would happen,' said Olivia. 'Bad footwear.'

'My feet need to breathe in this weather; sandals work better.'

'Let's sit over there for a bit.' Olivia pointed at a low wall under a tree. 'And let it be a reminder to you that private-eye work is not only driving around. It's walking around, too, and decent footwear is essential. Trainers, preferably.'

Training shoes, good for people who liked to walk, while Furlowe boots were good for murderers who liked to stalk. As she sank onto the cool concrete, Olivia was glad to take the weight off her feet. She stared at the footwear of the people who walked past them. Her eyes followed two fit-looking older men. Both wore trainers with shorts and vests, and had sports bags hanging from their shoulders. Not as physically fit as the athletes she'd admired in the newspaper earlier, but they looked quite healthy. The men crossed the road and entered a gymnasium. A thought began to grow in her mind.

'Are you finished resting, Amy?'

'Yep. Round two, here we come.' Amy stood up and stretched her arms to the heavens.

A wave of motherly concern hit Olivia. 'You know, we can buy some trainers if you want, or some comfy walking sandals?'

'Don't tempt me, Mom. I'll never walk in and out of a shoe store in five minutes. So many brands and styles. I need a good hour to indulge in the search.'

Olivia smiled. 'You're right – and we don't have an hour to spare.'

'Where's next on your list?'

'It wasn't on my list.' Olivia pointed across the road. 'You see that gym? That's where we're going.'

'Wouldn't have even noticed it,' said Amy. 'All that glass and stainless steel; I would've just thought it was another flashy store.' She glanced quizzically at her mother. 'What could we possibly want in there? They won't have an eye doctor.'

As they walked towards the pedestrian crossing, Olivia said, 'My old gym used to give out discount vouchers for opticians' visits, and dentists, too. You know, vouchers for twenty percent off glasses if you buy a one-year membership card? I don't know if they do that sort of thing in America.'

'Okay, but how does that help us?'

'I've been thinking maybe we're going about this in too broad a way. We need to narrow the focus.'

The digital image of a stick-like man flashed, and all the vehicles slowed to a halt. Olivia and Amy crossed four lanes of traffic to the other side.

'Narrowing the focus makes sense, Mom, but why the gym?'

'We know that the killer has something against well-built men. They may have been his clients. The gym may have a list of eye doctors who offer discounts to their members.'

Amy considered this for a moment. 'And one of those doctors might be our man. I get it, cool.'

Inside, the gym was just as impressive as it was outside, cool and light. Elliptical machines, stationary bikes, free weights, muscle machines. Males pumping iron, sweating and occasionally grunting. Although Olivia was quite comfortable with her soft, womanly middle, the many well-toned women made her feel body-conscious. Having long given up the fight to keep a washboard stomach, she would never dream of wearing a sports bra without T-shirt to exercise.

The bubbly receptionist was the sweet, excitable type who could keep up that front for the whole day. The gym did not have any eye doctors on their list, but she was enthusiastic about the idea of getting some. She wanted to engage Olivia in a conversation about England, but Olivia handed her a 'Wanted' poster and forced her attention in the right direction.

As they left, Amy said, 'Well, you made a new friend, and those skinny minnies made me think I shouldn't have eaten so many sausages. I'm sure that blonde woman by the water cooler lives on kale and cucumber.'

'Good for her, if she enjoys it,' said Olivia. 'You eat what you like in moderation, Amy. Get some enjoyment out of food. As long as you're not stuffing pizza and soda every day, you'll be just fine.'

Amy searched on her phone. 'There's another gym around the corner. Looks about a ten-minute walk from here.'

At the next gym, the receptionist was polite, but said they had no one offering medical benefits for gym members. The only discounts their members could get were for car rentals and trips to a casino. She barely glanced at the 'Wanted' poster when she discovered the newcomers had no interest in joining the facility.

In order to spare her daughter's feet – and her own ears from moans – Olivia hailed a taxi to the third gym. It was a chain gym, the kind that advertised on TV, promising to give clients a super-model's body in six months. When members swiped a card, the glass door opened to allow them in and slid closed a split second later. Olivia had to press a button to gain access to the lobby area, which was full of attractive people clad in the latest workout gear, bottles of expensive water in hand.

'What are they protecting in here that means people can't just walk in?' said Amy in disdain.

'Smile and look sweet. I know you can do it.'

Amy grinned and poked her mother in the back.

'Hey guys! You come to join us?' asked the receptionist, a small thing with a painted face that suggested she did not go in for the sweaty stuff.

Olivia offered a bright smile, which Amy replicated. 'Not today, I'm afraid,' Olivia said. 'I was hoping for some help though.'

'Ooh, I love your accent. Where are you from?'

Olivia maintained her smile, while thinking she needed to prepare a one-line answer to this often-repeated question. 'From London, but I'm on a working holiday.' She showed the woman her ID card.

'A private investigator from London? You're like Miss Marple?'

'She can only aspire to be as good,' said Amy brightly.

The receptionist showed sparkling teeth. 'What can I do for you guys?'

Olivia handed her a 'Wanted' poster. As the woman read it, Olivia glanced around the area. Another set of double doors provided a barrier to the gymnasium, so she could not see the clients inside. On the walls behind the reception countertop were posters of the interior of the gym, and of members posing beside various pieces of equipment. The top of a filing cabinet contained joining forms and brochures.

'Never seen him before. Awful man, going around murdering innocent people.'

'Do you offer membership benefits here?' asked Olivia.

'Sure do.' The woman picked up two single-page brochures and handed one to Olivia and the other to Amy. 'We pride ourselves on promising the best results out of any gym in the whole state.'

'Sounds good.' Olivia scanned the brochure quickly and looked up at the woman. 'My mistake, I don't mean the benefits they get from using the gym. I was thinking more like discount benefits your members get from using other people's services, like spas, dentists, eye doctors . . . that sort of thing.'

'Oh, that. Sure.' She reached for another brochure. 'Yes, full members can get great discounts from any one of these great sponsors. Let me see. We've got auto dealers, florists, cafés, dentists and yes, even an eye doctor . . . at least three of them at this one place.'

'Thank you, that's great.' Olivia almost snatched the brochure out of her hand. She scanned the sheet. A medical practice with a team of eye specialists. 'Do you know any of the doctors there?'

'Not personally, no. But I've only been here a year.' The woman raised her eyebrows and her eyes widened. 'Does this have something to do with the killer?'

'You never know,' said Olivia. 'Thanks for your help. We'll check them out.'

As they left the gym, Amy removed the brochure from Olivia's hand.

Olivia held out an arm and flagged down a yellow cab. 'I have no idea where that place is, but we're going to find it.'

'Champion Vision Care,' read Amy. 'Here we come.'

31

JACK TYLER FELT drained as he drove from site to site, seeing more of Philadelphia than he had known existed. The morning was hot, made more uncomfortable by the jacket and tie he was not used to wearing. He guided his vehicle into the slow lane. Needing some positive news, he called Tom.

'No luck,' said Tom. 'Director of ophthalmology at Penn Medicine took a good look at the posters, had no clue. Viewed the yearbook photos, talked to staff members: nothing.'

'Same here,' said Jack. 'None of the officers at the Military Academy at Elverson had any idea, either. I'm heading to Valley Forge as we speak.'

'You had any doubts about all this, Jack? Suppose we're out here chasing a phantom while the devil is headed west? Lamar Webster could have been leading you on. A special agent and a private eye turn up to see him. Told you what he hoped you needed so he could get your help. The eyedrops thing could be a coincidence. All the crying . . . might just be a good actor?'

'Thought about it a lot.'

Jack had thought about it more than he planned to share with Tom, especially having relayed both the jail meeting and his strategy to the director. Concerned that questions might be raised about his reliance on a private investigator, he consciously left Olivia's name out of the equation. While he retained the full confidence of his boss, he was aware that pressure was being brought to bear from higher levels, and murmurs of discontent were growing. If he did not get solid results soon, the ISB could be forced to hand control of his case to the FBI. His case. Jack squeezed his steering wheel until his knuckles turned white. Tom was one of the best men he knew, but the idea that he might be ordered to take over Operation Dean was too much to even contemplate.

'Lamar Webster has no prior convictions,' Jack said. 'He gets up one day and murders his best friend in broad daylight? No way. What clinched it for me is that the description he gave of the suspect pretty much matched the description he gave cops on day one. Four months later, he hasn't wavered. He didn't make it up.'

'What did the officers make of the whole thing at the time?'

'They pretty much reckoned Lamar did it. Said they thought Lamar and Nathaniel were more than friends . . . their thinking is the murder was a result of a lovers' tiff. I suspect that's why they didn't give it the attention it deserved. Whether he's gay or not is neither here nor there in my book; he wasn't lying about Nathaniel's murderer.'

'You met him, and I trust you, Jack.'

'Glad someone does.' Jack allowed himself a smile. 'Keep at it. We'll catch up later.' He hung up and called Perez. 'Tell me what you've got, Chesca.'

'Zach's parents say he's stayed at Larsson's campground before and never had any problems. Lived to walk in the wilderness, apparently. He's missing a bracelet they say he treasured. I've got a picture of it. Our killer definitely collected another trophy.'

'I hear you.' Jack was momentarily distracted by thoughts of the grieving parents.

'I'm still checking gas stations and convenience stores; haven't come up with anything interesting yet.'

'Stay on it. Is Marty with you?'

'He's out briefing the sheriffs' offices and state police.'

'I'll leave him to it. We'll do a team call tonight, nine o'clock, and see where we are.'

Jack drove through the leafy suburb of Wayne and turned into the hundred-acre campus of Valley Forge Military Academy, established in 1928. The centre boasted that it combined academic excellence and military expertise with a focus on building character, physical fitness and encouraging leadership. It was a private boarding school, training young men and women through middle school, high school and military college.

The colonel who greeted him was a tall, sharp-suited man with a strong jaw and close-cropped silver-grey hair. He walked with a purposeful gait and offered a firm handshake.

'Thanks for agreeing to see me, sir,' said Jack.

'Anything I can do to help Special Agent Tyler – though I must admit, although I know of the National Park Service, the Investigative Services Branch is new to me.'

'I get that all the time.' Jack smiled. 'Never let it hurt my feelings.'

Few cars were in the huge car park, and there were only one or two people in sight. Jack had hoped to see the marching cadets in their uniforms. Nothing beat the vision of people with united hearts and minds marching to the same tune.

'Still on summer break?' he asked.

'Yes, only the leadership detail is back this week. Next week the plebes, football, soccer and band return. The week after, the cadets. This institution is not the same without them.'

Jack handed the colonel the two 'Wanted' posters, which he studied as they walked through the stately grounds.

'I certainly don't recognise him, and I've been here for nearly thirty years,' the colonel said, a deep frown etched in his tanned forehead. 'You think this man could have undergone military training somewhere and then went on to become an ophthalmologist? It would be a new one for me. I don't know of anyone who took up medicine after life at Valley Forge, but I imagine some would have.'

'The man is killing people with precision. He seems to have a fascination with using knives, not guns. Maybe he bailed out of training at some stage, only did a year or two?'

'The fast-track military degree is only two years,' said the colonel. He drew back his shoulders, chest forward in pride. 'I say only, but the cadets leave here confident, strong in mind, body and soul, masters of self-discipline and ready to lead their peers.'

Jack hid the faint smile that threatened to creep to his lips. No one prouder than an army chief waxing on about his favourite subject.

'What about the dropouts?'

'Over the years, we've had very few students leave us. We've been in existence for nearly a century, and we're pretty proud of our high graduation statistics. We give up on no one. That said, you're welcome to have access to the data we hold on students who gave up on themselves.'

'I appreciate it, colonel.' Jack thought for a moment. 'And he's never been a part of the leadership detail?'

The colonel shook his head. 'No, not leadership, nor clerical or administrative. Can't identify him training the cadets in any way, shape or form. Sorry, Special Agent Tyler. This face isn't registering with me.'

'Are there particular eye doctors the academy uses?'

'Yes. I can give a list of the ones we've used, and others that are on our recommended list.' The colonel gave Jack a sympathetic look. 'Looking for that proverbial needle is a nightmare, isn't it?'

'We have to find the needle, sir. Would help to have an industrial-sized magnet, but the needle must be found.'

'Would you like to go inside and talk to some of the other leaders? No one has been at Valley Forge as long as I have, but you never know.'

'Lead the way, sir, thank you.'

32

CHAMPION VISION CARE was a single-storey detached building on the outskirts of the downtown business district. The beige structure didn't offer much to aesthetics, although the fragrant flowers and exotic plants surrounding the entrance gave it an inviting touch. Most of the parking spaces in the large car park were occupied by high-end vehicles. The signage at the entrance listed the names of three doctors, partners in the optometry practice.

Olivia and Amy entered into a spacious, open-plan, white-marble area. On one side was the reception desk, on the other side a waiting area with plush single-seater sofas. High-definition televisions were mounted on each wall, all showing the same wildlife programme with the volume muted. Olivia guessed that even with the twenty percent discount offered to gym members, these doctors were more expensive than their rivals.

Clients young and old occupied the padded chairs. A few of the men were powerfully built types who looked like they spent hours working with weights. A lone security guard paced in the rear of the waiting area, occasionally glancing out the casement window.

Two women clad in crisp white uniforms manned the front desk. Both were preoccupied dealing with phone calls. Their lanyards named them as clinical assistants. A female client leaned against the desk, waiting to get their attention and Olivia stood behind her.

Amy gestured to the wall behind the doctors' assistants. 'Look up there, Mom.'

Displayed were large framed photographs of the three ophthalmologists, together with their illustrious array of certificates. An Asian female with glasses mounted over her perfectly made-up eyes, giving her an owlish look. A white male who looked in his early thirties, blond-haired and shiny-eyed. The third was a silver-haired man with perfect teeth that would not look out of place in a Colgate advert. Doctor Aston Rafferty, Ophthalmologist.

Olivia stared at his features long and hard. She could see a resemblance, although this doctor had a longer face. His ears were not protruding, but anything could be done with Photoshop and she was pretty sure each of these images had been adjusted to show the doctors in their best light.

'What do you think?' said Amy. 'I think it sort of looks like the killer.'

Olivia took a deep breath. 'Well, if Rafferty's here in this building, it's unlikely to be him. The killer's probably heading west, or is still in South Dakota.'

'These doctors have every single letter of the alphabet after their names,' said Amy in awe. 'And they make sure everybody knows it.'

'If you spend the better part of a decade learning your craft, it's fair play to shout as loud as you want to.'

Although Olivia appreciated their career choices, she could not imagine studying anything for that length of time. The three years she had spent studying for a degree in marketing was bad enough, and what she'd learned was not worth her time. The working world provided her with far more training for real life than a classroom ever did.

She stood impatiently at the counter, waiting her turn. One of the assistants had put down her phone and was now busy writing notes. The security guard ambled past and gave Olivia a brief glance before continuing his slow stroll. She curled her toes as the other assistant dealt with the client in front of her. Eventually, that client moved away.

'Good afternoon. Is it possible to see Doctor Rafferty?'

'Good afternoon, ma'am.' The woman stared back, unsmiling. Her pink cheeks suggested she was flustered and overworked. 'He's not here. Not registered with us are you?'

'No, I . . .'

'Fill out your details if you want to register.' The woman pushed a blank form and a pen towards her. 'You'll have a long wait, but you can see one of the other doctors.'

Olivia picked up the pen and tapped it on the form. 'Oh, is he out to lunch or not working today? I only want to register if I can see him. I hear he's very good.'

'All of our doctors are very good, and Doctor Rafferty's not here.' The woman's look told Olivia she was wasting both the woman's time and her own. 'He's on a sabbatical. He'll be back in a couple of months. If your eyes are giving you problems, you don't want to wait that long to be seen.'

Olivia felt Amy's nails sink into her bare arm. 'Oh, I'm sorry I missed him. Did he go just recently?'

'No,' she said brusquely. 'Now, if you'd like to register, please fill out the form. If not, can you move aside so I can deal with the next patient?'

Olivia held onto the pen and form, nodded her thanks and moved away.

'Oh my God, it must be him,' whispered Amy.

'Okay, Amy, stay calm. I need to think.' Olivia pulled Amy along and they sat in the waiting area. She pretended to read through the instructions for registration. 'These ladies are not going to give me any information about when he left or where he's gone.'

'I bet he's taken a year out,' declared Amy. 'The murders started in November, and a couple of months takes us to October. One whole year.'

'Give me a minute. I'm just thinking what's the best move.'

'Call Agent Tyler,' said Amy. 'They'll have to talk to him.'

'He's busy doing his thing,' said Olivia. 'I'm going to do mine.'

Unless she had sound evidence of Doctor Rafferty's involvement in the murders, she would not call Jack Tyler. While the doctor's absence from work certainly raised his profile as a prime suspect, it was not enough to go on. Olivia surveyed her surroundings. A patient's name was announced, and she watched the man head down a wide corridor.

'Mom, you're in your zone. You're not going to do anything dangerous, are you?'

Olivia weighed up whether to lie or provide an explanation. Instead she opted to ignore the question. 'You see the security guard over there? I need you to distract him while I go find Doctor Rafferty's office.'

'Distract him? What am I supposed to say?'

'He's got those little Pac-Man images on his tie, he's a gamer. Bright smile, hand him your phone and ask him to help you find a game.'

'Hmm. As a mother, you don't get any flowers sending me to chat up strange old men.'

'Not the time, young lady. Just go.'

Amy did as she was told. Olivia watched as the security guard took Amy's phone and pressed the keys, while her daughter maintained a baffled expression. Olivia glanced at the reception desk, grateful that the assistants were busy and no one was looking her way.

Tiny bits of perspiration prickled on her brow, despite the

interior temperature being extremely cool. She set off down the corridor, which was lined with glass offices on one side and solid walls on the other. Most of the glass was frosted, so although she could see that people were inside, they were just blurry shapes. She could make out clinical rooms containing tools and machinery used for eye testing and operations. For a moment, she hesitated. If she could see into these rooms, the people inside could certainly see her. The doctors' private rooms must be on the side with the solid walls. Before she could move along, a door opened and the female doctor stepped out almost in front of her. Olivia noticed with some disquiet that the Asian woman's image had not been manipulated. She was a real looker.

Olivia faked confusion. 'Am I going the right way to the ladies room?'

'Patients' restrooms are the other way.' The doctor frowned as she pointed back towards reception. 'Go past the water cooler and you'll see the doors. Two unisex restrooms.'

'Oh, thanks.' Deep in frustration, Olivia turned and walked back the way she'd come.

She caught Amy's eye and shook her head at her. Amy resumed her conversation with the security guard and pointed out something to him on her phone screen. Olivia watched as the female doctor walked up to the reception desk and became engrossed in conversation with an assistant. Immediately, she turned around and walked back down the corridor, gazing at the name plates on the doors.

Doctor Rafferty's door was the furthest along. Unlocked. She entered the room quickly and closed the door behind her, breathing heavily. The huge windows allowed for plenty of light, revealing an office that had been left clean and tidy, as if its owner planned to be away for a very long time. A wooden desk and swivel chair, filing cabinets, bookshelves, more certificates on walls. On a side shelf was a line of wine bottles of different sizes and colours with international labels. Except for a lamp and a globe, the desk was bare.

She opened the desk drawers and glanced inside, searching for anything that could link Doctor Rafferty to any of the murder sites. The contents were mostly stationery, although there was a good hoard of drinking straws and paper napkins.

A hunting jacket hung from a coat stand in the corner. Good for camouflage, she thought. She felt around in each of the pockets, but came up empty-handed. She opened a cupboard. On the top shelf were a few books. Paper bags and plastic bags filled the lower section, along with a couple of umbrellas. She moved the bags aside and her breath caught in her throat. A pair of recognisable boots stared back at her. Brown Furlowe boots. With trembling hands, she picked them up and checked the soles.

The door behind her swung open, and the female doctor stood staring at her with a shocked expression. She backed up into the corridor and screamed, 'Security! Security!'

'Wait, doctor! It's okay, I'm not doing anything. I'll leave.'

Olivia walked towards the woman, who continued to shout for assistance. The security guard came running towards them and, to Olivia's alarm, a gun was pointed her way. Quickly, she raised her arms.

'Stop, don't shoot! I'm leaving!'

'Stay right where you are. Don't move.'

'I won't move.' Olivia stood with her back pressed against the wall. 'I won't run. Don't shoot me.'

'I'll call the police,' said the doctor, and ran towards the reception desk.

Amy came towards them. 'That's my mother. Don't point the gun at her!'

'We know what to do with thieves.' The guard cast a disgusted glance at Amy. 'You two working together, huh? Can't believe you came all the way from England to do this.'

'Neither can I,' murmured Amy, with a despairing look at her mother.

'What's in the bag?' asked the guard.

'Just my own things. I'll show you.'

'Keep your hands where they are. Move without my say-so, I shoot. What's in your pocket?'

'Just my ID,' said Olivia. 'I swear I didn't take anything. Look.'

Olivia slowly lowered her arms and removed her ID from her jeans pocket while keeping her eyes fixed on the gleaming gun barrel.

'My name is Olivia Knightley. This isn't what you think. I'm a private investigator.'

'Nobody's trying to steal anything,' said Amy.

The guard barely glanced at her, his focus still on Olivia. 'If either of you so much as sneeze, you'll regret it. You can tell the cops what you were doing.'

Amy stood beside Olivia, who hugged her daughter's shoulders.

'Can't you lower the gun, sir?' demanded Olivia. 'Do we look like a threat to you?'

'No, and yes,' he grunted.

'Can I make one phone call?' asked Olivia.

'No, you can do that at the police station,' said the guard. 'They'll read you your rights.'

'I'm only sixteen,' said Amy. 'There's no way this is legal.'

Amy broke away from her mother, typing on her phone as she walked away.

'Stay right there, ma'am!' shouted the guard. 'Ma'am!'

As Amy ran away, the exasperated guard turned back to Olivia. 'Don't even think about it. You're the one I caught red-handed.'

'Can I at least have a seat?'

'Sure. On the ground.'

A resigned Olivia slumped to the cool floor and crossed her legs. 'You don't know what you're doing. You're wasting so much time. I mean, really, it's an empty office. What's there to steal?'

'I wouldn't know. See, I don't go around breaking and entering people's private rooms.'

'Breaking and entering? The door was open. Nothing is broken.'

'Save it for the cops. I don't want to hear it.'

The police were in no hurry to attend. At least half an hour passed before Olivia heard a wailing siren. Her stomach plummeted. She hadn't been in the country two weeks, and was already about to have her fingerprints taken for a second time. She wondered how long the cops would keep her locked up. Surely they would not dare keep her overnight? Inwardly, she groaned. Jack Tyler would not be impressed by her getting herself arrested like this.

She stood up as the young uniformed officer came towards her. He seemed bored, as if he would rather be somewhere else. Olivia listened as the security guard related finding her searching through the office. She didn't interrupt when he accused her of attempting to steal a pair of boots. There was no point. The cop ordered her to put her hands behind her back and clamped on a pair of handcuffs.

The walk of shame was excruciating. She could swear the waiting room clientele had doubled, and a whole lot of people were mumbling and staring at her. Amy was nowhere to be seen. Olivia wondered where her daughter had got to.

Outside, piercing sunlight hit her eyes, and she rued not being able to shield them from the glare. Lowering her head, she felt like a criminal as she was marched to the squad car. The officer opened the back door and placed her inside.

'It's really uncomfortable sitting like this. If you must cuff me, can you put my hands in front?'

'Comfort isn't the goal, ma'am.'

He'd barely started the engine before the sharp sound of another emergency siren filled the air.

A car that Olivia did not recognise sped down the driveway and partially blocked the police officer's vehicle. A wave of hope, along with shame, overcame her as Jack Tyler jumped out, badge in hand. This was a Jack she had never seen, all professional in sharp suit and tie, with the triangle of a matching handkerchief peering from his breast pocket, and shiny black leather shoes. He had gone all out to spruce up for the military men. Inappropriately, considering the situation, she found herself thinking that he certainly scrubbed up well.

'What the . . .?' The police officer mumbled as he climbed out of his car.

There was a tap on the window, and Olivia turned, glad to see her daughter smiling at her. Amy tried to open the car door, which turned out to be firmly locked.

Olivia looked towards the two law enforcers, who were engaged in earnest conversation. She watched in dismay as the security guard joined them. It was impossible to hear what was being said. Occasionally, the guard shot a hostile glare in her direction. Eventually, he stormed back towards the lobby entrance.

With relief, Olivia watched as Jack patted the young officer on the back and both men smiled. They approached, and the cop unlocked the door. Olivia stumbled out awkwardly.

'Turn around,' ordered the cop.

Olivia obeyed, and soon her hands were free. She rubbed them together gratefully. The few minutes of confinement had been unsettling and she was thankful to be avoiding the drab interior of a cell.

'I've apologised for this misunderstanding, Olivia,' said Jack in a terse tone. 'Philadelphia police officers have enough on their plates.'

'Stay out of trouble.' The cop waved a warning finger at Olivia. 'You're lucky you've got such a good advocate for your character.'

'Thank you, officer,' said Olivia through gritted teeth.

The officer gestured with his chin towards the entrance, where onlookers stood watching. 'Good luck with the doctors, Special Agent Tyler. Let me know if you need a hand.'

'I appreciate it,' said Jack.

As the patrol car drove off, Jack turned to Olivia, a no-nonsense look on his closely shaved face. 'What the hell is going on? All I got from Amy is that a security guard had a gun on you. You broke into a doctor's office?'

'I think we might have found him, Jack. The killer. Well, he isn't here, but that's the point. If he was here, then it wouldn't be him.'

'In English, if you wouldn't mind?'

'His name is Doctor Aston Rafferty.' Olivia's words tripped over each other as she breathlessly poured out her story. 'He's on a sabbatical, expected back in two months. In his cupboard, there's a pair of brown Furlowe boots, size nine. But you know feet swell? He probably wears size tens too. Could have them on him right now.'

Amy declared, 'He's an eye doctor and a killer, and we've got him!'

'You two take a seat in my car.' Jack looked towards the building, where the guard stood, hands on hips, watching them.

'I'll come with you and show you where it is,' suggested Olivia.

'Security will not allow you back inside the premises.' He glared at her, his frustration evident. 'You remember what I told you about trespassing? About Stand Your Ground? People will shoot first and ask questions later. You should've called me the minute you suspected this doctor was of interest.'

Olivia was sheepish, yet her voice held firm. 'I didn't want to waste your time, if it didn't pan out.'

'That's not your decision to make. I'll decide who to take out of the equation.' He slammed the door as soon as Amy was seated beside her mother. 'Now somebody's bound to call Doctor Rafferty and tell him his office has been broken into. I've got to stop them warning him and find out where he is.'

Jack stormed off towards the office.

'Well, he could have said thanks,' said Amy. 'You helped him catch a killer, and he's mad about it.'

'He'll come around,' said Olivia with confidence. 'Once he's got his man.'

33

DESPITE THE FACT she'd just had a gun pointed in her face, Olivia experienced a strong sense of achievement. As time ticked by with no reappearance of Jack Tyler, though, she began to worry. What was he doing in there? Why hadn't Tom arrived? Surely the building should be swarming with officers by now.

Amy suggested he was ransacking the place single-handedly. Just when Olivia was beginning to think Amy could be right, the clinic's glass doors opened, and Jack came striding down the driveway.

'He hasn't taken a thing from the office, Mom. No Furlowe boots in his hands or anything. No gloves on.'

Olivia frowned. 'Maybe he's waiting to get a warrant and can't do anything without it.'

As soon as Jack approached the car door, Amy leaned out the passenger window and said, 'So did they tell you where Rafferty's gone on this sabbatical? Let me guess: Iowa, South Dakota, Ohio?'

Undaunted by his stern face and failure to answer, Amy continued. 'North Dakota? Look, I can't remember all the states he's been to. Where is he?'

Jack buckled his seatbelt. 'At the Wine School of Philadelphia, a couple miles from here. He's taking a full-time course for sommeliers. Sounds like a polite man.'

'You . . . spoke to him?' Olivia could not disguise her shock.

'I had to,' snapped Jack. 'They already had him on the phone when I got in there. I had to take over and try to placate him. He's threatening all kinds of legal action.'

Olivia wiped moist palms on her jeans. 'But I didn't take anything, so it can't be that bad right? Right?'

'Wrong. He wants to see his accuser.' Jack stared rigidly through the rear-view mirror. 'That's you. And he wants a formal apology.'

Olivia's throat went dry. 'Is that a good idea? To see him face to face, I mean?'

'You got a better one?' Jack started the engine. 'You're going to apologise, because a lawsuit is one astronomical check the ISB will not be inclined to pick up. If we don't make this right today, you'll probably be kicked out of the country.'

'What?' said Amy indignantly. 'I'm not even half ready to leave America yet. We've got to do Nebraska, Wyoming and LA. Mom, I swear if you get booted out, I'm not going with you. I'll travel alone.'

'Thanks for your support, love.'

'And I don't figure on being canned for having brought you on board,' added Jack.

'Wine School of Philadelphia.' Amy clicked away at her phone. 'Says here it's the top-ranked wine school in the USA. The place to find world-recognised, quality wine classes. Offering the required courses for well-rounded wine education. Promising plenty of fun and informative tasting classes. Who knew?'

Olivia sat back and buckled her seatbelt, her energy and enthusiasm drained. A wine college. With a bit of luck, they left the wine vats open, and she could drown herself in a vat of red wine.

*

Olivia tried to get her senses together as she entered the Wine School with Amy hanging onto her arm. The pleasing odour of fresh grapes seeped through the air. The absence of paintwork was noticeable, and she couldn't help but admire the exposed bricks and solid walls that gave the building an authentic feel. Students of all ages and races milled around, and but for their clothing it was like stepping back into an earlier century.

Jack strode ahead of them, avoiding all conversation. He merely looked at the signs on classroom doors, searching for the right one.

Olivia could have kicked herself. How had she got this so wrong? Why had she been so hard-headed? She could not blame him for giving her the cold shoulder, although it hurt more than she would care to admit. Her stomach churned. She had barely avoided one lawsuit in London; to get one across the pond would be a disaster. Anybody who knew anything about America knew that it was full of ambulance-chasing lawyers, encouraging citizens to seek seven-figure sums for the slightest aggravation.

Travel insurance wouldn't cut it. Visions of losing her job and having to sell her home to pay for this nightmare clouded her brain. If an apology was what it took for all this to go away, she would deliver it on bended knee, with head bowed if necessary.

Olivia whispered to Amy, 'I screwed up. No matter how mad Doctor Rafferty gets, I don't want you attacking him. Let him have his say.'

'I get it, Mom.'

Jack opened a classroom door. Doctor Aston Rafferty was

engaged in conversation with two fellow students, also middle-aged males. Holding a wine bottle, he pointed out words on the label. A swift flicker of bold eyes took in the new arrivals, before his attention went back to his immediate audience.

As expected, he looked slightly more creased than the glossy production at his medical practice, but he was still a chiselled man. Casually dressed in short-sleeved shirt, khaki slacks and canvas slip-ons, he looked relaxed and confident. Olivia hoped that feeling would rub off on her as she gazed around the room.

The classroom felt homely and cosy. The fixtures and furnishings were dark, yet contemporary and stylish, a mixture of modern highly polished wooden tables and chairs. The white ceiling, with its recessed light fittings, gave the room a bright and airy feel. An old-fashioned blackboard with a recipe written in chalk stood beside a large table at the head of the room. On the table were long-stemmed wine glasses and small ceramic bowls, as well as a selection of wine bottles and a stainless steel brew kettle. An angled reflective mirror high up on the wall overhead allowed the students to see what the instructor was doing without having to peer over shoulders.

The two students smiled and nodded at the new visitors as they left the room. The doctor closed the door behind them, and held out a hand to Jack.

'Good to meet you, Doctor Rafferty. This is Mrs Olivia Knightley and her daughter, Amy.'

'Hello, Doctor Rafferty,' said Olivia.

The doctor did not offer Olivia or Amy his hand, although his hard eyes sized them up for a while. Instead, he picked up a different bottle of red wine and studied the label. Olivia wished she could pick up a full bottle of white and drain the lot. Her insides were threatening to burst from tension. The man was enjoying her suffering, and seemed prepared to get his pound of flesh.

'Doctor Rafferty, I'm really sorry about what happened earlier,' she blurted out.

He remained focused on the label. 'I'm sure you are.'

'Are you a wine enthusiast, Agent Tyler?' The doctor poured a tiny portion of red liquid into a glass and held it up to the light. 'A miracle of viticulture. Light and heady, with overtones of almonds: an absolute delight.'

'Tend to stick to bourbon myself, though I do like a few beers.'

'Beer.' The doctor's tone was dismissive. He swished the wine around the glass and sniffed it. 'This red is one of best I've ever tasted. Good for rare steak and medium lamb.' His eyes bore into Olivia with undisguised dislike. 'Not so great for mutton.'

Olivia gritted her teeth. The nerve of the man. Were it not that he was the difference between homelessness and security, she would have snatched the glass and thrown the contents in his smug face. It took all her mental strength to grate out her words.

'Entering your office without permission was the wrong thing to do. I swear I didn't take anything. Nothing at all.'

The doctor slammed the bottle onto the table. 'That's what you say, but until I go into my office, how do I know?'

Olivia thought about how she would feel if a private eye rummaged through her Camberwell home in her absence. Angry, yes. Violated – oh, boy. 'I had no business in there, Doctor Rafferty. I was out of line. But you won't find even a paperclip missing.'

'That's the truth, doctor,' said Jack. 'Nothing was removed from your office, and your security can confirm it. I couldn't say everything I wanted to say on the phone for reasons that will become obvious.' He handed the doctor both versions of a "Wanted" poster. 'Olivia Knightley is a private investigator working on our search for this killer.'

Doctor Rafferty took the posters and skimmed both. His eyes

focused again on Olivia. 'You wouldn't be trying to suggest that I look like a murderer?'

'It wasn't just to do with looks. And no, I have to say, you certainly don't look like a murderer.'

'And tracking this person led you straight to my office?'

Olivia swallowed as his unblinking eyes fixed on hers.

'My clients may now believe I am involved in a crime. There's no smoke without fire, and all that. Smacks of defamation of my good character.'

Jack shook his head. 'Neither your colleagues nor patients know what Mrs Knightley was doing in there. I didn't tell them, didn't show around the "Wanted" posters. No reason for them to think anything bad about you. The one who looks bad to them is Mrs Knightley, who they've tagged as an opportunistic thief . . . and her sly lookout.'

'Oh great,' murmured Amy. 'I'm a sly lookout.'

Olivia's cheeks burned, and she wished death would just claim her already. Knowing she was in the wrong was bad enough; admitting to it was painful. 'I'm really sorry, Doctor Rafferty. I'm an investigator, and thought I was on the right track. The killer has murdered nine men so far. Right now, there's a man in jail awaiting trial for a murder we're pretty sure he didn't commit. Catching the real killer is something I have to do.'

'That's exactly how it is, Doctor Rafferty,' said Jack. 'Think of the bigger picture before you think of lawyers and courts. We have to nail this killer so people can enjoy the beauty of our parks again, feeling safe and secure. Everything we do is in the interests of national safety.'

The doctor appeared to mellow, and his mouth curved slightly at the corner. He waved the older poster in the air and met Olivia's gaze. 'I admit there is a slight likeness.'

'You're much more handsome,' she said, with an apologetic smile.

'I must say I haven't been following the news much lately. Pennsylvania, Ohio, Illinois, Iowa — and his latest in South Dakota. He's been very busy.' The doctor stared at Jack. 'There must be thousands of men out there who bear a resemblance to this image. Whatever led you back to Pennsylvania — and, in particular, to me?'

'I believe he lives or used to live and work in this state,' said Jack.

Olivia squirmed. 'I sort of put two and two together and got an eye doctor, which led me to a gym, to membership discounts, and then to your clinic. And when I went into your cupboard and saw the boots I just thought . . .'

'Boots?' The doctor stared at her quizzically.

'A pair of brown Furlowe boots,' said Olivia.

'Oh, those.'

'We believe the murderer wore a similar pair, in a different size,' added Jack.

'Great boots for walking and hiking. I've had them for about four years now. Well used, and they remain in excellent condition.' The doctor smiled wistfully. 'You know, I'd never even heard of Furlowe's before they were recommended to me. Funnily enough, it was by another ophthalmologist.'

Olivia's breath caught in her throat. 'Another ophthalmologist?'

'Yes. He's retired now, though. A doctor I met through Unite For Sight . . . that's a volunteer group that takes on patients who can't afford to pay for eye care. Group of us used to go hiking for a few days every year. My old boots always had me suffering heel pain by the end of the day, while he was unaffected. Out of all of us, he was the only one who never complained of foot pain.'

'What's his name?' asked Olivia.

'Doctor Gregory Callender.'

'He look like the man in the poster?' asked Jack.

Doctor Rafferty looked at Jack incredulously and let out a laugh. 'Oh, come on now, Special Agent Tyler. You don't think Greg is a killer?'

'Look again, doc.'

The doctor did as ordered. 'I concede there is a close resemblance. Haven't seen him in four years, but he couldn't have changed much. Greg wouldn't hurt a flea, though, let alone stab someone. He's the kindest, sweetest, most polite person I ever had the pleasure to know.'

'Do you know him well?' asked Olivia. 'Sometimes we think we know people and we really don't.'

'I mean, we only ever hiked together. Greg's not someone I ever performed surgery with or shared a medical practice with. He's not someone whose cell I call. He's not active on social media, either.'

'Do you have a photograph of Doctor Callender?' asked Jack.

'Not one that I've taken,' said Doctor Rafferty. 'But you could check the Unite For Sight webpage. They used to post pictures of the adventurers among us on the trail every year.'

Both Jack and Olivia immediately took out their phones and searched for the website.

'Would either of you care for a drink?' asked the doctor. When no one answered, he filled his glass and downed a mouthful, savouring the taste with an appreciative sound.

Before either Jack or Olivia could raise their heads, Amy waved her phone in the air.

'Found the website,' she said. 'I've got the photo section, but I can't see any with you in them.'

'It will be in the archived section,' said the doctor. 'Look for the Silver Fox Crew. There are five of us in a photo, planting a flag on a hill in Ohio. They kept that one, because one of the leading doctors in that photo died – of natural causes – and it was the best image they had of him. Even used it in his funeral montage.'

Amy's fingers worked, fast and furious. 'This is it.'

Olivia took the phone and enlarged the image. Her heart stopped as she focused in on the smiling faces. One in particular, a man wearing a red puffer jacket, held her attention. There was no mistaking the eyes or the facial structure.

'I've seen this man before.' She pointed him out to Jack. 'I'm pretty sure I have, but I'm trying to remember where.'

Jack frowned and turned the image to Doctor Rafferty. 'Which one is Doctor Gregory Callender?'

'Red jacket, big smile.'

'So many people have engaged me in friendly conversation,' Olivia closed her eyes briefly. 'He spoke to me once. I don't think it was at Hawkeye. He wore a hat, but I could see dark hair. Must have dyed it. He said something about his knees. I remember looking down at his knees. He was wearing sandals, though.'

Amy said, 'I don't remember him.'

Olivia's eyes flew open suddenly. 'It was when you were rock climbing at Palisades. I'd been up and come back down. I was rubbing my injured finger, and he spoke to me.'

'Oh my God, Mom, you talked to a serial killer!'

'Come on, you must be mistaken,' scoffed Doctor Rafferty. 'Even if you did see Doctor Callender at a park, he would never do such a thing. He's a fifty-six-year-old, highly respected, retired eye doctor, not a murderer.'

'Does Doctor Callender have a military connection?' asked Jack. 'Any army or marines in his immediate or extended family?'

'Strange you should ask that. I remember when we were musing on one climb, about how our lives had panned out against how we'd imagined they would be after high school.' Doctor Rafferty paused as his memory refreshed. 'It was the only thing I ever heard Greg complain about, and he was quite bitter about it too. He had wanted to join the army as a young man, but they wouldn't have him.'

'Why not?' asked Olivia. 'He's way above the minimum height requirement. About five-seven, five-eight, right?'

'That's right.' the doctor nodded. 'He wasn't passed over for his height, Mrs Knightley. It was his weight. They told him he wasn't fit enough for all that strenuous training and stealth that army officers need. He was quite affronted by that. I think he got teased a lot for being plump back in the day.'

Olivia locked eyes with Jack and sensed his excitement.

'He's not overweight now, though.' said Doctor Rafferty 'At least, he wasn't when I knew him.'

'No, he's quite slim now,' whispered Olivia.

'He said his parents were delighted that the army rejected him. They were firmly against him joining the military. They were overbearing types, apparently, especially the father. They demanded he go to medical school. He said they argued all the time about education. Eventually, he gave in and did what they asked of him.'

'He's resented the men of the army his whole life,' murmured Jack. 'He's showing the world that he would have been a great soldier. No one ever gave him a chance.'

Doctor Rafferty looked alarmed. 'Do you really think he could have committed these murders?'

'Absolutely,' said Jack. 'Doctor, do you know where Gregory Callender lives?'

The man shook his head. 'I do not, I'm afraid.'

'Do you know what kind of vehicle he drives?' asked Olivia.

'Back then, he had a green Chevvy Silverado. Don't know if he still has it.'

'The other men in the photo – give me their names and numbers.' Jack wrote as Doctor Rafferty read the details from his phone.

'Sure you wouldn't like a drink?' the doctor asked. 'It really is sublime.'

'We're good. Thanks for your help, doc, much appreciated.' Jack shook the man's hand. 'Please do not relate any part of this conversation to anyone.'

'I wouldn't dream of it.'

'Come on,' said Jack, looking at Olivia. 'We have to get out of here.'

Olivia stared awkwardly at the man she had thought was a murderer and mumbled a goodbye before following behind Jack. She ushered Amy in front of her.

'Oh, Mrs Knightley,' the doctor called.

Olivia closed her eyes tightly for a brief second, then turned around, apprehension evident on her face.

The doctor raised a glass of wine. 'Thank you for trying to keep America safe.'

She smiled back at him. 'Thank you, doc.'

34

JACK PHONED THE local police as he climbed into his car. Olivia got in beside him, while Amy headed for the back seat. With the phone on speaker, he tapped the steering wheel and awaited a response from the police dispatcher.

The officer's voice crackled over the airwaves as she read out a Lancaster address. 'Two people registered at that location: one male, Gregory Callender, aged fifty-six; one female, Vera Callender, aged eighty-two.'

'I need a patrol unit at the address right now,' said Jack. 'No one goes in. I'll meet them there.'

'Will do.'

Jack hung up and stepped on the gas. With a screech of tyres, the car peeled out of the wine school parking lot. 'It's about eighty miles from here. Should take just over an hour to get there.'

'Must be mother and son,' said Amy.

'Could be wife and husband.' Olivia's mind conjured up an image of a sultry, stick-thin woman draped in furs, blowing rings of cigarette smoke in the air. 'Maybe Vera Callender is a glamorous Joan Collins type?'

'Unlikely,' said Jack. 'We're talking suburbia, not Hollywood.'

Jack tapped on the phone again and called Tom. He read out

the suspect's address, and Tom agreed to meet them there. Next he patched in Perez in Iowa and Morelli in Ohio on a three-way call.

'The suspect's name is Doctor Gregory Callender, an ophthalmologist from Lancaster. We're heading to his last known residence right now. I don't expect to find him, but it looks like his mother lives there. I'm sending you a recent photograph. Distribution is to law enforcement only; the media gets nothing.'

'You absolutely sure that's our guy, Jack?' asked Morelli.

'As sure as I've ever been,' said Jack.

'Good enough for me,' said Perez.

'I need you and Marty to quietly put every park, forest, campground nature reserve on alert. Stress the need to keep his name away from the media.'

When Jack finished the update, he hung up and focused on cutting through the traffic, siren blaring.

Olivia agreed that the Lancaster suburb was not Hollywood. The wide roads were clean, with well-kept lawns and neatly trimmed hedges. None of the premises had gates. Quaint mailboxes sat on stilts at the edges of most lawns, and signs on a few houses warned of an effective neighbourhood watch. The Callender house was an unassuming bungalow with a double garage and spacious driveway. A patrol car was parked outside a house two doors down from the target, and Jack pulled up behind it. He got out and held a brief conversation with the officers before returning to his car.

'This is unbelievable. I'm looking at a murderer's house,' Amy stated in awe. 'I can go inside too, right, Agent Tyler?'

'No way,' said Jack. He drummed on the steering wheel and stared in his wing mirror as if checking for approaching vehicles. 'And let's keep it as "murder suspect", not murderer. The power to declare him such lies elsewhere.'

'Are we going in?' asked Olivia.

'When Tom gets here. That is, if Vera Callender will let us.' Jack studied the windows of the house. All were closed. 'We don't even know that she's inside.'

'So where's an eighty-two-year-old woman going to be?' asked Amy in a sour tone. 'Out dancing?'

'My mother is eighty, and yes, she goes out dancing,' said Jack.

Olivia's phone rang. She was relieved it was neither Bill nor Chris, but she did not recognise the number. She answered, and told the caller they were safe and well.

'What was that about, Mom?'

'Palisades campground. They were just checking that we were okay, as nobody's seen us in the caravan and Tango hasn't moved.'

'Nice of them,' said Amy.

'Yeah, nice lady.' Olivia tucked away her phone. 'She did warn that they'll still charge my credit card whether we make use of the facilities or not.'

'If all goes well here, we'll fly back west tonight,' said Jack. 'Right to wherever the doctor is hiding out.'

A sedan pulled up behind them, and Olivia watched as Tom emerged. As usual, he looked dapper, in a tailored suit with a bright-red bow tie, and a trust-me face. Jack immediately leapt out of the vehicle and walked towards him. The two police officers joined the two special agents in conversation.

Olivia slammed her door shut and leaned in through the open window. 'Wait here until we get back.'

'Why, though?' Amy's face contorted in annoyance. 'The killer's hundreds of miles from here, and his mother's hardly likely to attack me, is she?'

'I don't know if any of that is true – and you don't, either.'

Olivia followed the officers up the short driveway to the Callenders' front door, a solid wooden door with mosaic glass panels on each side.

The doorbell rang to the tune of 'Jingle Bells' and Olivia frowned, wondering who in their right mind could listen to that tune, one she found bearable only in December. A shadow moved behind the glass panels. Someone was inside.

'Vera Callender!' shouted Jack.

'Who is it?' The voice was female and strong.

A patrol officer shouted, 'Police, ma'am!'

The door opened wide and Olivia stared at the homeowner. Vera Callender was no Joan Collins. The woman's thin grey hair hung limp around her narrow shoulders, and behind thick lenses, watery grey eyes moved keenly. Her hands were concealed beneath a long, flowery apron speckled with grease. She took a few paces backwards and brought up trembling mottled hands. Olivia's lips parted in shock as she stared into the barrel of a rifle.

'Whoa, gun!' shouted a police officer, and immediately reached for his holster while backing away from the door. Jack pushed Olivia towards the wall, away from the line of fire. He pulled his own gun and stood square, pointing it at the rifle-toting octogenarian.

'Ma'am, drop the weapon!' shouted Jack. 'Put it down.'

Olivia pressed herself against the wall beside the door. She placed her warm forehead against the cool concrete and wondered whether bullets could pierce it. Her breath came ragged as her heart pounded in fear. She turned around so her back was to the wall, as if a bullet to the rear of her skull would be less damaging than one to the forehead.

'Don't make me shoot you. Drop it!' shouted the police officer.

'Vera, look at me.' Tom slowly moved into the old woman's line of sight. 'Vera, look at my hands. No gun. Put it down.'

Jack immediately moved forward with his gun angled past Tom's side, aiming it at the old woman. Olivia's view was of the officers and the street, of the car in which her daughter sat. In her mind's eye she pictured stray bullets flying everywhere and landing in the passenger seat. She prayed that Amy would not get out to stretch her legs, or, even, worse defy orders and walk up to the house.

Olivia drew her eyes to Jack, who was fully focused on the woman. His gaze did not flicker. Tom stood beside Jack, talking calmly to the woman. To Olivia, he looked like a friendly door-to-door salesman, and she hoped no salesmen had ripped off Vera Callender recently. She closed her eyes.

'Vera, no one is here to hurt you,' said Tom. 'We're law enforcement. Just put down your weapon so everyone can be safe, alright?'

'You sure you're not tryna trick me?'

'No one's trying to trick you, Vera, I promise,' Tom crooned. 'That's great, Vera. Put it on the ground.'

Olivia stared at Jack as, inch by inch, he lowered his weapon. Sheer relief took over as she peeled herself off the wall and grasped her knees. 'Dear God,' she murmured.

The police officer burst past them into the house and retrieved the weapon. 'Safety's still on,' he said.

Jack holstered his gun. He leaned against the door frame and wiped his brow with the back of his arm. 'Phew!' he breathed. 'Vera, don't you ever do that again, do you hear me?'

Olivia's cotton blouse was soaked, and even her braids felt heavy with perspiration. She looked into the hallway. The woman stood, hands on hips, an unfriendly glare on her weathered face.

'Got a constitutional right to carry my rifle, don't I? Don't know who's coming to my door, have to protect myself.'

'You don't need to protect yourself from us. We're the good guys,' said Jack. 'Anybody else here?'

'Just me and my dog. He don't bite. Come on in.'

As he stepped into the hallway, Jack pointed at a body

camera, a small device attached to his waistband. 'I'm going to turn this on to record us while we talk, is that okay?'

'I guess,' Vera pushed back her straggling hair, as if self-conscious of being filmed. She focused her glazed vision on Olivia. 'This one police, too?'

Olivia placed a hand over her disturbed heart. 'When I was alive, I was a private investigator.'

'She's an honorary officer.' Jack introduced each of his colleagues by name. He took the rifle from the police officer and weighed it in his palms. 'Heavy. Must be a hundred years old.'

'Still works, though,' grunted Vera. 'Puts out a bullet just like when it was first pieced together.'

'I believe it,' said Jack.

'Does everybody in this country have a gun?' asked Olivia.

'No,' said Jack. 'Some people have five or six. Got any more, Vera?'

'That's the only one. Don't take more than one if your aim's good.'

Olivia surveyed the interior as they walked from the hallway to the sitting room. The decor looked as if it had not been changed since the early eighties. Chunky furniture, floral wallpaper, thick patterned carpets brushed by matching curtains. Religious paintings lined some walls. Certificates of Gregory Callender's educational achievements were framed and proudly displayed at eye level.

A strong odour of dog filled the air. The tiny culprit, an elderly chihuahua, rested in a padded basket close to a rocking chair. The chair was still moving slightly, as if Vera had occupied it before being disturbed by the unexpected visitors. Vera reached down and stroked the dog's head. He gave a weak yap and went back to sleep.

'We're looking for Doctor Gregory Callender,' said Jack. 'He your son?'

'That he is. What you wanting with him?'

'I won't lie to you, Vera. I think he's done some bad things. The best thing for him to do is to come forward and talk to us. I don't think he plans to do that.'

'Done some bad things?' She gave a short, stifled snort. 'Greg? You don't mean to tell me he's gone and killed somebody, do you?'

Olivia raised an eyebrow, surprised by the woman's odd behaviour. If police had come to her house looking for Amy and claiming she'd done bad things, the last thing she'd think would be that her daughter had killed someone. Chained herself to a government building, participated in a sit-down demonstration, climbed a statue to topple it — plenty of things would come to mind, but not committed a murder.

'Do you know where Greg is, Vera?' asked Tom.

'No, I don't. Hasn't been around for months. Christmas was the last I saw of him. Couldn't tell you where he is now.'

'Got his phone number?' asked Tom.

'Had it in my phone, but I know he changed his number. Last time I called it and called it, with no answer. When I finally saw him he told me he got a new number. He never put it into my phone, though. He's the one used to put all numbers in my phone, 'cause I don't get how to. Now I won't know when he's coming home till he shows up at the door.'

'Yours is the only address we have for him,' said Jack. 'He live here with you?'

'Pretty much. He's always lived here since he was a boy, except when he was at university. Then there was that time he got married to some strange broad for a few years and went and lived with her. I say she was strange 'cause she must have been strange to marry Greg.'

'You know where the ex-wife lives?' asked Jack.

Vera shrugged. 'She's Texan; that's about all I needed to know about her. Twenty years since I set eyes on her.'

'What vehicle does he drive?' asked Jack. 'You have the papers anywhere?'

Vera Callender narrowed her eyes. 'Suppose you tell me what he's gone and done?'

'Recognise this man?' Jack handed her the 'Wanted' poster which she held close to her face.

'Writing's too small,' she said.

'Face isn't too small,' said Jack dryly.

Vera shot him a dark look.

'He's wanted for the murder of at least nine people that we know of,' explained Jack. 'He's been moving steadily west, killing people, and we need to stop him.'

'I seen it on the news.' The woman swallowed and put a hand to her throat. 'You mean you think my Greg did all them murders?'

'Yes, we do,' said Jack. 'What does he drive?'

'Last time he rolled up here in a dark grey Ford Bronco, just like his pa used to drive, God rest his soul. I don't know the plates.'

'Mind if we take a look around?' asked Jack.

'No, go look wherever you want. I got nothing to hide.'

Jack and Tom pulled on latex gloves. Jack handed a pair to Olivia.

'Try not to touch anything unless you really have to,' he said.

Tom picked up an old photo album and flicked through it. He held up a photo of a Ford Bronco with an elderly man leaning against it. 'This your husband?'

Vera squinted at the image. 'Yes, that's him. Edgar loved his Bronco.'

Olivia strolled around the sitting room, taking in the cluttered walls. No family photos on display anywhere. Interspersed between educational certificates were posters of famous sports stars popular in the eighties. She noted lists of ten best things were framed on each wall. Ten best cities to visit, ten best movies quotes, ten most unique animals. To Olivia, it seemed odd that anyone would use such things to decorate walls, but this was an odd family.

'Vera,' said Olivia. 'You don't mind me calling you Vera, do you?'

'It's my name.'

'Seems like Greg is quite an intelligent man.' Olivia chose her words carefully. 'Why did you think it strange that someone would marry him?'

'He was always a sad sack. Don't know how me and his pa had a boy so shy. His pa used to call him stupid, but I never thought he was stupid. Just weak. Always overeating and stuffing himself. No self-discipline.' She grinned suddenly. 'He wanted to join the army. That gave us a good old laugh. Even his friends laughed at him. Poor fat little Greg. Slimmed down by the time he got to his forties, though.'

Tom, who had been busy flicking through some note papers on top of a cupboard, turned to look at her. 'Did you ever love your son?'

'Course we loved him. Still love him. Wouldn't have forced him to go get a proper education if we didn't love him.'

'Doesn't sound like he enjoyed his life here much,' said Jack.

'Course he did.' She smiled a knowing smile. 'Always comes back home eventually. Ain't no place like home, as they say.'

'Does Greg have any friends or girlfriends who might know where he is?' asked Olivia.

'Greg wasn't one for friends. When he was young, yes, but as he got older . . . no, it was just him and his books and his radio and TV.'

'I know the feeling,' Olivia smiled at her.

'Tom, looks like the truck's papers.' Jack held up a vehicle registration document. 'I'll call it in to Perez and Morelli only. He'll ditch the Bronco if he knows we're looking for it. We have to pin him down and flush him out.' He put the phone to his ear and began relaying instructions.

'Can you show me Greg's bedroom, Vera?' asked Olivia.

Vera led the way to the back of the house and into a bedroom with an ensuite shower room. The space carried the unlived-in odour of stale air that came with keeping the windows locked and the door closed.

As well as a king-sized bed, it contained a wardrobe, a chest of drawers, a desk and two bookshelves. The desk and book-shelves were covered with notepads, papers, books, newspaper clippings, drawings, an old laptop, a portable hard drive, an old camera. There was a wall calendar, frozen on December. Military symbols were everywhere: memoirs of army generals, antique medals and dog tags. A scarred baseball bat and threadbare mit-tens lay in a corner.

Jack and Tom entered the bedroom and continued the search, rifling through the desk and bookshelves. Jack picked up a well-leafed *Guide to Combat* book and a sheathed combat knife.

'Interesting he has something as sharp and efficient as this, but prefers to use ordinary kitchen knives,' he said. 'Showing the world how good he can be without expert equipment.'

'Stressing the fact that he missed his calling,' added Tom.

'Good set of teeth on him.' Jack held up a portrait of the smil-ing suspect holding the chihuahua to his chest. 'Greg looks better, too.'

Olivia studied the portrait. A cheerful-looking, professional man with a clear love for his family pet had somehow crossed the line and decided to commit a run of murders. Part of him main-tained some humanity, as he clearly cared for some people: young disabled people, mainly. The doctor's work with Unite For Site was exemplary; he had helped dozens of youngsters either regain or improve their sight, and had never charged a penny for the surgery.

'Get this.' Tom removed a silver key chain from a matchbox. 'Initials A. H. Anthony Hall, the very first victim from French Creek. Exactly as his wife described it.'

'Never seen that before. Don't know nobody with those initials.' Vera's voice faltered as she stared at the key chain. 'My Greg couldn't have killed all those people.'

Olivia took her arm and helped her onto a chair. 'He did it, Vera. I'm sorry, but this is no mistake.'

Despite Mrs Callender's anxiety, Olivia felt a flush of excitement. Even with a distinct lack of evidence and very few clues, they had identified the killer. There was no longer any doubt Doctor Gregory Callender was Dean, The Parkside Killer, one of the most wanted men in America. All they had to do now was find him.

While Jack and Tom continued their manual search, opening drawers, flicking through papers and books, Olivia studied the environment without touching a thing. On other walls hung more lists of tens. Ten best things about Pennsylvania. Ten most successful racehorses. Taking pride of place on his bedside table was a framed montage of ten men, two of whom Olivia recognised as game-show masters Regis Philbin and Steve Harvey. Beside it was an old hardcover book: *Who Wants to Be a Millionaire?*, based on the TV quiz show. Stacked on the other bedside table were puzzle books: a mixture of hard and cryptic crosswords, trivia, and brain teasers.

Above his bed was a large watercolour painting of a grand old wooden ship, *Mary and John*, at a dock. Olivia had never seen a ship with two names before. She leaned in close, but could not read the artist's blurred name. In slanted, flowing letters was the legend 'Massachusetts Bay Colony, 1630'.

Jack emerged from the shower room with a hairbrush. 'Vera,

it's important that we take some of Greg's things with us. Some will be evidence, and others might help us trace him. I can get a warrant to do that, but it will take time that we don't have. Do I have your permission to take what I need?'

'Sure, it's my house. I allow my son to live in it. If he murdered people, he's got to face up to it like a man.'

Olivia was taken aback that Mrs Callender had recovered so quickly from the revelation that her son was a prolific murderer. No tears, no wringing of hands. The earlier quiver in her voice had gone. She had brushed off the news, almost as if she had been notified that the church fete was cancelled. Not even the sight of agents packing her son's belongings into boxes elicited a tear. Maybe, deep down, the woman had known it would one day come to this; perhaps she had been ignoring the signs, despite knowing that her son had shown odd behaviours.

Olivia pushed away the thought as she headed out the front door. No one would ever dream their highly educated child who came home for Christmas would become a mass murderer.

As Olivia climbed into the car, Amy said, 'See, I could have gone in if all they were going to do was collect boxes from an old lady.'

Olivia tugged her daughter's plait, thinking how she nearly collected a bullet from said old lady. 'You don't know the half of it.'

'I'm listening, Mom.'

35

THE NEXT DAY, the taskforce gathered at the FBI field office in South Dakota. The haul of items taken from the Callender home was strewn out on the long table, the empty boxes tossed in the corner.

As Olivia took her seat, she was surprised when Perez and Morelli chose chairs on either side of her. She could not ignore the warm feeling that engulfed her, and she smiled as they settled in. Tom took up a seat at the end of the table and grinned.

'Rose between the thorns,' he said.

'Like an endangered California Redwood, Olivia has protected status,' said Perez.

'And nobody's going to fell her on my watch,' agreed Morelli.

'I'm honoured,' said Olivia playfully. 'Thank you.'

She picked up one of the doctor's crossword books and flicked through the pages of half-finished puzzles as Jack replayed the video of his interview and the search of the Callender house.

'You nailed the army connection, Jack. Or rather, lack of connection,' said Morelli. 'Didn't see that one coming.'

'Only person I've ever come across who's obsessed with the army but doesn't seem to like firearms,' said Perez.

'You're right, it is unusual,' said Jack. 'His mother is the gunwoman.'

'Wish I'd met old Shotgun Annie,' said Morelli with a grin.

Olivia looked up from her book as Jack moved over to the death wall and added the name of the latest victim, Zach Harrison. Most of the newspaper clippings had been removed to make space for an enlarged image of Doctor Gregory Callender hugging his pet chihuahua.

Jack stared at the suspect's smiling face. 'He must enjoy living rough, putting himself in situations he assumes army officers have to bear. He ditches his vehicle elsewhere and trudges through the woods, probably does a good bit of crawling through the undergrowth.'

Perez held up two matchboxes. 'The matchbox I found is identical to the one you took from his bedroom. Barcode numbers are consecutive; they came from the same pack.'

'He was there in the woods, watching, the whole time,' said Olivia with a shudder. 'Probably even saw when I found Rick's body.'

'Most likely,' agreed Jack.

'We've had a few possible sightings, but all turned out to be false,' said Perez. 'Still, if I was the killer doctor, I'd be getting nervous.'

'We've got eyes on the ex-wife's house in Amarillo,' said Morelli. 'The man registered at her address looks like he's the current husband, a Colombian.'

'The software guys are going through the doctor's hard drive for information,' said Tom. 'It'll take a while; he's got a lot on it.'

'Jack, you still sure we shouldn't put this doctor on blast?' asked Perez. 'Tell the whole world who he is? Maybe pick him up faster?'

'We might lose him to the woods.' Jack shook his head. 'I can't risk him going deep when he's got millions of acres to hide in. We're in a much better position to track him down while he's still confident he's unknown.'

'He's obsessed with ten of this and that,' said Olivia, as she flicked through another of the doctor's puzzle books. 'He's done nine victims so far, and I'm thinking he must be itching to get ten.'

'I agree ten is a number significant to him,' said Jack, nodding. 'A milestone he plans to reach.'

'He's never killed more than two people in any state, so I'm guessing he'll soon be on the move, if he hasn't already left South Dakota,' said Tom. 'The pattern suggests he might take a break before finding another victim.'

'In another state, going west,' added Jack.

'He might try out an elaborate disguise.' Olivia walked up to the death wall and studied Doctor Callender's photo. She wondered if she would notice his distinct features if he changed his appearance again and they met face to face. 'Not just dyed hair. Full wig, moustache, beard, darken his complexion; he could completely change how he looks.'

'He still has to go out and buy the things needed to make that change, and that's risky. He'll be worried the cashiers will spot him, or he might get caught on CCTV.' Jack tapped the whiteboard with his marker pen. 'Nine innocent men. In his mind's eye, Doctor Callender must have replaced the faces of each one with the army recruiters or friends who taunted him.'

'That's one hell of a grudge,' said Perez. 'I don't even remember half the people who used to annoy me when I was a kid.'

'You were a kid, like, yesterday,' said Morelli. 'If you don't remember them, you've got way bigger problems than you think.'

Perez threw a pen at her colleague, who ducked as it flew past his shoulder.

Olivia leaned down and retrieved it. She threw it back to Perez, who snatched it from the air.

'You see that, Marty? Olivia threw it straight to my left hand.

I've known you for six years, and you've never shown me that courtesy.'

'That's 'cause I'm trying to teach you to use your proper hand,' said Morelli. 'Call it professional development.'

Jack turned and stared at the suspect's poster. 'Doctor Gregory Callender, where the hell are you?'

As the hours ticked by, the team waded through the mountain of possible evidence, sifting through documents, diaries and notebooks, as well as combat training books and manuals. They talked amongst themselves, each giving theories about where their suspect might strike next. There were dozens of possible locations, each now under the watch of local police officers eager to apprehend the killer.

Olivia concentrated on the puzzle books, hoping to find the names of the parks Doctor Callender had targeted and a clue as to where he might strike next. So far, nothing: no sign that he'd been careless enough to write anything down. The man was so fond of word games and quizzes that she firmly believed the answer was there to be found.

Morelli flicked through the book *Who Wants to Be a Millionaire?*. 'Is this show still on? I really need to try get on it.'

Jack's phone rang and he held up a warning hand, commanding immediate silence. 'Great, where is it?' he said.

Olivia and the special agents stared at him expectantly. The flash of excitement in his eyes told her that this was something big.

'On our way.' Jack clicked off the phone and grabbed his keys. 'State trooper found the Bronco in a superstore parking lot. It's been sitting there overnight, covered under tarpaulin.'

The special agents rushed for the door. Olivia stuffed a handful of puzzle books into her tote bag and ran behind them.

*

Jack peeled off the tarpaulin to reveal the Ford Bronco truck. He glanced up at the structures around the car park. Plenty of CCTV cameras, and one was pointing in the right direction. He looked at the state trooper.

'Do we know if the cameras are working?'

'Didn't check. Called as soon as I saw the tag.' The officer handed Jack a piece of paper. 'Manager's name and number. He's inside, if you want to talk to him?'

'Good job, I really appreciate it. We'll take it from here.'

All four special agents slid on latex gloves. Olivia watched as Perez forced a thin piece of metal down the Bronco's window, which soon resulted in a popping sound as the door unlocked. She opened the driver's door. Soon all four doors were wide open, and the agents studied the interior.

Morelli opened the glove box. 'Look at this.' He held up the die-cast Harley toy.

'That's it,' said Olivia. 'It was hanging from Rick's trailer.'

Morelli rummaged again. He held up an eternity ring. 'The little star is on it, just like his mother said.'

'Whose is it?' asked Olivia.

'Victim number two,' said Tom. 'Fitz Murray.'

'Whole lot of bright, shiny things in here,' said Morelli. 'This SOB's got more stolen valuables than a downtown Miami pawn shop.'

'We'll get the vehicle towed back to base for a full examination,' said Perez. 'Close it up, Marty.'

'You do that,' said Jack. 'I'll check if anyone knows the driver or saw where he went. Let's go talk to the store manager.'

Inside the superstore, the manager escorted Olivia, Jack and Tom through rows of fashionable clothes and shoes to the back office.

'The Bronco was left last night,' said the manager. 'Thought it was kinda strange, but we usually only get involved if a vehicle sits there more than twenty-four hours.'

'Seems like a long time to ignore a vehicle?' said Olivia.

'Some folks sleep in their cars.' The manager shrugged. 'We give them a chance, but one night is usually it. Sometimes we'll allow them two, then they have to move on. When the cop came to ask about the owner, I thought maybe we need to change the policy, because you never know who you're harbouring. Sometimes it doesn't pay to be kind.'

The manager set aside a half-eaten pizza and soda cups before he rewound the tape. The footage that played out on screen was grainy, but there was no doubt the man concealing the vehicle was Doctor Gregory Callender.

'Can't see where he goes afterwards,' said Jack in frustration. 'Either he's staying near here or he took off in another truck.'

'Could have stolen a vehicle from inside the car park?' suggested Olivia.

'Not from our parking lot,' said the manager. 'At least, no theft has been reported to us this month.'

'I'll check with local police if any vehicle has been reported stolen in the vicinity,' said Jack.

'We can try and get footage from the store next door, see if any other cameras have picked him up,' suggested Tom.

'Let's do that,' agreed Jack. He gestured to the manager. 'Can I get a copy of this footage?'

'No problem.'

Olivia and the special agents visited other nearby stores and watched CCTV footage for hours. Summer nights were deceptive, and she did not even notice the rapidly darkening skies until they'd left the third establishment. She desperately wanted to remain in pursuit of Doctor Callender, but her motherly instinct kicked in. Even though the preying boys had now abandoned

Palisades for pastures new, she was still affected by overwhelming guilt about leaving Amy. When she'd waved goodbye to her daughter earlier that day, she'd been in the company of some new arrivals, two fresh-faced college girls.

'I have to get back to the campsite, I'm sorry.'

'Sure, Olivia,' said Jack. 'You've been great.'

'You do what you have to do, Olivia,' said Tom. 'Apologies for keeping you out so late.'

'Oh, I really wanted to be here,' said Olivia. 'I wouldn't have forgiven you if you'd left me behind.'

'I can run you back?' suggested Jack.

She thought he stared at her for rather longer than usual. There was no doubt in her mind that a spark existed between them, and as much as she liked the idea of being alone with him, she had to resist temptation.

'No, don't.' Olivia waved off the offer breezily. 'You guys have got a lot on. I'll get a cab. Good luck with the search and keep me up to date.'

36

OLIVIA ARRIVED BACK at Palisades campground in the dead of night. She assumed Amy must already be fast asleep in bed, as she had not answered her calls. Most of the motor homes and campervans were dark and silent. A few couples were lounging outside on deckchairs under the faint moonlight, beverages in hand.

Even before she pushed open the caravan door, Olivia sensed the vehicle was empty. She tried Amy's phone again, and felt growing nausea as it rang without answer.

'Keep calm,' she whispered to herself. 'This place is safe.'

She headed towards the motor home of the two girls Amy had been with earlier. From a distance, the vehicle appeared dark, but as she drew closer, she could see a dim, flickering light coming from inside. Then she heard an unmistakable sound that lifted her heart. She almost cried with relief. Amy laughing. A squealing laugh that told her the girl was having a good time.

Olivia stood on an upturned bucket and peered through the window. The three girls were all in pyjamas, sitting on a bunk bed, focused on the screen of a tablet, watching what she did not know or care. They found it funny, and they were safe.

She stepped down and slumped onto the bucket, waiting for

her mind and body to become composed enough to interrupt the girls. As far as Amy was concerned, her brown skin and female status would protect her from the serial killer, but Olivia was not so sure. Doctor Callender might change his MO to thwart the efforts of law enforcement. She was sure he had seen her beside Rick's body and watched her with the investigators, which had then driven him to boldly engage her in small talk below the cliffs.

Olivia rested her head on her knees. Part of her wanted to throttle Amy for not answering her phone, while the other part felt pure guilt for having abandoned her all day. Why should Amy sit alone in a caravan if she didn't want to sleep?

Whether Olivia liked it or not, Amy had grown up. Soon she would be an adult, and fretting over her would not slow the process down one bit; in fact, it was more likely to alienate her. Olivia wondered at what point Vera Callender had lost her son Greg. At what stage did a woman stop mothering her child and just let them be, let them learn from their own mistakes and grow into who they were always meant to be?

Olivia fixed a bright smile and knocked lightly on the door. 'Hello, ladies!' she called. 'Amy, you in there?'

Amy quickly opened it. 'Oh, hi, Mom. This is my mom, Olivia.'

The girls chorused their greetings.

'Hi, Amy's mom!'

'Hi, Olivia!'

'Apologies for disturbing you guys, looks like you were having fun.' Olivia kept her voice cheerful and upbeat, surprised at her ability to do so. 'Just wanted to make sure everybody was okay. Go back to what you were doing.'

'Cool, Mom. I'll be back by midnight.'

'See you later, love. Goodnight, ladies.'

Olivia was sticky from the long day and the heat of the night.

She crossed the campground to the communal shower area and took great pleasure from the cool water spraying her face and body. Her limbs were tired, but her brain was running on adrenaline and juggling numerous thoughts about the killer.

She returned to the caravan determined there could be no letting up. The rest of the taskforce were still hard at work trying to locate Gregory Callender, and the idea of going to sleep felt almost like being a traitor to the cause. She kept her phone close by, hoping that a call would come in to say they had found the killer before he found his much-wanted tenth victim.

She gazed at the image of him cuddling the senior chihuahua: such a warm face, but behind it hid a maniacal mind and a thirst for a neat, bloody kill. She sifted through photos of the deceased males and stopped at the picture of Rick Seagal. Poor Rick. A man she never got to know, yet whose death had spurred her on from the outset. She looked at Nathaniel Jeynes, a man she'd never met, whose innocent best friend was in danger of spending the rest of his life in prison.

She poured a glass of white wine and turned to studying the puzzle books. Nothing clicked; neither the set questions nor the doctor's answers inferred any particular park or forest or campground. Though frustrated by her lack of progress, she ploughed on, desperate to find the killer's secret within the pages.

Way after midnight, a glowing Amy burst through the door. Glad to take a break, Olivia lowered the book and greeted her daughter. She listened to the breathless girl chat excitedly about her new friends and the comedy show they had watched. She threw in a question or two whenever Amy paused for breath.

Almost as if in afterthought, Amy said, 'So I guess you guys still didn't track down Killer Callender?'

'Oh, is that his title now?' She pinched her daughter's chin.

'Not yet. Keep your mind on the comedy shows. You don't want to be thinking of him just before you go to bed. You'll have nightmares.'

'Oh, Mom.' Amy rolled her eyes. 'I'm not going to have nightmares. I used to have nightmares when you and Dad argued and you thought I was sleeping.'

'You are joking, right?'

'No. I used to remember the movie *The Shining*. I'd pull the sheet over my head and imagine Dad going all crazy and coming for us with an axe.'

Shocked at this disclosure, Olivia said, 'Wow, have I ever failed.'

'Of course you haven't, Mom.' Amy got up and locked the caravan door. 'See? Keeping us both safe.'

'You really should answer the phone, particularly at night, you know. That's one rule I need you to stick to. It's not so bad in the day, but at night, all sorts of terrifying things flood my mind. Even a text would do.'

'Oh, sorry. I put it on mute and forgot.' Amy sat and buried her head into Olivia's shoulder.

'You must be knackered.'

'Not really.' Amy picked up one of the brain teaser books. 'I know you too well to think you're in here relaxing. This is all work, isn't it?'

'You've got me.' Olivia closed her eyes.

'Are you zoning again?'

'I'm looking around his bedroom for as many items as I can remember.' Olivia's eyes remained closed. 'There's a picture of game-show hosts right beside his bed, along with these books. He's got a thing about quizzes.'

'As well as his thing about ten,' said Amy. 'Have you looked at question number ten in all of the books?'

'First thing I did. No luck.' Olivia's brow furrowed. 'There's a lovely painting of an old ship on his bedroom wall. One of those with tall masts and huge sails, like you see in the pirate movies. A ship named *Mary and John.*'

'Strange name for a ship.'

'It is,' agreed Olivia. 'Docked in Massachusetts Bay Colony in 1630.'

'He hasn't killed anybody in Massachusetts, has he?' Amy pulled up a map on her screen. 'Hmm, that's not west, anyway. That's way north-east, past New York.'

'I'm wondering if it's just a painting he bought because he liked it, or if there's some meaning behind it for him. It has pride of place in his bedroom, where he would see it day and night. Put in the *Mary and John* and see if anything comes up.'

After a few moments, Amy said, 'Well, it brought the first colonists from England to Dorchester, Massachusetts, in 1630.'

Olivia frowned. 'Did it carry any famous passengers?'

Amy's fingers worked at an impressive pace. 'The only claim to fame I can see is that two people who arrived on it, Matthew and Priscilla Grant, are the ancestors of Hiram Ulysses Grant, born in 1822.'

'Never heard of him. I've heard of Ulysses S. Grant, though, the president on the fifty-dollar bill.'

'Says here it's the same man. He ditched the Hiram for some reason,' said Amy. 'You do know President Grant is also the Yellowstone National Park president, right?'

Olivia's heart skipped a beat as she stared at her daughter. 'The what?'

'He's the one who opened Yellowstone as the world's first national park in 1872.' With speed, Amy searched for the information. 'Here, I'll show you.'

Together, they read all about Ulysses S. Grant, military officer, politician and eighteenth president. As Commanding General, he led the Union Army to victory in the American Civil War in 1865.

An American hero who worked to implement Congressional Reconstruction and remove the vestiges of slavery.

'You learn something new every day,' said Olivia. 'In the past ten years, I've learned more about American presidents than I ever wanted to learn, but this man is interesting.'

'Says here he prosecuted the Klan, pressed for treatment of Black people as human and American, and pushed for an innovative Native American policy.'

These achievements were impressive to Olivia, yet only one sentence stood out in her investigative mind. On 1 March 1872, Ulysses S. Grant had signed a bill establishing Yellowstone National Park. A military president admired by an eye doctor who had dreamed of joining the military service. A spectacular national park created by his idol: the ideal setting for a final murder.

'He's going west to Wyoming,' whispered Olivia. 'Victim ten will be at Yellowstone.'

37

AFTER ONLY FOUR hours of sleep, Olivia and Amy set off for Wyoming. According to the sat-nav, a twelve-hour journey lay ahead, and Olivia was determined to beat the traffic.

The rest of the taskforce were headed in the same direction. Jack and Tom were in one vehicle, Perez and Morelli in another. Despite intense conversations on a group call during the journey, no one had been able to identify a possible date on which Doctor Callender might strike. The consensus was that it would happen soon, and there was no time to waste. They ran through every important date they could think of that might apply to President Ulysses S. Grant: birth, death, election, swearing into office. Nothing clicked. Despite the killer's fascination with the number ten, he had not murdered on the tenth day of any month, and the tenth day of August had already passed.

Olivia tried to concentrate on the traffic while glancing at her tablet screen every few seconds and asking or answering questions. Another unanswerable question was where in Yellowstone National Park's two million acres the doctor would seek out his victim. They discussed whether Ulysses S. Grant had stood at a particular place in the park to cut a ribbon or shake hands, but this could not be ascertained.

'Okay, I'm looking at a website,' said Jack. 'There's a group called the Ulysses S. Grant Society. It's not showing Doctor Callender as a member, but they might be able to help.'

'What are you thinking?' asked Perez.

'The Society can lure him to Yellowstone, put him right where we want him,' replied Jack. 'First things first: we need a press conference purely for Doctor Callender's benefit.'

When Olivia signed off from the group call, she was confident that Yellowstone's would be flooded with law enforcement from that moment. Wyoming police, sheriffs, US Marshals, even a fugitive apprehension team: everybody they could spare would be in and around the massive park.

At noon, Olivia and Amy watched the latest ISB press conference on screen. Yet again, there were at least a dozen reporters with fluffy microphones arranged close to the speaker's plinth. The spokeswoman purposely displayed the earlier version of the killer's composite image, and spun the line that Jack had insisted on.

'The suspect is believed to be in the state of Montana or headed there. All citizens of Montana are asked to be on the lookout for this man. Do not attempt to apprehend him. Contact your local police, the sheriff or the ISB on the following numbers . . .'

Olivia was glad she was not involved in deceiving the media, especially after the abuse from blogger-turned-investigative-reporter Kimberly Grant. She had begged Jack to give Kim the exclusive if they apprehended Doctor Callender. Jack was of the view that the woman did not deserve it, but Olivia had said, 'It's a girl thing.' She understood the woman's anger, and felt she owed her.

Amy's voice interrupted her thoughts. 'Suppose he really does go to Montana, Mom?'

'Trust me, the thought had crossed my mind.' Olivia frowned. Although Jack and the team had accepted her proposition that the tenth victim would be taken out at Yellowstone, no one really knew for sure. She fought off the self-doubt that plagued her and said, with certainty, 'This is a big deal for Gregory Callender. He's going to Wyoming for his grand finale.'

The spokeswoman continued. 'We appeal to the suspect again to turn himself in for questioning without further delay.'

A reporter asked, 'Why are you so sure he's heading to Montana? We know he's been steadily going west, but why not some other western state?'

'Our intelligence and information gathered, including help from the public, suggests that Montana is the likely destination. Montana is a state of over one million people. He could be hiding anywhere, although we know at some point he will make for his chosen ground, be it a park, campground or forestry reserve. We ask individuals in those areas to be on the highest alert.'

'Are you any closer to naming the killer yet?'

'Identifying the killer is, of course, our priority. We are asking friends or family who know the person committing these heinous acts not to offer him shelter. Let us take him off your hands calmly and safely, without any violence.'

'That media lady is good,' said Olivia in admiration. 'Straight to the camera, clear voice, confident. If I was Doctor Callender, I'd believe her.'

'Me too.' Amy nodded.

'When we stop for food, remind me to find a beauty salon or a hair shop.'

'You're going to do your hair?' Amy was incredulous.

'No. I'm going to get us some wigs.'

38

TWO DAYS LATER, the team were in Yellowstone National Park, a vast region atop a volcanic hot spot, featuring lush forests, dramatic canyons, alpine rivers and hot springs. Visitors gained unparalleled opportunities to view geologic wonders like the Grand Canyon of the Yellowstone River. Signs of wildlife were abundant, including warning notices on how to stay safe and keep your distance from bison, elk, bears and wolves.

New and hastily erected signs throughout the park pointed visitors to the Ulysses S. Grant Society's tent and talk. Olivia had to admire the speed with which the organisation had put together the mock event with the help of the special agents and park rangers. For two days straight, before and after news broadcasts, advertisements for the one-off event were aired. Olivia prayed Doctor Callender would be unable to resist the opportunity to attend in person.

The taskforce members spread out, swallowed amongst the enormous crowds of tourists. Each of them had arrived at different times in unmarked vehicles. Olivia glanced around, wondering whether the people she walked past were sheriffs' deputies, local police or other officers. All were in plain clothes. A man ambling along, admiring the plants, could be an officer, as could the lithe woman doing yoga moves. The couple who cycled past on mountain bikes could also be law enforcement.

Olivia had never seen the special agents in such casual clothing before, blending in perfectly with the masses. Jack wore chinos with loafers and a short-sleeved shirt that hung loosely from his frame. Tom was clad in knee-length shorts, polo shirt and moccasins, not a bow tie in sight. Morelli wore the uniform of a groundsman, complete with rake and enormous black plastic bag. Perez had on a tracksuit and trainers, her ponytail tucked into a tight bun. Everyone wore dark shades as well as discreet ear pieces.

Olivia was irritated by the ear piece. She was not used to wearing them, and found herself scratching her ear every few seconds. The other annoyance was the blonde bob wig, of which she was fully conscious even though a broad-brimmed hat covered much of it. A pair of dark aviator glasses took up much of her face, but her visibility was good.

'Mom, you look just like Mary J. Blige, honest,' gushed Amy. 'It suits you.'

Amy wore a long auburn wig under her baseball cap. Olivia was not sure whether the doctor had noticed Amy before, but thought it was a good idea to alter her look somewhat just in case.

'Never thought I'd see myself in a blonde wig,' said Olivia. 'It would take a lot of getting used to.'

The two wandered over to Old Faithful, the most famous geyser at Yellowstone National Park. Not the largest of the park's five hundred geysers, but the most popular for its regular sprays, which appeared up to seventeen times a day. The water could reach a height of 184 feet. It was little wonder that crowds jostled for space to see the spectacular event.

Benches were laid out in Old Faithful's five viewing areas, and all were full of eager tourists. Those who could not fit into the bench space walked further down the horseshoe-shaped walkway and stood by the rails.

When Old Faithful blew, Olivia could not help but be distracted. She joined Amy, staring up at it in awe as the boiling water rushed to the blue skies, expanding and falling back, spray glinting in the sun. She forced her attention elsewhere. Today, she could not play tourist. Her focus had to be the job. She searched the crowds for the face she knew, the killer who had once dared approach her and talk about his knees. How he must have laughed afterwards.

Olivia and Amy stayed a good distance away from the marquee of the Ulysses S. Grant Society, under which white plastic chairs were arranged in rows to facilitate an audience of two hundred people. Olivia watched as visitors arrived and took up seats, guided by Society members. She squinted while studying the male faces. No sign of the target, and it was thirty minutes before the scheduled midday talk would begin.

Close to noon, the long-awaited call came in from an officer. A man closely resembling Doctor Gregory Callender, in khaki trousers, white shirt and white Panama hat, had been spotted on a trail approaching the marquee. Unfortunately, the officer had lost sight of him in the crowd.

At first, Olivia could not see Jack or any of the special agents, and realised she might be the closest person to the suspect. She kept her phone clutched in moist fingers, and had to keep swapping hands to wipe her palms on her jeans. Eventually, she spotted Perez talking to one of the park rangers, all of whom had maintained their usual dress code in order to avoid raising Doctor Callender's suspicions.

Olivia caught a glimpse of a face and her heart thudded nonstop. The man came towards her, wearing similar clothes to those described by the officer. She held her breath and then slowly released it as he went past. It was not the killer. The hair and colouring were right, but not that face or ears.

Suddenly, Olivia realised that Amy was not beside her. She swung around, her eyes darting from side to side. The crowds were huge, but the doctor was not interested in hurting women . . . unless he decided to make an example of Amy. If he knew her mother was part of a team seeking to apprehend him, he might just want to teach her a lesson.

Olivia spun around and saw Amy standing beside the rail, staring at another geyser. Almost immediately, she caught sight of a man walking past in the background. She removed her glasses and narrowed her eyes as she watched him. The man locked eyes with her for a brief second. His look was one of shock and disbelief. Enough for Olivia to know the recognition was mutual.

'Mom, look at this,' called Amy, beckoning to her.

The man was less than two feet from Amy. He shot her a swift glance before returning his stare to Olivia.

For a moment, Olivia froze. He could kill her daughter with one swift, easy motion, if he wanted to. His gaze told her he knew this too. A pain such as she had never experienced before pierced her chest as she willed him not to touch the most precious person in her life. He turned away. Fumbling with her phone, she pressed a thumb against the call memory.

'I see him, Jack,' she shouted. 'He's running up a trail towards the woods.'

'Where? I can't see him. What's your location?'

Olivia pushed a boy off a bench and climbed up. 'Sorry, excuse me.'

'Hey, lady!' the boy grumbled.

Olivia waved frantically in the air. 'Jack, can you see me?'

'I see you, where is he?'

Olivia pointed in the direction the suspect was running. She jumped from the bench, apologised to the youth again and started running around the horseshoe-shaped viewing area.

'Amy, stay right here. We're going after him.'

'I'm not staying here, are you crazy? I'm coming with you.'

Olivia did not stop to argue. There was no time to reason with her daughter. Up ahead, Jack held his phone close to his face, shouting and gesturing. The crowds parted as the plain-clothed law enforcers sprang into action. Some tourists paid scant attention and focused instead on what they'd come to see, the impressive actions of Old Faithful and the surrounding geysers.

Olivia caught up with a panting Jack. He craned his neck and stared over the heads of the tourists, then shouted into his phone. 'He ditched the hat and I've lost him. You see him?'

She heard Morelli's distinctive voice at the other end. 'Suspect jumped into a tan Mitsubishi truck, cannot see the plates. He just blew past. I repeat, he's in a tan Mitsubishi truck. He's going east on Craig Pass.'

'Come on, we'll get my car,' shouted Jack as he ran. 'All units in pursuit. Suspect headed east, tan Mitsubishi truck, east on Craig Pass. It is not known whether suspect has firearms. Proceed with caution.'

Olivia and Amy jumped into the Jeep's back seat. Soon, Jack was in the middle of a procession of cars that whizzed past startled sightseers, ignoring the park's speed limits of forty-five miles per hour. Signs imploring drivers to 'Give the animals a brake' went by as a flash of silver.

'Make sure all five entrances are covered.' Jack spoke urgently into his phone. 'We have thousands of square miles of wilderness, but he'll run out of track.'

Another voice crackled on the airwaves. 'Suspect is proceeding west. There are slow-moving vehicles in the area. He's not stopping for them. Hang back to avoid casualties.'

Olivia closed her eyes as Jack cursed under his breath and swerved to avoid a cyclist with earphones, unaware of the tonnes of metal flying towards him. The cyclist pulled off the road so quickly his wheels buckled, and he ended up lying in the grass.

'Do not shoot unless you come under fire,' ordered Jack. 'We want him alive.'

'And us, too,' murmured Amy as she swung to one side and clutched the passenger door. 'Alive, I mean.'

Olivia glanced at Amy, expecting to see sheer terror. Instead, Amy's excited, flushed face was pressed against the passenger window, watching the scenery speed by. Olivia reached down and double-checked that both of their seatbelts were firmly secured. She did not relish the speed of the pursuit, and clutched the driver's backrest while Jack sped along. Eventually, he overtook one of the lead cars.

In the wing mirror, Olivia observed two patrol cars behind them, lights flashing, sirens wailing. She closed her eyes. One blown tyre and they were all gone, with a multiple pile-up behind them.

'Hang on, Mom.'

She felt Amy's fingers sink into her arm, and was grateful that her daughter had sensed her discomfort.

Static crackled over the airwaves and a voice announced in alarm: 'He just side-swiped a private vehicle, but he's continuing. Vehicle's occupants are now standing in the road. His truck does not appear to have suffered much damage.'

'I can't wait to learn to drive,' said Amy, delight etched on her face.

'God help Londoners when you do,' said Olivia.

The officer's voice again: 'Suspect has turned north, driving along the lakeside, road leads to Bridge Bay. Any units in the north close to Bridge Bay, head south and cut him off. Spike strips ready to deploy.'

Olivia's spirits lifted. The man would surely be cornered now. Almost as soon as that feeling of relief grew, it died again at the officer's next words.

'Suspect is slowing, he's stopping beside the lake. Watch out for the tour bus. All units get down to the lake, he's ditched the vehicle. Suspect is on foot, running towards the mooring area at the lake.'

'Foot patrol, that's all I need,' mumbled Jack. 'This guy has way too much energy.'

'Nothing wrong with his knees, then,' said Amy. 'He must be a really fit old boy if he can swim across a lake. Like he's doing an Ironman Triathlon.'

'Are there alligators in the lake?' asked Olivia.

'No 'gators, but there are boats.' Jack muttered a curse and then raised his voice. 'Do not let him get onto a boat.'

Olivia estimated they must have travelled over twenty miles before they finally gained sight of the killer's vehicle. Two patrol cars with their doors wide open were parked on either side of the newly abandoned truck. One of the officers waved his hands frantically and pointed towards a small speedboat making off across the lake. The other officer tended to a woman lying close to a mooring post. A group of tourists were trying to comfort the distraught victim. Three other vessels floated lazily on the dark waters, two of which were speedboats and one a sailboat.

Jack brought the Jeep to an abrupt halt, grabbed a loud-speaker and leapt out. Olivia and Amy chased after him. More patrol units arrived in a whir of noise, closely followed by Tom Walsh in his sedan.

'Stop him, that's my boat!' wailed the woman on the ground.

'Doctor Gregory Callender, stop!' Jack's voice echoed, loud and deep. 'Don't make me shoot you. Doctor Callender!'

Olivia was in no doubt that the killer had heard the warning words. Half of Yellowstone park had probably heard him. Doctor

Callender was now bareheaded, his silver hair shining in the sunlight. He barely glanced behind him as he pulled the throttle. The speedboat raced away.

A park ranger, also wielding a loudspeaker, urged the fugitive to stop and give himself up. The fleeing boat continued to distance itself from the shore.

Tom looked at the ranger. 'What direction is he going?'

'That's east. If he makes it across, the closest road is Sylvan Pass, but even if he hijacks a vehicle, he'll never get out the east entrance. It's locked down tight.'

'What's over there?' Jack gestured towards the area with his chin.

'Couple of log cabins. Other than that, it's wilderness . . . and grizzlies.'

Olivia sucked in air. 'Grizzly bears.'

Jack holstered his gun under his shirt and retrieved his knapsack from the Jeep. 'Don't worry, we're well equipped for wild animals. Bear spray, binoculars, flare gun . . . extra pistol, if you need it?'

'No, thanks,' said Olivia.

Jack called Morelli and Perez, and ordered them to get onto Sylvan Pass. He then looked at the other boats. 'Can anyone steer one of these?'

A young man standing close by answered. 'That one's mine, yeah. I can drive it. Can only take three passengers, though.'

The owner of the other speedboat piped up with, 'Mine's not as fast as that one, but sure, we can follow him.'

Jack looked at Olivia. 'Stay here. He may not be armed, but he's still dangerous.'

'Stay here? Are you out of your mind?' Olivia quickly climbed into the boat with the youth.

'Hey, that's my line!' Amy jumped in after her mother.

'I won't ask who you take after,' said Jack, as he joined them.

Tom, a patrol officer, and a park ranger climbed into the other speedboat.

Doctor Callender stayed comfortably ahead of them as he raced across the rippling green waters, leaving a spray of white foam in his wake. The breeze beat against their faces, cooling the balmy temperature as they pursued the suspect. Under other conditions, Olivia would have cherished the ride and taken time to appreciate the stunning scenery. As it was, she clenched the safety rail and stared ahead, anxiety written on her face. There was no mooring dock on the other side of the lake. The fugitive jumped off in a swampy area and waded across to the bank. He made no attempt to anchor the vessel, which began drifting away.

'Doctor Callender, give it up!' shouted Jack.

The youthful captain brought the boat as close to the shoreline as possible. The area was wild and unkempt, with low-hanging leafy trees brushing against the water.

'You're gonna get soaked, sorry guys. I can't go any closer.'

The calf-deep water smelled of algae and slime. They waded through the morass and up the slippery bank. Olivia held Amy's arm to steady her.

'You should have stayed where you were safe,' said Olivia.

'I wouldn't have missed this for anything,' said Amy. 'Going to need some new trainers, though.'

Ahead of them were densely packed trees and thick bushes, which the law enforcers broke through with their arms to create a path. No sign of Doctor Callender. As they trudged further inland, the soil became drier, and Jack brought them all to a halt. He held up a hand for silence.

'That way,' said Jack. 'I can hear crackling branches.' Holding his bear spray aloft, he led the way as they changed direction. 'If we come across any animals, stand still. Do not shoot. They won't attack unless they feel threatened.'

'Look there,' said Olivia pointing. 'He's ditched his white shirt.'

Tom snatched up the damp shirt. 'He'll try to blend in with the trees,' he said, as he stared around.

'Go that way.' The park ranger pointed. 'Area looks disturbed over there.'

They walked and searched and shouted the suspect's name. The only response came from the birds high above in the trees, tunefully alerting each other to the trespassers' presence.

'I see him!' exclaimed Olivia. 'He's crouching by that tree; he's covered himself in mud. He's seen us.'

The fugitive started to run again. Olivia was amazed at the man's stamina. For a fifty-six-year-old he sure knew how to move. Had she been in his position, she would have collapsed from sheer exhaustion by now.

'Doctor Gregory Callender, you're surrounded,' shouted Jack. 'Give yourself up!'

'Doctor, we will shoot!' shouted a police officer. 'Stop and put your hands up!'

The doctor ignored their warnings and continued to distance himself from the pursuing team. Soon, they lost sight of him again. Eventually, they came upon a log cabin. All was quiet. The silence was suddenly broken when a terrified woman came running from the rear of the building, screaming and pointing.

'He's gone that way, he's got a knife!'

'What's this place called?' asked Jack.

'Reefside Lodge,' she said, through gushing tears.

Jack spoke into his phone as they raced behind the cabin. 'He's near to Reefside Lodge. Stay back on the perimeter. He's got nowhere to go when he emerges.'

'He's over there!' Tom pointed.

'He's going in the wrong direction for the road; he'll go over a cliff,' said the park ranger. 'There are warning signs, but no barricades.'

'Steep cliff?' asked Jack.

'Fifty-foot drop.'

The doctor disappeared from view yet again, and Olivia's stomach sank at the idea that he might run right off a cliff. She wanted this man to be taken alive and able to speak. As they emerged from the bushes, she stopped in shock at the alarming sight ahead. Doctor Callender held a park ranger in a chokehold, with a kitchen knife against the man's neck.

'Drop your weapons,' the doctor warned. 'Now!'

'He's got Sam,' murmured the ranger standing beside Olivia.

Jack instantly placed his gun on the ground and beckoned for the others to do the same. 'Doctor Callender, there's no way out,' he said. 'It's time to give up.'

The doctor dragged the ranger backwards until they came to a halt, teetering on the edge of a steep cliff, his eyes wild, panting with exhaustion. The sharp blade gleamed in the sun. Olivia looked at Sam, the hostage, who appeared terrified, and she knew he was well aware of exactly what his captor could do.

Jack took two steps forward. 'I want you to listen to me, Greg. I'm Special Agent Tyler.'

'I know who you are,' the doctor panted. 'National Park Service. Got to hand it to you, you're smarter than you look.'

'I won't argue with you, Greg,' said Jack. 'But this has to end now.'

Doctor Callender peered over the edge of the cliff. 'Stay where you are!'

'Don't do it, Greg. You won't survive,' said Jack. 'Let Sam go. You know he's not your type.'

'Worked it all out, didn't you?' snarled the doctor.

'Actually, someone else did, but let's not get into that,' said Jack. 'I want everybody to get out of this safely. Do the right thing, Greg.'

Silence filled the air, and all Olivia could hear was her own heart beating. She jumped when Amy squeezed her arm.

The sound of breaking branches echoed through the woods,

and Perez and Morelli emerged. Jack immediately said, 'Hang back, guys. We got this.'

Gregory Callender again contemplated the sheer drop, never moving the knife away from the ranger's neck.

Olivia approached the special agent. 'Jack, let me try.'

Jack stared at her for a moment, then nodded.

'Watch his knife, Mom.'

'You've done some great things, Doctor Callender.' Olivia removed her blonde wig and twisted it in her hands as she edged forwards. 'I've seen the brilliant work you did for Unite For Sight. You helped all those people regain their sight, did a lot of free eye surgery, bought thousands of glasses for the needy. Lots of people have only good things to say about you.'

A flicker of interest crossed his eyes, yet his voice remained firm. 'Stay away from me.'

Olivia glanced at the cliff edge behind him, and fought off the quiver of fear that ran through her body. No ropes and harnesses. Anyone who went over there was done for good. She took another step towards him, forced a bright smile and tried to keep her voice upbeat.

'Do you remember a little girl named Susan . . . you called her Sunny Sue? You operated on her eyes, removed her paediatric cataracts. She remembers you. Says you're the best doctor in the whole wide world.'

Olivia saw the recollection in his eyes. He blinked a few times, but his mouth stayed set in a firm line.

'And Charlie, the lifeguard? You fixed his detached retina. He said he would have gone blind in days if you hadn't operated on him. Would have had to give up the job he lives for. He says, next to his father, he loves you more than anyone. A lot of people look up to you, Doctor Callender.'

The doctor suddenly released his captive and pushed him away. The ranger ran past Olivia, towards safety.

'That's great, Greg,' said Jack, once Sam was out of danger. 'Now, drop the knife and you come too.'

To Olivia's surprise, the doctor's body racked with sobs. After all the terrible things he had done, emotion and empathy still lived within him. He held the knife blade to his chest and took another step backwards. Olivia stifled a scream as pieces of the cliff face crumbled and fell away.

'I might as well be number ten,' he whispered.

'No!' shouted Olivia.

'Olivia, back away from him,' said Jack.

She wanted to heed the warning, to turn and run, but knew she would never forgive herself if she did and he jumped to his death. The victims' families badly wanted answers to their questions. Lamar Webster wanted to face the man responsible for his imprisonment and the death of his best friend. 'Don't do it,' she said. 'That's not the legacy you want to leave behind, doctor. It's not what an army man would do, you know that.'

The doctor gradually lowered the knife and sat on his haunches, sobbing openly. Jack walked slowly past Olivia, extending his hand to the fallen man.

'Come on, soldier,' he said, as he sank to his knees. 'Take my hand. Crawl forwards; take your time, now.'

The doctor obeyed. He clutched Jack's hand and the ISB man moved backwards, inch by inch, until both were a safe distance from the cliff edge. Perez and Morelli lifted the weeping Doctor Callender to his feet.

'Nice work, Olivia,' said Jack.

'Great work, Mom!' Amy grabbed her mother and held her in a tight hug while Olivia stroked her daughter's hair.

'You're under arrest.' Jack handcuffed the doctor and read him his Miranda rights. 'Gregory Callender, you are one hard man to catch.'

Though physically and mentally drained, Olivia gave a smile

of relief. 'Good to see you can arrest suspects without shooting them.'

Jack grinned. 'Never waste a good bullet.'

Olivia stared down at the doctor's feet. 'Furlowe boots.'

The doctor blinked a few times and lifted his eyes to Olivia's. She tried to read what was going on in his mind. Was he angry to have been stopped in his tracks, or relieved it was all over? This man had looked into the eyes of unsuspecting patients for decades, wanting to plunge a knife into them. Thanks to him, she would never get an eye test again without wondering about the mental status of the practitioner.

'Thought you were on vacation?' said Doctor Callender, his words coming in starts.

'Kind of got side-tracked,' said Olivia. 'I am, as of now.'

39

THAT NIGHT, THE taskforce ate dinner in a dimly lit Irish tavern, decorated with both Irish and American flags. The atmosphere was warm, and the air smelled rich with a variety of alcoholic beverages. Wall-mounted flat-screen television screens showed a range of sports to the boisterous patrons.

'Hey, Olivia, slide the salt over here,' said Perez.

Olivia leaned over and slid the salt across the table, straight to Perez's left hand.

'You see that, Marty? Told you she wouldn't forget.'

Olivia smiled at them. 'You guys wouldn't have been talking about me behind my back again, would you?'

Morelli manifested pain and put his hand on his heart. 'Who, me?'

The team all laughed, their spirits lightened by the end of a successful operation.

'I can just guess the gist of it,' said Olivia. 'My ears haven't stopped burning for days now.'

Perez decided to plead her innocence. 'Hey, I said you've got a great accent. I did, didn't I, guys?'

'She did,' said Tom.

Jack smiled and said, 'We're all agreed that you're the best private eye we've ever worked with, and we wish you could stick around.'

'I know my worth,' said Olivia slyly. 'ISB could not afford me.'

'Whoa!' Laughter rose and grew amongst the team.

'Only kidding!' said Olivia.

The waiter hovered beside them, keen to be of assistance.

'You'd better put the toothpicks down as an extra side dish,' said Perez. 'My colleague here will chew all of them.'

'Hey, I only had two,' said Morelli. 'So far.'

The waiter beamed at him. 'That's fine, sir. They're free.'

Olivia looked at Jack. 'Did you talk to the public defender and the DA about Lamar?'

Jack nodded. 'They went before the judge for a lower bond. Lamar bonded out.'

'But he's not free, right?' she pressed.

'They've got paperwork and procedures to deal with, but it won't be long before the charges get dropped. He won't go to trial.'

'Glad to hear it. Amy will be delighted, too.'

'Olivia, you know you can claim the twenty thousand Nathaniel Jeynes's parents offered as a reward for finding his killer?' said Morelli.

Olivia shook her head. 'Ask them to give it to Lamar. He needs it way more than I do. He lost his job and has loads of back rent.'

'You know how many drinks we could buy with that twenty thousand dollars, Olivia?' asked Perez.

'We're never gonna find out.' Morelli jiggled his empty glass under Perez's nose. 'But you can put in twenty dollars, kid.'

Olivia's phone rang. At first, she thought it must be Amy, who was dining with her new young friends at the Yellowstone campground. Her daughter was enjoying the sudden limelight as a mini celebrity, having played a role in catching a notorious killer.

Olivia looked at the phone number and excused herself from the table before answering.

'Hey, Olivia. Just wanted to say thanks again for the exclusive. I appreciate it.'

'That's fine Kim. You deserve it. Great write-up.'

'You're a great gal. You take care now, and enjoy the rest of your vacation.'

'I will. All the best to you, too.'

Olivia went to the ladies' restroom and stared in the mirror as she washed her hands. This was her last night with the task-force. Leaving them would be bittersweet; she had grown used to being part of a team of focused individuals determined to catch a killer. One killer down, thousands of them out there. Still, it would be good to get back into holiday mode, to continue exploring the wonders of Yellowstone National Park at a leisurely pace.

Olivia sighed as she dried her hands. As much as she hated admitting it to herself, she would miss the man with whom she had worked so closely. Jack Tyler had grown on her, and would not be easily forgotten. That shiny gold band was still on his ring finger, though he had stopped playing with it. Still, she was a professional, not about to get drawn into anything, despite the attraction. Now was the time for goodbyes. It was over, and she would have interesting memories for years to come.

On her way back down the corridor, her progress was blocked by Jack.

'Oh, you startled me!'

'Sorry, Olivia. Thought you were unshakeable by now?'

'No chance.' Olivia smiled. 'I'll probably be jumpy for a few days.'

'Glad we haven't scared you into running off back to London.'

'Amy would never let me. Yellowstone was already on the agenda, and looks like a fascinating place. Must also be the safest place on earth right now. After that, unless we get distracted again, we'll end up in Los Angeles.'

'City of Angels,' murmured Jack. 'You a gambler?'

'I never gamble.'

'Even at the worst odds, you can luck out.'

'So I hear.'

Jack nodded with a rueful look. 'I wasn't kidding, you know. If you decide to ditch Bill Tweedy, I'm sure I can pull some strings, get a full visa for you.'

'You know something, Jack Tyler? You're not a bad bloke.'

'Bloke?' he smiled. 'No one's ever called me that before.'

'It's not a bad word, honest.' Olivia held his gaze. 'You never know what I'll do. I have your number.'

'You have my number. I have yours.'

THE END